Julia James lives [...] peaceful verdant [...] of Cornwall. She a[...] so rich in myth and history, with its sunbaked landscapes and olive groves, ancient ruins and azure seas. 'The perfect setting for romance!' she says. 'Rivalled only by the lush tropical heat of the Caribbean—palms swaying by a silver sand beach lapped by turquoise water… What more could lovers want?'

Jackie Ashenden writes dark, emotional stories, with alpha heroes who've just got the world to their liking only to have it blown wide apart by their kick-ass heroines. She lives in Auckland, New Zealand, with her husband, the inimitable Dr Jax, two kids and two rats. When she's not torturing alpha males and their gutsy heroines she can be found drinking chocolate martinis, reading anything she can lay her hands on, wasting time on social media or being forced to go mountain biking with her husband. To keep up to date with Jackie's new releases and other news sign up to her newsletter at jackieashenden.com.

THE HEIR SHE KEPT FROM THE BILLIONAIRE

JULIA JAMES

ENEMIES AT THE GREEK ALTAR

JACKIE ASHENDEN

MILLS & BOON

First published in Great Britain 2024
by Mills & Boon, an imprint of HarperCollins*Publishers* Ltd,
1 London Bridge Street, London, SE1 9GF

www.harpercollins.co.uk

HarperCollins*Publishers*, Macken House, 39/40 Mayor Street Upper, Dublin 1, D01 C9W8, Ireland

The Heir She Kept from the Billionaire © 2024 Julia James

Enemies at the Greek Altar © 2024 Jackie Ashenden

ISBN: 978-0-263-32004-6

04/24

THE HEIR SHE KEPT FROM THE BILLIONAIRE

JULIA JAMES

MILLS & BOON

For my editor, Emma Marnell.

Many thanks for all your work on this,
our first novel together.

PROLOGUE

ALAINA ASHCROFT WATCHED the hotel limo ease away from under the shaded portico, setting off down the long, hibiscus-lined drive towards the highway. She swallowed. Hard.

So he was going. Heading back to the airport, back to Italy, back to his own life—just as he had said he would. Demolishing all her hopes that he might extend his time here on the island, spend more time with her. That he might want to do so. Might want, perhaps, something more than holiday time with her...

Might want to take me back to Italy with him...

There was a tightness in her chest, as if something sharp was piercing her. Hadn't her mother warned her, from her own pitiful experience, how careful she must be lest she end up like her? Wanting what she could not have...yearning for it... For a man who did not want her...hoping all the time that he did...

As I have been hoping...

She swallowed again, turning away. Her hopes had been dashed. Now all she could do was get on with her own life. She had work to do, and work must be her therapy.

He's gone—and there's an end to it. Nothing more will come of it, and my life will go on just as it did before. As if we'd never met. Never romanced at all...

But in that, as it turned out, she was completely mistaken...

CHAPTER ONE

Five years later...

RAFAELLO RANIERI STRETCHED out his long legs and crossed his ankles in a leisurely manner, relaxing back into the capacious first-class airline seat, then extracted a law journal from his briefcase to while away the flight to London.

As one of Italy's top lawyers, in great demand by a large number of the country's elite families for whom he and his law firm provided invaluable services when it came to tricky matters of tax efficiency, inheritance conflicts, troublesome offspring or annoyingly avaricious ex-spouses, he needed to keep abreast of his field—not just in respect of the Italian legal system, but wherever his wealthy clients might find themselves in need of his highly respected and extremely well-remunerated, expertise.

It was just such a client who necessitated this trip to London, to consult with his counterpart law firm based in the city's Inns of Court. He would be arriving too late to see them this evening, and as he was flying back to Rome the next day he had decided to overnight not in his customary hotel on Park Lane but in one of the nearby airport hotels. Tomorrow he would have a working lunch with his counterpart, then take a late-afternoon flight to Rome. A brief visit to the UK, but nothing untoward about it. Which was the way he liked to live his life. Calmly and smoothly.

His face shadowed a moment. 'Calmly and smoothly' had not been the way his mother had lived her unhappy life. His father, now living in semi-retirement from the highly prosperous family law firm, the management of which he had handed over to Rafaello, his son, had condemned her as neurotic and needy. His parents' disastrous marriage had only confirmed to Rafaello that his own chosen path—judiciously selected affairs with women who never wanted more than he was prepared to offer them, never wanted more than he wanted from their time together—was the wisest course for himself.

He felt his thoughts flicker. There had been one woman, once...

On a Caribbean island, with silver sand beaches, palms swaying in the tropical breeze...a perfect place for romance. And she had been perfect for a romance in such a place. Beautiful, passionate, ardent. He had desired her the moment he had seen her, and their affair had been all that he had wanted it to be.

Until she'd shown that she wanted more time with him than he had been prepared to offer her.

Then he'd driven away from her in the sleek hotel limo, towards the airport that would take him back to Italy, to the life that suited him very well—the life he was still leading now and intended to go on leading. Smooth and unruffled—just the way he liked it to be.

Alaina was harassed, but was not letting it show. That would be unprofessional. As one of the assistant managers at the hotel, she was well-schooled in presenting only an air of calm competence. So the fact that she was manning the reception desk because two of the staff had gone off sick and one was still a trainee must remain quite invisible to incoming and outgoing guests. So, too, the fact that she was running late to collect Joey.

She'd managed to put a call in to Ryan, with whom she'd 'paired' at the nursery, to bail each other out if work got in the way of the strict collection times enforced by the extremely good and therefore extremely popular nursery where Joey was enrolled. Thankfully he had agreed to collect Joey, along with his own four-year-old daughter, Betsy. He'd give both children tea at his house, then deliver Joey to her after he'd returned Betsy to her mother, who lived not very far away with her second husband. By that time the evening reception staff would be on, and Alaina could go off duty, clocking back in after she'd delivered Joey to nursery in the morning.

The system worked well—if sometimes stressfully, as today—allowing her to continue her job, which was both financially necessary and good from a career perspective. But being a full-time working mother of a small child brought its own pressures.

And unlike Ryan, who shared custody with his ex-wife, she was a full-time single parent.

But that was my choice.

Because otherwise she'd have had to disclose the existence of a child who'd never been planned or anticipated to a man who had no interest in her. However much she might have wished otherwise.

It was not to be—leave it at that...

The entrance of a flurry of guests delivered by the airport shuttle—one of the secondary London airports, situated out in the Home Counties, away from the capital, but always extremely busy for all that—demanded her attention.

She had just finished registering the guests when she heard the front doors open again. She glanced up, professional smile ready on her face. It wasn't time for the next shuttle, so it must be a self-drive or taxi arrival. But as she lifted her head the smile froze on her face.

To be replaced by an expression of complete and absolute disbelief.

Rafaello stopped dead. Unconsciously, his grip on his briefcase and the handle of his carry-on tightened. Then, as his eyes met those of the woman standing behind the reception desk, he said, *'Alaina?'*

He walked towards her, aware of conflicting emotions in his head. Shock was uppermost—that was to be expected. But there was something more, too, which right now he did not have time to analyse. He was dealing with the moment—that was all.

He schooled his expression as he approached. With his trained sense of observation he saw she had paled, and her face had tensed. Then, like him, she schooled her expression into neutrality.

'Rafaello—how extraordinary!'

Her voice was light, but he could tell she was deliberately making it so, that it was an effort for her. The tension in her face—and in her immediately veiled eyes—remained.

He allowed himself the very slightest of smiles. 'Well, these things do happen,' he answered, with a quizzical lift of one eyebrow.

'You're not on my reservation list,' she responded blankly.

He gave a shake of his head. 'No—I made the decision not to bother with going into London tonight on the flight. I take it you have availability?'

He saw her swallow, and it was clear to him that she was fighting for a veneer, at least, of normality. He could see a pulse beating at her throat, the faintest flush of colour staining her cheeks. It only enhanced her beauty...

He pulled his thoughts back. It was five years since her striking beauty had beguiled him on his visit to the Caribbean island where one of his most lucrative and much-divorced clients lived and had required his presence to initiate yet another divorce. Client dealt with, he'd indulged in a holiday for himself—and indulged, too, in a very enjoyable romance to enhance his time there.

Alaina had been working not where he himself had been staying—one of the fabled Falcone hotels—but at a more modest four-star hotel next door. He had seen her sunning herself on the beach as he'd strolled along one afternoon and that had been all it had taken.

She had been as responsive to his interest in her as he had wanted.

Perhaps too much so...

For all her very beguiling charms, he had been aware that she would have been more than happy for their encounter to become more than a mere holiday romance. He had drawn back from closer involvement—as he always did. It was more prudent so to do.

Yet, prudent as it might have been, he'd been conscious of faint regret as he'd headed back to the airport at the end of his stay.

His eyes rested on her now. She had matured in the five years since their time together, and unlike on the laid-back island she looked brisk and businesslike, in a crisply styled suit with neat lapels, her hair drawn back into a tight French plait, and only minimal make-up on her face.

Despite his best intentions, he felt memory spear.

Her...lying in bed...her glorious mane of dark hair tumbled and tousled and her luminous eyes holding his...her lush mouth soft as velvet...

He tamped it down. Stamped it down. It was not appropriate for this completely by-chance, unsought encounter.

'Yes. Yes, of course.'

Her voice was staccato, and he knew why. Knew why her eyes had veiled, even though she was looking at him straight on. She broke her gaze to look at the computer screen, flicking it to another page. Then looked back at him.

'Would you prefer a garden view or a lake view?' she asked politely, the dutiful hotel receptionist.

'Which is quieter?'

'Both are quiet, but the lake view rooms are closer to the car park.'

'Garden view,' he answered. 'Only one night,' he added.

She gave a distracted nod, tapping the keyboard. Not bothering to ask his name, which she knew perfectly well, or his nationality.

She knew so much else that was personal as well...

Again, to his displeasure, he felt memory distract him. She knew every centimetre of his body...how he liked his coffee...what food he liked.

How he liked to make love...

As did he know her. In the time they'd spent together they had acquired a lot of information about each other.

Too much?

Oh, not just lifestyle details, or even their respective sexual preferences—not that he would dwell on that right now—but more than that.

Information about what each wanted from life.

And from each other.

He shut down the memory. Unnecessary, unwanted. Unwelcome.

'Will you be dining with us tonight?'

Alaina's politely professional enquiry was timely. He

gave a nod, and she entered the information on the screen, then turned to reach for his room key.

For just a moment, Rafaello found himself on the point of saying, *Have dinner with me.*

Good sense silenced him. For a start it was unlikely she would be allowed to dine with a guest, and anyway...

Seeing Alaina again like this, out of the blue, was to no purpose. His time with her all those years ago had been good—OK, he allowed mentally, *memorably* good—but it was long over, and that was the way it should remain. He'd made his decision back then not to take things any further, and there was no reason to question that.

His veiled gaze rested on her as she handed him his key with a professional smile accompanied by her own equally veiled gaze. Was there the slightest tremble in her hand as she held the folder out to him?

'I hope you enjoy your stay with us,' she was saying to him now, in her smiling, impersonal, professional way.

He gave an answering, equally impersonal smile as he took the key, then took hold of his carry-on again, turning to walk towards the elevators at the far end of the lobby. He was conscious he should have said something—made some innocuous remark acknowledging that they knew each other, some passing pleasantry. And he asked himself why he hadn't.

He didn't get an answer.

Alaina gazed at Rafaello's retreating figure, heart thudding. Memories were clamouring—memories of her brief but unforgettable time long ago with Rafaello, on that magical Caribbean island. For a moment she just stood there, almost faint with the aftershock of seeing Rafaello walk back into her life.

'*Mummee!*'

She gave a gasp. Joey was emerging from the rotating door into the hotel, his hand held by Ryan. The instant he was clear he tore free and hurtled towards the reception desk, little face alight with delight.

In horror, she felt the world turn in slow motion, paralysing her. She could not move—not an inch.

Joey reached the desk, placed his little hands on the edge, standing on tiptoes to see her, his smile beaming. But her eyes were not on him. They had gone, as if dragged by weights she could not counter, to the bank of elevators.

She saw Rafaello pause in the act of pressing the button to call one. Saw his hand drop away. Saw him turn around. Saw his eyes go to Joey, hear him cry out *'Mummee!'* again, in excited greeting.

Saw Rafaello's expression change. His body freeze.

Then Ryan reached her desk as well. 'Hi,' he said easily. 'Here he is.' He ruffled Joey's hair with familiar affection.

She couldn't reply. Was incapable of doing so—incapable of anything at all except standing there, chest crushed, breathing impossible.

Rafaello had started to move. But not into the elevator, whose doors were now sliding open. He was coming towards her. Towards Joey. His face had no expression.

For a second—a fleeting instant—Alaina's mind raced. She would imply that Ryan was Joey's father, greet him as such...*anything* to disguise the truth. But as her eyes dropped to Joey she knew that trying to pass him off as Ryan's son—Ryan so fair, so completely unlike Joey—would be impossible.

The evidence of Rafaello's paternity was in Joey's face. Incontestably visible. The dark hair, dark eyes, the shape of his face—all declared it. Oh, there was something of herself in him as well, but he was Rafaello's son. What use would it be to try and deny it?

And Rafaello's gaze was riveted on Joey. Frozen. His every feature pulled tight like a wire.

He reached the desk. Both Ryan and Joey turned to look at him. Ryan stepped away, assuming he was a hotel guest wanting to ask Alaina something. Joey dropped his hands from the edge of the desk, looking curiously at Rafaello but knowing, as Alaina had trained him to know, that when Mummy was working he was not to interrupt.

For one endless second Rafaello just went on looking at Joey. His face was expressionless. Completely and absolutely expressionless. Then his eyes flicked to Ryan. Dismissed him. They shifted again, refocussing on her like lasers.

'Perhaps,' he said, his voice as chillingly expressionless as his face and his eyes going back to Alaina, 'you would care to explain?'

The blood drained from Alaina's face.

Rafaello could feel his heart slugging in his chest, like hammers beating at him from the inside. But he paid no attention. Paid no attention to anything at all except what he had just seen.

'Well?' he prompted, in the same tight, taut voice.

Her face had paled. Gone white as a sheet.

He'd seen witnesses in court look like that, when their alibies were demolished, their lies uncovered.

Lies of commission...

Or lies of omission...

He felt emotion spike somewhere inside him, like the skewering thrust of a knife, but he blanked it. It was essential to do so. Essential to do what he was doing now. Keep his face without expression, his voice without inflection.

She did not answer him. Instead, she came around the

desk, her face still chalk-white, and spoke to the man who was surely irrelevant to this situation.

'Ryan...' her voice was low '...could you take Joey into the café for a few moments? Let him have a diluted orange juice.' Then she was hunkering down to the little boy. 'Joey, darling, nip off with Ryan for five minutes.' She gave him a tight hug, and a kiss on his cheek. Then she straightened, casting another look at Ryan.

Rafaello saw the irrelevant man pause for a moment, exchange a look with Alaina, and then cheerfully take the little boy by the hand and say, 'Come on, Joey, let's get you an OJ!'

They headed off to the café that opened off the lobby at the opposite end from the elevators. Rafaello watched them go for a moment. He felt that knife-thrust inside him again. Sharper this time. More skewering. But still his face was expressionless. Then he turned back to Alaina. She was still as white as a sheet, and he could see a nerve working in her throat.

She'd moved slightly to address one of the young women further down the reception desk, and he heard her ask her to hold the fort for a few minutes.

Then she looked back at him. 'My office,' she said.

She walked into a room behind the reception desk, her gait jerky, her entire body as tense as steel.

Rafaello followed her.

Closed the office door behind him.

Confronted the woman who had lied to him.

Lied to him for five years...

'He's mine.'

Alaina heard the words. They were quite expressionless. Her eyes went to Rafaello and she swallowed. Every muscle in her body was strained. Her throat tight.

'No,' she said, 'he's mine. Joey is my son.'

Did something move in his eyes? Those dark, lidded, completely expressionless eyes? She didn't now—knew only that the office had suddenly become stifling, suffocating. He dominated it. Dominated the room. Dominated everything.

But not me.

She could feel rebellion inside her. Resistance. Her eyes met his, full-on.

'Joey is my son, Rafaello,' she said again.

Her voice was steady, and she was proud of it, because it was costing her everything to keep it so. She took a breath—a careful one, because her lungs felt drained of oxygen.

'When we parted,' she went on, 'five years ago, it was a permanent parting after a very temporary affair. I knew that then. I have known it ever since. I know it now, still. You had no further interest in me and I accepted that. What became of my life thereafter was not your concern.' She paused. 'It still isn't.'

She saw something flash in his eyes, but it was so fast it was soon gone, like a lightning bolt. She went on, doggedly trying to keep her voice steady, ignoring the tremor in it.

'I'm sorry this has happened. It's a shock to you. It's something I would never have imposed on you. My lack of contact these past five years must indicate that to you.'

She swallowed. There seemed to be a brick in her throat, but she swallowed all the same.

'I ask only that you...withdraw from the situation.'

Those lidded, expressionless eyes were still holding hers.

'Is Ryan your partner?' His brows drew together momentarily. 'Your husband?'

With all her heart Alaina wished she could give an answer that would protect her. But she shook her head.

'We help each other out with childcare. Nursery pick-ups

and so on. He's divorced and has a little girl Joey's age he shares custody of. He's…a friend.'

'Good.'

The single monosyllable fell from his lips. It was as un-inflected as anything else he'd addressed to her. Yet something seemed to ease across his shoulders—some of the stiffness, the tension she could see, the shock which, in fairness, he was entitled to feel.

But that was absolutely nothing to the thunderbolt of shock that slayed her at his next words.

'So there will be no impediment to our marriage, then,' he said.

CHAPTER TWO

RAFAELLO HEARD HER GASP. Saw the colour that had drained
from her face suddenly shoot back in. Saw her eyes widen
as if she could not believe what he had just said. Heard her
voice echo his.

'Marriage?'

His mouth tightened. Somewhere, very deep within him,
controlled with absolute insistence, something was moving.
He would not acknowledge it. Would not permit it. Would
deal only with what had to be dealt with right now.

'Just so,' he said.

Her eyes flared. Those expressive eyes that had always
been so much a part of her beauty. But her beauty was irrelevant. There was one focus now. Only one.

'Are you mad?' She stared at him disbelievingly.

He gave a quick, impatient shake of his head.

'Prevarication is without purpose,' he answered. 'Do not
waste my time contesting me.'

He paused, with purpose. The dark, subterranean emotions that were scything through him were strengthening,
but he must continue to control them. Must make clear
straight away the inevitable conclusion of the situation that
had just presented itself like a bullet to his head, requiring
an immediate decision.

'Neither now, nor...' he paused again, to drive his message home '...in court.'

Her face froze again.

'Court?'

He looked at her for a moment. Looked into the pallor of her whitened face.

'For five years,' he said, 'you have had my son. Now I will have him too...'

Alaina heard him speak, but his voice seemed to be coming from a long, long way away. Shock was still going through her—shock after shock after shock.

She felt herself sway...

A hand shot out, gripped her arm.

'Don't pass out on me, Alaina. There is no need.'

For the first time, through the mist that seemed to be rolling in all around her, she heard in his voice something akin to expression. Then she felt herself pressed down, a chair placed beneath her. She sank down on to it with nerveless legs that were suddenly jelly.

'Put your head down...let the blood get to your brain.'

The grip on her arm was released and of its own volition her head sank. Slowly the drumming eased, the mist rolled away. Heavily, she lifted her head.

He was looking down at her. He seemed different now. She didn't know how, or why, but he was. His voice was different too.

'Alaina, we can and shall be civilised about this. But you will need to co-operate with me. I have no wish—none!—to resort to legal proceedings, but please believe me that I will do so if you do not accept that we must now marry. I will give you time to accept that necessity but not a great deal.'

She gazed up at him blankly. Watched as he calmly sat

himself down on another chair, and got his phone out of his jacket pocket, crossing one long leg over the other.

'There is a considerable exchange of information we must make, but we shall begin with the essentials.' He flicked his phone on, ready to tap in information. 'Let's start with your address.'

Rafaello lay on his hotel bed, looking up at the ceiling. There was a lot to get done and he needed to stay focussed. Absently, as if detaching part of his mind from the rest of it, he wondered how he was staying so calm. But he knew how. He had, instinctively, automatically, gone into the mode he adopted when he was being his professional self, and was treating what had happened this evening in the same dispassionate, forensic way. Analysing the situation swiftly, reaching the necessary conclusions, cutting to the chase, disposing of anything unnecessary.

Such as how he must process the information that had been thrust upon him a bare few hours earlier—the existence of a child, concealed from him, for whatever reason, by a woman he had assumed would never cross his path again.

He pulled his mind away from what did not matter right now to what did. To what he had spelt out to her with brutal but essential bluntness, ensuring the message hit home. He started to work his way mentally down the list of things that needed to be done. To be put in order. To be set to rights.

The same emotion that had scythed through him earlier swept its cutting blade through his chest again, extinguishing his breathing momentarily. For a timeless moment it demanded attention, demanded that he acknowledge it—acknowledge its existence and the reason for its existence. With an effort, but with ruthless self-discipline, he defied it.

This is not the occasion.

Then it passed, leaving him back in control. He returned to listing all the things that needed to be done. That neither he nor Alaina had any choice about.

Alaina lay huddled in her bed, duvet pulled tight around her, trying to shut what had happened out of her head. The disaster that had befallen her.

She would have given so much to have had it not happen. Not now.

Five years ago I had to choose—and I've stuck by that choice.

She had resisted, though it had cost her so much strength to do so, the overwhelming temptation to let Rafaello know that their affair had resulted in her pregnancy. It would have given her a means to call him back into her life. But she had known, brutally and inescapably, that he would not welcome the news.

He didn't want me, and he certainly would not have wanted a baby.

That was the blunt reality that had shaped her life since then. That had made her a single working mother, juggling her career and her baby, now an adored child, to give him the best life she could.

But now…

Now a question was pounding in her head—had been pounding ever since Rafaello had informed her he would be calling on her the following evening, to take matters further, then got to his feet and walked out of the office.

She'd sat there numbly for a moment, then jerked to her feet, hurrying out into the lobby. *Was he going to find Joey?* Fear—or an emotion something like fear—had clutched at her, but he had simply been striding towards the elevators and in a moment had disappeared.

Hurriedly, she'd dashed into the hotel's café, where

Joey had been happily finishing his orange juice. Ryan had looked up as Alaina came in, and in his face had been an open question. She hadn't said anything, not with Joey there. She'd dropped a kiss on Joey's head, desperately trying to be normal, sound normal.

'All ready, poppet? Good, then let's say goodnight to Ryan and we can be off very soon. I just need to sort a couple of things, and then we'll get going.'

The three of them had gone back out into the lobby. At the hotel door Ryan had said quietly to her, 'I'm here if you need—'

She'd shaken her head instinctively. His concern had been obvious, but what could she have said to him? That a bomb had just exploded in her life, shattering her into pieces?

He'd patted her arm, his gesture sympathetic, and taken his leave.

Somehow she'd got through the business of handing over to her replacement, getting Joey, very tired by then, back home and into bed. In her head, circling like vultures, Rafaello's chill, expressionless words had gone round and round and round in tighter circles, tighter and tighter. They were circling still.

'Do not waste my time contesting me. Neither now nor in court.'

Oh, God, would he do that? Fear stabbed her.

What am I going to do? Dear God, what am I going to do?

The question echoed in her head. Finding no answer.

Rafaello's taxi pulled up at a small, modern semi-detached house in a quiet, tree-lined road on the residential edge of the town closest to the airport and he got out. He'd been busy that day. Very busy. He'd gone into London, had his meeting with his client, cancelled his homeward flight, changed his room reservation to an open-ended stay, then started the process of checking UK law on disputed child custody and the fastest way to marry.

Alaina could take her choice. He would allow no other.

He set that out plainly to her as he sat himself down in the compact but comfortable modestly appointed sitting room.

Tension was racking through her—that was obvious enough. She sat perched on the sofa opposite his armchair, hands clasped tightly in her lap so that the knuckles showed white. Though his own habitually well-schooled demeanour displayed no tension, he was aware that it was present all the same.

But how could it not be, given the revelation that had ripped into his life twenty-four hours ago? Tearing it apart...

'So, what decision have you come to?' he asked.

His eyes rested on her. She was pale, but not as ghost-white as she'd been the night before. Her hair was still drawn back off her face, and she wore not a scrap of make-up. She was wearing long black trousers and a dark green polo-neck jumper emphasised her pallor.

In spite of that, her beauty was undimmed.

He could feel it drawing him—just as it had five years ago, when he had first seen her, catching his lingering eye as she sunned herself on the beach. But he pulled his wayward thoughts to heel. It had been her beauty then, her allure for him, that had resulted in this situation. The situation which must hold his sole focus—without the distraction of recognising that her beauty was undimmed. That did not matter—he would not allow it to.

He gave himself an admonishing mental shake. All that mattered was that upstairs his son was sleeping— the son who, a bare twenty-four hours earlier, he had not even known existed. Emotion came again, slicing through him—that same dark, unnameable emotion that had scythed through him last night as he had taken on board the realisation of what had been hidden from him, deliberately and determinedly.

But this was no time for indulging in emotions. They only made for confusion and conflict. It was a lesson he'd learnt early in life. His father had been very clear about the importance of that lesson. Life ran far more smoothly without excessive emotion getting in the way.

So now he would apply that hard-earned knowledge. Would resolve matters as swiftly and as expediently as necessary. He had given Alaina a clear choice. Now she must make it.

'Well?' he prompted.

He saw her swallow, lick her lips—and ignored the flicker inside him that the unconscious gesture caused. That, too, was utterly irrelevant to the situation. His keen legal mind would allow no distractions, no deviations.

He saw her hands clench more tightly. She swallowed again, then spoke.

'Before…before I answer you, you must tell me why… why you want anything to do with…'

'With my son?' He completed her sentence, unable to keep the edge out of his voice. 'The answer is in the very statement. *My son.*'

Something flared in her eyes. Fear, or rejection, or protest. He didn't know. Didn't care.

'But *why*? What we had—it was a holiday romance! You said as much. You made it crystal-clear you didn't want anything more!'

'No,' he answered. 'I didn't.' Truthful. Brutal. But protecting her feelings right now was not his priority. 'But I want my son.'

'Why?'

The word was wrung from her. He looked across at her.

'Why do *you* want him?' he countered.

Her face contorted. 'That's a stupid question!'

'No more stupid than you asking me.' He could hear the edge back in his voice, like a honed blade. 'I want him.'

'But you've had nothing to do with him! You don't know him. You're a stranger—a complete stranger!'

That nameless emotion scythed through him again, more powerfully this time, and this time he could not bank it down. His mouth thinned, like a whip.

'You sit there, having kept my son from me, kept from me all knowledge of him, and presume to say that to me?' He held up a hand. Peremptory. Impatient. As when a witness attempted to prevaricate. 'Alaina, you will believe me on this, if nothing else. I am my son's father. I have responsibilities that come with that. Responsibilities I have no intention of reneging on. I will be part of his life, as his father. All that is to be decided is whether we do this the civil way...or the uncivil. I can't tell you which to choose—only you can do that. So...choose.'

He paused.

'Custody battles can be vicious, expensive and destructive. And...' his voice changed '...unnecessary.'

He paused again, not letting her eyes drop from his. When he spoke his voice had changed again.

'The alternative,' he said, 'is what I will outline to you.'

He drew a breath. Her hands were still clutched together, knuckles still white. There was tension in every line of her body, her face drawn and pale. He made his voice calm, composed, unemotional. Setting out the situation the same way he did with his clients.

'If you agree to a marriage between us,' he said, spelling it out, his voice neutral, his expression likewise, 'it will be on the following lines. We make a civil marriage in as short a time as the law allows. You resign from your job. You travel with me, with our son, and you come to live in Italy with me. I will provide a suitable home, and our marriage will be civilised and without hostility. You will accept the situation as it must be.'

He paused again, his gaze resting steadily, unreadably, on her. 'Is that not a less destructive option?'

He saw her shut her eyes, shake her head slowly. But not in rejection. More in exhaustion. Her head drooped.

Rafaello surveyed her. Long experience usually told him when his point had been taken. When his goal had been achieved. His eyes rested on her. Memory mixed with the present moment. Conflating. Confusing.

He did not care for confusion. He required clarity at all times. Clarity and control. Or chaos ensued.

Her eyes opened, meeting his. She was making them meet his, he could see.

He spoke again and his voice was conciliatory. Collusive, even.

'Alaina, whatever my opinion on whether you should have told me our affair had left you pregnant, you made the decision you did. Now that I know about my son, however, you must decide again. I would infinitely prefer not to go down the ugly route that leads to a courtroom, which is why I will argue in favour of the alternative I have put to you.'

He paused for a moment, letting her absorb what he was telling her, just as he did with his clients, getting them to accept what they might not wish to, but what the law would insist on.

He was insisting now. But his tone of voice was still conciliatory as he picked up his speech again. Her hostility would not be helpful—would only hinder the outcome that he wished to achieve.

'If it helps you accept it, consider that this need not be

permanent. For a young child, a stable home with both parents provides the most secure childhood. But...'

Even as he spoke memory burned in him, like a cigarette being extinguished on his skin. Had his own childhood been secure, for all the married status of his ill-matched parents? In his head he could hear his mother's weeping voice, calling in anguish to her husband, could see his father dislodging her clinging hands, walking out of the room in stiff, exasperated strides. Then he saw his mother, stooping down, face ravaged by tears, clutching him to her, still weeping hysterically. His own body had been as stiff and tense as his father's...

He thrust the memory from him. Whatever this marriage he now had to make would be, he would ensure it was nothing like his parents'. It would be calm, and civilised, and emotion would be completely unnecessary.

His mouth compressed for a moment and then he continued, setting the scene for this woman who had, without any intention on his part, borne him a son.

'But an older child, able to express his own views in a rational way, would have no objection to us divorcing and making our own individual lives again. That is for the future—but bear it in mind as you make your decision now.'

He paused for a moment, letting the information be absorbed. Then he spoke again, his voice as calm as ever.

'Give me your answer tomorrow. Then I will make the appropriate arrangements—whatever they are to be.'

She lifted her head, looked at him without expression. Closed in on herself.

'You know,' she said. 'You already know what those arrangements will be. You have spelt it out to me. A custody battle would be hideous and—' he saw her mouth twist '—what kind of lawyer could I possibly afford to stand against you?'

Something moved in her eyes—an expression he could not read. Then she said, with emphasis in her voice, 'I would never, *never* put Joey through that! Anything has to be better than that. *Anything!*'

He gave a slow, considered nod. Her face was still pale, her tension unabated.

'I am glad that is how you see it,' he said. He paused, then spoke again. 'Alaina, understand that my responsibility for my son is absolute—as is yours. Our decisions can only be based on that.'

He got to his feet, moved to the door of the sitting room.

'I'll take my leave—don't see me out.'

He walked out of the room. As he passed the staircase his glance went upwards. Somewhere up there the son of whose existence he had had no idea was sleeping...

Once again that scything of emotion cut through him. Then, with a quickening stride, he let himself out, climbing into the taxi he'd ordered to wait by the kerb, and was gone.

Alaina sat on the floor beside Joey's little bed. He was fast asleep, teddy clasped to him. Her heart was heavy, and she was hearing again Rafaello's voice in her head—but from long ago. Five years ago.

'I'm sorry if you've read more into our time together than there has been in reality. Perhaps the island is to blame— palm trees and silver sand and a tropical moon can send the wrong messages.'

Was that all it had been? The working of the moon on the sea? The gentle soughing of the warm breeze in the fronded palms? The soft sand beneath her feet as they'd walked along the midnight beach? The velvet seduction of his mouth on hers as he took her into his arms? Had it only been the romance of the place that had made her so susceptible to him? That had made her want to chuck in her job, be whisked back to Rome with him, to want her time with him to go on and on…?

Because Rafaello was a man like no other she had known. She had known that vividly, from the very start. Oh, the setting out in the Caribbean had helped—she acknowledged that—but that was not the reason she had been so smitten. It was Rafaello himself.

From the moment she'd glanced up from her sunbathing to find herself being leisurely, appreciatively perused by a tall, good-looking, sable-haired man strolling along the beach from the Falcone hotel next door. His lean, fit body had been displayed very nicely by dark green shorts and an open-fronted moss-green short-sleeved cotton shirt. His eyes had been shaded by designer shades, making him look—she'd gulped silently—darkly glamorous and enticing.

From that very moment she'd been hooked. When she'd encountered him again, the following evening, going across to the Falcone with some off-duty colleagues to the famous weekly barbecue there, she had not made the slightest objection when he'd singled her out and, with effortless ease, taken her off to share a quiet coffee and liqueur with him on the far side of the crowded pool and barbecue area.

It was all that had proved necessary. His eyes, his attentions… All had told her he found her desirable. And she… Oh, she had found him even more so…

She had gone along with his skilled, effortless seduction with full, enraptured co-operation. Giving herself entirely to the romance of it all. Snatching every moment she could to be with him. Knowing, instinctively, powerfully, irresistibly, that this was a romance like no other…knowing how very, very close she was to falling in love with him…

She had known, above all, that had he asked her to stay with him she'd have given only one answer. Known she was standing on the edge of the very cliff her mother had warned her of.

'Be careful...oh, so careful, my darling daughter! Do not give your heart to someone who does not want it—as I have done.'

But she had pulled back from the edge of that cliff just in time. Saved herself from her mother's heartbreak.

Rafaello had not asked her to stay with him.

Yet now he was demanding just that—because of Joey.

There was an irony in it somewhere—one that had an edge to it. A sharp and cutting edge.

She got to her feet, still looking down at Joey, sleeping so peacefully. In the morning, his life would change for ever—and there was absolutely nothing she could do about it. And her life would change for ever too. She would uproot herself, give up her job, leave her little house, the friends she'd made, leave her familiar life to move a thousand miles away, settle in a foreign land. And there was absolutely nothing she could do about that either...

And, since there was nothing she could do about it, she shut her eyes for a moment. What else could she do but accept it?

Nothing...nothing at all.

Slowly, she opened her eyes again, looked down at her precious son, sleeping so peacefully. Her heart was full, and heavy, as she walked quietly from the room.

CHAPTER THREE

RAFAELLO STEPPED OUT of the taxi that had just pulled up outside Alaina's house. This time it was morning, not evening. This time there was no confrontation awaiting him. Alaina had yielded to what was the only sane and reasonable outcome for the situation in which they both found themselves.

But even if there was no confrontation, what *was* awaiting him brought far more tension. He would be meeting his son.

For a second, blankness descended on him. What did he know of fatherhood? Nothing. It was a skill he'd never required. Never contemplated or thought about. But now he must.

How do I do this?

The question was blunt and stark, and memory flashed suddenly—unbidden and unwelcome. His father. Shooting a frowning, displeased look at him, telling him brusquely to lower his voice, enquiring acidly whether he had completed the assignments set by his school for the summer holidays… Then making some crushing reply to his mother, who had immediately protested, telling him something about the holidays being for relaxation and enjoyment. Then walking out of the room, his displeasure evident, back to his study, where no one was permitted to disturb him.

He thrust the memory away. Whatever kind of father he made for the son whose existence he had just discovered, he would not be harsh, like his own father. Never that.

I will do my best by him.

Whatever that 'best' was.

His expression set. After all, wasn't he prepared to give up the life he had enjoyed immensely till now? Give up his freedom, his comfortable, self-considering existence, to marry, to change his life completely, change his way of living? He would do that for his son, unhesitatingly, un-flinchingly.

Resolved—steeled—he pressed the doorbell.

'Joey, darling, there's someone I want you to meet.'

The doorbell had just rung and Joey had looked up from his train set, which he was laying out on the sitting room floor with Alaina. She got up and went to the front door, conscious of a tightening in her lungs, a rise in her heart rate.

Rafaello, on schedule, was standing there. Dressed in the same charcoal-grey suit with its immaculate Italian tailoring, his shirt pristine, his silk tie stylish but understated, a brief glint of gold from his cufflinks. A completely irrelevant kick went through her at the impact he made, but she stifled it.

Rafaello greeted her coolly, and she made herself answer in the same way. Yet for all his self-contained composure she was aware of a tension in him that mirrored her own. Well, that was hardly surprising...

She led him into the sitting room.

Joey looked interestedly at him. 'You're the man at the hotel,' he announced.

Alaina saw Rafaello nod gravely. She was standing

slightly to one side, and she could feel her already elevated heart rate racking up a notch.

'Yes, I am,' Rafaello said. 'And you are Joey.'

'Hello,' said Joey. He cocked his head to one side. 'I am playing with my trains,' he informed Rafaello.

'So you are,' Rafaello agreed, in the same grave manner.

Alaina could see a nerve working at his cheekbone, but he gave no other sign that he was, for the very first time in his life, talking to the son he had never known existed.

A shadow passed over her face.

Did I do the right thing, keeping Joey's existence from him?

It was a troubling thought—and a familiar one. She had struggled with it all through her pregnancy, and the decision not to tell Rafaello, to make no contact with him, had not been an easy one. She felt her chest tighten painfully. Now the struggle was over—whether she liked it or not.

Rafaello knew about Joey.

Knew about him. Wanted him. Was determined to have him, whatever it took.

Even to the point of marrying her.

She felt a lump inside her, hard and heavy. Five years ago, had Rafaello asked her to marry him, had he swept her off her feet and back to Italy, she'd have thrown herself into his arms and been carried off by him in a state of romantic bliss, a whirlwind of longing fulfilled...

Now it was different. So very, very different.

Joey was telling Rafaello about his trains. Rafaello had an attentive expression on his face. The two faces were so alike in appearance. She watched them both, her emotions confused. Father and son...

'Won't you sit down?' She gestured to the sofa.

'Thank you,' said Rafaello, still speaking gravely, and did so.

His tall figure seemed to dwarf the small sofa, as it had the previous night, when he'd given her the option of marrying him or fighting him for custody.

She felt emotion churn within her—and not all of it was on account of that impossible choice. As her gaze went to Rafaello, she felt again the impact of his presence. Again, she pushed it aside. She must not dwell on how her gaze wanted to drink him in, must not conjure memories, nor allow emotions that had no place.

I banished them a long, long time ago. I let them wither and die, and never gave them air or light to breathe and survive.

And it was essential—utterly essential—that she never let herself remember her time with him. It would serve no purpose. The only purpose was Joey.

She took a breath, hunkering down beside him on the carpet.

'Joey, darling, there's something I must tell you.' She took one of his little hands in his. Took another breath, conscious of how tight her throat suddenly was. 'This is your *papà*, Joey. Your daddy. Like Ryan is Betsy's daddy.'

Joey's gaze went to Rafaello, open and direct as only a child's could be.

'Hello,' he said. Then he frowned. 'Why were you not here before?' he asked.

Alaina felt her throat constrict even more. Oh, dear God…out of the mouths of babes and innocents…

Her eyes flew to Rafaello. What would he say? Panic beat briefly.

'I have been abroad, Joey,' Rafaello said calmly. 'I live in Italy. And now,' he said, in the same matter-of-fact manner, 'you and your mother are going to be coming to live with me there too.'

Joey's gaze had gone back to Alaina. 'Are we, Mummy?' he asked for confirmation.

She nodded, her throat still tight. 'Yes,' she said. 'It will be fun.'

He looked at her consideringly, then at Rafaello, then back at Alaina. 'Can I bring my trains?' he asked. 'And all my toys?'

'Yes,' said Rafaello.

'Good,' said Joey.

That, it seemed, was all he needed to know. He went back to laying out the track, talking to his trains and answering back for them as he moved them along the track.

Rafaello got quietly to his feet, and Alaina stood up too.

'Would…would you like a coffee?' she asked, not quite knowing what to do or say now.

She led the way into the kitchen—Joey would be happy for a while now, occupied with his train set. Rafaello followed her, perching himself on a stool by the narrow breakfast bar.

She busied herself putting on the kettle. 'It's only instant,' she apologised.

'Fa niente,' he answered.

She swallowed. 'That…that seems to have gone off… well,' she said. 'Maybe children just…just accept things.'

'As we must too,' Rafaello replied.

She nodded, went back to measuring the coffee into mugs. 'What happens now?' she asked.

She was being very calm and was grateful for it. Maybe staying calm, not letting emotions cloud and confuse and upset her—emotions for which there was no place, surely?—was the best or rather least worst way of coping?

Rafaello was being calm, cool and dispassionate—and she would be too. Somehow it made this entire unreal situation less…

Less real?

She felt her heart rate quicken, adrenaline starting to run. How could she possibly be standing here, making coffee for a man who'd told her she must marry him or face a custody battle for her beloved son? A man she hadn't seen for five years? A man she'd never thought to see again...?

How unreal is this? Totally, totally unreal!

Except that it wasn't—and she had to deal with it, process it, adopt a façade, at the very least, of being as calm as he was as they coolly discussed the practicalities of what was going to change their lives for ever.

He was answering her, and she dragged her wayward mind back to what he was saying.

'Paperwork,' came his reply. 'Setting in motion the necessities required for our marriage. Does Joey have a passport?'

'Yes. We went to France on the Eurostar last Christmas, with Ryan and Betsy.'

Rafaello's face suddenly hardened. Alaina pre-empted what was obviously going to be his next question. 'I told you—he's just a friend. In France he shared with Betsy and I shared with Joey. We went to the big theme parks just outside Paris—the children were over the moon.'

Even as she explained, she felt resentful. Why should she defend herself? Even had she wanted an affair with Ryan— had she wanted more than an affair—what business would it be of Rafaello's?

He didn't want me. He made that clear.

Just as he was making it crystal-clear it was Joey he wanted now, not her...

She made herself say it in her head. That, and nothing more, was to be the basis of their marriage. The reason for it. Nothing else.

We'll just be Joey's parents—that's all. Nothing else...

She shut down her thoughts. She was coping as best she could. Forty-eight hours earlier her life had been what it had been for the last five years. Now it was turned upside down. She would cope only by taking one step at a time. Looking no further than that.

It's all I can deal with.

She filled his coffee mug, placed it in front of him. He drank it black, she remembered. But then there was such a lot she remembered about him…

She pulled her thoughts away. Back to something she wanted him to tell her.

'What is Joey to call you? I mean… Dad, or Daddy, or something in Italian? What?'

'Papà will be fine,' Rafaello said.

She nodded, pouring milk into her own coffee.

'He will need to learn Italian,' Rafaello went on. 'You as well—it would be helpful.'

'OK,' she said. 'Joey will probably pick it up faster than I will—they are like sponges at that age. I'm sure he'll be speaking it in no time.'

A sudden convulsion went through her. It showed in her face, she knew, but she could not stop it. This was not the childhood she had thought Joey would have—being taken from his home to another country, having to learn that language, taking the nationality of his father…the father who didn't know him at all.

And why is that?

The question stabbed at her, but she stabbed back.

I had to make that call! I had to decide whether a man who had made it crystal-clear I was a holiday romance only would regard his son's existence as anything but an unwelcome nuisance. Would wish he didn't exist at all.

But she couldn't and wouldn't rehash that argument. Nor was there any point in doing so. It was the present she had to deal with—not the past. Rafaello had walked back into her life. She had never thought he would, but he had. And he'd announced that he wanted a role in Joey's life.

He was going to have one.

And that was all there was to it.

So there are no more decisions for me to make. I'm going along with this because the alternative would be a nightmare I could not endure and could never risk.

She dropped her eyes to her coffee, mechanically stirring in the milk. A question was stirring in her head as well. A question she didn't want to ask—let alone answer.

But what are you risking this way?

She thrust it away. Refusing to heed it.

The taxi was back yet again, outside Alaina's house, but this time Rafaello was not going in. She was coming out. And when she did it would be to lock the door after her and leave her life in England behind.

She will join her life to mine.

It was not the way he'd intended the years ahead to play out, but necessity—in the form of their son—required it. And Alaina, too, acknowledged that necessity. Accepted the necessity of their marriage as composedly and dispassionately as he did—for that he was decidedly appreciative.

He shut his eyes for a moment, felt memories of his own childhood pressing in again. His mother's endless out-of-control emotion, her hysteria as his father coldly condemned it, always weeping and wailing…

What if the woman he was having to marry was anything like that?

He felt an inner shudder, followed by a sense of relief.

We shall make it as good a marriage as circumstances permit. We will primarily be parents, make a stable home for our son.

Anything else...

He felt his mind shy away. Anything else would be dealt with as and when it occurred. It was not necessary to think about it now.

Through the taxi window he saw her emerge and lock the door behind her. She stood, just for a moment, looking at the house she owned. The house she was leaving. Then, with a straightening of her shoulders, she turned and walked towards the taxi at the kerb, pulling her cabin bag with her. Their main luggage had been air-freighted out that week, was now awaiting her in Rome.

They would marry that afternoon, collect Joey from nursery, then fly out to Italy. Their marriage would begin today.

That was all there was to it. It was necessary, and it would be done.

He stepped out, went to relieve her of her cabin bag, usher her into the taxi. She was pale, but calm, wearing her business suit, her hair neat in its French plait, her make-up minimal.

A frown of sudden displeasure crossed Rafaello's face. Whatever their priorities in Italy, one priority was clear. She must dress according to her role as his wife. Displeasure turned to a glint in his eyes. Playing down her beauty, as she now did, would no longer be required.

He shook off the thought. That was for later. For now, there was a wedding to get through.

He turned to her. 'Ready?' he asked.

Did her fingers tighten over her handbag? He wasn't sure. But her voice was calm, if taut, as she answered him.

'Yes,' she said.

It was all that was necessary for him to hear.

The taxi moved off. Taking them to their wedding.

Alaina stood beside Rafaello in the register office. Other than a floral display on the table, there was no sign that something as celebratory as a wedding was taking place. Rafaello was wearing a business suit and so was she—she'd finished her last shift at the hotel that morning, and her employment there. Joey was at nursery. His last day too.

They would be flying out to Italy after this brief but legally binding ceremony made her Rafaello's wife.

To begin their new life there.

In the weeks that had passed since Rafaello had discovered the existence of Joey, Alaina felt—in so far as she was allowing herself to feel anything at all—she had come to passively accept what was going to happen now. In that she had been helped by Rafaello's own attitude, and she found herself mirroring it. It was the simplest way to deal with the situation. He was calm, composed and matter-of-fact. So was she.

That matter-of-fact attitude was good for Joey, too.

If he sees me accepting what is happening, then so will he. He seems, in his simple, childlike way, to have accepted Rafaello's appearance in his life. And if Joey can accept him—so can I.

Because this marriage she was making—entering into right at this very moment—had nothing to do with her or with Rafaello. It had nothing to do with what had once been between them—with what she had wanted and he had not. It had nothing to do with her having once stood so close to the brink of falling in love with Rafaello—or with the fact that she had pulled back just in time when he'd returned to Italy. It had nothing to do with their feelings, or what they themselves wanted or might want.

It was for Joey's sake. That was all.

Only Joey.

And that, she knew, as she stood there giving the responses the registrar required, speaking in a voice that was as calm and composed as Rafaello's as he gave his own responses, was what was going to make it possible for her to make this marriage work.

Joey was gazing out of the window at the Rome traffic, but was too sleepy to take in any of it. He'd enjoyed the flight over, asking Rafaello endless questions, which had been patiently answered—from why the plane didn't fall out of the sky to why the packet of unopened crisps had gone so puffy.

Alaina had been glad to leave them to it, staring blankly out of the window at the white cloudscape beyond. Now, leaning back in the luxurious interior of the chauffeured car into which Rafaello had ushered them at the airport, she felt thoughts circling in her mind, slow and incomprehensible.

This is my wedding day...

But it was best not to dwell on that. Better to focus only on practicalities, as she had ever since she had accepted the choice Rafaello had put before her.

Landing in Italy had brought home to her just how much she was changing her life. It had made her glad that she had laid down some stipulations of her own. Joey would keep his British citizenship, and so would she. Her passport was still in her own name, and his too. She would keep her house, bought with an inheritance from her late mother. She would keep her own credit cards and bank accounts, and all her financial affairs—such as they were—would remain hers.

Whatever she was to become as Rafaello's wife, she would remain who she was as well. Rafaello had made no demur at all, and she was glad of that too.

His words came back to her now.

'We can do this—we can make a civil, civilised marriage.'

And that was what they would do. She drew a breath, fingers tightening over her handbag. Yes, a civil, civilised marriage. It could be done. It must be done. It *would* be done.

'We're nearly there.' Rafaello's low voice penetrated her thoughts. 'My apartment is in an old nineteenth-century mansion in the *centro storico*. As we discussed, it will be our base for now, but Joey will want more space, so we'll take a house outside the city as well. Finding something suitable will be a priority.'

She nodded, and when a short time later she stood in the elegant surroundings of Rafaello's apartment, she could see how it was not an ideal home for Joey. Occupying the *piano nobile* of the grand old house, with a cobbled inner courtyard its only outdoor space, it was furnished with antiques and displayed what she suspected were very expensive *objets d'art*. Not at all appropriate for a lively four-year-old.

Not that Joey was lively at the moment, leaning against her half asleep and yawning.

Rafaello showed them into a bedroom where a truckle bed had been set up next to a beautiful carved one swathed in a richly embroidered counterpane that she swiftly removed and folded to place safely in the equally beautiful carved wardrobe.

Then, focussing on getting Joey to bed, she led him into the en suite bathroom, as opulent as the bedroom, and gave him a very cursory 'up and down' flannel wash. She whisked him into his pyjamas, and tucked him into the truckle bed with his beloved Mr Teds clutched to him. He was asleep in moments.

She stood looking down at him, her heart feeling strange. For the sake of this so beloved child she had uprooted herself from everything that was familiar, from the life she had painstakingly made for herself. Had committed to a marriage that felt more unreal than anything else...

She bent to bestow a swift, emotional kiss upon Joey's forehead, a wave of love welling out from her.

I can do this! I can do this for you, my darling boy! And it will be all right! I promise you I will do everything to make it all right for you!

She straightened, still gazing down at him in the soft light from the bedside lamp on the far side of the other bed. Then, with a breath, she turned and left the room.

She found Rafaello waiting for her in the apartment's dining room. Beautifully draped dark green velvet curtains shaded the sash windows, and a polished mahogany table was set for two with silverware, crystal glasses and linen napery. For the first time it struck her that Rafaello Ranieri was a substantially wealthy man.

Oh, she had known that ever since their first encounter—no one staying at the Falcone, next door to the four-star hotel she'd worked at, could ever be anything other than wealthy. But he'd been on holiday, and it hadn't really registered. They'd dined out at expensive restaurants, true, and his clothes—even the beach casuals he'd worn—had clearly not come from chain stores, but for all that she'd paid little attention to his material circumstances.

Now, as he greeted her in his cool fashion, enquired after Joey and then invited her to take her place at the table, she glanced around her at the ultra-elegant apartment, at the antiques and *objets d'art*, at the old-fashioned landscape paintings on the walls that might as well have been in a museum, it was hitting home.

The emergence of a manservant through a service door only emphasised it.

Rafaello introduced her, and the middle-aged man bowed his head politely. He proceeded to beckon to a maid, who came forward with their *aperitivo*, then presented to Rafaello a bottle of wine from the marble-topped sideboard.

Carefully, Alaina spread a pristine linen napkin over her lap, hearing again Rafaello's introduction of her to his staff.

'This is Signora Ranieri.'

It was the first time she'd heard it, and she could feel a jolt of disbelief go through her.

'Alaina?'

Rafaello was indicating to her, asking whether she would care for wine. She nodded, and he poured her a glass. The maid was placing plates in front of them, and Alaina murmured her thanks. Then the staff left them to it and she was alone with Rafaello. The man she had married that afternoon for the sake of the little boy now fast asleep in that bedroom.

'I think,' Rafaello announced, 'we should drink a toast, Alaina.'

She saw him lift his glass, tilt it across the table towards her.

'To making this a successful marriage,' he said.

His voice was as cool as it ever was, but there was a strange expression in his dark eyes.

'We can do it, Alaina,' he said quietly. 'If we put our minds to it.'

She nodded numbly, lifting her own glass. She could not quite return his toast, but took a mouthful of the ruby liquid. It tasted rich, and expensive, and she hadn't the faintest idea what it was. But it went with the restrained elegance all around her—with the cool, composed man sitting opposite her, so good-looking in his austere way, with his slate-dark, long-lashed eyes and a sensual twist to his well-shaped mouth...

Out of nowhere, she felt danger lick at her. Danger... and memory.

She must permit neither. Not in a marriage like theirs.

She set down her glass with a click.

'Yes,' she said, 'I think we can.'

A faint smile curved his mouth and he lowered his glass, picking up his knife and fork to do justice to the buttered scallops on his plate, bathed in a saffron *jus*.

Alaina picked up her cutlery too, and started on her dinner.

The first meal of her new life with Rafaello.

Her husband.

It still felt completely and totally unreal.

CHAPTER FOUR

DESPITE HER ASSUMPTION to the contrary, Alaina slept well and dreamlessly. So did Joey—for which she was very grateful. He woke her, as he always did, by clambering into bed with her, Mr Teds clutched in one hand, and snuggling up to her.

'Morning, munchkin,' she greeted him drowsily.

His little body was strong, and warm, and precious to embrace.

'Are we on holiday?' he asked.

She smiled. 'It will feel like a holiday, yes,' she said. 'But it's a sort of adventure too.'

'I like adventures,' he replied happily.

Alaina was glad of his answer. Even if it only applied for now. The whole question of how he would adapt to the way his life would be now hung unanswered and unanswerable.

A piercing longing filled her to get a taxi to the airport, take the first flight home, back to the life she had made for herself these last five years.

But that life was gone.

It was this new one she had to get used to. And so did Joey.

She busied herself getting Joey up and dressing him in cotton trousers and a checked shirt. She dressed herself in sleek black trousers and a lightweight knitted top, drew her hair back into her customary French plait. She was not bothering with make-up because there was no need for any. In the dining room, already seated, was Rafaello, surrounded by breakfast. He rose to his feet as she came in.

'*Buongiorno,*' he said, pleasantly enough.

His glance went to Joey. Did it change? Alaina couldn't tell. She was too preoccupied with controlling her own reaction to seeing Rafaello, feeling that kick in her pulse coming again. Would she get used to it? Well, she must—that was all, she resolved.

The novelty will wear off before long.

That was the way to think of it. She was not letting him get to her.

He wasn't paying attention to her at the moment, and that was good at least. He pulled out a chair beside him, already supplied with a booster seat, and Joey trotted forward enthusiastically, clambering up, as Alaina took another chair. Three breakfast places had been laid, and on the table was a jug of orange juice, a pot of coffee, hot milk, and a generous basket of delicious-looking bread rolls and pastries, with pats of butter, jam and honey.

'Yummy!' said Joey, eyeing it all in a pleased fashion.

Alaina poured some orange juice for him, diluting it with iced water from a jug also on the table, then buttering one of the bread rolls for him.

'Bread roll first, then you can have one of the croissants,' she told him.

'In Italy, croissants are called *cornetti*,' said Rafaello.

'Like ice-cream cornets,' said Joey, looking at him.

'Yes, because both are horn-shaped, and "horn" is the root Latin word,' supplied Rafaello.

'What is Latin?' Joey asked, biting into his bread roll.

'It is the language spoken by the ancestors of the Italians—the Romans. The Romans lived very long ago, and ruled Europe, and many of the words they used we still find in our languages today. Like cornet and *cornetti*.'

Alaina sat quietly, pouring herself some orange juice and then a cup of strong, aromatic coffee, which she diluted with hot milk.

Memory struck her: breakfasting with Rafaello on the balcony of his room at the Falcone, sunshine blazing on the azure sea, her wrapped in the cotton bathrobe that came with the room, Rafaello in a grey silk knee-length dressing gown, its wide lapels showing his smooth chest, long legs stretched out, both of them languorous from their morning lovemaking...

She snapped the memory shut. That was then. This was now. And there were five long years in between.

Her eyes dropped to her son, munching on his bread roll while his father told him more about the Romans and he listened interestedly.

All that links me to Rafaello is Joey—nothing else.

That was what she must remember. She was here, back in Rafaello's smooth, ordered life, simply because there had been a failure of contraception. An accident. Unintended... unintentional.

She felt her heart contract as her eyes rested on Joey, her expression softening automatically. A wave of love so overwhelming it was almost unbearable dissolved her. Out of that 'accident' had come the most precious baby in all the world...the most beloved son.

And for his sake—only his—I am going to do anything! Anything at all for him!

Including what she had done yesterday.

Her eyes lifted to Rafaello, still talking with Joey. His face was unreadable.

Emotions, strange and inchoate, ebbed and flowed within her, making little sense.

But it didn't matter what she felt or didn't feel, nor that she couldn't work out what she was feeling. The die had been cast. Yesterday she had become the wife of Joey's father, and from now on that was what she must steer her course by.

Their discussion of the ancient Romans came to an end, with Joey diverted by finishing his buttered roll and remembering what she'd said about the *cornetti*. She gave her permission, and he helped himself to one, soon getting stuck in in a crumby sort of way.

She turned to Rafaello. 'What is to happen today?' she asked him.

He took a mouthful of his coffee. 'I plan on driving us out beyond the city. I have a shortlist of houses to view, and you can choose which you think most suitable.'

They set off on just that mission shortly after breakfast.

Joey, cleaned up from the stickiness he'd acquired over breakfast, happily climbed into the sleek saloon car waiting for them at the kerbside. Alaina took a moment to look about her at the cobbled *piazza*, lined by elegant, terraced mansions and sporting an ornate stone fountain in the centre, from which water was issuing sedately. The ambience was one of distinct but understated wealth.

It suited Rafaello, she thought.

'This apartment is very conveniently situated,' he said, dismissing the chauffeur as Alaina took her seat beside Joey and taking the wheel himself. 'A good base for when we are entertaining or going out by ourselves.'

'By ourselves?' Alaina spoke sharply.

'Whichever house outside the city you choose, it will be staffed,' Rafaello said. 'So there will always be care for Joey there. As my *wife*, Alaina,' he said, and his voice had changed, but she didn't quite know how, 'you will be required to do some socialising.'

She didn't answer, only settled Joey into his child seat. She wasn't sure what to make of what Rafaello had just announced.

Maybe I just haven't thought that far ahead.

She pushed it out of her mind as Rafaello drove off, and both she and Joey looked out of the windows with interest as they turned into a wider street and the vibrant city of Rome leapt into life. The traffic was appalling, and she made a comment to say so.

'Notorious!' he agreed. 'It's why I seldom drive myself. Being driven means I can get work done while stuck in traffic.'

It seemed a justifiable explanation for such luxury, but it was also, Alaina knew, another indication that Rafaello Ranieri was a wealthy man. She didn't know how wealthy and didn't much care. She knew only that he had the funds— and his own legal skill, of course—to mount a formidable custody challenge, should she have defied him about what had taken place yesterday at the register office.

She felt her hands tighten in her lap. Surely anything was better than that?

She shook the question from her. It was too late to have questions or doubts—the deed was done. Like it or not, she had uprooted her life—and Joey's—and now she was Signora Ranieri... Rafaello's wife. She took a quick breath. Whether it felt real or unreal made no difference to that truth whatsoever.

She just had to get on with it. With as good a grace as she could muster.

Rafaello paused at the exit of the driveway of the third house that Alaina had rejected and consulted the estate agent's list on his phone. Would the next house fare any better? She had rejected the first three on the grounds that they were too large, too grand and too formal.

'Isn't there anywhere more…well, *ordinary*?' she asked now.

He turned to look at her. 'Is that what you would prefer?' His voice was studiedly neutral.

'Yes,' she said.

'Very well.'

He set off again. The villa they were now heading for had not been in his top three, and it was a little further out from the city than he'd planned, but when they drove up to it Alaina smiled.

'Oh, but this is charming!' she exclaimed. Her voice was warm.

They got out of the car and he could see her looking about, her expression also warm. The narrow road beyond the stone wall girding the perimeter had been very quiet, and certainly there was no audible traffic here, only birdsong in the plentiful trees all about. The villa was Mediterranean in style but of indeterminate age, and it seemed to nestle into the large gardens encircling it. It was only two storeys, in white stone, with arched windows and colourful flowerbeds running along the frontage.

They went inside, and Alaina continued to be charmed. For himself, Rafaello thought it could do with refurbishment, and he said as much.

Alaina cast him a look. 'Your standards are a clearly a good deal higher than mine—it all looks beautiful. And homely.' She glanced around. 'What about the furniture?'

'There's an option to include it, but I assume you would want to start afresh.'

She shook her head. 'It suits the house. And anything new would have to be made Joey-proof! Besides…' she cast him another look '…you can't tell me this house isn't going to cost a great deal of money. You might as well save on furniture.'

Rafaello looked at her. Was she serious?

But she was already wandering off, smoothing the back of a long sofa absently and heading towards the arched French windows that opened onto a terrace beyond. Joey was intently studying a painting on the wall that depicted nymphs lounging around in a classical landscape.

'Those ladies have no clothes on,' he observed. 'Aren't they cold?'

'Fortunately, it's summer time for them,' Rafaello said. 'And in Italy the summers are always hot.'

'So will we go around without clothes in summer?' Joey enquired.

'Not entirely,' Rafaello answered. 'But when we are in our garden we may not want to wear much. Especially when—'

But Joey was running forward excitedly. He'd been leading the way to the French windows, and Rafaello had followed him. Beyond the covered terrace, plentifully arrayed with planters rich with greenery and verdant with bright flowers, azure water sparkled in the sunshine.

'A swimming pool!' he exclaimed ecstatically. He started to jump up and down in enthusiastic excitement.

'I think that seals the deal,' Rafaello murmured.

Alaina gave a laugh. It struck him that it was the first time he had heard her laugh since five years ago...

She was walking forward, coming to Joey, who was still jumping up and down in glee.

'Can Joey swim?' Rafaello asked.

'Yes, but not without water wings yet. We were allowed to use the hotel's indoor pool sometimes. He loved it!'

'Good,' said Rafaello. 'But I think, all the same, it would be prudent to put some fencing around the pool.'

'Yes,' agreed Alaina.

She looked about her.

'This really is a lovely garden! I know the gardens of the other villas we saw were fabulous, but they were very formal. Here, like I said, there's a homely feel. Plus, the pool is close to the terrace, so that makes overseeing Joey easier.' She frowned slightly. 'Does a gardener come with the place? It's going to take a lot of upkeep!'

'As I have said, there will be staff. This particular villa,' he went on, 'comes with a staff cottage, though we can't see it from here.'

Alaina looked at him. 'I think I'd find it easier if the staff weren't in the house itself. That would make me feel a bit... well, awkward. More like a hotel, I suppose. I wonder what the bedrooms are like? Shall we take a look?'

'There are only five,' Rafaello remarked.

'Sounds plenty!' she answered, calling Joey back to check out upstairs.

Upstairs found as much favour as downstairs, and as Joey ran in and out of the bedrooms eagerly, Rafaello turned to Alaina.

'Decision made?' he asked.

She smiled, and it was a warm smile.

'Yes, please,' she answered.

'Good,' he replied. He caught hold of Joey as he careered around. 'Time for lunch, I think, young man.'

Joey looked up at him. 'Are we going to live here? With the swimming pool?'

'Yes,' he said.

'Hurrah!' said Joey.

Rafaello laughed. Joey's delight was infectious.

He felt his mood lift and his eyes met Alaina's. 'You see,' he said softly, 'we can make this work.'

For a moment he held her gaze, not sure what he was seeing in her expression. Then Joey was tugging at his arm.

'You said it was time for lunch,' he reminded him plaintively. 'And my tummy is *very* hungry.'

Alaina stepped forward, taking Joey's other hand. 'Come on, then, let's go and eat. Careful on the stairs, munchkin, no rushing!'

She set off down the wide stone stairs and Rafaello looked after her for a moment. She walked very gracefully...

He felt memory flicker like the replaying of an old film: their brief time in the Caribbean. How long ago it seemed. And yet—

Joey was calling out for him, telling him again that it was lunchtime, and Rafaello followed them downstairs— his son and the mother of his son. The woman who was, against all expectations, his wife.

He wondered what he was feeling about it other than strange. Then he put it out of his mind. It didn't matter what he was feeling about it. He had done what had to be done and that was all there was to it. Now it was just a question of getting on with it.

Alaina took her place at the table, looking about her with pleasure. The three of them were seated outdoors at a pleasant and to her mind very typical Italian trattoria. It was not the restaurant that Rafaello had first chosen in this little town out in the Roman countryside—which, she had seen at a glance, had been far too elegant for Joey.

She'd said as much, pointing across the *piazza* to a much more humble and therefore child-friendly establishment. Besides, it looked more attractive, with its colourful awning, red-checked tablecloths on the pavement tables, cheerful bright red geraniums in big pots around the perimeter.

Much more attractive than the pristine white linen table-cloths and the modernistic clipped box hedges and sculpted topiary of the expensive-looking restaurant.

Rafaello had made no demur, but it was clear it would not have been his choice to eat so cheaply. Memory struck her. On the island, as they'd toured around, she'd opted once for eating lunch on a beach, supplied by a ramshackle bar from which vibrant reggae music had been audible. She could remember her own cajoling banter with Rafaello as she'd squeezed his arm encouragingly.

'Come on—it's local—it looks fun!'

She blinked and the memory was gone.

The trattoria's waitress arrived with menus and a beaming smile which became even more beaming when she laid eyes on Joey. She broke into voluble Italian at the sight of him and Alaina heard *'bambino'* several times. She realised that the Italians' love of children was in full flood and Joey, she could see, was basking in it. Even though he could not understand a word, he knew when he was being praised to the skies.

Then the middle-aged waitress—presumably the proprietor's wife, Alaina thought—made a remark that she did get the gist of.

'So like his *papà!*'

She bustled off, leaving the words ringing in Alaina's head. Leaving, too, a difficult thought in its wake. What if Joey *hadn't* been such a dead ringer for Rafaello? What if his looks had taken after hers, instead? Would Rafaello have thought him to be his child? Or assumed Ryan was the dad?

Then I would not be here now, in Italy, at Rafaello's behest, reshaping my entire life...changing everything I thought it would be...

Emotion flushed through her, but she wasn't sure what it

was. Regret for the lost life that she had so carefully made for her and Joey? Or unease at the thought that she had kept all knowledge of Joey's existence from Rafaello? Or was it an even more difficult thought?

Her eyes went to him now, as he paid attention to Joey, going through the menu with him, telling him what the dishes on offer were. His manner towards Joey was hard to decipher. But one thing was obvious. It was not...

Not *what*, precisely? How could she describe it? He was attentive, patient, calm—but not...

Not affectionate. Not paternal. Not loving.

Joey might be any little boy...

A pang pierced her, and yet she had no right to feel it. She had been the one to exclude Rafaello from Joey's life. It had been mere chance that had blown that out of water. But all the same, she argued to herself now, staring at her own menu without taking it in, his dispassionate attitude towards Joey only showed her that she had made the right decision five years ago?

He thinks of Joey as a responsibility. So he's stepped up to the mark to take that on board.

He, too, after all, was changing his life for the sake of the little boy. She felt those strange, confusing emotions tangle inside her again, and then, realising that it did no good to dwell on what she could not change, she set them aside. She was going along with what Rafaello had stipulated—bringing Joey out here, legitimising his existence by entering into marriage with his father—and now she had to deal with that as positively as she could. For Joey's sake.

'Joey's decided on *spaghetti napoletana*,' Rafaello announced.

'Excellent.' Alaina smiled. 'Me too.' She set her own menu down.

'That makes three of us.' Rafaello smiled too, but more faintly.

His words echoed in Alaina's head.

Three of us...

But was there really an 'us' at all when it came to the strange unit they made? Outwardly so normal, yet in reality so totally not...?

But that was going to be their future now, wasn't it? Looking like a normal family—*mamma, papà e bambino.*

Her gaze went to Rafaello, who was beckoning the waitress over to give their order. She felt her breath catch. Dear God, five years had only made him even more good-looking! Whatever it was about his looks—and she knew they were not to all female tastes, with the fine-boned, even austere features, their sometimes saturnine cast, and the lidded eyes that were so often veiled—they reached to her own female susceptibilities as no other man's ever had...

She'd known it five years ago, as she'd embarked on that irresistible affair with him. And with a painful swallow she knew it now, too.

What she was going to do about it, she had no idea.

Except resist it.

Five years ago he didn't want me. Now what he wants is Joey.

Her eyes shadowed.

And what do I want?

Well, that was obvious too. She wanted Joey safe, with her, and happy. That was her priority. The only priority she could have...could allow herself.

Nothing else.

And certainly not what, if she were not strong and resolute, she might be weak enough to want.

For that time had gone. Finished five years go. Rafaello had made that very clear.

* * *

The move to the villa was accomplished within a week, Rafaello having insisted on immediate occupancy and expedited all the legalities.

Alaina was relieved. She'd spent the week taking Joey out and about, exploring Rome, treating it as a holiday. Rafaello was at his office daily, but returned to dine with her every evening, usually returning after Joey was in bed. Her conversation with him was mostly about what she and Joey had done that day, and practicalities pertaining to the villa and moving in as swiftly as possible. She'd deliberately kept Joey's toys in their bedroom, which had become a playroom as well, so as to minimise the risk to Rafaello's antiques.

Her relief as they set off for the newly acquired villa was palpable. And not just on Joey's account. On her own, as well.

She was getting used to Rafaello's presence in her life. But it was not easy. That sense of unreality that had hit on their wedding day washed over her periodically, and sometimes she awoke in the mornings longing so much to be back home, in her own life, the way she had been living it. But that was impossible now. It had gone.

Now I just have to get on with this life.

Was it any easier for Rafaello? She had made more of a change to her life than he had—except, of course, she had to acknowledge that she wasn't dealing with discovering that she was a parent…

It was hard to tell what he was thinking…feeling. He was unfailingly courteous and accommodating towards her, unfailingly patient and attentive to Joey, and his calm, unruffled demeanour was, she had to acknowledge, making it all that much easier for her. Or at least less difficult…

'You will be glad to know,' he was saying to her now, as they headed out of the city, 'that the married couple who looked after the villa's previous occupants are happy to stay on. I hope they prove satisfactory.'

The greeting that Maria and Giorgio afforded them on their arrival indicated to Alaina at least that they would indeed prove satisfactory. They were middle-aged, with smiling, kindly faces, and Maria's English was perfectly adequate. Giorgio's was enthusiastic, if less fluent, and their faces lit up when Joey descended from the car.

Joey had clearly acquired two more fans, and beamed angelically. Then Giorgio was fetching the luggage and Maria was bustling off, promising lunch *'prontissimo'*.

They ate in the pleasantly appointed dining room, the doors open to the terrace, and Joey made a hearty meal of his pasta, fussed over by Maria, who was still demonstrating her enchantment with him.

Through the open French windows Alaina could see the sun sparkling off the water of the swimming pool—and saw, too, that a metre-high fence with a lockable gate was now encircling the pool area.

'That was swiftly done!' she exclaimed.

'Essential things can always be done swiftly,' Rafaello replied. 'When there is pressing need and the will and the means to do them.'

Her eyes went to him. Thoughts raced in her head.

Like marrying the woman you've discovered has had your child... Then moving them both out to Italy and into a villa that will be their new home...

Well, it was done now. She was married to him and here she and Joey were. At the villa. Their new home. She felt emotion stir somewhere inside her but would not pay it any attention. There was no point in doing so. No point in doing anything other than accepting the situation in which she found herself.

Rafaello was speaking again.

'I'm going to leave you and Joey to settle in,' he was saying, in that cool, imperturbable way of his. 'Let you find your feet—that is the expression, is it not? I'll go back to the apartment, and then later this coming week I have to fly to Geneva for a few days. I hope Maria and Giorgio will look after you well, but of course you must phone me if there is anything you need me to do.'

She nodded. It was true—it would be easier for her and Joey to settle in here without Rafaello being around. Without him she could relax. Did he see that in her expression now? His gaze was resting on her unreadably, but she felt he could read her all too easily.

He gave his familiar faint smile. 'Take your time, Alaina. It will get easier, I promise you. For both of us. We shall… get used to things.'

She nodded again. 'I know, but—'

She broke off. What was there to say? They would *have* to get used to things, that was all.

She deliberately put a more upbeat expression on her face. 'Thank you for agreeing to this villa, Rafaello. I think it will suit us very well. And Maria and Giorgio too. As you say, given time, we'll…get used to things.'

Her gaze slid away, for all that, moving around the room in this villa that was now going to be her home. Hers and Joey's. The strangeness of it lapped at her, and she heard a low sigh escape her.

Then, giving a little start, she felt Rafaello's hand lightly touch hers as it lay on the table. It was lifted away swiftly, as she heard him speak again.

'We did what we had to do, Alaina—both of us.' He nodded towards Joey, who was busy polishing off his *dulce*—a sweet, nutty cake confection bestowed upon him by Maria. 'For his sake,' he said.

And that, in the end, was what it came down to—what it always came down to.

What else could she do but remember it and accept it?

She blinked, and realised with a disquiet that had nothing to do with this new life being forced upon her, that she could still feel the echo of his brief touch to her hand...

Rafaello's touch...

CHAPTER FIVE

RAFAELLO SLID THE key into his hotel room door and entered with a sense of relief. He'd shower, shave, and dine out. He felt he needed it. His client, objecting to a particularly hefty tax bill, had been difficult and demanding, and clearly displeased with the recommendations Rafaello had made, which did not reduce the amount payable as much as he wanted.

Rafaello's mouth curved cynically. Since he wanted to pay none of it, he was bound to be dissatisfied.

A mood of irritation swept over him. He wanted to be done with this particularly irksome client, however profitable he was to the firm. He wanted, he thought, as he methodically stripped off his jacket and constricting tie, followed by his shirt and the rest of his clothes as he headed for the en suite bathroom, to get back to Rome.

He wanted to see Joey.

And not just Joey.

The realisation came to him as he stepped into the shower and turned the water to max.

I want to see Alaina.

The water, hot and forceful, was sluicing over him powerfully, stinging on his skin. The sensation was physical, potent. Almost...

No!

He reached to snap the temperature down. Stood there, shocked, as colder water poured over him.

But as he started to wash himself, rigorously and swiftly, he was physically aware of his own body in ways he was loath to acknowledge. Yet the knowledge impressed itself upon him all the same.

As he rinsed himself off, cut the water, and seized a towel to snake around his hips, another to pad his torso dry, his thoughts were...difficult. Shaking his wet hair, he stepped up to the sink, reaching for his razor, starting the familiar ritual of a wet shave. As he did so, he stared at his reflection. Scrutinising it as if it were a hostile witness.

He wanted to find out the truth he was concealing.

From himself.

He paused, razor in hand, his gaze boring into his own eyes.

From the very moment his gaze had gone to the little boy at Alaina's desk in the hotel, and realisation had struck him like a tsunami pulverising him, he had gone into a mode of behaviour that was what the situation—an unimagined situation—demanded of him. Of him and of Alaina. Nothing else had been permissible. He had pushed it forward remorselessly, ruthlessly, demolishing everything that might stand in the way of getting to where he now was. Where Alaina was too.

Everything else had been put to one side.

Including the past. His gaze narrowed. The past that had created the very situation he had now dealt with. Was still dealing with.

They had married for the sake of the son they had unintentionally created. That was as far ahead as he had thought—had allowed himself to think. But now they were married. Now Alaina and Joey were safely installed in the villa he had found for them. Now their new lives were underway. And so was his new life.

Alaina, the woman he had romanced all those years ago, was back in his life. Married to him. His entire focus had been on getting to this point. He had barely thought beyond it. But now, deed done, marriage accomplished, he knew with unavoidable clarity that he had to do just that—think beyond simply making Alaina his wife.

They were married, yes. But…

But what kind of marriage are we going to have?

Oh, he had said they would be civil and civilised about it, and that was what they were being. And, yes, he had talked of a vague future when separation might not be out of the question, when Joey was old enough and they might go their separate ways. But till then…?

He reached for his shaving foam, applied it with smooth, methodical strokes, brought the blade of his razor down his cheeks, along the line of his chin. Familiar, routine movements… And all the time his eyes were boring into those in his reflection. Asking a question to which he already knew the answer.

The question about what kind of marriage he and Alaina were going to have.

The answer literally stared him in the face, shaping itself in words that spelt it out with clarity and concision and compelling logic.

I desired her once.

He had desired her from the moment he had seen her, her lovely body displayed to the sun, so long ago on that silver sand beach under the hot Caribbean sun. He had desired her, courted her, seduced her—and she had come with him every step of the way. Her lovemaking had been as ardent as his…her passion, unleashed at his touch, as hot as his.

So why should it not be so again?

Because how else was their marriage going to work?

The logic of his thoughts clicked ineluctably into place, making him accept it as his gaze bored into his reflection in the glass. Adultery was abhorrent, unthinkable—either hers or his. And celibacy...

A glint showed in his dark eyes. Well, he knew himself well enough to know that the prospect of celibacy—indefinite, on-going celibacy, for any length of time—would be...challenging.

But why should he—or she—be contemplating either unpalatable prospect? There was no reason for it. There was proof positive, after all, of just how compatible they were in that respect. And nothing had changed, after all, had it?

Five years on he acknowledged that Alaina's beauty, though matured now, was every bit as breathtaking as it had been when they'd first romanced. He had suppressed his awareness of it because it had been a distraction from his focus on getting his son into his life the way he had. But now—wedding over, their removal to Italy accomplished, her settled at the villa with the son he had claimed—now he could indulge that awareness.

As for Alaina... Well, the same logic drove his thoughts forward. Why should she be immune to the charms that she had once found as irresistible as he had found hers? She, after all, had made it clear at the time that she would have liked their time together to continue.

The glint came into his eyes again. Well, now their time together *could* continue. With a little encouragement on his part...

Into his head came the words he had said to her.

'We can make this work.'

The glint in his eyes intensified and he set aside his razor, its work done, bent to rinse his face and pat it dry. Then he looked once more at his reflection.

They could indeed make this marriage work.

And not just for the sake of their son and the stability of his family life.

We can make it work for us—for Alaina and myself—as well as our son.

He dropped the towel beside the basin, strode out into the bedroom and swiftly dressed again—more casually this time—for dinner at a nearby restaurant.

His mood was better than it had been for quite some time. Tomorrow he'd be heading home. To Joey—and Alaina.

Anticipation filled him.

Alaina stretched languorously. She was face-down on a flat sun lounger, out on the villa's sunlit terrace. This early in the summer it was deliciously warm, but not too hot, and the afternoon sun felt extremely pleasant on her bare back.

Somewhere in the gardens she could hear water sprinkling, and Joey's piping voice every now and then, coupled with Giorgio's deeper one. Birdsong came from the bushes, and the scent of flowers. A little way off she could hear the lap of water in the pool, slapping gently against the filter. Sleep drifted over her and she drowsed lazily in the warmth. It really was gorgeous to be able to sunbathe like this, knowing she had the leisure to do so and that Joey was happy without her attention.

Memory plucked at her. How long ago it was that she had sunbathed on that silver sand beach in the Caribbean…?

She dozed off again, sleepy under the sun.

Why she awoke, she did not know. Footsteps on the paving stones?

She lifted her head, expecting to see Giorgio returning with Joey. It was not.

It was Rafaello.

Looking at her from the shade of the covered terrace,

standing in one of the arches, completely still. Just looking at her.

Looking her over.

Past and present rushed together. That was exactly the way he'd looked at her—looked her over—that long-ago afternoon in the Caribbean. In that chance encounter that had led to the present moment...

She felt her cheeks flare, a heat flush through her that had nothing to do with the sun and everything to do with the way his gaze was resting on her. So very, very familiar...

In those few heady weeks that she'd spent with him how often had she seen his gaze on her like that? Countless times! And every time it had melted her, sent a dissolving heat through her, quickened her pulse, licking at her senses.

Faintness washed through her and she dipped her head.

Then she heard: 'Where's Joey?'

Rafaello's voice was sharp, and her head shot up as he strode towards her.

'Joey...?' She said it vaguely, as if the name were unfamiliar to her.

Her eyes were riveted on him. She hadn't seen him for several days and now he was walking towards her, his impeccable business suit moulding his tall frame. She took in the silk of his grey tie, the pristine cuffs. He looked sleek, and expensive, and lethal...

'Where is he?' he demanded again, and his gaze raked the pool, even though the gate was firmly shut.

She pulled herself up, careful to ensure that she took the sarong she was lying on with her as she did, remaining punishingly aware that if she let it slip she'd be naked to the waist, for the strings of her bikini were undone.

'He's with Giorgio,' she retorted, stung at the implicit accusation in Rafaello's question. Deftly, she managed to knot the sarong over her breasts, and got to her feet. 'They're watering the plants in the shade.'

Rafaello frowned.

Alaina went on, with an indulgent smile in her voice. 'Joey,' she informed Rafaello, 'happens to adore watering the garden! And Giorgio has a hose...*much* more fun than a mere watering can.' She gave a fond laugh. 'I can only hope that the plants are getting some of the water at least!'

She saw Rafaello's expression relax. At least as far as Joey's safety was concerned. But then his eyes came back to her, and in them was, once again, the same look as before. She stood for a moment, knowing that the thin material of the sarong was moulding the shape of her breasts, and that her shoulders were completely bare. Her hair, roughly pinned on her head to get it off the back of her neck, threatened to descend at any moment. She felt caught off-guard.

Her colour slightly too high, she made an attempt at nonchalance. 'How did it go in Geneva?'

'Tedious,' he replied. 'I'm glad to be back.' He looked about him, taking in his surroundings, his expression changing. 'This was a good choice of yours...this villa.' His tone was considering—and approving.

Alaina's expression softened too. 'It's lovely, isn't it? Perfect for Joey, too. He's been loving the pool, I promise you. He's really settling in.'

Rafaello nodded. 'Good,' he said. 'And, speaking of the pool, it looks pretty tempting right now, I must say.' He turned away. 'I think I'll join you,' he said, heading back indoors.

As he left, Alaina sat herself back down on the lounger with a plonk. Her heart rate was up—she could tell. And it wasn't just because she'd been startled by Rafaello's appearance. Her cheeks felt heated, and she stared out over the sparkling water in the pool, thoughts churning, willing herself to calm down.

Finding it harder than she thought.

Wishing she didn't. But not wanting to examine why.

Rafaello shrugged off his business clothes, pulled on bathing trunks and a white tee, slipped his feet into pool sandals and headed downstairs, pausing only to put his head around the kitchen door and greet Maria, in the throes of making fresh pasta, and ask for coffee and refreshments to be served on the terrace.

Then he went outside, slipping on a pair of sunglasses against the bright sunshine. Wanting to see Alaina again. Knowing just why.

Restlessness filled him, together with an incongruous sense of purpose. He felt conflicted, and at the same time knew his decision had been made. Knew that he wasn't going to unmake it—nor regret it.

As he stepped out on to the cool, shaded and covered terrace, his eyes went straight to Alaina, now sedately sitting on her lounger, its backrest upright. Her upper body was now in shadow under the parasol she'd pulled over the lounger. Only her bare, honey-coloured legs stretched out into the sun.

His decision was confirmed.

He felt again that instinctive quickening of his body, but repressed it. Now was not the occasion.

She looked up from the magazine she'd apparently been perusing intently. She, too, had donned dark glasses, and she had also retied the strings of her bikini, though her body was still securely veiled by her colourful sarong.

'Oh, there you are. Do come out and enjoy this sun,' she said to him lightly—and self-consciously, he could tell.

She indicated another sun lounger, and he pulled it into

the half-shade of the parasol, facing the glittering water of the pool.

'This really is blissful!' she went on, still in that light, self-conscious voice.

'Definitely an improvement on Geneva—it was raining,' Rafaello responded dryly. He opened the book he'd brought out with him, a popular police thriller. 'I've asked Maria for coffee—and something for Joey too, when he's done with soaking the plants.'

'And soaking Giorgio too, I suspect—and himself!' Alaina added with a smile.

She flicked a few pages of her magazine—an Italian homes and gardens one, Rafaello could see.

He indicated it with his hand. 'Any good ideas for the villa?' he asked casually. 'You must feel entirely free to refurnish and redecorate, you know. It is your home now.'

'It's lovely as it is,' she assured him. 'But maybe I'll get some new cushions and ornaments…things like that. Oh, and some pool toys!'

'We can get them tomorrow,' Rafaello said genially. 'Joey can help choose them.'

'He'll love that!' Alaina laughed.

Maria emerged from the house with a tray of coffee, juice, iced water and some tempting-looking *biscotti*, setting it down and then disappearing again.

Rafaello watched Alaina busy herself pouring for them both. He took the proffered cup, knowing his fingers lightly brushed hers. Knowing that she knew they had…

He sat back, sipping his coffee. He would take this slowly. Not rush things but savour them… As he had before.

The prospect was pleasing.

He took another mouthful of his coffee, relaxing his shoulders back. After all the last few weeks had necessitated, it was time to relax. Relax and…enjoy.

His eyes flickered sideways for a moment. In profile, Alaina was as beautiful as in full face: the delicate line of her cheek, her hair in tendrils around her jaw, her mouth tender and sensuous. All of it as alluring to him now as five years ago.

Every bit as alluring...

Alaina clutched her magazine a tad more tightly than required and knew why. She was punishingly conscious of Rafaello, sitting beside her on the adjacent lounger. Punishingly conscious of how his long, bare, lithely muscled legs were stretched out...how the white tee moulded his lean torso. Conscious, most of all, of how she wanted to twist her head and drink him in.

Memory was crowding her head. Of how they'd sunned themselves on the beach in the Caribbean, heating up only to cool off in the turquoise water, she in her skimpy bikini, he stripped to the waist. Then they'd gone to his room, in the cool of the air-con, and he'd slid his arms around her, drawn her down onto the bed, removing the frail barrier of her bikini to have her naked in his arms, to make love to her...

She tried to push the memory out, but it was reluctant to go. She felt colour flush her cheeks, and hoped Rafaello was not looking at her. Let alone realising why she blushed.

She felt danger flicker inside her. In the weeks since Rafaello had walked back into her life with such devastating consequences she'd done her best not to let herself remember, not to let herself acknowledge that whatever it was he possessed that had been so lethal to her, he still had it. She had let herself think no further than what he was demanding of her—that she marry him, that she uproot herself, settle in Italy, make her home here with Joey.

And with him.

And now it was done. She was here. Married. Settled in their new home.

And what happens now? Between Rafaello and me?

The question floated inchoate, barely formed. But she didn't want to give it shape or substance. Didn't want it there at all. She had thought no further than getting to this point because she had had no alternative but to do so. But now…

'Mummee!'

The patter of Joey's feet was a welcome interruption to thoughts she did not want to have…questions she did not want to ask. He came running up to her, his tee shirt, as she'd predicted, soaking wet.

'We've been watering—Giorgio and me! He let me have the hose! We got wet!'

'So you did, munchkin,' she agreed.

'Very wet,' Rafaello confirmed beside her.

Joey noticed his presence and ran around the lounger to him. 'Papà!' He tugged at Rafaello's arm. 'Come swimming! Come swimming!' he begged excitedly.

Rafaello swung his legs round, getting to his feet. 'You'll need your water wings,' he reminded Joey.

Alaina handed Joey some diluted juice to gulp down, with a *biscotti* to munch on, while she peeled off the soaking tee shirt and stripped off his shorts—almost as wet—getting his wriggling body into swimming trunks, then sliding the inflated armbands on as he jumped from one foot to the other impatiently.

Then Rafaello was taking his hand, walking to the pool with him, unlocking the gate.

'Jump in! Jump in!' Joey cried excitedly, and proceeded to do just that.

Alaina watched Rafaello enter the water more sedately as Joey batted around in his armbands. She watched them, emotion moving within her.

Father and son…

But what kind of father would Rafaello make? He talked of responsibilities, and he was unfailingly patient with Joey, but what else?

It will come in time, won't it? That bond must surely form?

Yet it did not always.

A shiver went through her. Had she been a boy, perhaps her father would have taken more notice of her. Or had she developed the same interests he had when she'd reached her teenage years. But that had never happened. It was her mother she had been close to—the mother who had warned her, from her own bitter experience, to be careful where she gave her heart. Never, never to give it to a man who could not return her love…

A shadow seemed to fall over her and she heard again in her head her mother's sad warning.

Her gaze, of its own volition, went to the two figures in the pool. Her son, so eager and excited, and the man who had fathered him. The man to whom she had once given herself in passion and desire, coming so close to wanting more than he could offer her, to wanting what she had come so close to offering him…

And once again danger flickered all around her. Impossible to dispel.

CHAPTER SIX

'MARIA, THANK YOU. This all looks splendid. We'll serve ourselves.' Rafaello gave a cool, but appreciative smile to the housekeeper.

She bustled out, having set the plentiful array of dishes on the table for them to help themselves.

Rafaello reached for the wine he'd selected. He'd had a delivery from the wine merchant he patronised, and now he poured carefully for Alaina and himself. She was sitting opposite him, and his eyes rested on her with appreciation.

She'd come down from checking on Joey in bed, and Rafaello's glance had immediately gone to her. Though not formally dressed—for that was not necessary here at the villa—she wore a calf-length shift dress in warm amber tones, with a light lacy cardigan. It flattered her slender figure. Her hair was in a casually upswept style that was equally flattering to her bone structure. She had not put on make-up...but that hardly mattered. Her eyes, wide-set and long-lashed, barely needed enhancing, and nor did the tender curve of her mouth. In the soft light from the wall lamps she looked effortlessly lovely.

'So,' he announced, lifting his wine glass, 'our first weekend here. *Saluti.*'

He tilted his glass and took a considering mouthful before giving the wine his approval. Then he set his glass back on the table, lifting the lids of the various serving bowls placed on chafing dishes to keep them warm. Maria had prepared a rich beef ragout, with slices of grilled polenta and assorted steamed vegetables.

He gave a generous helping to Alaina, and then to himself. 'Well, I see we won't starve with Maria in charge of the kitchen!' he remarked drily.

Alaina gave a little laugh. 'No, indeed. She's feeding Joey up on pasta and pastries very nicely—though I make sure he's eating lots of salad and fruit as well,' she added. 'He's taken to Italian cooking like a natural!'

Rafaello's eyes glinted as he made a start on the delicious ragout. 'Well, he is half-Italian. And now,' he said pointedly, 'he can give free rein to that side of his heritage.'

He saw colour stain her cheekbones as she picked up her fork.

'He's adapting well,' was all she said in reply.

'And you?'

Her eyes met his across the table. 'I'm doing my best,' she said.

Was there defensiveness in her tone of voice? There was no need for it.

'I appreciate, Alaina, what you've done.'

Something changed in her expression and her eyes dropped away. She gave a little shrug, barely a gesture at all.

In a deliberately lighter tone, he went on. 'How have you busied yourself this week?'

She took the cue and answered in a similarly light tone. 'We've unpacked, and Joey's chosen his bedroom—that's his playroom too, so his toys shouldn't spread too widely! We've done a lot of pool time—Joey's favourite! And Giorgio very kindly drove us into the nearby town so we could explore and stock up on some bits and pieces.'

'I must ensure you have a suitable car for yourself and Joey,' Rafaello remarked. 'Can you face driving out here?'

'I must,' she answered. 'I don't want to rely on Giorgio—or you—the whole time. But maybe I should take a few lessons—learn how to drive on the wrong side of the road!' she added humorously.

She paused, taking another sip from her wine, then went on.

'I'm wondering whether it would be good to find some kind of nursery for Joey. Oh, not a full-time nursery, obviously, but maybe a few mornings a week...to help him socialise, and most of all to help him learn Italian. He's picking up some from Maria and Giorgio—and you, of course,' she acknowledged. 'He's made a start, but it's best he becomes as fluent as possible, as swiftly as possible.'

'I agree,' Rafaello answered. He looked across at her. 'And what about you? Do you want an Italian tutor?'

She made a face. 'That sounds very formal. I brought a couple of grammar books out with me from the UK. I bought them when...when I knew I was going to have to come out here,' she said, and he could hear the awkwardness in her voice. 'And there's the Internet too, of course—loads of how to learn Italian podcasts!'

'Well, if you want one-on-one tuition, just say. Of course,' he added, his voice smooth, 'I can always provide that myself.'

He let his gaze rest on her for a moment. She'd flushed a little, and he liked the effect it had on her. Liked it considerably...

His mood mellowed even more.

'I seem to remember,' he said musingly, his gaze still on her, 'that you showed an aptitude for acquiring a...specialised vocabulary when we first knew each other...'

The flush increased, and he knew exactly why.

Memory washed within him of how she had lain in his embrace, after lovemaking, her mouth gliding over his anatomy, asking him the Italian for each place where her lips were languorously exploring…

She bent her head, busying herself with the business of doing justice to Maria's cooking. He knew why. He let her be. To pursue the subject would be crass.

Instead, he took another mouthful of wine and made some remark about it, which she picked up on, asking him a question about what kind of wine it was. He told her, and let the subject be a suitable topic for anodyne discourse. He saw her heightened colour subside, and she visibly relaxed once more.

'Well, as you can tell, I know nothing about wine,' she said lightly. 'But this…' she indicated her glass '…is certainly very good.'

'Thank you,' he murmured, half amused. 'I shall look forward to building a cellar here, I think. I must explore the kitchen and decide the best position for installing it.'

'Doesn't it have to be a hole in the ground?' she asked, surprised.

'Not at all. These days climate-controlled cabinets are superior in many ways. Adjusting them minutely for temperature and humidity and so forth is a fine art.'

'I'm sure you'll have fun with it,' she answered, her voice dry. But he heard amused indulgence in her tone as well.

'What is that phrase in English?' he queried lightly. 'Boys' toys? Is that it?'

She gave a laugh. 'Spot on,' she agreed.

He was glad of the light mood, and of the mild, but significant rapport it betokened. He felt his good mood improve even more and reached again for his own wine glass, relaxing back in his comfortable dining chair.

Things were coming along nicely…

Alaina pushed her now-empty dessert bowl away from her with a little sigh. Maria had concocted a delicious *semi-*

freddo and Alaina had been unable to resist it. She sat back, replete but relaxed. Surprisingly relaxed…

There had been a couple of awkward moments during the meal, but they had passed and conversation had become more general…easier. Yet for all that those moments had been disquieting. Oh, not when Rafaello had pointedly reminded her that Joey was half-Italian, but when he'd reminded her of other things.

Lying in his arms…asking him what the Italian word was for the place where I was kissing him…

She pulled her mind away—but not sufficiently to blank all those memories…memories only too easily aroused simply by dining with him here, by the French windows open to the terrace, with the sound of cicadas beyond, the mild warmth of the air, the perfume from the night-scented flowers in the gardens.

All of it was weaving memories into her head.

Rafaello taking her to dinner at a seductively situated restaurant…dining out on a terrace overlooking a moonlit beach below. The murmur of waves, the caressing warmth of the evening, the candle glowing in its glass holder as he poured wine for her, refilled her glass… His lambent gaze telling her how very appealing she was to him and her own gaze resting on him in return, reciprocating the message.

He'd lifted his glass to her, and she hers to him, and his hand had reached for hers across the table, softly letting his long, sensitive fingers play on the delicate contours of her exposed wrist—a prelude, tantalising and arousing, of what the rest of the night would bring…of the sensual pleasures that awaited her in the midnight hours…

She could feel the allure of those memories—and knew the danger they held. A danger she must resist, even as she must resist the memories. They had no place in her life now.

She gave her head a little shake, as if to dispel them. 'I ought to check on Joey,' she announced.

'No need,' came the reply. 'We'll hear him on the monitor if he wakes.'

She watched Rafaello get calmly to his feet and cross to the sideboard where Maria had deposited the coffee tray when she'd cleared the table and left their dessert and *formaggio*.

'Let's have coffee on the terrace—it's warm enough, I think,' Rafaello was saying now.

He picked up the tray, gestured towards the French windows for her to go through first. She did so, stepping out on to the terrace.

'The moon has risen,' Rafaello remarked, following her out.

He placed the coffee tray on the low table in front of a rattan couch set back under the arched perimeter of the terrace, sitting himself down beside her, pouring her coffee and his own, handing it to her.

She took it, but knew she was too conscious of Rafaello's presence beside her…the faint, familiar catch of his aftershave, the closeness of his long, lean body that once, so long ago she had known intimately…

She was too conscious of the silvered moon riding high in the heavens, of the shimmering iridescence of the pool water, lit from underneath, the murmurous chorus of cicadas all around, the warmth of the early summer evening lapping at her. All conspired to evoke memory within her. Memory she should not allow.

It came all the same.

She and Rafaello, sitting out on the balcony of his room at the Falcone, with the moon glancing over the Caribbean, the tree frogs audible in the velvet night. Rafaello loosely holding her hand in his, then raising it to his lips, caressing it lightly with the softest silken touch and drawing her to her feet. Rafaello taking her inside, into the air-conditioned cool, where the sensual burn of their passion would give all the heat they needed.

And she going with him so willingly, heat building up in her, pulse quickening… The arousal that had teased her all evening being finally, gloriously, blissfully, meltingly sated as she feasted on him and he on her… Until dawn broke from the east and slumber finally took their spent, exhausted bodies…

She dipped her head, closed her eyes, wanting only to banish the memory. And yet—

She felt the slightest, lightest touch at the nape of her bowed neck. For a second—less than a second—she was sure she felt it. The merest drift of the tips of his fingers, resting on the delicate exposed arc of her neck, playing in the stray fronds of her upswept hair.

A wave of weakness went through her. The sensation was so slight—and yet it was slaying her…

She heard her name spoken. Felt her coffee cup being removed from her suddenly nerveless grip. Still with her neck bowed forward, her eyes still closed, she felt the fingers of Rafaello's other hand shape her jaw, her cheek, turn her head towards him.

Her eyes opened, wide and fearful. This must not be— she must not let this happen. Must *not*.

But he was leaning towards her, his face half shadowed. The skilled, sensual mouth she had once known so well, whose power to evoke sensations in her that must melt her, beguile her, was reaching for hers now…impossible to prevent.

Impossible to *want* to prevent.

He said her name again, soft and low, and then his mouth was cool on hers. Light, undemanding, and yet with a certainty that told her she must resist.

But how? How to resist what he was drawing from her? How to stop the silken sensation of his mouth moving on hers slowly, lightly, leisurely? How to stop the feathering of his fingers at the nape of her neck? Her head was rising now, as his mouth moved on hers and his hand shaped her cheek. How to stop her own hand lifting with a will of its own to press against the lean, hard wall of his chest, so close, so tantalising, temptingly close to her now?

She let her eyes flutter shut, helpless to do anything but sink into the sensations playing at her mouth, her nape, at the lobe of her ear, into the sensual pressure he brought to bear.

His kiss started to deepen. Her hand against his chest splayed out, her mouth started to move against his, desire quickened within her...

With a cry, she pulled away. Urgently—fearfully.

She forced herself to her feet, stepped back...away.

'Rafaello, no—*no*!'

He was untroubled by her refusal. He sat back, one arm stretched out along the back of the rattan seat, looking up at her. His face was still in the *chiaroscuro* of the moonlight, his body lean and long, as he casually hooked one leg over his knee in a relaxed gesture.

'Why?' he asked.

His question was interested, no more than that, as his half-shadowed gaze rested on her.

'Because...' she said.

Her voice was tight. Her whole body was tight. Yet her heart was pounding—she could feel it. Could feel the adrenaline rush that had come. Whether from his kiss—or her fear of it—or both.

She saw his eyebrows rise. 'Because...?' he prompted.

She clenched her hands at her sides, still feeling her heart pound. Still feeling how dangerously close she had come to that doomed, destructive edge she must never approach.

'Because I don't want to go back into the past!'

He gave that faint, familiar smile, effortlessly demolishing her desperate defence.

'But this is not the past, Alaina. This is the present. And we can acknowledge, with honesty and clarity, that what once drew us together is doing so again.'

He stood up, stepping towards her as he spoke, lifting one hand, letting one finger drift lightly down her cheek.

'You are more beautiful now than ever,' he said, and his voice was low, husky, and did things to her she must not allow. 'So...' He paused, and his eyes, lidded and dark... so dark...held hers. 'Why should we not once more indulge in each other?' His grew even more husky. 'I promise we would find much pleasure for us both...'

She gazed up at him, helpless, in thrall to that darkly lidded gaze, that low, husky voice. She felt her body sway, weakness drumming though her. Weakness and wanting...

How easy it would be—how very, *very* easy—to let her hands lift to his chest, to feel that hard, familiar wall beneath her fingers, to lift her mouth to his, feel his lips descend on hers to taste and take...

To fall into his arms...his bed...

As she had before.

She felt herself take an unsteady, jerking step back.

'I... I must check on Joey!'

The words were broken, her breath ragged, her pupils dilated.

She turned and fled.

Rafaello watched her go, his expression unreadable. Then, after leaving her sufficient time, he strolled back into the dining room and crossed to the sideboard where he would find the very good single malt his wine merchant had also delivered.

He poured himself a glass, hearing Alaina's hurried foot-steps on the stairs. He knew just why she was hurrying—and it was not to check on Joey.

A smile played about his mouth as he strolled back out on to the terrace and lowered himself down on to the rattan couch, stretching out his legs in a leisurely fashion, cross-ing them at his ankles while he sampled the single malt, his gaze resting on the iridescent water in the pool beyond, hearing the gentle slap of the water interspersed with the night music of the cicadas.

He would not rush her. He would take his time, and she could take hers too. Take all the time needed for her to accept what he had said to her. That there was no reason—none at all—for them to deny what still ran between them. Five years ago he had had his life to return to—the familiar life he had made for himself, comfortable and well chosen. But that life was gone now—for the foreseeable future. So what reason was there not to make the most of what this new life offered? When both of them so clearly desired it…

Because what he had revealed to her had been just that—desire. What had been between them five years ago was still there, needing only a touch, a caress, a kiss, to be re-awakened…

He relaxed back against the padding of the couch, taking another indulgent mouthful of his whisky, feeling the ma-ture, fine and fiery heat ease down his throat. He savoured it—just as soon he would be savouring all that his reawak-ened desire for the woman who was now joined to him in marriage would bring him.

It was a marriage he had never planned to make, but now that he had made it, it would bring pleasures of its own to both of them. His dark, lidded eyes glinted in the moon-light, filling with anticipation.

* * *

Alaina sat beside Joey as he lay asleep in his bed. Her hand was resting lightly on his head, as if in blessing. Love poured from her, overwhelming and all-consuming. How she loved him! He was everything to her—everything! A precious, wonderful gift she had never looked for, never asked for, and yet his coming had transformed her. She would do anything for him—anything!

And she already had, hadn't she? She'd uprooted her life, turned it upside down, moved to a new country. Rafaello had said that this very evening. Rafaello...the man she had married to protect Joey. Oh, she had done so much for Joey, and she would do more for him! Anything...

Her face shadowed and she lifted her hand away.

But what Rafaello was asking of her now—could she do that?

She got to her feet, looking around blindly for a moment. Feelings washed around inside her like water let out from behind a sluice gate. A sluice gate that had remained shut for five long years.

Her eyes were blind in the dim light of Joey's bedroom, with only the soft, shaded glow of the nightlight plugged into the wall socket at floor level lifting the dark. Joey's breathing was silent, and the room was still...quite still. The only sound was the beating of her heart. That uncertain, troubled beating. She stood there, with questions in her head she could not answer. Did not want to answer.

Then, as if on a sudden impulse, she stooped to drop a feathered kiss on Joey's brow and left the room.

Still she heard no answer to her troubling thoughts, her unanswerable questions.

CHAPTER SEVEN

RAFAELLO STOOD IN front of the cheval glass in his bedroom, tying his black tie with deft, economic movements. Alaina had arrived here at the apartment after lunch, and he had cut his working day short. Joey was safely at the villa, being looked after by Maria and Giorgio.

Tonight he was taking Alaina out with him for the very first time. She had been reluctant at first, but he had simply said, 'Alaina, I won't hide you away at the villa! There is a certain amount of socialising that I do, and it is fitting that you are at my side. Besides...' he had lidded his eyes '...don't you think I want to show you off?'

He'd said it lightly, and lightly was the way he'd been behaving towards her since she had run from him after he'd kissed her that evening after dinner, on the moonlit terrace two weekends ago. He had known he would not... *must* not...rush her...must give her time to accept what he had already accepted.

We can have again what we had before.

It was as simple as that—to him. But if she needed more time...well, she could have it.

The day after she'd run from him he'd made sure to make no reference to it...to behave as they had come to behave with each other—civilly, calmly, congenially, even. They'd spent an easy day enjoyably, taking Joey to buy a selection—a large one!—of pool toys, and then they had gone to have lunch at the same little trattoria Alaina had chosen when they were house-hunting. Then they'd gone back to the villa, and Joey had blissfully tried out all the pool toys.

That evening the weather had been warm enough for Rafaello to suggest a barbecue, and Joey's bliss had gone overboard. By the time he'd consumed the very last burger, the very last grilled banana with ice cream, he'd been all but asleep. Rafaello had carried him upstairs, feeling strange, for it had been unfamiliar, how good it had felt to do so.

Downstairs once more, he had whiled away an hour with Alaina watching a popular crime drama on TV, set in Sicily, and handily provided with subtitles in English for her. It had been an easy, enjoyable evening, without him making any indication or giving her any reminder of what had passed the previous evening.

Sunday morning had seen Joey and himself spending most of their time in the pool again, and then, following a leisurely salad lunch, eaten *al fresco*, he had taken his leave and returned to Rome, ready for the working week.

The next weekend had followed a similar pattern, but he'd also driven Alaina and Joey out into the depths of Lazio, to visit a lakeside resort, where they'd gone out in a boat—much to Joey's delight—and then visited a nearby petting zoo, to Joey's even greater delight.

After two such child-centred weekends, though, Rafaello acknowledged that he was looking forward to something more sophisticated this evening.

He felt that glint come into his eyes as he finished tying his bow tie. He was to have Alaina to himself. Anticipation filled him.

On her arrival at the apartment that afternoon Rafaello had whisked her off again, heading for the Via Condotti, filled with high fashion boutiques.

'You'll need a gown for tonight,' he'd told her. 'It's quite a formal occasion.'

She'd made her choice and now he wanted to see her in it.

He reached for the slim black case on top of the antique tallboy, sliding it into the pocket of his jacket, and strolled from the room, heading for the *saloni* to await Alaina.

She was already there.

He stopped short.

Never had he seen her more beautiful—not even in the Caribbean all those years ago.

Her full-length gown was a delicate pale blue plissé silk that cupped her breasts and fell in graceful folds to her ankles. Her shoulders were bare, only a diaphanous stole, subtly interwoven with silver thread, covering them lightly. A narrow silver belt circled her slender waist. Her hair was styled high in a top knot, from which delicate strands framed her face.

And her face...

His connoisseur's scrutiny told him everything he needed to know. Full *maquillage*, but applied with a lightness of touch that only enhanced the natural sculpture of her cheekbones, the depth of her luminous eyes, lengthening her lashes and widening her gaze, just as the pastel lipstick enhanced the lovely curve of her mouth.

He let his gaze explore her beauty in a leisurely fashion, knew there was appreciation and approval in his regard of her. With part of his awareness he saw that colour was flaring slightly but significantly across her cheekbones. He was glad of it. It was what he wanted to see. He wanted her to know just how beautiful he thought her.

A sentiment he echoed now in words.

'You look,' he said, strolling towards her now, 'quite breathtaking.'

He felt a smile tug at his mouth. Part warm and genuine…part something else. And a touch—just a touch—saturnine.

'You require only one further adornment,' he said.

He withdrew the jewellery case from his pocket, flicked open the satin top. A river of diamonds lay within. He heard her breath catch as he lifted out the necklace, came near to her to drape it around her throat.

'Rafaello—I couldn't possibly—'

He fastened the safety catch and lightly turned her around, so that he could see the effect of the necklace.

'Exquisite,' he said. 'And quite perfect for you.'

He stood a moment longer, surveying her, admiration open in his eyes. In the Caribbean, when they'd gone out in the evenings, she'd dressed with flair and allure, her chosen colours vibrant to match the climate—vivid vermilions and sunshine-yellows and sea-green blues—but here, for the formal affair ahead of them, her air of mature sophistication, of Italian couture, was exactly appropriate.

'Shall we go?' he murmured, and ushered her forward.

Out on the pavement his car was waiting for them. He opened the rear door for her, letting the driver stay at the wheel.

As she settled herself into the capacious leather seat, drawing the seat belt across her, she spoke.

'Tell me more about this evening, so I'm prepped for it,' she said.

She was speaking in a tone that told him she was putting aside the compliments he'd paid her…the way his gaze had openly admired her.

Rafaello fastened his own seat belt, taking his cue from her. 'Well, as you know, it's the annual gathering for one of the law societies I belong to. A dinner dance, I think is the English expression. I know many who will be there, and networking is always useful. There will also be friends to introduce you to.'

He paused for a moment as the car moved off.

'It's part of the life I lead, Alaina. I hope you will accept it as such.'

She gave a faint, flickering smile by way of an answer. But nothing more.

Rafaello sat back.

He glanced at her momentarily now, her head averted from him as she looked out of the window at the passing streets of Rome, and felt his breath catch yet again at just how breathtakingly lovely she looked in her evening splendour. The evening would bring what it would bring, but he knew with certainty that the very least of it was the dinner dance ahead of them.

That was only the start of what he was looking forward to…

Alaina stepped carefully out of the car, walking beside Rafaello into the lobby of the Viscari Roma, where tonight's function was to be held. She was burningly conscious of her high heels, her fabulous, terrifyingly expensive gown, and the diamonds around her throat. And conscious, most of all, of the man at her side.

She glanced about her. Knowing her heart rate was elevated not by the prospect of the evening ahead, but of spending it with Rafaello.

That was the challenge.

Since the night he had kissed her out on the villa's terrace in the moonlight, and she had fled from him…fled from herself, he had, to her abject relief, reverted to the way she had got used to him being since he had turned her life upside down with cool, casual ease. His focus had been on Joey, and that was what she could cope with.

But now…tonight…

She was on show. She knew that. Knew that she was

there to be Signora Ranieri, the wife of a prominent lawyer, a member of Rome's high society, or whatever it was called out here, and she did not want to make mistakes.

She looked the part, at least, in a gown that had come with an eyewatering price tag and a necklace of diamonds whose value she dared not even think about.

He ushered her up the grand flight of stairs to the floor where the hotel's banqueting suite was. Like the Falcone, out in the Caribbean, the Viscari was head and shoulders above the hotel chain she'd worked at in England, but she would not be cowed by it. OK, so she was here to be Signora Ranieri, and that was what she would be.

Her chin lifted, and she glided forward, getting used to the extra elevation of her heels.

Guests were mingling in the bar area, and Rafaello was drawing her forward. She put a faint smile on her face, conscious that she was getting some curious looks directed her way, which were soon explained when he introduced her—to exclamations of open surprise.

'Alaina and I go back some way,' Rafaello said in his smooth, urbane way, offering no more than that.

Most of the conversation was in Italian, however, and all that was required of her was to smile and take little sips from her glass of champagne. Soon they were taking their places at their table, and Alaina felt herself relax more. There were only three other couples there, and they all clearly knew each other well enough to be convivial.

The dinner started to be served, and as the dishes went round and the conversation swapped back and forth from Italian to English, divvied up between the guests around the table, Alaina found her nerves subsiding. Everyone was good company, and even if the conversation turned to the law from time to time it was sufficiently general. She was asked polite questions about the part of England she came from, and how she liked living in Italy, and that led to Rafaello mentioning that he'd taken a villa outside of the city.

'It's more suitable for our little boy,' he announced.

He'd said it in English, and Alaina realised, with a tremor, that he'd intended her to understand the announcement he was making. And the fact that he said it so coolly told her he wanted her to do likewise.

'He adores the pool there!' she said, and smiled.

To their credit, no one probed further, and Joey's unexpected existence seemed to have been tacitly accepted.

'How old is he?' one of the women asked.

'Four—and a handful!' Alaina smiled again.

'Oh, ours is five—and even more of a handful, I promise!' The woman laughed.

'Wait till they hit their teens,' another man warned humorously.

The conversation turned to children, and Alaina relaxed. The announcement had been made, absorbed and accepted. Whatever discussion there might be about why Rafaello Ranieri had turned up with a brand-new wife and a brand-new four-year-old son, out of the blue, it could take place later, Alaina decided.

The woman with the five-year-old leant towards her. 'Maybe we should arrange...what is that English term?... some play dates?'

'Oh, that would be lovely—thank you!' Alaina responded genuinely.

She liked the other woman's easy-going air. Her husband was genial too, and was currently chatting to Rafaello— something about some new legislation going through Parliament, Alaina thought.

By the time the lengthy dinner had finished Alaina was feeling decidedly more at ease. Liqueurs and coffee and petits-fours were circulating, the master of ceremonies was announcing the guest speaker, to polite applause, and Alaina settled back with a glass of orange-scented liqueur and a cup of rich coffee, prepared to be bored by a speech on a subject she knew nothing about in a language she did not understand.

Rafaello leant towards her. 'It won't last too long,' he murmured. 'Then the dancing will start.' He paused. 'You're doing splendidly—thank you.'

Alaina gave a flickering smile, lifting her liqueur glass and taking a sip of the fiery but fragrant liquid. Rafaello's breath had been warm on her throat, the hint of his aftershave potent, the heat of his body close. She'd been very cautious in what she'd drunk all evening, but the modest amount of wine had entered her system, she knew. Or something had...

Rafaello sat back, paying dutiful attention to whatever it was the guest speaker was saying. Her gaze rested on his profile and she felt that 'something' reach inside her again. That slight faintness catching at her. Oh, but she could just gaze and gaze at him! She really could just drink him in...

The way I did when we were together. Just sinking my chin into my hands to gaze and gaze. And he would see me gazing and sometimes laugh, sometimes smile, and sometimes... Sometimes he'd lean casually forward across the dinner table and taste my mouth with his, knowing there was only one way the evening would end—impatient for it, yet savouring the journey too. Toying with each her so as to enhance the consummation when it came...

A silent sigh of longing went through her. How much she had wanted him—desired him—yearned for him... How she had counted the hours till she could go off duty... How she'd badgered her boss to get days off ahead of schedule so she could take off with him...climb into the Jeep he'd hired, or the motorboat he'd commandeered, and head off across the island or along the coastline to find other bays and beaches…

She had been in a state of bliss.

Until the end of the affair came and he put her aside—no longer desired, no longer wanted.

Holiday over…time together over.

He had told her, without intentional cruelty, that theirs had been an interlude of the greatest pleasure—but it had now come to an end.

'You have your life, and I have mine,' he'd said, a faint smile on his face.

And she had felt him withdrawing from her…closing her out. Detaching her from his life. Telling her with his body language and that faint smile and his cool voice that this was something she must accept.

And I did. Because what else could I do except be grateful that it was only the edge of the precipice that I had come to—not the fatal falling over that I might so easily have done had we had longer together…

She heard again, now, the mantra she'd adopted, telling herself, night after night, in the aftermath of his departure, *You got out in time—just in time.*

The way her mother had not…

Applause roused her, and with a start she realised that the speeches were over and an air of relaxation was settling over the room as people got to their feet and started to mingle. At the far end there was a dance floor, and music came from a band that had materialised, striking up old-fashioned melodies from the inter-war years.

'Shall we?'

Rafaello was murmuring his invitation, accompanying it with a smile. Others at the table were getting to their feet too, and Alaina had no option but to do likewise. Otherwise she would be left alone with Rafaello, and that would probably be worse. Besides, she was here to perform her role as Signora Ranieri and this was simply part of it.

He took her hand, drawing her to her feet, ushering her past the tables towards the dance floor. Then he took her into his arms…

Rafaello felt her body tremble—a fine vibration going through her that transmitted itself to him, telling him just how she was responding to being in his arms like this. It was exactly the response he wanted. But he kept his hold on her light, all the same, not drawing her closer to him, letting her get used to the touch of his hand at her waist, guiding her around the dance floor to the gentle age-old melody.

He could tell how self-conscious she was—saw the faintest stain of colour on her cheek, her face turned away from him, her hand touching his shoulder as lightly as she could. He felt…heard…the swish of her silk skirts, caught the delicate fragrance of her perfume.

He made no attempt to speak to her, wanting her simply to get used to the sensation of dancing with him. Then, as the music stopped and they halted with the other dancers, he smiled down at her.

'That wasn't too bad, was it?' he said.

'I haven't danced in a long time,' she said, swallowing.

She slipped her hand from his, dropping her hand from his shoulder. Taking her cue, he let go of her waist and walked with her back to their table. Another couple joined them—Gina and Pietro Fratelli, with whom Alaina had discussed play dates earlier. Rafaello had no objection— he liked he couple—and if Alaina palled up with Gina, and Joey and their little boy got on…well, that was all to the good.

He chatted to Pietro, a senior lawyer in one of the government departments, letting Alaina talk small children with Gina. Then another couple returned to the table, and the man gallantly asked Alaina to dance. Rafaello promptly asked his wife in return, and the four of them made their way out on to the dance floor again.

Rafaello soon had another chance to dance with Alaina himself, and this time he felt she was less tense, more relaxed, more accepting of their contact. He made no reference to it, only made small talk to her as they danced, though he was never not conscious of her body so close to his...

The evening wound down and people started to take their leave. Soon he and Alaina were among them, heading downstairs, out to their waiting car, then being driven back to his apartment.

As they settled into the car and it moved off, he turned towards her. 'Survived the ordeal?' he quizzed with a half-smile.

'I enjoyed it,' she replied. 'And I'm glad to have met Gina. I think her little boy and Joey could have fun play dates, and it's just what Joey needs. We're going to fix something for next week—we've exchanged phone numbers. She said she doesn't live far away.'

'No, not that far,' Rafaello agreed. 'And, yes, the Fratellis are a nice couple.'

They chatted a little more about the evening as a whole, and then they had arrived at the apartment. He helped Alaina out, feeling once again her hand trembling very slightly as she let him draw her up. She had become self-conscious again—he could tell.

Inside, he turned to her.

'A nightcap to round off the evening?' he suggested.

He kept it light. No pressure—that would not help his cause.

He saw uncertainty flicker in her face. He thought she

was about to agree, but then, with a shake of her head, she demurred.

'It's been a long evening. I think I'll just head straight for bed. Thank you for tonight, Rafaello—it was…well, nicer than I thought it might be.'

He gave a low laugh. 'We'll build on it from there,' he said.

He watched her make her way to her bedroom, swaying elegantly on her high heels, the drape of her skirts swishing gracefully, her head poised, as beautiful from this perspective as from the front. A stab of regret went through him. Should he have tried harder to get her to defer retiring? But he was trying to pace it carefully—a little delay would cost nothing.

As her bedroom door shut he heard her murmur a low 'Goodnight', which he echoed absently and headed for his own bedroom. It adjoined hers and had a communicating door—the staff would think it strange otherwise, and he had no wish to cause gossip of any kind. But the communicating door itself was locked from her side, not his…

He let himself into his bedroom, closed the door quietly behind him. Started to pull loose his bow tie.

He was very conscious, glancing at the communicating door between their bedrooms, of Alaina just beyond…

CHAPTER EIGHT

ALAINA SET DOWN her evening bag on the dressing table, easing her feet out of her high-heeled shoes, feeling relief when her feet were flat again. She flexed her toes. She had implied to Rafaello that she was tired, but she wasn't. She was restless. Her heart rate was elevated. She wanted to feel sleepy, but she didn't—and she knew why.

It had been dancing with Rafaello that had done the damage. Oh, she'd covered it as well as she could, and she'd only danced twice with him anyway, but once was all it had taken.

All it had taken to let memory come rushing back in, to breach her careful defences against him, to make her shamelessly, disastrously, want to hold him closer to her in their dancing embrace, to wind her arms around his neck, lean against him, feel his strength, his masculinity, let desire build, arousal quicken...

She gave a half-smothered cry now, turning away sharply. But that meant she now had a full view of herself in the long mirror inset into the wardrobe. She gazed, wide-eyed at her reflection. Her gown was truly beautiful, graceful and flattering as only a couture gown could be.

For a helpless moment she just went on gazing at herself. Then restlessly she turned away. No point standing there admiring herself! Her hands went to her spine, reaching for the zip, pulling it sharply down, peeling the gown from her. She draped it over the back of a velvet armchair—she'd hang it up in the morning. Just as swiftly she stripped off her underwear, determinedly looking nowhere near her reflection, and grabbed her dressing gown to cover herself. The silky material was cool on her skin, and she was glad.

Then she unpinned her hair, shaking it down. With a start, she realised she was still wearing the diamond necklace Rafaello had adorned her with that evening. Her hands went to her nape, fiddling with the clasp. She started to frown—the safety chain was on, and she couldn't get any purchase on it somehow...it was too intricate.

Several attempts later she gave up the battle. Her face set. She was either going to have to sleep in the damn thing or...

Without conscious volition, and without thinking about it—because to do that would have been to stop her in her tracks—she went towards the communicating door. The key was in her side and she turned it, giving a slight knock as she twisted the handle and pressed the door open.

'I can't get the safety chain unfastened,' she said.

Rafaello was standing by his tallboy, slipping his cufflinks from his dress shirt. His jacket was abandoned and his bow tie untied, the top button of his shirt undone. He turned at her abrupt entry. Turned and stilled.

Alaina had stilled too. Absently, in her mind, words ran. What *was* it about a man in evening dress with his bow tie loose and his top button undone? It should be nothing... nothing at all! And yet—

She gulped silently. Oh, dear God, but he looked so... so...

'Come here.' He held a hand out to her. 'You'll need to stand by the light.'

He was under one of the wall sconces, where the pooling light enhanced the play of shadow across him.

Numbly, she walked towards him. This had been a bad, bad idea…

But she walked towards him all the same.

He took her shoulder, turned her lightly, stood behind her so the light from the wall sconce was shining down on the nape of her neck.

'Hold still.'

She held still. She could do nothing else *but* hold still. Except in every cell of her body that same faint tremor that had been set off when he had taken her into his arms to dance with her was set off again. And she could not stop it, or calm it, nor do anything about it at all.

She felt his fingers, cool and expert, brush her loosened hair over one shoulder, then release the tricky safety catch… felt the necklace sag forward. She caught it with her fingers, turning to hold it out to him.

'Please, Rafaello, keep it. It's too valuable for me to want it in my room.'

He took it absently, dropping it as if it were nothing more than costume jewellery from a market stall on top of his tallboy. His attention was not on the diamond necklace, but on her. On her silky dressing gown with its silver facings.

'I remember this,' he said. There was a husk beneath the cool murmur of his voice, and his eyelids had drooped. 'You had it on the island. I admired its effect then, as I recall. I also recall…' before she had time to realise what he was doing, his hand had dropped to her waist, was drawing at the tie of the belt '…relieving you of it…'

She couldn't move. It was as if every nerve in her body were paralysed.

'Rafaello—no—'

Her voice was faint, a thread. But she could feel her heart rate rocket. Protest rose. And then panic.

I didn't come in here for this—I didn't…

Her eyes flew to his, dismay flooding her. That look in his face, in his eyes, that glint of gold so distinct within their hooded depths, the faint curve of his mouth....

I don't want this.

She heard the words again in her head. But they were fainter now. Drowned by the thudding of her heart, by the heat suddenly, disastrously, rising up in her.

'No?'

A lift of his eyebrow, his voice low and husky...quizzical. She felt his hand pause.

'Are you sure, Alaina? Are you really, really sure?'

Yes!

The single essential word shouted in her head. She was as sure as she had been on the moonlit terrace at the villa when he'd kissed her. Nothing had changed—*nothing!* She must go...must step away, walk away, go back to the communicating door, back into her bedroom, shut the door behind her, lock it...

But she did not move. Could not move. Could do nothing at all except, in a voice that was so faint it was a sigh, a whisper, say his name. Only that.

'Rafaello...'

She felt herself sway—a movement without conscious volition, a kind of instinct beyond her control. Beyond reason.

'Alaina...'

He echoed his name with hers, and she could hear in it... Not humour...no, not that.

Desire.

He drew her towards him, folding her against him, and his mouth found hers lifted to him. Like the softest silk... like the richest velvet...his mouth moved on hers. Faintness drummed through her, and so much more.

Then, at her waist, she felt his hand slip the belt of her dressing gown, loosening it from her.

And she was lost…

She was naked in his arms, her warm, silken body pressed against his.

With effortless ease he lifted her up, carried her to his waiting bed.

Past and present fused.

He laid her down on the waiting sheets, his breath catching. Her naked beauty inflamed him, and he felt his body surge, desire coursing through him. But he held it back, held it in check. He must not rush her.

He lowered himself beside her, sitting on the bed, leaning over her, for a moment simply gazing down at her. Her eyes, wide and distended, clung to his. He said her name again—a low, hushed murmur. Then reached his hand forward.

Slowly, intently, he touched her breasts, the warm, soft mounds silken against his palm. They flowered at his touch, and a low, aroused moan came from her throat. He lifted his hand away. Replaced it with his lips. Slowly, sensuously, he laved the coral peaks, hearing that low moan come again. He heard his name, and then her hands were curving around his back, seeking to draw him down to her.

He felt the impediment of his clothes with a sudden impatient rush. He jack-knifed up, shedding them swiftly, disposing of them as unnecessary hindrances to what he now most wanted in all the world. Then he returned to the bed where she lay waiting for him, as she had lain and waited for him before—so many times. Each time in the overture to a night of passion and of pleasure.

As tonight would be…

He came down beside her, his body rich and ripe with

desire. More than his body... How beautiful she was. How much he wanted her. Wanted her to want him...

And she did. He could see it in her face, in her dilated eyes holding his, alight with all that he wanted there to be in them. He could hear it in the quickening of her breathing, feel it in her exquisite, engorged, coral-tipped breasts, the slight but oh-so-telling slackening of her thighs.

Her hands reached up to him to wind around his waist and draw him to her. His mouth closed over hers, his body moved over hers, his own arousal surging. She was warm and soft and silken, her mouth tender beneath his, her lips parting as his kiss deepened to feast on all that she was offering. His body pressed on hers and he felt her thighs widen under his, felt her give a gasp, low in her throat, as she felt the strength of his manhood.

Still he held back, memory possessing him. He was re-calling how she liked to make love...just what it was that he could do to her that would bring her body to wild thrashing, make her voice cry out in sensual ecstasy.

His mouth lifted from her, gliding down the contour of her throat, beneath the sweet valley of her ripened breasts, over the satin slenderness of her waist and further still, lower now, to where she was most achingly sensitive. His hands held her flanks, his mouth and his lips skimming her with arousing caress. Her hands had slid caressingly up the strong column of his back, and her fingernails were indenting now on his shoulders. He felt her back straining to arch beneath him.

She said his name, helpless, pleading, as he readied her for his possession, wanting her desire to reach its peak so that the pleasure he would give her would soar above his own. He lifted his mouth away and she gave a cry, as if of loss, but then he was moving his body up over hers again, his mouth finding hers, fusing her lips with his in the mounting passion between them.

His arousal quickened, urgency filling him. She, too, was quickening, her thighs pressing against his, widening under his, and her spine was arching again, hips lifting to his.

It was an invitation that he could not refuse…that was impossible to refuse. She was saying his name again, through the passion of their kisses, and he knew the moment had come—the moment was now…*now*…

He entered her without hesitation, with a hunger that sought its own satiation, and she cried out, her hands coming down to his hips, pressing him, pulling him against her, more deeply into her. He thrust forward, feeling their bodies fuse, and it was right, so right, for them to do so. He folded her into him, felt the delicate tissues of her body embracing him, taking him deeper…deeper yet.

And then he felt her body flame all around him, felt her convulse in sudden, throbbing pulsation, heard her cry out, more wildly now, in an ecstasy that was almost anguish. Her hands snaked around his back, either side of his spine, pressing and splaying as if she would never let him go, would hold him within her for ever.

He said her name, ragged and beyond control, his head lifted, thrown back, as all through his body the power of his own moment forged through him. Absolute possession. Absolute fusion. Absolute union of their bodies. Shuddering through him, taking him, and her, to the apotheosis of desire fulfilled, sated and consumed.

For an ageless moment he was blinded by it, possessed by it, then slowly…very slowly…he felt his body subside. Grow heavy and lax. He could feel little whorls of pleasure still echoing in her body, tangible to him, and smiled to feel them. With a shaking hand he smoothed the dampened tendrils of her hair. She was gazing up at him with the same blindness, the same wonder.

He kissed her softy, gently, but the need for sleep was drumming through him…the body's exhaustion, the mind's oblivion. He said her name again, slipping from her only to fold her close against him, against the hectic beating of his heart. Her softness, her tenderness, was all that he craved now.

His last barely conscious thought, before oblivion took him, was that he knew with a certainty that filled every cell in his body that reclaiming her, making her his own again, was all that he had wanted it to be…could ever want it to be…

Past fused with present, and present with past—and *now* was what was good. So very, very good…

Then sleep took him as she was held fast in his arms. The only place he wanted her to be.

Alaina stretched languorously in the dawn light, one thigh warm against Rafaello's. Memory, familiarity and a wonderful sense of happiness suffused her. It was as if those five long years since she had last lain like this alongside Rafaello, their bodies intertwined so sensually, had never been.

Words, inchoate, welling up from deep within her still drowsing consciousness, formed in her mind.

I belong here…

She slid her arm around his lean waist, wrapping herself to him, one cheek on his hard, smooth chest, her long hair trailing over him as he slept.

She hovered between waking and drowsing and more words formed, silent but sibilant in her mind.

This is right—this is how it should be.

She had been right—oh, so right—to abandon her struggle to resist him and to yield to what she knew, despite all her verbal denials to him, she wanted…

What she had wanted from the moment Rafaello had walked back into her life, reigniting that old flame…

How could she quench it again? Five years ago she had had to. Five years ago he had wanted her no longer…had taken his leave of her. Left her life for good.

But now he was back in it—and she was back in his.

And he wanted her.

Not just as the mother of the child they had unintentionally conceived—the little boy who had lit up her life, who was an undeserved gift and so, so precious. And surely she should be glad—and grateful, and relieved—that Rafaello wanted Joey! Wanted to be in his life.

A sliver of cold went through her. Rafaello might have rejected Joey, wanted nothing to do with him, played no part in his life. Might have considered him a burden, unwelcome and unacknowledged. That was what she had feared five years ago, on discovering her affair with Rafaello had left her pregnant.

But her fears had proved groundless. Rafaello had not hesitated—had not questioned or doubted or delayed. He had rearranged his entire life so that Joey could be part of it. Joey…the son he wanted.

And he wants me too—wants me as he wanted me on the island.

And she wanted him to want her—wanted to want him. She knew that now, with a certainty that filled her.

She felt him stir, felt the arm around her shoulder tighten, drawing her closer to him, felt his other hand reach to rest on her rounded hip. She heard him murmur something in Italian, soft and fluid. Then his body relaxed again and he lapsed into sleep once more.

Drowsiness, sated and sensual, eased through her, and her thoughts and her consciousness faded. She let the dark, and the night, and the warmth of Rafaello's embrace, draw her back down into sweet, honeyed slumber. Happiness and gladness suffused her, and she had only one last drowsy thought.

How good it was to be here in his arms again…how very, very good…

It was the right place for her to be. So, so right…

CHAPTER NINE

RAFAELLO GLANCED BRIEFLY in his rear-view mirror. Alaina was sitting beside Joey in the back of the car, reading a story to him as they sped along the autostrada leading south out of Rome. They were heading to Amalfi, and Rafaello was not looking forward to reaching their destination.

He was taking Joey and Alaina to meet his father.

He'd written to inform his father of his marriage as soon as they'd arrived in Italy, knowing it would not be welcome news. But his father had merely indicated he should visit, and now they were. But it was a duty visit, nothing more. He already knew what his father would say.

Trapped you, did she? You should have known better! At least tell me the prenup is watertight!

Would he be interested in Joey? Oh, not in the boy himself—Rafaello knew that with the unsentimental clarity engendered in him by his own upbringing; his father hadn't taken much interest in his own son while young—but as his grandson, his genetic progeny?

He shrugged mentally. His father's interest, or lack of it, would make little impact on Joey, or indeed on Rafaello either. If his mother had still been alive, though...

He pulled his mind away. That was not something he wanted to think about either. If his father would be predominantly indifferent to Joey's existence, he knew his mother would have been over-emotional and over-indulgent, possessive and neurotic, with an excess of sensibility...

No, he did not wish to dwell on that. It was all so long ago. The past was gone, and it was the present he must focus on. The present which, he thought, his mood mellowing as he cruised along the busy autostrada, had so much to commend it.

His glance went to the rear-view mirror again. Alaina's head was turned towards Joey, delineating her lovely profile, and he felt his mood improve yet more. Since the night she had come to him after the dinner-dance, every night had been as good. There was no holding back, no reluctance or questioning or denial of what had been rekindled between them. She was as ardent, as eager, as he could wish. And he was glad of it—very, very glad.

And that was a good feeling to have. Surprisingly so...

His life, which the discovery of Joey's existence had turned upside down, was settling again. Running, once again, on smooth, oiled wheels, with nothing to disrupt or unsettle it again. He had Joey, the son he was doing his best to be a father to, and he had Alaina, whose beauty aroused him as strongly as it once had. Their desire was rekindled—and now there was no reason for that flame to be extinguished.

No reason at all...

Joey was restless, bored with the long car journey. And there was still about another half an hour to go before they reached their destination.

Alaina felt tension dart within her. She was not exactly looking forward to this visit. Rafaello's father did not sound like an easy man.

Not that she had said as much to Rafaello. She understood this was a necessary visit—introducing her and Joey

to Rafaello's surviving parent. Severino Ranieri was sup-
posedly retired—but, as Rafaello had made clear to her, he
still kept a sharp eye on the family firm, even though these
days it was run by Rafaello himself.

'My father speaks his mind,' Rafaello had informed her.
'He knows the circumstances of our marriage, obviously,
but what he will make of Joey I am unsure. He will be glad
of a grandson—an heir, so to speak, to continue the family line. But—'

'But less glad of me,' Alaina had finished drily.

Rafaello had glanced at her. 'He will be civil to you,'
he had said.

'And I,' she had replied, 'will be civil to him in return.'

But for all her assurances, when the introductions were
made on their arrival at the imposing-looking residence in
an affluent region of the dramatic Amalfi coastline, she
was on her guard.

Rafaello's father was tall, like him, and good-looking,
in a severe fashion, even in his seventies. But, she thought,
his distinguished appearance did not hide the chill in his
eyes. If Rafaello presented his keen intelligence within an
outwardly smooth, urbane manner, his father was more like
a blade with its cutting edge unconcealed.

'So.' Severino's tone was clipped, as he addressed his
son. 'This is your…unexpected wife and son.'

His inexpressive glance went briefly to Alaina, then
dropped to where Joey stood beside her, holding her hand.

'Well, no point questioning his paternity,' he remarked.
His eyes went back to Alaina. 'You will wish to refresh
yourself after your journey. My housekeeper will attend to
you. Rafaello, a word…'

He indicated that his son should follow him, leaving
Alaina to be shown upstairs, with Joey trotting beside her,

looking about him interestedly, by a timid-looking middle-aged woman.

Joey was asking questions, and Alaina answered as best she could.

'Yes, the elderly gentleman is your grandfather,' she said. 'And, like I told you, because he's elderly, you will need to be quiet, darling. He won't like a lot of noise or excitement.'

And that was not all that Rafaello's father would not like—that was obvious. But she kept that to herself. Welcoming he had *not* been. As to whether he would even be civil was questionable. It was perfectly clear he would have preferred her and Joey not to exist at all.

Well, that was no concern of hers. The timid-looking housekeeper was showing her into a guest bedroom, indicating the en suite bathroom, where she could make use of the facilities. Alaina was glad they were not staying with Rafaello's father, but were booked into a hotel nearby. All she had to get through was lunch, some conversation—however stilted—and then they could leave.

Even so, lunch was not a relaxing affair. Joey, mindful of her admonition, was on his best behaviour, and was looking smart in long trousers and a shirt with a little waistcoat, his hair neatly brushed. He got a measured, unsmiling look from the man who was his grandfather. She got one as well.

Alaina suspected he was pricing her outfit—a stylish designer two-piece in pale green, purchased in the Via Condotti—and, she surmised, thinking she had done well out of marrying his son.

The conversation, conducted in English, centred on herself. And it was less of a conversation than a cross-examination.

Alaina answered the clearly leading questions composedly.

'Yes, Rafaello and I met on holiday. It was a relationship

that was not intended to last. I chose to be a single mother for that reason. However, Rafaello, meeting me again by chance, convinced me that a two-parent family was preferable—hence my presence now, in Italy and in his life. That's all there is to it really,' she said, calmly continuing to eat.

'Indeed,' Rafaello's father said tightly.

'Indeed...' echoed Rafaello.

Alaina could hear the ironic timbre in his voice. It drew a sharp glance from his father and a swift utterance in rapid Italian that she could not understand and was probably glad not to. Whatever it was—and she had a shrewd idea that it was not complimentary about herself—it drew no response from Rafaello. He was, she could see, indifferent to it. Or at least appearing to be so.

His father reverted to English. 'You have legitimised the boy?'

He put the question to Rafaello.

'As I told you, yes.'

Rafaello's reply was as composed as hers had been.

His father's mouth tightened. 'It will never be as satisfactory as a child born in wedlock,' he remarked.

'We are not a dynasty,' Rafaello replied, his manner seeming still unruffled by his father's implied criticism. 'There is no title or nobility to be affected.'

'Nevertheless, it is not a desirable situation.'

The chilly eyes flickered over Alaina again, with a dismissive expression in them, and then returned to Rafaello.

'But what is done is done.' He reached for his wine. 'I can only be relieved that your mother is not with us any longer. Her emotionality would have been tiresome in the extreme.' His glance now went to his grandson, dutifully and silently eating his food. 'She would have spoilt the boy completely!'

Alaina smiled sweetly, and decided to intervene. 'But

that is the role of a *nonna*. It is sad that Joey has no grand-mothers to make a fuss over him. My own mother died some years ago.'

Sharp eyes came at her. 'And your father?'

'He remarried shortly after her death. I am no longer in contact. He lives in Scotland.'

'And his circumstances?' There was a discernible edge in the terse enquiry.

'Like you, he is retired. He worked as a scientist for one of the government departments.' She paused minutely, tak-ing a sip from her water. 'He is quite respectable,' she said.

Severino Ranieri's face tightened. He did not, it was evi-dent, care to be answered back to—or to have his own as-sumptions called out.

Thoughts ran through her head as she resumed eating. Rafaello might have inherited his father's good looks and his keen intelligence, but that was all—and Alaina was glad of it.

Severino Ranieri made another remark in Italian to his son, and even though she did not understand it completely, she caught enough to know that he was making a waspish comment about women and sharp tongues. As before, Ra-faello made no answer.

Alaina decided she had had enough of this not so co-vert inquisition.

'I am looking forward to seeing something of this dra-matic part of Italy,' she declared. 'Though I'm not sure about Pompeii and Herculaneum—probably best to wait until Joey is older and at school, learning about the Romans. A boat trip to Capri might be more fun for him. What do you think, Joey darling?'

Joey, still mindful of her previous admonitions to be on his best behaviour, said 'Yes, please, Mummy,' in an ultra good-boy tone.

She smiled, then looked across at Rafaello's father. 'Would you join us?' she asked limpidly.

There was a sound that might have come from Rafaello's throat, but she wasn't looking at him and wasn't sure. His father's face had tightened again.

'I will leave that joy to yourselves,' he answered acerbically.

Alaina hadn't for a moment imagined that he would agree to come, and nor had she wanted him to. A shaft of sadness went through her. She hadn't expected Rafaello's father to be a doting grandfather, but all the same…

As for my father—he doesn't even know Joey exists, and I will never tell him. What for? So he can ignore him as he ignored me all my life? As he ignored my mother?

Severino Ranieri was addressing his son now, and Alaina looked at him. He and her own father were cut from the same cloth. Unemotional, cerebral, self-contained, uncomfortable with emotion.

They don't want other people loving them.

No, that was a dangerous path to go down.

Involuntarily, her gaze went to Rafaello. Tension netted her suddenly. Rafaello was not chilly, like his father, but there was a detachment about him that came across as coolness—a dissociation from the rough and tumble messiness of human affections. As if he were, however urbanely, keeping the world at a distance.

Keeping people at a distance.

Whoever they were.

A troubled expression clouded her eyes. This was the man she had married…the father of her son. The man whose physical appeal to her was overwhelming, and whose bed she now shared. She was no longer fighting what was impossible for her to fight. This was the man who could inflame her with a skilled, sensual passion she could not resist, and yet…

A question was trying to shape itself in her head, but she did not want to allow it do so—let alone answer it. She batted it away, dismissing it. Silencing her disquiet.

There is no need for that question—because there is no purpose to it. We are married, and making a home for Joey, making a sustainable marriage, making something for ourselves as well as for our son. So why think any more about it?

She moved her thoughts away from this dangerous ground.

'So, is Capri overrated?' she asked, addressing the question to both Rafaello and his father.

'It depends what you want,' Rafaello answered smoothly. 'It's extremely popular, as you know. I expect Joey will enjoy the boat ride.'

Rafaello's father looked at him disapprovingly. 'You must not over-indulge him,' he said.

Alaina felt herself bristle, but banked it down—there was no point in reacting to her father-in-law.

She saw Rafaello's expression become veiled.

'Definitions of over-indulgence may vary,' he replied. His tone was as veiled as his expression.

His father moved on to another line of criticism.

'What is happening about his schooling? It should not be delayed by his lack of Italian.'

Alaina got her reply in before Rafaello. 'He'll be starting in the autumn term at the infant class of the International School near the villa Rafaello has taken.'

Cold eyes rested on her. 'School is good for children—and not just for their education. It makes them independent of any maternal possessiveness.' His glance went to Rafaello. 'For you that was essential,' he said.

That veiled look was on Rafaello's face once more…inexpressive. Alaina was glad that the housekeeper came in at that point, to remove their plates and set down a platter of cheeses and biscuits. Rafaello made some genial remark to the housekeeper, and Alaina saw the woman's face light up. But then her employer made a terse remark and the frightened expression reappeared. Alaina merely thanked her as she took her and Joey's empty plates away.

Clearly cheese was instead of any dessert course, and Alaina selected a mild-tasting one for Joey, with a couple of biscuits, taking a sliver for herself of something that looked like Camembert—more out of politeness than anything else.

Conversation limped on, stilted and formal, with her polite enquires about the Amalfi region receiving only clipped replies from her father-in-law, ameliorated by Rafaello's more expansive ones. Joey, she could see with a sense of foreboding, was running out of ultra good-boy mode and getting restless.

Her attention would keep his restlessness at bay, she knew, and she left the conversation to Rafaello and his father, who reverted to Italian. A covert glance told her that neither father nor son were at ease. She wondered if Severino Ranieri even knew the meaning of the word.

A sense of depression edged over her. Rafaello's father was, indeed, cut from the same severe, unyielding material as her own father. It was a blessing Rafaello was not like that.

Yet there were elements of that in him. She knew she had to acknowledge that. He made no accommodations when his course was set. He'd placed those stark options before her—to marry him or face a court battle over Joey. Memory stabbed at her. Five years ago, on their last day together on the island, he had had closed down the conversation she'd tried to have with him about whether their time together must really be over.

'We each have our own lives to lead,' he had said.

He had not said it harshly, or coldly, but he had meant it…
Her expression shadowed.

And now our lives have come together again—because of Joey.

Emotion plucked at her, but she could not identify it. Did not want to. It was dangerous to do so. Much better to pay it no attention, not to address it or give it entrance. Much better to accept the life she was now leading.

I have Joey and I have Rafaello. All I could possibly want.

That was good—very good indeed. So very, very good…

Rafaello was getting to his feet, his father likewise.

Rafaello looked at Alaina. 'I think we must make a move,' he said.

Relieved, she stood up too, telling Joey they were going now.

They took their leave, with the poor housekeeper holding open the front door, and Alaina smiled her thanks as she went out, holding Joey's hand. They all got back into the car that was parked on the carriage sweep and Alaina settled Joey into his child seat, strapping him in as Rafaello got into the driving seat and gunned the engine.

She looked back to the front door, expecting to see his father there, bidding them goodbye, but it was already shut.

She said nothing, and nor did Rafaello. But was there a tenseness across his shoulders and in the stiffness of his neck as they drove off the property and on to the highway? She wasn't sure, but she could well understand if there was. She herself felt as if she could finally breathe easily.

She made no remark about their visit, though, only saying brightly, 'How far to the hotel?'

'A few kilometres,' came the answer. Rafaello's tone was short.

She said no more, busying herself pointing out the passing scenery to Joey. He was getting sleepy, she could see, especially now he was back in the car, and she let him doze off. Rafaello still didn't speak, but she let him be.

At the hotel—an old-fashioned but luxurious-looking edifice perched atop a steep cliffside—they checked in and went up to their room. Joey had surfaced, and was becoming chatty again, but it was only Alaina who answered his questions and acknowledged his observations.

The afternoon was still warm, though the sun was lowering over the azure sea gloriously on view from their balcony.

'Mummy, there's a swimming pool!' Joey said excitedly, pointing down to where he had spotted a rectangular patch of blue set in the gardens, sparkling in the sunshine.

'You two go down,' Rafaello said. 'I'll follow. I must check on some work matters.'

He was getting out his laptop, setting it on the desk. The tense look was still evident and, again, Alaina let him be. He needed time on his own. And she… Well, the pool looked just as enticing to her as it did Joey.

She threw open the lid of her suitcase and rummaged for their swimming gear, extracting it, then quickly changing Joey into swim shorts and a tee, and herself into a one-piece with a sundress over the top. She grabbed sandals for their feet, and a tube of suncream for them both.

'We're off,' she said cheerfully to Rafaello, who barely looked up from his laptop.

He had a closed, focussed expression on his face, his eyes scanning a document on the screen.

She set off with Joey, who was tugging her along eagerly. Ultra good-boy mode had vanished, and she, too, felt that she'd just come off duty. Daughter-in-law duty, which was supposed to have shown her presence in Rafaello's life as something other than a gold-digging adventuress foisting her bastard son on Severino's family.

But she wasn't angry about it. She'd learnt long ago that anger achieved nothing. Had learnt that lesson as her father's daughter. She could remember trying to convince her mother that both anger and tears were pointless.

'It's not his fault, Mum. He doesn't possess the faculty for love. It's missing in him. All we can do is not love him ourselves. That's the only protection we can have.'

Sadness filled her. It had been easier for her, she knew, to survive without her father's love. But not for her mother.

She just went on craving it...all her life. Desperate for him to love her back. And he never would, and never could—it wasn't in him.

She stepped with Joey into the elevator, letting him press the button as he loved to do.

As the car plunged down, it took her stomach with it. Echoing the plunging emotion that was stabbing at her.

Never fall for a man who does not and cannot love you back.

It was the warning she'd lived by all her life, thanks to her mother's sad and sorry example of the fate awaiting any woman who made that fatal mistake.

A warning she must never forget...

It had saved her...*just*...on the island. And it must keep her safe now.

What I have to do now with Rafaello is only to make our marriage workable, for Joey's sake.

That was all she must allow.

CHAPTER TEN

RAFAELLO WALKED OUT on to the pool deck. The hotel was not full, and he could see Joey and Alaina, the pool's sole occupants at this late hour of the afternoon, disporting themselves in the water. A large degree of splashing was involved.

He gave an involuntary smile. Out of nowhere, he felt the tension that had netted him since the morning suddenly evaporate finally. His duty visit to his father had been necessary, but an ordeal. Now he and Alaina, and Joey, could have the rest of the weekend to themselves.

Joey caught sight of him and called out excitedly.

'Mummy and me are having a splashing competition! I'm winning!'

Rafaello let his eyes rest on the little boy, who was back to splashing frantically at Alaina, who was ducking exaggeratedly. They were at the shallow end, Alaina standing, Joey buoyant in his water wings.

Memory shafted in him—or rather an absence of memory. His mother had disliked the water, and they had had no pool anyway, nor gone on beach holidays. Their holidays, such as they were, had been walking holidays, up in the Dolomites. His father had led the way, striding wordlessly forward, his mother next, fearful of falling, but insistent on coming along anyway, desperate to do anything her husband might want to do, and not to be excluded. As for himself, he'd plodded along in their wake, not expecting to enjoy any of it.

There was little of his boyhood that he'd enjoyed at all. School—boarding school, as soon as he could be despatched by his father, who had been insistent on getting him away from the baleful influence of his neurotic mother—had been a respite. There he had made his select friends, discovered that being intelligent gained the teachers' approval. And being good at sports such as fencing and climbing had given gave him sufficient social cachet not to be written off as a nerd.

In his teenage years he'd discovered that good looks and a cool manner served him well too. His cool manner had predominated, keeping both his father's implied criticism and his mother's neurotic clinginess at bay. It had also, he knew, made him attractive to females keen to get past that air of dispassionate reserve, which he'd punctuated with smooth attentiveness when he'd felt like it, for those females he'd considered qualified for his interest in them. All had been keen to be selected by him for such affairs as he was prepared to indulge in when the occasion had suited him.

Such as on the island, with Alaina.

And now...?

Well, now choice had been removed from the situation. Not for a moment would he have reneged on his responsibilities towards the child Alaina had borne him. Did he wish she hadn't? An irrelevant question. He dealt in realities—anything else was pointless. And this reality came with distinct advantages.

His eyes rested on Alaina now, on the way the sleek one-piece moulded her figure, the way the water lapped her breasts in a very pleasing manner. He found his mood lifting more. Found himself wishing he had not reserved a family room but a suite, wondering if it could be changed at this late hour. But even in an adjoining room, if |Joey did not settle then there would be no point.

Just as there had been no point thinking that his father would have been any different today than the way he had always been. Alaina had coped well—he must congratulate her. As for Joey...

His smile quirked at his mouth. Joey most definitely deserved a treat for his ultra good-boy performance!

He shrugged off his short-sleeved, open-necked shirt and shucked off his pool shoes.

'Time to even the score,' he informed Joey, who was still mercilessly batting water at his mother.

He slid into the pool, welcoming the cool water lapping at his thighs.

Joey gave a cry of excited glee, paddling frantically in his direction, splashing mightily as he did so. Rafaello fisted both hands and brought them crashing down into the water, sending out a mini tsunami towards Joey. Joey shrieked and battle commenced.

In his head, Rafaello heard his father's admonition not to over-indulge Joey.

The sound of splashing water drowned it out.

Or something did.

Rafaello did not trouble himself to listen to it again...

That night they decided to dine on their balcony, making use of Room Service. Joey, sufficiently tired out by a lot of fun in the pool, was fast asleep in his little bed inside. He'd had his supper out by the pool—a large helping of pasta, followed by a bowl of ice-cream.

Out on the horizon the sun had set. Lights were pricking on along the coastline and out on the sea itself, from fishing boats and night cruisers. It was still warm, but not so warm that Alaina did not welcome the light shawl around her shoulders.

Rafaello had a cotton sweater knotted around his neck, over an open-necked shirt with the cuffs turned back, and wore dark blue chinos that matched her own navy-blue cotton trousers and elbow length top. She hadn't bothered with make-up, just washed her hair after its immersion in the pool, and was now letting it dry by itself, scooped off her forehead with a hairband. Rafaello hadn't shaved, given the informality of their dining.

'Very piratical,' Alaina observed as they took their places at the little table on the balcony as Room Service departed, leaving dinner tucked under covered serving dishes.

Rafaello rubbed his darkening jawline ruminatively. 'Not a good image for a lawyer,' he remarked.

'You'd have to grow it into a proper beard—that would lend appropriate gravitas. Maybe when you hit fifty?' she suggested. 'You might be a judge by then!'

He laughed. 'Not my line of the law,' he replied.

She reached for her glass of wine, taking a considering sip. 'I could see your father as a judge,' she said. 'Though I wouldn't like to come up against him when it came to sentencing.'

'He'd be the type to throw the book at you,' Rafaello agreed. He took a mouthful of his wine, then set it back on the table, looking directly at Alaina. 'Thank you for coping with him as well as you did today.'

She gave a demurring, brief smile. 'Thank my training in the hospitality business! We are taught to handle difficult hotel guests by being the three Cs—calm, composed and collected. Don't argue, merely state, and stay polite at all times, whatever the provocation.'

Rafaello's eyes glinted. 'You lapsed only once,' he replied. 'Telling him your father was "quite respectable".'

She made a face. 'Guilty as charged.' Her expression changed. 'They're very alike,' she said slowly. 'Aloof is probably the best one-word description.'

Rafaello looked at her. 'You said you were no longer in touch with him.'

He reached for their plates on the serving trolley beside them, lifting the domed covers away and placed hers in front of her, doing the same with his own. The *primo* was a seafood salad, and Alaina got stuck in, glad they were not facing another gruelling meal with Rafaello's disapproving father.

'No,' she said. 'There didn't seem much point. He remarried within six months of my mother's death, and I went off to college. I didn't go to his wedding—it seemed far too hypocritical to do so, given the rapidity with which he had remarried. I've never met his second wife. She was a colleague, he told me, when he informed me he was marrying again and they were moving to Scotland. She's a scientist too, so probably better suited to him than my mother was.'

Rafaello was silent for a moment, making a start on his own *primo*.

'Curious that we both have parents who were not suited to each other,' he said. 'Why did yours marry in the first place?'

'My mother was in love with him. She thought...' Alaina could hear the edge to her voice '...thought that she could break through his aloofness. But she couldn't.' Her voice changed. 'I've always thought that she sort of bled to death from her heart—'

She broke off, reached for her wine.

'What about your parents?' she challenged. 'Why did *they* marry?'

'My mother's family was wealthy and socially well connected. She was a good match for my father in that respect. But…'

He paused, and Alaina knew why, for it echoed her own pause.

'But because she was very beautiful, and a social butterfly, she was used to being adored by men. My father was the exception. She only irritated him. So she focussed all her emotions on me instead.'

His voice had become expressionless. But he continued, all the same.

'My father found that irritating too, and he disapproved of it. So he sent me off to boarding school to remove me from her malign influence.'

Alaina was silent for a moment. 'My father did the opposite. He left me to my mother. He himself ignored me… just as he ignored my mother.' She frowned. 'Had I been a boy, perhaps, or even if I had been scholarly—especially if I'd turned out to have a yen for science—he might have paid some attention to me. But…' she gave a slight shrug, as she had shrugged off, long ago, her father's indifference to her existence '…as it was, he had no reason to be interested in me.'

She pushed her now-empty plate aside, reached for her wine again.

She looked across at Rafaello. 'I've come to terms with it long since. I don't let it affect or upset me any longer.'

She said the words, but they plucked at her all the same. It wasn't her own relationship with her father that upset her—it was her mother's. The lesson her mother's fate had taught her. Never to love when it was not returned…when it could never be returned. When it was impossible that it should be so.

She took another sip of her wine, then set down her glass.

'I was eighteen when my mother died—she was knocked down by a car. How…how old were you?'

'Twenty-three. I'd just qualified as a lawyer. My father was pleased with me. Though he was less pleased when he learnt I was going to visit my mother at her clinic.'

Alaina frowned. 'Clinic?'

'Yes.' Rafaello's manner was calm, and he lifted her empty plate, along with his, placing them on the trolley, then handing her their *secondo*—a delicately spiced lamb tagine. 'She'd been there a while…my father thought it for the best. Her nerves were not good.' He started to eat, his manner still calm.

'What…what happened?'

'There was some confusion over her medication. It caused an adverse reaction.' He tapped his plate. 'This tagine is excellent. And the wine goes well with it.'

He was changing the subject. Alaina let him. They had both gone into deep waters—time to wade back.

'Yes, both are delicious,' she agreed. 'Tell me, are you OK with going to Capri tomorrow? I think we might have to get out on a boat, at least, as Joey will be disappointed otherwise. But it needn't be to Capri—any boat ride will do!'

In her head she heard Rafaello's father warning against over-indulgence. Her face tightened momentarily, her glance going to Rafaello. His expression was unperturbed.

The three Cs applied to him too, she thought. Calm, composed and collected. Applied constantly really. It was his normal manner. Very little, if anything, ruffled him. He dealt with life rationally. Coolly. Smoothly.

'Let's see how things go,' he said now. 'Capri can always wait. As you say, a boat ride is what Joey will be keen on. And the lift down to the swimming platform.'

The conversation moved on to ways in which Joey would

be entertained on the morrow, and then on to the Amalfi coast in general, Vesuvius and its impact on the area.

'As I said at lunch,' Alaina remarked, 'I don't really want to take Joey to Pompeii or Herculaneum. He's too young, and the ruins wouldn't mean much. And, quite frankly, it's too upsetting anyway, thinking back to that nightmare disaster for all those people.'

'Yes,' replied Rafaello, 'it was a cruel fate for them. Nature can be very harsh.'

'People, too,' Alaina heard herself say. 'But...' she frowned '...sometimes they don't mean it—as in, they don't do it intentionally to hurt others. They just lack the capacity to be otherwise.'

She'd moved the subject back to their respective fathers again, and wished she hadn't. Her eyes rested on Rafaello in the dim light. The table lamp was throwing his features into *chiaroscuro* as the evening gathered around them. The play of shadow and illumination seemed to make his features more austere. More like his father's.

Well, they look alike—just as Joey looks like Rafaello. It's natural.

Yet just for an instant she felt uneasy.

Then it dissipated.

Rafaello was making some remark about the likelihood, or not, of Vesuvius erupting again, and how the rich volcanic soil benefited agriculture and viticulture.

'Better harvests to enjoy—but living in the shadow of danger.'

He reached for his wine, and took a leisurely mouthful, the lamplight giving his face a flickering saturnine cast.

'Yes,' Alaina replied. 'There's always a price to pay,' she observed.

Again, for an instant, she heard her own words hanging in the air...

She set them aside. That wasn't a path she was going to take. She was sticking to the safe path, the predictable route. Creating a way for Joey to know his father and for Rafaello to know his son. And for her and Rafaello to enjoy each other, as they had the first time around.

Thinking of which…

Her expression changed. A familiar frisson shaped itself inside her. His rough jawline was really making him very, very attractive right now…

He caught her gaze. Exchanged it for a similar look that changed to one of humour charged with irony and regret.

'We'll have to take a rain check,' he told her, his mouth quirking. 'We can't disturb young Joey's slumber…'

Alaina gave an exaggerated sigh. 'Ah, well, so be it.' She pushed aside her empty plate. 'OK, if that's one appetite I can't indulge, I'll compensate with indulging in a generous *dolce* instead. What do you think is on offer?'

It proved to be a delicious, rich and delightfully sweet *crema*. She demolished hers happily, then sat back, replete. Rafaello poured coffee for them both, and they sat awhile in the still-mild evening, chatting amiably, with the spectacular night view to gaze on and the stars above to dazzle the heavens.

Alaina relaxed back in her chair, contentment filling her. *This is good. This is more than good.*

A phrase of Italian drifted through her head.

La dolce vita.

Oh, it was that all right! A very, very sweet life. She had her beloved Joey, she had Rafaello—she had all she could possibly want.

La dolce vita indeed…

Unseen, around the curve of the bay, Vesuvius slumbered. Dormant and safe. For now.

CHAPTER ELEVEN

'AND SO,' RAFAELLO declared with an air of finality, 'they all lived happily ever after. The end.'

He looked down at Joey. He had his arm around his shoulder as he half lay on his bed, propped against the headboard, while Joey snuggled against him, already almost asleep. Rafaello closed the book and set it aside. With his free hand he turned off the bedside light, leaving only the nightlight to illuminate the bedroom. He could see Joey's eyes closing and hear his breathing slow, felt his little body still cradled against him. Warm and trusting.

Memory flickered in him of the way he had wondered, on first discovering Joey's existence, how he would feel being a father—how he should be one to Joey. He'd known he would never be as his own father had been to him... known he would always acknowledge his responsibilities for his son, would be as good a father as he could be. He'd known he would apply patience and attention to him, would do his best.

So, how *did* it feel?

For a while he just went on sitting there, listening to Joey's breathing, feeling the warmth of his pyjama-clad body against his shoulder.

He heard his own question answered as his son leant trustingly against him, sleeping in the crook of his arm.

It felt good.

Good that he should have read the customary bedtime story as he fell asleep beside him—as he always did when he was at the villa. Good simply to be here with him.

Life had settled into a new routine. He usually stayed in Rome during the working week, or went to the airport for his occasional business trips abroad, but sometimes he arranged matters so he could have a couple of days working from the villa remotely. And he spent every weekend either at the villa, as now, or sometimes Alaina would join him in Rome for an evening, and they would either go out, or entertain at the apartment, leaving Joey in the doting care of Maria and Giorgio. They entertained out here at the villa too—and not only his own established friends and acquaintances. Alaina was building a circle of friends too, including women such as Gina Fratelli, and a few other mothers she'd palled up with at the nursery Joey was now attending three mornings a week. Her and Joey's command of Italian was coming along apace. And Joey, as they'd told his father, would be starting at the International School come the autumn.

Everything, Rafaello thought appreciatively, continuing to sit there with Joey's little body soft against him, was really very...

Very...what?

He wasn't sure what it was...what word would describe it. He frowned slightly. Did it really matter what he thought of the life he lived now? There was no alternative possible, so why analyse it? Why examine or scrutinise it?

Of course, one essential ingredient was Alaina's passion for him... His frown dissipated, replaced by a considering glint in his eyes. It had been awakened again so very satisfyingly and it had not abated—and nor had his for her. The glint intensified. He desired her just as much now as on their first night together in Rome all those weeks ago, back at the start of the summer, when he'd shown her how very enjoyable their reunion could be—how essential, in fact, to making their marriage work.

Thoughts flickered in his head. He did not usually find that his desire for a woman lasted this long. He had always been very…careful in his selection. Avoiding any female who wanted more from him than he was prepared to give. His expression changed. Alaina had once been such a female—not wanting their time in the Caribbean to end, wanting their affair to carry on. Perhaps lead to more…

There was an irony, he was suddenly aware, in the fact that now Alaina had got the 'more' she had sought then because of his son's existence…

His frown came again, and a mental dismissal of the intrusive thought. His life…her life too…was as it was. Joey's existence necessitated it. So speculation and memory were equally irrelevant. It was the present that mattered. And right now that meant the evening ahead.

Realising Joey was fast asleep, he eased his arm away, getting carefully to his feet to draw the quilt around him and ensure Mr Teds was snuggled up to him. He walked quietly to the door, opening it, turning to look back at the sleeping infant one last time before stepping out on to the landing, leaving the door ajar and the landing light on. Then he headed downstairs.

'Fast asleep?' Alaina looked up as he went into the sitting room, where she was curled up on one of the sofas, leafing through a magazine.

'Fast asleep,' he confirmed.

He sat himself down beside her. As she usually did, she had placed a bottle of chilled beer and a glass, plus a bottle opener, on the coffee table next to her own glass of white wine. He opened his beer, poured it out, and she reached for her glass, clinking it against his lightly.

'Maria says dinner in ten minutes,' she told him with a smile, taking a sip of her wine.

'Perfect,' Rafaello said, making a start on his beer. He stretched his long legs out. 'How was today?' he asked.

'Play date with Gina's little boy, and then we came home. Joey had his usual lively session in the pool—he's looking forward to having you share in the fun over the weekend! Then we did some number games, made a jigsaw, did a bit of reading… Then he had his tea and you came home. The rest you know. Bath time and bedtime with Papà.' She smiled. 'How was your day?'

'Office, staff meeting…lunch with a client, court appearance appealing a divorce settlement…back to the office, then fighting my way out of the city to make it back here for Joey's bath time,' Rafaello answered. He took another mouthful of his beer, feeling the good of it. 'I am very glad it's the weekend. What have we got planned? Remind me.'

'Lunch party tomorrow—parents and kiddies from the nursery—but dinner just on our own here. Sunday is free. What shall we do? Any preferences?'

'Just…what's that English term…? Chillaxing. That sounds good to me!' Rafaello smiled and helped himself to Alaina's hand. 'Too dull for you?'

She smiled. 'Dull is the last word I'd ever use for spending time with you,' she answered.

He raised her hand to his mouth and brushed it lightly with his lips.

'What an ideal wife you make,' he murmured, his eyes glinting.

Something changed in her eyes. For a moment it disquieted him, then it was gone. Maybe he'd only imagined it.

She slipped her hand from his, setting down her wine glass. 'I'll go and give Maria a hand in the kitchen,' she said.

Her voice was light, and yet...

He watched her get up and leave the room, her walk as graceful as ever. The evening stretched ahead of him very pleasantly indeed. They would enjoy a well-cooked dinner *à deux*, chatting about whatever it was they usually found it so easy to chat about, and then, assuming Joey didn't wake—which he seldom did—they would have a nightcap out on the terrace.

And then he would take Alaina to bed and they would make love very pleasurably indeed.

Very pleasurably.

He took another easy sip of his beer, savouring the chill and the flavour...the sense of the end of the working week. The sense of an enjoyable weekend underway.

His mind worked contemplatively as he flexed his ankles, drinking his beer unhurriedly. His thoughts went back to what he had contemplated upstairs as Joey had fallen asleep. Since discovering Joey's existence his life had changed fundamentally. The question was...

Do I regret it?

The answer came back the same. That choice had not been possible. So therefore regret or no regret was irrelevant. He had an unavoidable obligation to shoulder the responsibilities that came with his son and he had always honoured his obligations in his life, even conflicting ones. He had been the son his father had wanted him to be, but he had done his best by his mother, too—as much as he'd been able to.

Right to the very end he had at least tried to be patient with her—as his father had not—but he had always known that she craved so much more than he was able to give her. He had held back for his own protection and self-defence.

And once he'd reached his teenage years, his young adult-hood, he had been as kind as he could, but keeping an essential *cordon sanitaire* between them. Accepting that the situation was as it was, and nothing could change it.

Just as he had now accepted his current situation.

He downed the last of his beer, setting the glass back on the coffee table with a click. Life, after all, was seldom black and white—his clients' convoluted affairs told him that. There were rights and wrongs on both sides all too frequently, and his path was stepping carefully between them towards whatever outcome best benefited whoever was paying his fees.

And the life he now had to take on most definitely came with very clear compensations...

He felt his expression change. A half-smile tugged at his mouth.

Getting to know Joey meant getting to enjoy Alaina.

He got to his feet. Time for dinner.

As he headed towards the dining room, taking the open bottle of white wine with him, he gave a mental nod. His life had changed direction, but it was once again running smoothly.

The way he liked it to be.

Alaina glanced across the table at Rafaello. She was glad he was back for the weekend, and had arrived in time to see Joey before bed. That quiet, end-of-day reading time was important for their bonding. It wasn't something her own father had ever bothered with, and she'd bet that Rafaello's grim father hadn't either, with his son.

Rafaello, she thought sadly, didn't really have anything of a role model when it came to fatherhood—he was having to learn from scratch.

And *was* he bonding with Joey? She could only hope

so. Because with Rafaello it was so hard to tell. He kept himself so...

She tried to think of the word that described Rafaello's character. She could come up with *private*, or *elusive*, or *unreadable*, but none of those really fitted him. He was always cordial, pleasant, unruffled, good-humoured, charming, co-operative—there were any number of complimentary adjectives she could use about him, both in the way he was with Joey and with her.

It was just that...

Again, she drew a blank. And as she watched him chat pleasantly with Maria, setting out the dishes, there really was nothing she could criticise him for. With Joey he was always attentive and patient, and with her... A slight blush rose up her cheeks. As a lover he could not be faulted! She melted for him...just *melted*...

And afterwards he would gather her still-trembling body into his arms, smooth her tumbled hair, kiss her softly, hold her in his embrace. He was sensitive, caring, considerate...

Everything a lover should be...

But he's not my lover. He's my husband.

Her eyes shadowed. Yes, Rafaello was her husband—but only because of Joey. Not for any other reason.

Thoughts glided across her head as if on ice...ice that was dangerously thin. She needed to get off that ice lest it crack beneath her...

Maria was bustling out of the dining room and Rafaello was refilling her wine glass with crisp white wine, filling his own glass too. The *antipasto* before them looked appetising: slivers of fresh melon and mint with finest *prosciutto*, garnished with a delicately fragrant raspberry vinaigrette.

She started on her portion, making some absent reply to the comment Rafaello had just made.

Rafaello—her husband.

And my lover.

Again, she felt the thin ice beneath her. Husband… lover—did it make any difference?

Confusion filled her, and a deep reluctance to let such thoughts, such questions, have any place in her mind. In Amalfi she had called the life she was leading with Rafaello *la dolce vita*…and that was still true. Because what else could it be? She had Joey, she had Rafaello, and life was surely very sweet indeed.

'Alaina?'

Rafaello's quizzical voice recalled her to the moment. She blinked, refocussing. 'Sorry—I missed that completely,' she said.

He gave a slight smile as he started on the *antipasto*. 'Run me through who's turning up for lunch tomorrow,' he said.

She did so, giving him a thumbnail sketch of each of their guests and their offspring who would be there to play with Joey. As she did, her thoughts—incongruously—went to Joey's nursery playmate in England. She ought to invite Ryan to come out…bring Betsy with him for a little holiday. She frowned slightly. But maybe that might be unsettling for Joey—remind him of a life that was no more. And besides… She doubted Rafaello would care for her playing host to an unattached male, even if she and Ryan did go back a long way and between them there had only ever been friendship, nothing more.

No, best leave Ryan and Betsy in the past. Leave her former life in England in the past. Her future was here, in Italy. With Rafaello.

Her gaze went to him now, and softened as it always did when she looked at him.

I thought I would never see him again. Thought our ways had parted for ever. And now…

Now he was an indissoluble part of her life.

She felt emotion rise within her.

I have everything I could ever want.

And surely she had—because what else could she want? What could she possibly lack?

She let the question hang there, floating. Putting no weight on it. Wanting it to drift away, dissipate. Leave her to enjoy this sweet, sweet life she had. Here, like this, with Rafaello.

And to want nothing more…nothing more at all.

CHAPTER TWELVE

'IT'S A LONG DRIVE,' Rafaello was saying, 'but we'll do plenty of stops along the way, Joey.'

'Lom-bard-ee,' said Joey in a sing-song voice, as Rafaello eased the car along the villa's gravelled drive and out on to the highway.

'That's right,' he confirmed. 'Right in the north of Italy. Just before the mountains. Do you remember what the mountains are called?'

'Dol-o-mites,' intoned Joey.

'Quite right. Clever boy,' approved Rafaello.

He went on chatting as he made his way on to the autostrada heading towards the north of Italy. Unlike the grim duty visit to his father in Amalfi, this time he was looking forward to a long weekend away.

He addressed Alaina, sitting beside Joey as she always did when they travelled long distance with him, in order to be on hand for toys, audio books, drinks from his no-spill beaker, fortifying snacks and being on hand in general.

'I hope you get on with Dante—he and I go back a long way. And, as you know, his wife is English too.'

'And their little boy is around eighteen months, I think you said?'

'Thereabouts. I'm his godfather, so I should know. But, well...' Rafaello gave something of a shrug 'I wasn't really into babies when he was born. Luckily, Dante is totally besotted—as is Connie.' He sounded amused.

'I'm looking forward to meeting them all,' said Alaina.

'You'll like Connie—it's impossible not to. She has a very sweet nature. It's a shame they live so far away. But Dante's work keeps him in Milan—he's in finance. Connie's a stay-at-home mum, like you.'

He gained the autostrada, settling into a steady pace that ate up the miles. The scenery became more dramatic as they edged along the Apennines, and he went back to telling Joey about the regions they were passing through. They stopped for lunch off the autostrada, then resumed their drive.

By the time they reached the lush, flat landscape of Lombardy Joey had dozed off, but he surfaced, refreshed, as Rafaello turned into the drive of Dante's villa. He was glad to visit his old friend. Although conscious, all the same, of a sense of irony that he would be turning up with not only a wife but a four-year-old in tow.

Dante had already ragged him about it over the phone, and Rafaello knew, resignedly, that he would be on the receiving end of his friend's open amusement at this abrupt change in Rafaello's lifestyle in person.

And so it proved.

'Raf—the married man and fond *papà*! Who'd have thought?' Dante greeted him, slapping him heartily on the shoulder as they all disembarked from the car.

His wife's greeting was less teasing. 'Raf, how lovely to see you again—it's been far too long! I'm dying to meet Alaina—and the gorgeous, *gorgeous* Joey!'

Connie kissed him on the cheek, but her attention was on Alaina, now extricating Joey from his child seat. Rafaello watched Dante's wife smile warmly at her.

'Welcome, welcome! And this is Joey—oh, you are just *so* adorable!'

Joey was clambering down, looking interestedly around him. Alaina was returning Connie's greetings, and Dante came up to her, holding out his hand.

'Alaina—good to meet you.'

Rafaello could see Dante's eyes alive with interest in the woman he had married.

'Come on in. I can see that you don't manage to travel any more lightly than Connie and I do!' His voice was amused. 'It's amazing just how much stuff a baby needs— and it looks like it just increases as they get older!' He turned his attention to Joey. 'Hello, young man—I'm Dante. This is Connie. Come inside and meet Benito. He's younger than you, so you'll have to be gentle with him.'

They all made their way indoors, with Dante leading them through the villa out into the garden beyond.

'A pool!' Joey exclaimed happily. His contentment was guaranteed, and he ran forward eagerly. 'Can we swim now?' he asked.

'In a while,' Dante told him. 'Time for cake first.'

This was a sufficient diversion for Joey, and he quickly settled himself at the wooden table set out under a wide awning. Connie had re-emerged from the house, holding the hand of an infant who was wobbling forward.

Now it was Alaina's turn to exclaim.

'Oh, but you are just *darling*!' she enthused.

Lifting Benito into his highchair, Connie beamed. Rafaello watched as she and Alaina settled into mum-talk and turned to Dante.

'OK, get it out of your system,' he said dryly. 'The obvious hilarity of my finding myself a ready-made father and taking a ready-made wife…'

Dante's dark eyes glinted with appreciative humour. But it was not solely directed at Rafaello. 'I'm hardly one to talk, Raf—Connie was a gift I never saw coming too. And it looks like you've struck just as lucky with Alaina.'

He laid an arm around Rafaello's shoulder, but it was a comradely one.

'Tell me all about it later, when the girls are cosying up. It will be nice for Connie to speak English. I hope they get on…'

'No one could fail to get on with Connie,' Rafaello said.

They laughed, sitting themselves down as a maid came out of the house bearing a large tray of tea things.

Connie turned to Alaina. 'I'm so glad you're here—I've baked a Victoria sponge for us, and chocolate fairy cakes for the infantry. Do you drink tea, or have you converted to coffee completely?'

'Tea would be lovely, thank you,' Alaina was answering. 'I can't cope with *espresso*, though I love *cappuccino*. Rafaello has a fearsome machine in the kitchen, but I'm terrified of using it. I leave it to our wonderful housekeeper, Maria. But mostly I drink tea. It never quite tastes the same, though, even with imported tea.'

'It's the water,' Connie was saying. 'Or the British weather! Or something. Yes, Benito…' she turned her attention to her son '…choccy cake *is* coming. I promise. But guests first. Now, Joey, would you like a fairy cake with a flaky chocolate bar in the icing, or one with chocolate buttons?'

'Both!' announced Joey happily.

It was not long before a substantial amount of chocolate icing had transferred itself to both Joey and Benito, and the atmosphere had settled into one of complete conviviality. Rafaello could see that Alaina was hitting it off with Connie, chatting away in English, while he and Dante lapsed into Italian for a casual catch up.

After tea, as promised, a swimming session beckoned.

Rafaello saw his friend's eyes soften and linger on Connie's lush figure as she stood in her one-piece swimsuit, a wriggling Benito in her arms.

Dante caught Rafaello's eye. 'Every day I give thanks for her!' he said, his voice heartfelt. Then his expression changed. 'And you, old friend, do you give such thanks?'

A real question was there in his tone, however lightly spoken. Rafaello did not quite meet his eyes, looking back, instead, to where Joey was now vigorously splashing away, batting himself forward on his water wings. Alaina was gracefully swimming alongside him.

'I give thanks that I found my son,' he said.

He was aware that Dante was still looking at him, but did not turn his head to face him.

'Why did Alaina not tell you that she was pregnant?'

Dante's voice was neutral. But Rafaello knew perfectly well the question wasn't neutral at all.

He was silent for a moment, then spoke carefully.

'We had an affair, Dante. That was all. I made it clear that was all it could be when I became aware, I acknowledge, that she might have liked…something more. But I was flying back to Italy…she was working out there in the Caribbean. And I— Well, as you know, I was perfectly happy with the way I lived my life.'

'Avoiding commitment,' Dante said dryly.

Rafaello's eyebrows rose, and now he did glance at his friend. 'As you did—before Connie.'

'For very different reasons, Raf,' Dante replied. 'I'd never had time to commit—nor met anyone I wanted to commit to.'

'The second reason I share with you,' Rafaello answered.

'And now?' Dante's voice was probing, his own eyebrow raised questioningly.

Rafaello looked away again. Dante was too old a friend to prevaricate with. So he spoke the truth. Blunt, but honest.

'My commitment is not of my own making. The situation is as it is and I accept it. Joey is my son. I have a lifelong responsibility for him and to him. He comes with Alaina. And Alaina,' he said, 'comes with very significant...compensations.' His gaze went back to Dante. 'She and I get on perfectly well. She, like me, has accepted the necessity of our current situation and has adapted to it. I treat her, I hope, with respect and consideration. We are making a good home for Joey, and that is our priority. As for ourselves... Well, the compensations are, as I say—and as is obvious—' his glance now was pointed '—significant.'

Dante held his gaze. 'But you would not have chosen this of your own free will—compensations or not? Is that really what you're saying?'

The question hung in the air. Rafaello wished Dante had not asked it. Because the answer was irrelevant.

His own words just now to Dante echoed in his head.

'The situation is as it is and I accept it.'

That was the only answer to be given.

Whatever else it was that Dante was probing for...

How can he understand my situation? The arrival, out of the blue, of a ready-made son I had never envisaged? The necessary and completely essential reaction I had to give to that? Neither I nor Alaina had any say in what that reaction had to be—we simply had to accept it and adapt our lives accordingly. For Joey's sake. And we have. We have done just that.

Dante's questioning eyes were still on him. Rafaello wanted him to back off.

Then Connie's voice pierced the moment, and he was glad.

'Dante! Can you throw in that inflatable for Joey?' she called from the water. 'It's just over there by the pool house.'

Rafaello welcomed the diversion. Dante was probing where it was pointless to go. He got to his feet along with his friend. Time to join the pool party. Not to think about things that had no purpose, no place in the life he now led.

Had no choice but to lead.

The long weekend passed very enjoyably. Dante and Connie were the most welcoming and hospitable of hosts, and just as Dante and Rafaello relaxed back into what was clearly, Alaina could see, a long-standing friendship, so a new friendship was being forged between herself and Dante's wife.

As Rafaello and Dante, helped by Joey, packed up the car, ready for them to set off back to Rome, Connie warmly invited them to come again.

'Or you come to us,' Alaina returned smilingly. 'Though I know that travelling with a little one is less easy than it is with Joey.'

'I'm sure we'll manage something between us.' Connie smiled. 'And as the boys get older it will become easier. Unless, of course, we start all over again with another sproglet. Dante and I are keen, but these things are never certain. What about you and Raf?' she asked.

Alaina was silent for a moment. Then, slowly, she spoke. 'Rafaello and I aren't a…a normal family, Connie. When I had Joey I never expected Rafaello to play any part in his upbringing—in his life, really.'

Connie was staring at her, a frown on her face. 'But why?' She took a breath. 'I'm being tactless, and I'm sorry, but it seems so strange to me not to tell a child's father that he is one!'

Again Alaina was silent for a moment before she answered, and she knew she spoke hesitantly.

'I just didn't think he'd welcome the news. We…we only

had a holiday romance, Connie. It was all very magical and glamorous—romancing under the tropical moon and all that stuff!—and Rafaello...' she made a face '...he's a pretty hard guy to resist. And, to be honest, I didn't want to resist him at all.'

'Not many women do,' said Connie dryly. 'He's quite different from Dante in his appeal, but I know he's got it in spades! Even I could see that when I met him—and I was totally besotted with Dante! Raf is Mr Cool personified. He...' she frowned '...plays the field. Well,' she amended, 'he used to—'

'That,' said Alaina, 'I can well believe. And it only lends weight to my argument. I didn't think he'd welcome discovering that one of his passing romances was pregnant. I didn't think it fair to burden him with it. I don't need financial support, and there are plenty of other single mums around. And also—'

She broke off, took a breath, and looked Connie straight in the eye.

'Also, I didn't want Joey having anything to do with a father who would have preferred he didn't exist. *No* child should grow up knowing that!'

Now Connie was staring at Alaina with concern in her expression.

Alaina gave a half-shrug. 'My father made it pretty obvious he had no interest in me. He found it hard, if not impossible, to be affectionate. If he didn't exactly resent my existence, he certainly didn't take much interest in it. So...' she took another breath '... I didn't want to risk that for Joey.'

'But Raf's so *good* with Joey!' Connie protested.

'Yes,' said Alaina, 'he is. But he might not have been.'

He might have been like his own icy, condemning father, as well as like mine.

The thought was chilling.

'And Joey clearly gets on like a house on fire with Raf!' Connie continued.

Alaina's expression softened. 'Joey's accepted him in his life and I'm so very glad of that. He's adapted incredibly well to coming out to Italy, to the new life we lead now.'

Connie looked at her, another question in her eyes. 'And what about you? Have you adapted well?' She paused. 'It must have been a big thing,' she said quietly, 'giving up the life you'd made for yourself and Joey and moving out here. And, of course, marrying Rafaello.'

'Yes, it was,' Alaina replied. She kept her voice measured. 'But it had to be done. Rafaello had to do it and so did I. I hadn't planned it—but once he'd declared he wanted to be in Joey's life permanently there really wasn't an alternative. As for adapting to it…well, I suppose I have.'

She dropped her gaze, aware that Connie was still looking at her.

'And are you happy?' she asked.

Alaina could feel her heart beating. Did it seem louder than it should be? And if it did, why should that be?

'I'm as happy as the situation permits,' she said carefully. She turned back to Connie and met her gaze full-on. 'I have so much, Connie! I have Joey… I have an easy, luxurious life! I live in a beautiful villa just outside Rome. I have staff to run it and I have a glittering social life as well, with fabulous gowns and jewels! I have a husband who is attentive and considerate, who has taken Joey into his life, and I can't fault his treatment of him! And I can't fault Rafaello's attentions to me either!'

She coloured slightly, but went on, woman-to-woman— both of them, after all, were married to men any other woman would envy them for as far as sexual attractiveness was concerned, let alone the wealth and glamour that went with them.

'He's made it crystal-clear that whatever flared between us five years ago is still there, and that there's no point denying it or quenching it. So...so we don't. And...and that's very good. I mean...' She coloured again, giving a half-laugh. 'Well, I'm sure you know what I mean! You don't need diagrams! Rafaello is incredibly attractive, and I'm no more able to resist his Mr Cool charm now than I was five years ago. And there's no need for me to do so anyway. In fact...' she drew a breath '...our marriage probably wouldn't work without it, I can be honest enough to admit that.'

She dropped her gaze again, still feeling that stronger heartbeat inside her. This was a strange conversation to be having—and had Connie not been the wife of Rafaello's closest friend she'd never have had it. Certainly not, she realised, with any of the new mothers she'd been meeting as she settled into her new life.

She realised Connie was starting to speak again, and heard the careful question in her voice.

'And is that enough?' she asked.

The thudding in Alaina's heart was louder than ever. Her voice was thin as she eventually answered.

'I don't know,' she said.

But even as she spoke she felt that dangerously thin ice beneath her crack and fracture.

She looked away, the answer she'd given Connie echoing in her head.

I don't know.

But she did know. Yet she dared not say it. Dared not admit it or the carefully constructed life she'd made for herself and Joey out here in Italy would plunge through that dangerously thin ice...

Taking her with it.

* * *

Rafaello depressed the accelerator and the car shot forward along the autostrada. He had enjoyed their stay with Dante and Connie—impossible not to, given his long friendship with Dante and his fondness for Connie. Yet it had disturbed him too.

Dante had talked to him openly about the marriage he'd made with Alaina for Joey's sake, and Rafaello had answered as openly. Yet he'd felt an unspoken criticism—a challenge—coming from Dante. His mouth tightened. Dante had an idyllic marriage—what could he know of how it was between himself and Alaina?

On the surface, Dante and Connie and their little boy were identical to himself, Alaina and Joey, apart from Benito's younger age. But there was a difference all the same.

His friends had chosen the life they were leading.

I didn't. It was imposed on me. And however much I enjoy the...compensations it affords me, nothing gets away from that blunt truth. I didn't choose the life I now lead.

In his head he heard again the question Dante had put to him. Asking him bluntly whether he would have chosen the life he was leading now of his own free will.

It was a question he never allowed himself to ask. Because there was no purpose in asking. It was hypothetical...irrelevant.

His glance went to the rear-view mirror. He could see Alaina, quietly reading to Joey one of his favourite train stories. She seemed subdued, he fancied. Did she, too, feel the difference between themselves and Dante and Connie?

But what did it matter if she did? There was no more point in asking her the question Dante had put to him than it had been to ask it of himself.

She accepts the situation...as do I. What else can we do?

Thoughts moved across his mind. Was this how his father

had felt when he'd realised how completely ill-matched to each other he and the woman he'd married were? Yet he'd accepted the situation.

But their marriage was a disaster!

His and Alaina's was nothing like that. He was nothing like his father, and Alaina was nothing like his mother. There was no comparison—none. He was not cold or resentful, as his father had been, and Alaina was not needy and clinging as his mother had been.

We are fine as we are—as fine as we need to be.

And that, in the end, was all that could be said. All that could be done.

And yet his hands tightened over the wheel and his expression, as he accelerated again to overtake another car, was set.

CHAPTER THIRTEEN

ALAINA WAS STUDYING the calendar. In little more than a month Joey would be starting school. The summer had flashed by. She frowned. How had that happened so quickly?

She felt her thoughts go off at a tangent. With Joey at school every day, she'd need to find something for herself to do. Maria and Giorgio ran the villa perfectly, so maybe she could get a job of some kind? She wasn't sure what—this wasn't a touristy part of Italy, and hospitality was really all she knew. It would need to be something that could be worked around Joey's school timetable, of course, and his school holidays. And around any socialising Rafaello wanted her to share in.

Speaking of which, there was a fancy bash coming up this very weekend—some glittering charity gala in Rome, for which she would need to look her very best. She had a hair appointment booked already, plus an appointment for getting her nails done too, and a facial. All would be needed for her to be Signora Ranieri, doing her husband proud.

Her mind ran on to which evening gown would suit—her wardrobe now held plenty to choose from—and what jewels would best go with it. Rafaello had presented her with additions to the diamond necklace, and her jewellery case now held sapphires, rubies and emeralds, as well as some very beautiful pearls.

Not that she considered any of them *hers*. They were Rafaello's, and she merely wore them as his wife. The same was true of the exorbitantly expensive designer evening gowns she wore the jewellery with. The same was true of her whole lifestyle out here, really...

The lifestyle that came courtesy of Joey.

Deliberately, she changed her expression. She hadn't asked for this lavish lifestyle—and she hadn't asked or expected Rafaello to provide it.

Or even to marry me.

Thoughts flickered in her head. She'd have been perfectly happy staying in England, continuing to work as she had, juggling her career with motherhood. Rafaello might have simply been a regular visitor, or she might have gone for part time working, maybe, and brought Joey out here for regular visits. As Joey had grown up he would have spent time on his own with Rafaello, if that was what they'd both wanted. These days parents did not always live together, and their children were none the worse for it. It could work flexibly and very well. Her friend Ryan managed being a divorced dad perfectly, after all.

She headed towards the kitchen, where Maria was showing Joey how to make fresh ravioli, wanting to put such thoughts out of her head. This was the life she led and that was all there was to it. No point thinking about anything else.

No point remembering that weekend with Dante and Connie. Seeing them together with their little boy. A truly happy family. An adored baby, and parents who adored each other too...

A pang struck her, like an ache in her side. She banished that too, for there was no point feeling it. Dante and Connie were lucky—so lucky. They loved each other, were made for each other. She was not jealous of them...only envious...

No, don't go there! Theirs is a marriage based on love—a normal marriage! They were married and then they started a family...the normal order of things. For Rafaello and me it was not like that.

She shut her eyes for a moment. Hearing the words in her head. Tolling like a bell she could not silence.

Nor can it ever be like that.

She pushed the kitchen door open.

'Mummy, come and see!'

Joey's voice was gleeful as Alaina went into the kitchen. He was kneeling on a chair at the long, scrubbed wooden kitchen table, diligently working away under Maria's supervision. Dutifully she admired the somewhat ragged-looking, zig-zag-edged pasta squares that Joey was busy cutting with a zig-zag roller.

'I hope those are for our lunch,' she said, and smiled.

'He is learning very fast!' Maria beamed.

'You're an excellent teacher,' Alaina complimented her. 'And thank you for looking after him this weekend while I'm in the city. All next week, I know, you and Giorgio are off to visit your son and daughter-in-law in Puglia. I haven't forgotten. It's a well-deserved break for you both!' she assured Maria.

They discussed practicalities for a few moments, then Alaina left them to it. A restlessness filled her, and she didn't know why. Nothing had changed, after all, had it?

She halted in her tracks.

Maybe that was the problem. Nothing *had* changed. Her life here was flowing smoothly and would go on doing so. What had she to complain about? Yet into her head came the question Connie had put to her as she'd outlined her smooth, untroubled life, her *dolce vita* here with Joey and Rafaello.

'And is that enough?'

She heard her own answer echo.

'I don't know.'

It hung there again, in her head. And beneath her feet the smooth thin ice of her smoothly flowing life once again seemed to be suddenly dangerously thinner.

The charity gala was a glittering affair indeed, held at one of the huge aristocratic Renaissance *palazzos* in Rome. Alaina looked stunning, she knew, in an off-the-shoulder gown in lemon glacé satin and a pearl choker, her hair swept up into an elaborate style, with drop pearl earrings and pearl combs completing the extravagant look. At her side Rafaello, in white tie, looked as knock-out as he always did.

Compliments came their way, with appreciative looks from females at Rafaello and from males at herself. Conversation was easy, many faces familiar now, and the evening was sumptuous.

When they returned to Rafaello's apartment he undressed her slowly, sensually, and then just as slowly and sensually made love to her in a way that reduced her body to molten lava...

Over a late, leisurely breakfast, Rafaello poured himself some coffee.

'I'm afraid I won't be coming back with you to the villa today,' he told her. 'A business trip's come up at short notice and I have to fly out first thing.'

'Where this time?' Alaina asked conversationally.

'Long haul, alas...'

There was a slight air of hesitancy about him that she picked up on. It was explained as he went on.

'The Caribbean. The same client that called me over there five years ago. He's getting divorced again. From the woman he'd left his then wife for when I handled the divorce for him that time.'

The cynical note was there in his voice quite openly—

Alaina could hear it. But it was not that that she paid attention to.

A ripple of something she could not name had gone through her.

'Will…will you be away long?'

He took a mouthful of his coffee and shrugged. 'I hope not, but he's a difficult character. He'll want to dispose of this wife as cheaply as he can.'

Alaina looked at him. 'So few of your clients seem like very agreeable people,' she said.

His mouth twisted. 'They're the ones I charge the highest fees for.'

She let that pass. What did she care about clients who didn't like paying their taxes, or liked to divorce their wives on the cheap? But he was speaking again, and she made herself listen, wondering why it was so disquieting to think of Rafaello going out to the island where they had first met. What had happened there had led directly to her sitting here having breakfast with him at his opulent Rome apartment, sharing his life.

'I was wondering…' he was saying, and she heard uncertainty in his voice, which was unusual for him. 'Whether you might like to join me once I'm done with work there. Have a holiday out there.'

She looked at him. 'Joey's too young for a long-haul flight,' she said.

'I was thinking of just you,' he replied. He looked at her. 'For old times' sake, perhaps.' His voice was light. Dispassionate. As if he were feeling his way…

She swallowed. 'I wouldn't like to leave Joey and be so far away. And besides, Maria and Giorgio are away all next week, visiting their son in Puglia. I can't ask them to change their plans…it wouldn't be fair.'

He gave a slight shrug, as though it were of no importance. Reached for his coffee cup again.

She heard herself continue, wondering why she did, and whether it was wise to do so.

'And besides, maybe…maybe it wouldn't be a good idea, Rafaello. Maybe it's best to leave the past alone.'

She looked away for a moment, blinking. In her mind's eye she was under that hotel portico, watching Rafaello drive away from her.

She felt the same pang that had smitten her when she'd compared Dante and Connie's loving marriage to her own with Rafaello.

Five years ago she had watched Rafaello leave her life. Watched and known with quelling awareness just how very close she had come to stepping off the brink of that dangerous cliff her mother had warned her about her all her life. She had almost stepped off and plunged down, down, down… Into a love that could never be returned. Never be requited. Never be shared with the one person she most longed to share it…

I stepped back then—I managed to do it. Managed to save myself from my mother's fate.

Rafaello was changing the subject, making some innocuous remark about the charity gala the night before. Alaina pulled herself together, made some appropriate reply.

She got through the rest of breakfast. Then, getting to her feet, she said, her manner unchanged, 'Why don't I head back to the villa now? I'm sure you'll be prepping for whatever will be required of you next week with your client, and you'll want to pack and so forth. Maria and Giorgio will want to pack too, I expect, so I'll take over on the Joey front this afternoon.'

'I can drive you back—' Rafaello began, but she shook her head.

'No, stay here—Joey will be disappointed if he gets to see you and then you disappear again. If your driver is off duty I'll just take a taxi to the villa.'

Which was what she did.

As she took her leave of Rafaello she kissed him good-bye, as she always did when they separated. Her kiss was light, her manner as it always was with him. As was his with her. He saw her into the taxi, lifted a hand in casual farewell as it moved off.

He did not see—could not see—that Alaina had sat back, tilted back her head, and that in her face was a look that had not been there for a long time. For five long years…

On Monday morning she saw Maria and Giorgio off, with Joey waving manically to them as they drove away. Then, slowly, she went back indoors. The same restlessness that had assailed her before the weekend came again. Plucking at her…disquieting her.

On sudden impulse she stooped down, catching Joey.

'Joey, munchkin—Papà is away, and Maria and Giorgio have gone away, so why don't we…?' She took a breath. 'Why don't we do the same? Let's have an adventure of our own—a little holiday! Let's go and see…' She swallowed, but then she said it. 'Our old home.'

Joey looked at her. 'Is it still there?'

She nodded. 'Yes,' she said slowly, 'it's still there.'

By the end of the day she was letting herself into her little house in England, wondering if she had just made the worst decision of her life or the only one she could make.

The only one that would not destroy her utterly.

Rafaello stood out on the balcony of his hotel room, resting his hand lightly on the balustrade. The t air was warm, much warmer than at home, and he could hear the soft lapping of the sea on the beach beyond the lush gardens. The noise of tree frogs chirruping unseen in the palm trees made a different chorus from that of the cicadas he was used to. Above the azure sea the sun was a blaze of gold.

Memory shafted through him. A memory of standing like this, but with Alaina at his side. The Alaina of five years ago. The Alaina he had seen, desired, and seduced so very pleasurably. And it had been completely mutual.

Mutual right up until the end.

His expression changed, and he frowned. It was not his fault he had not wanted what she had wanted. Nor her fault that she had. They had simply wanted different things, that was all.

I wanted the life I'd always led and saw no reason for anything different.

Joey's existence had changed all that for ever.

What if I still didn't know Joey existed?

Images crowded into his mind. Joey splashing in the swimming pool. Joey running around the garden. Joey sitting in his car seat, asking him questions. Joey playing with his building bricks and toy trains. Joey drowsing against him as he read him his bedtime story...

Abruptly, suddenly wanting to hear Joey's piping voice, he reached for his phone. The time difference was such that it was already the eveningin Italy. He phoned Alaina's mobile, but it went to voicemail. Probably she was getting Joey to bed already. He would have to trt again in the morning.

He set down his phone, conscious of a feeling of disappointment that he hadn't been able to speak to Joey, and stood looking out over the lush gardens of the Falcone again, palm trees waving in the warm breeze.

And it was not only Joey's voice he wanted to hear. It was a shame Alaina would not be joining him. It would have been good to see her here again. Recapturing what they had once had.

But we had only a brief romance—nothing more than that.

And what was the use of seeking to recapture something so brief?

He abandoned his thoughts, heading down to the dining room to enjoy the Falcone's celebrated cuisine.

Tomorrow he had to face his difficult client. Alaina's words over breakfast the day before echoed in his head. Found resonance. Why did he bother with clients like this one, whose treatment of women was shameful, however well he paid his lawyer to dispose of them? Or the Geneva-based client reluctant to spend any of his vast wealth on paying the taxes he owed? Or any similar unscrupulous if lucrative clients?

Maybe he should prune his client list when he got back to Rome. Get rid of such clients, however much revenue they brought in. His father would not approve—but then his father wasn't running the firm any more.

But it was best not to think of his father. He had heard nothing from him since their brief duty visit earlier that summer. As predicted, his father had taken not the slightest interest in his grandson.

His thoughts flickered. Had it been his mother who was still alive…

No, best not to think of his mother either. Besides being all over Joey, she would have woven ludicrous, unreal dreams around the marriage he had made, never accepting that his marriage to Alaina was the way it was for the reason it was. Nothing more than that.

'Signor Ranieri, how good to have you with us again!'

The maître d' was greeting him fulsomely, exhibiting the Falcone's reputation for faultless service in remembering a guest who had not visited for five years, dispelling pointless thoughts about what his mother would have wanted his marriage to be—when it was simply not.

He took his place at the table he was ushered to, memory flickering yet again. He'd brought Alaina to dine here and she'd sat gazing at him, her eyes alight, blazing with all that she had never hidden. All that she had offered.

But he had taken only what he'd wanted to take then. Wanting no more of her than that.

And nothing has changed.

Neither the five years between, nor Joey's existence, nor their marriage, made any difference to that.

It's all I want of her—what I had then, and what I have now.

Nothing else.

Alaina heard her phone ping. She ignored it. It would be Rafaello again. The call had gone to voicemail, but she hadn't played it back yet. Her thoughts were too troubled to do so. Joey was in bed, in his old bedroom, tired after the journey from Rome and disorientated too.

She too was disorientated—how could it be otherwise? It felt so strange to be back in the UK, and had felt even stranger to climb out of their taxi from the airport and go into the little house that had once been her home. For Joey's sake, though, she had to hold it together, however strange she felt. And however tight her insides were at the thought of the step she'd taken so precipitately.

I'm not thinking about it—not yet. I can't. I'll think about it later.

But when later came—with Joey safely asleep, clutching his teddy—and she had had a sketchy supper of tinned soup and unpacked their suitcase, she was lying in her old, familiar and yet now so strange bed, the thoughts came anyway.

Difficult, confusing, painful thoughts, that went round and round in her stubbornly sleepless head.

Thoughts she didn't want to think—didn't want to face. Thoughts she didn't want stirring up emotions she didn't want either.

Though she finally fell asleep, it was not a peaceful, restorative sleep, and when in the early hours she heard Joey cry out, calling plaintively for her, she went into his room, getting into bed with him and hugging him, holding him close until he fell asleep again, reassured by her presence in what had become an alien place for him.

And yet again the question circled in her head.

Have I done the right thing or the wrong thing? The right thing or the wrong thing?

And right—or wrong—for who?

For her—or for Joey?

Because if it's only for me, then I shouldn't do it.

She gazed blankly at the ceiling as daylight crept into the room through the drawn curtains.

But at what cost to me?

And that, she knew, was the hardest question of all to ask. Let alone answer...

Rafaello was reading Alaina's text. It was the only communication he'd had from her since leaving Italy. She hadn't returned his calls. Was it just the time difference being awkward?

But as he read her text, his brows snapping into a frown, he realised that it was nothing to do with the time difference. He stared down at the phone in his hand. Her text incised itself upon him.

She had gone to England. Taking Joey with her. She'd given no explanation, and certainly no indication of how long she would be there.

His frown deepened.
Slowly, he texted back.

What brought this on?

No answer came.

He slid his phone away. He had to go and meet his client at the appointed hour this morning. He would do that, then try and get hold of Alaina.

But his calls went to voicemail and she did not phone back or text again.

By the evening he had made his mind up. He phoned his client, cancelled their next meeting, ignored the angry protestations heaped upon him, and booked the first flight off the island.

What the hell is going on?

The question circled. Unanswerable and unanswered.

Alaina could hear the sound of a raucous cartoon playing on the TV in the living room, keeping Joey entertained. She was standing in the kitchen, holding her phone. There were more texts from Rafaello, more voicemails. Sounding more frustrated, increasingly terse. She had to answer... find something she could say.

Carefully, she texted him.

I wanted to check on my house. This seemed like a good time, with you away all week.

His reply came immediately.

When are you back? I'm in Rome. I have cut short my time in the Caribbean.

She stared at the screen, knowing her heart rate was thudding. Why had he cut his trip short? Because she'd said she wasn't in Italy?

She texted back:

Not sure.

Again, his reply came instantly.

Tell me when you are.

She turned her phone off. She didn't want him phoning her. Could not cope with it. Could cope with nothing right now—not even Joey.

She could cope with nothing at all. Least of all the knowledge of what she had done.

Or why.

Rafaello lay in his bed at his apartment. It was impossible to sleep, and jet lag had nothing to do with it. He was just lying there, staring blankly at the darkened ceiling. The bed was too large, and he was alone in it.

But he often slept alone when he was in the apartment without Alaina during the working week, so why, now, did it feel so...?

So wrong.

It was a question he could not answer. But there were a whole stack of questions piling up that he could not answer.

Only Alaina could.

And she was not giving any answers. None that made sense.

He lay, staring unseeing into the dark. Conscious that his heart rate was elevated, tension netting him. What was Alaina playing at—and why?

And why, above all, was there a churning in his guts that should not be there. Should not be there at all...

Joey was fretful. His initial excitement at being back in the house he'd once lived in had dissipated. He was finding fault with it. His toys were all in Italy and there was no swimming pool. Nor was there Maria and Giorgio.

And he wanted his *papà*.

'Papà is away on business,' Alaina told him evasively. She put a smile on her face. 'I'm going to see whether we can visit Betsy. That would be nice!'

But on texting Ryan to tell him they were unexpectedly back in the UK she learnt that Betsy was off with her mother on holiday.

Ryan phoned her. 'How come you're back?' he asked. 'Is it just a flying visit?'

'I'm not sure,' Alaina replied, conscious of Joey nearby, discontentedly watching TV.

Alaina took the phone into the kitchen, not sure what to tell Ryan.

Because I'm not sure of anything.

But that wasn't true, and she knew it. She was sure of something. Something that was starting to feel like concrete, setting in a lump within her, heavy and hard.

She heard only silence from Ryan. Then, 'Alaina, is everything all right? I mean, with...with you and Rafaello?'

The silence now came from Alaina. Then, 'I'm leaving him, Ryan.'

She had said it. The words she had been trying not to say. The words she had been silencing all the way from Italy. The words which now, like that concrete setting inside her, were the hardest and heaviest she had ever had to speak.

I'm leaving him...

CHAPTER FOURTEEN

'RAF—GOOD TO see you.'

Dante settled himself down at the table in the restaurant where Rafaello, with extreme reluctance, had agreed to meet him for lunch during his friend's impromptu business trip to Rome.

The timing could not have been worse.

He let Dante order martinis for both of them.

'How's things? The *bellissima* Alaina and the cherubic Joey?'

'They're in the UK,' Rafaello answered. He was aware his voice was light…deliberately so.

'Oh, shame. I'm under instructions from Connie to visit while I'm here and report back.'

'Report back on what?' Rafaello's voice had sharpened, and he set his water glass on the table with a click.

Dante stared. 'Just how they're doing—how you're all doing.' He leant forward a fraction, his expression changing. 'Raf…?'

Rafaello sat back. Tension had formed across his shoulders. To others he might seem to withdraw behind his customary cool demeanour, holding the world at bay, immune behind his honed-to-perfection guard—the guard that enabled him to lead the life he liked to lead, staying observant, amused, sardonic, distanced from any personal involvement—but Dante knew him better than any other person in his life.

And he knew Dante. Knew that Dante took life by the shoulders and shook it till it did what he wanted of it. Rafaello took a far less combative stance, stepping with faultless precision along the path of life even when that path had to be altered and rerouted in directions he had never envisaged in the light of completely unforeseeable circumstances.

Like the discovery that he had a son.

And his making a wife of the woman who'd borne him.

'Raf?' Dante prompted again.

The waiter placed their martinis in front of them and took himself off. Dante ignored his martini, still eyeballing Rafaello.

'OK, what's up?' he said abruptly. 'And don't brush me off, Raf. This is me, Dante, remember? I don't take brush-offs.' He took a breath. 'So…?'

Rafaello's focus slid past him. For a moment he did not answer. Could not. Then his eyes went back to Dante, meeting his bullishly insistent gaze straight on.

'Alaina wants a divorce,' he said bluntly.

'Divorce?' Ryan's voice was openly shocked. 'Good God, *why*? I thought it had all worked out OK with Rafaello.'

Ryan had turned up after work and was now sitting in Alaina's tiny garden. Joey was still parked in front of the TV, though Alaina felt bad about it. Tomorrow they must go and replenish his empty toybox and bookshelf. And she'd have to contact the school he'd been going to go to here in the autumn, and hope they still had a place for him. Then she needed to see if the hotel would take her back.

Restart my life.

Her eyes went to her old friend, saw the shock open on

his face as well as hearing it in his voice. She swallowed. It was like swallowing concrete.

'I thought I could do it…being married to him like that,' she said. 'But I didn't… I didn't think it through.'

She went silent, dropping her gaze away from Ryan.

He waited a moment, then spoke, his voice both careful, and gentle. 'So…what went wrong?' he asked.

Alaina lifted her eyes to him. Her throat had closed. In a voice that was almost impossible to get out, she told him…

Rafaello was at the villa. He'd gone there deliberately, immediately after his lunch with Dante. Maria and Giorgio were still away, and the emptiness of the place echoed all around him.

No piping sound of Joey's voice greeting him. No Joey running up to him and hugging him, waiting for him to stoop down and scoop him up, return the hug…

No Alaina's voice to break the echoing silence, welcoming him home…

Only the echo of Dante's voice in his head. Challenging. Demanding.

So, what are you going to do?

He heard his own answer, given in his cool, contained voice:

I'm considering my options.

Dante had glowered at him.

'This is not one of your damn clients you're talking about! This, Raf, is your wife and your son.'

Rafaello had looked at him.

'You mistake the situation. It is my son and his mother.'

Dante's eyes had narrowed.

'Is that so?' he'd asked.

Rafaello had met the narrowed gaze full-on.

'Yes,' he'd answered coolly. *'Alaina is my wife only because she is the mother of my son.'*

Now, as he stood out on the terrace in the dusk, the noise of the cicadas was incessant in the vegetation beyond the pool. The pool lights were turning the water to glowing iridescence, a moth was fluttering nearby, and the scent of honeysuckle caught at him from where it clambered up a trellis.

He heard Dante's taunting question again.

'Is that so?'

He stared at the emptiness ahead of him. The emptiness all around him. The emptiness inside him. The emptiness that was echoing with thoughts he did not want to think. About someone he did not want to think about.

Alaina.

The mother of his son. The son she had not told him about because she had known he would not welcome the news or the responsibility it would impose upon him. The responsibility he had now taken on—that had made him change his life completely, made him take Alaina as his wife…take her to bed…take only what he'd wanted of her before, all those years ago in the Caribbean. Then in an affair—only that. But now in a marriage…because of Joey.

I married her because it kept things simple. It gave me Joey without a fight, and it made creating a home for him straightforward. It regularised things. Legitimated them. Normalised them. Mother, father, child.

A family unit.

Except family units were made after marriage, not before. Before family units came husband and wife. That was what came first.

You choose your spouse and then, and only then, do you start a family. When you know your choice of spouse was right.

His mouth twisted painfully. Half his clients never chose right…

Nor had his parents.

Theirs had been a disastrous marriage from the start. But they'd had a son, all the same. A son who had grown up witnessing the non-stop car crash that his parents' marriage had been. A son who had found the self-protection he needed by emotionally withdrawing from it all.

It was a self-protection he still relied on implicitly. It served him well. Always had.

Until now.

His gaze went out over the empty pool, then back to the empty house. No Joey tucked up in bed, falling asleep as his bedtime story finished, his dark eyes closing in drowsy slumber as Rafaello smoothed his hair and left the room on quiet feet. No Alaina curled up on the sofa sipping her white wine, leafing through a glossy magazine. Lifting her lovely eyes to look at him. Smiling up at him…

And suddenly, out of nowhere, a knife plunged into his side. Vicious…brutal. Striking into his ribs, his lungs, cutting off his breath. It was a pain like nothing he had ever felt. Ever allowed himself to feel.

But now it skewered him.

He shut his eyes, unable to bear it.

Alaina let Joey scramble out of the car seat in her little car, then headed for the front door. They'd been shopping, including buying some toys and books, but Joey's mood was still subdued. He'd asked when they were going home… Alaina had been evasive.

Anxiety and so much more plucked at her. Had it been rash to tell Rafaello by text that she wanted a divorce? But how could she possibly speak to him? And her position now, surely, was stronger than it had been when he'd first talked about custody battles. She was his legal wife, and even with the prenup she'd signed surely that would mean she could afford a lawyer as tough as him?

But would it really come to that? Please, God, no... Could they not just work out something that would give her back her own life, but keep Joey sufficiently in Rafaello's too? She didn't know. Only knew that *something* had to be hammered out.

Because I can't go back—I just can't. I can't, I can't, I can't.

Joey had run on indoors and she turned to shut the front door behind her, shopping bags in her hands. As she did so, she saw a taxi pulling up at the kerb. One of the airport taxis.

Alaina froze.

Rafaello stepped out on to the pavement. Glanced towards the narrow house. Saw Alaina at the doorway. Her face had gone paper-white. He walked up to her, his gait steady, his face expressionless, as the taxi moved off behind him.

He heard her say his name faintly, as though it were costing her a lot. Costing her as much as it was costing him to keep his face expressionless, to keep all emotion out of his voice as he said her name in return.

'I would like to talk to you,' he said. He paused a moment. 'Is Joey here?'

She nodded, as though speech were beyond her. She was still paper-white, but there was something in her face, her eyes...

She stepped aside, jerkily, and he walked in. Headed into the sitting room.

'Hello, Joey,' he said.

Joey whirled around. His face lit up like the sun. With a cry he hurled himself at Rafaello, and Rafaello swept him up. Joey's little arms wrapped themselves around his neck, his legs around his waist and Rafaello clutched him tightly, his heart pounding…hammering. Slowly, he lowered Joey to the floor.

Joey danced around him, exclaiming rapturously. 'Papà! Papà! Papà!'

Alaina was walking into the room. Joey went running up to her.

'Papà is here!' he told her, excitement vivid in his voice. Then he turned back to Rafaello. 'Are we going home?' he asked him.

Rafaello's eyes went to Alaina. For one impossible moment he held her stricken gaze. Then he lowered his to Joey.

'I need to talk to Mummy,' he said. 'Can you go up to your room and play on your own for a while?'

Joey looked fearful suddenly. 'You won't go, will you?'

Rafaello shook his head. 'No,' he said, 'I won't go.'

'OK, then,' Joey said. He rummaged in one of the shopping bags, pulled out a sizeable box. 'I've got a new train set!' he announced. 'I'm going to play with it!'

He thundered up the stairs.

Rafaello turned his attention to Alaina. She still looked white as a sheet.

A sense of déjà vu swept over him. She'd gone white as a sheet that evening he'd arrived here all those months ago, to tell her that now he knew of Joey's existence he would be a permanent fixture in his son's life. And that the most civilised way of achieving that was for them to marry and make a home for him in Italy.

It had seemed so simple. So straightforward. So obvious… But now…

He saw her lower herself jerkily into the armchair opposite the small sofa, perching at the edge of the seat, just as she had all those months ago.

Then, she was simply a woman I had romanced five years earlier and then parted from.

But now…

The same words came again. Brief words…changing everything.

He drew a breath, let his eyes rest on her face.

'Why did you leave me, Alaina?' he asked.

Emotion was churning within her. Emotion that was impossible to control, to contain, to suppress or repress. It was filling her, consuming her, overwhelming her. Possessing her.

Her hands, clutching at each other, tightened their grip.

'I couldn't stay,' she said.

Her gaze was hooked on him.

He's here—real, solid, sitting a couple of metres away—and I can't bear it… I can't…

Something changed in his face. It had already been unreadable. But somehow it had become more so. Tension pulled across his shoulders, moved in every line of his body as he sat there.

So close to her.

So far away…

In the months she'd been with him—in the months since they had become lovers, come to know each other's bodies so intimately she could have recognised him in pitch-dark by touch alone—she had been able to reach for him, to be casually and easily in bodily contact with him. Leaning against him on the sofa…brushing his arm in passing…all those easy signs of companionship… Yet now he seemed a million miles distant from her.

And I've done it! I've made it this way.

Anguish clutched at her like a vice.

But I had to do it! I had to!

He was speaking again, and she made herself listen,

block out the anguish that was crushing her like a vice, the same way her fingers were crushing each other in her lap.

'Can you explain to me why?'

His voice was neutral. As if he were addressing a client, drawing out from them just what their problem was.

She tried to find words. The words that would explain to him without explaining.

'I… I thought I could make it work…the arrangement we agreed on. I really thought I could. But—' the lump of concrete inside her throat made speaking difficult '—in the end I couldn't.'

'Can you say why?'

Again, he spoke in that neutral tone, drawing her out, gathering the information he needed to analyse the situation and then make his recommendations, as he would to a client, presenting them with their options.

But I don't have any options—only the one I've resorted to. The only one I can bear!

She tried to find a way of answering him that would not answer him. Not with the truth. The truth she could not speak.

Because what purpose would it serve? None. He would hear it, and note it, and then…

Then what? The truth of why she had left him, why she was divorcing him, was irrelevant. It would change nothing, and since it would change nothing there was no point telling it.

'It wasn't what I wanted,' she said. She sounded curt, but didn't mean to be.

His eyes rested on her. She couldn't read them. She never could. The only expression in his eyes she had ever been able to read was desire. That, and that alone, he had not veiled. Oh, she'd seen amusement in his eyes—wry, mostly, but warm, too, sometimes, when it was at something that

Joey had done or said—but there had never been anything else. Approval, perhaps, when she'd appeared in an outfit he'd considered becoming on her, and said so. But his thoughts, his moods, his feelings—all those were never visible.

He was neither cold, like his father, nor hot. Just…cool. Cool and in control—not harshly so, but only ever composed and collected, calm and unruffled, unperturbed and unreadable. He was easy to be with. He was courteous and friendly, conversational and relaxed. But…

He holds the world at bay.

He held *her* at bay.

Oh, sexual desire had burned between them—dear God, how it had burned! But…

But nothing else.

She looked at him now. Accepted who he was.

I can't reach him.

The words fell into the space inside her head, sounding like a death knell.

He was speaking again, and she made herself listen—though to what purpose she did not know. How would this conversation help at all? It couldn't.

'So what *did* you want?' he asked.

She heard the words, and in her head a thousand answers came. But none were any use—none at all. So there was no use saying them.

And yet…

She propelled herself to her feet. 'I wanted,' she said, 'what it is not in you to give.' She took a breath, and it was like a razor passing over her throat. 'I wanted to give what it is not in you to accept. And I'm sorry. I truly am. I tried… I tried not to want it. But it was too late.'

She looked down at him as he sat there on her little sofa, his long body showing tension in every line, though his face was still unreadable. She felt the concrete inside her swell until it possessed her whole body. He was so close to her—and yet he was a million miles away. In a place she could never reach.

She shut her eyes, defeated.

'I wanted you to love me,' she said.

CHAPTER FIFTEEN

RAFAELLO HEARD THE WORDS. They hung in the air. She had closed her eyes and he was glad of it. It let him go on looking at her.

He felt himself get to his feet. There seemed to be two of him suddenly, but he wasn't sure why.

I wanted you to love me.

The words had an echo of their own. An echo all around him. An echo reaching back...

And suddenly he wasn't there. Wasn't in this neat but unremarkable room, with its budget furniture and reproduction prints on the wall, its modest TV in the corner. He wasn't there at all.

He was in a hospital room. Well, not a hospital...a clinic. A discreet, very expensive clinic—for money could buy discretion, and that was important—tucked away in the Dolomites, where patients could benefit from the fresh mountain air. Patients who found life a little difficult from time to time. Patients with families who found *them* difficult...

He was looking down at the figure lying in the bed. Lying very still. In his head he heard the words the clinician had said to him, speaking very carefully—to a client...to a lawyer...

Explaining how there had been an adverse reaction to some medication...so very unfortunate...and impossible to foresee, given that the patient had—without the clinic's knowledge, of course—taken some medication of her own that she had secreted away…medication that had unfortunately not been compatible with what the clinic had prescribed.

'I am so very sorry,' the clinician had said.

Then he had left the room.

Leaving Rafaello alone.

With the body of his mother.

Who had wanted him to love her.

Alaina opened her eyes. She could not keep them shut for ever. She opened them, and swallowed, though there was still a razor in her throat. It was slicing through her vocal cords one by one, silencing her. But too late.

She had said the words to Rafaello she had sworn she never would because there would be no point saying them.

He was standing there, quite immobile. As immobile as she was. His face still had no expression in it. And yet…

There was something in his eyes. Something in those lidded, dark, occluded eyes that out of nowhere flashed with a light that was actually no light at all—but darkness. A visible darkness.

She felt her hand jerk forward—then pulled it back.

'I'm sorry,' she said. Her voice was low, all she could manage…a bare, strained husk. 'I should not have told you. There…there was no point in doing so. And it's…it's an irrelevance.'

She shut her eyes again for a moment, to give herself a moment's respite, then they flew open again.

'Rafaello, I'm sorry—I truly am. I tried so hard to stop myself. Just as—' She pressed her lips together, then spoke again. 'Just as I did five years ago. Then I succeeded. I had to. You drove away…you were not around any longer. I had to get on with my life. There was nothing else to be done. You weren't there.'

She felt her fingers tighten into fists, hanging by her sides.

'But when I was with you again...after we'd married... day after day...night after night...it started again. I tried to stop it—truly I did—but I failed. I *tried* to treat our marriage as you were treating it, for all the reasons you did. I truly thought, I could succeed! But when I saw Dante and Connie together, saw their marriage, saw what they are to each other...as we were not...could never be... I... I could not bear it—'

She gave up, defeat in her voice, a terrible weariness dragging at her. She rubbed a hand across her brow.

'I can't live with you, Rafaello, knowing that this time around I can't stop myself wanting what I wanted five years ago. Can't stop myself doing now what I managed at such cost not to do five years ago. I can't stop myself falling in love with you. Even knowing...' she felt her throat tighten in agony '...knowing nothing has changed since we first met. That falling in love with you now is as pointless... hopeless...as it would have been five years ago.'

She made herself take a breath, forced herself on.

'And...and because of that, I... I can't be with you on the terms you set out—the terms we live by in our marriage. I just can't do it. So please, *please* can we come to some other arrangement for Joey? Something that will give him an equal share of us both...that will be fair to all of us. Surely...oh, surely, with good will and effort we can achieve that. Can't we?'

Her voice was openly pleading. How could it be otherwise? So surely—oh, *please*—Rafaello would agree? Because he would no more want to live with a woman always wanting what he could not give than...

But he was speaking again, and his words were like stones. Dropping on her pleas. Crushing them to pieces.

'No,' he said. 'I don't think we can.'

She was staring at him. Her eyes—so very beautiful—distended and wide. Filled with anguish. She was going to speak, to say something, but he held up his hand.

'I don't think we can,' he said again.

Something was happening inside him. He could feel it. Those two people—that separation into two that he had felt as her words had echoed down the long years to him standing looking down at his mother's body, lying so defenceless in the bed at the clinic—were blurring.

'I don't think we can,' he said once more, letting his arm fall to his side. 'Because, you see, it would be quite impossible.'

She started. 'But we must… We *must*—for Joey's sake—find another way—'

'Yes,' he said. 'I think we must.'

He looked away for a moment. He knew there was a frown in his eyes. And something was pressing on him from the inside. He did not know the source of the pressure, but it was building with every moment. His eyes went back to Alaina. She was still standing stock still, her eyes huge, anguish in her face…

He felt that pressure still building within him. And then—in a moment, in an instant—it was gone—

That knife had plunged into his side again—between his ribs, into his lungs. It was an agonising pain. The same as he had felt by the empty pool at the empty villa. With Alaina and Joey gone.

His wife and his son—gone.

But now they're here. I'm with them again.

He felt the words rise up in him, moving through the pain possessing him.

They are here—and I will never—never!—lose them again.

Because to lose them would be an agony he could not endure.

I thought of her as the mother of my son—the woman I had to marry for that reason alone. Had to make my wife for that reason alone. A wife I did not choose and the son I felt responsible for, whose conception I would not have chosen either. But now...

Now everything was entirely and utterly different.

It's taken me till now to realise—to see. To feel what I am feeling now... To know.

To know that to lose either Joey or Alaina would be intolerable...unbearable...

He tried to speak, but his words were halting. He could not find them—though he had to. Words that must be framed in a language he had never spoken, never thought to speak.

But now he spoke.

Because not to speak would be an agony he could not endure.

'There is...there is a way,' he said, halting, hesitant, feeling his way into a land that was stranger to him than a distant planet.

How can I find it? How can I make my way there? How can I?

He felt despair fill him, possess him utterly.

And then suddenly there were more words—but not his. It was the pleading, impassioned voice of the mother who had wanted him to love her, as she loved him, and loved the man she had married, who had no love to give to her or anyone. He heard her voice now as clearly as if she were alive still—had never met that sad, mistaken end all those years ago, bereft of all that she had so longed for.

'Oh, my darling—my darling one! You can find the way! You left it—but you can come back to it—find it again.'

Then his own words came. The words that would reach out, bring him to where the pain possessing him would stop, cease and be assuaged.

'You said…' The words were still hesitant, but growing in power as he spoke them. He could feel it…know it. 'You said you wanted me to love you.' His eyes held hers. 'What if I wanted the same? What if…?' he said—and now he felt his feet move, as if on an impulse that was not his own and yet at the same time more his own than any step he had ever taken. 'What if I *wanted* you to love me?' He took a breath. 'To love me back.'

She did not move. Only stood there. And for a moment— a terrible, agonising moment—he was back in that room in the clinic, his mother's lifeless body there in front of him. She had wanted him to love her, but it was too late…too late for him to do so…to tell her…

But now it was not too late—not too late to say what he must say…could not bear *not* to say.

'Alaina… I, too, thought that the marriage we had made would work. That it would give our son a happy home…that it would give us a life that would work on the terms that we had come to. I thought that right up until you left me. But when I went to the villa and you were not there, and Joey was not there, and the place was empty, and you were gone—then…then I knew the folly of it all. The depths of my self-delusion.'

He took a step towards her. Reached for her hands, lifted them in his. Hers were cold, so cold, and he closed his own around them. She was staring up at him still, her eyes so wide, so beautiful. He felt the pain slice into him again, tightened his grip on her hands.

'All my life,' he said, 'I've kept my distance. It made life...easy. When I parted with you five years ago it was easy to do so. Then, when I found out about Joey's existence, it seemed...not easy, but less difficult to do what I have done. To take you and him into my life, accommodate you, fit you in, adapt to you. Honour my responsibilities to my son...my obligation to you as his mother. That you just happened to be even more beautiful now, as Joey's mother, than you were five years earlier on a Caribbean island, was, I admit, an attraction—a compensation, if you will, for my having to change my life entirely because of Joey.'

He heard his voice twist, the wry note that came into it.

'And we were, you must admit, highly compatible in that respect.'

A sensual note entered his voice—he could not help it— and he lowered his eyes.

He saw colour run up her ashen cheeks and was glad of it. His grip on her hands tightened yet more, lest she seek to withdraw them. But she made no attempt. No movement at all.

'I thought,' he said, 'that everything was as sorted as it needed to be, and that between us there would be what we had together five years ago. As much as that, but...but nothing more.'

He took a breath, searching for words. Finding them. And now his voice changed yet again, became edged with the pain that was still hollowing him.

'But what I did not realise was that something else was happening. Joey—the son I was not sure how to be a father too...the kind of father he needed...the kind that I needed to be for him—was reaching into my heart.'

He stopped, taking another breath, holding her hands still fast in his.

'And so were you.'

For a timeless moment there was silence, and she was completely still. Her eyes stayed fixed on his, wide and distended, and in them...

He spoke again. Saying all he wanted to say...needed to say.

'I was becoming...dependent. On you,' he said. 'For staying alive. For breathing. For my very heart to keep beating...' His expression changed. 'I don't know love, Alaina. I've kept it far away. So I didn't recognise it. Never realised. Only when you left. Then your absence taught it to me in the desolation I felt in that empty house. Without you.'

He drew a breath, stepped closer to her, closing the distance between them. Closing it for ever. He could catch the faint perfume of her body, feel the warmth of her hands in his now.

'Do you think,' he asked, 'that now we might find a way forward? A way,' he said, 'to make our marriage work? A marriage in which we love each other—now and for ever.'

Tears were welling in her eyes. Like diamonds, but more beautiful. The most beautiful thing in the world. He heard her say his name, her voice catching, and it was all he needed.

His mouth kissed her tears away, then grazed her trembling lips as he drew her into his arms. A sense of relief so profound that it shook him possessed him. Her hands were slipping from his, wrapping him to her, and his arms came around her, holding her tight, so tight. Never, never to let her go.

And still he went on kissing her as he had never kissed her before. Because never before had she been the woman he loved.

As she was now.

Now and for ever…

A hand was tugging at his sleeve, a little voice piping up. The only voice he would ever attend to more than to that of the woman he now knew, with that sense of relief that shuddered through him, he loved for ever and for good.

He drew back, looking down at Joey.

'Come and see my new train set!' Joey said. 'Mummy too!'

Rafaello took his hand. His son's hand was so small in his, and so infinitely precious. The same love that swept through him for Alaina now swept through him for his son as well. Shaking him to the core with its intensity.

'Show me,' he said. 'And Mummy too.'

Joey needed no second invitation. He grabbed his mother's hand as well. She gave a laugh, carefree and joyous, and Joey tugged them both forward, then vaulted up the stairs.

Behind him, his parents followed.

Taking each other's hands again.

Never to let them go.

Alaina leant back against Rafaello on the banquette in the nearby popular family hostelry they'd repaired to for lunch, after admiring Joey's new train set.

Joey was busy with the crayons and colouring sheet the child-friendly restaurant had provided. Contentment radiated from him.

As for her…she felt a happiness so golden that she could not believe it.

La dolce vita—that is what I now truly, truly have! True, and wonderful, and blissful! The sweetness of life—loving Rafaello—him loving me back.

She turned now to Rafaello, his arm strong and safe around her shoulder, heart filled with love for him.

His eyes were shadowed. 'I was always torn,' he said, his voice low. She could hear the tension in it...the pain. 'Between my mother and my father. I tried to be a bridge between them, but it was impossible. They were so entirely different—extreme in their ways. You've met my father—cold and detached. My mother was the very opposite. Impassioned and emotional. She loved too much.'

'She loved,' said Alaina, her eyes full, never wanting to see that shadow in his eyes again, that grief, 'as my own mother loved. She loved a man who could not return that love.' Her face convulsed. 'Which is why I was so scared, Rafaello—so scared! Five years ago I pulled back in time—I had to. I told you. But this time...seeing you...living with you...being intimate with you... How could I stop myself? How could I?'

She seized his hand, pressing it close.

'Are you sure, Rafaello? Are you really, really sure? Because I couldn't bear it—I just couldn't—if you woke up one morning and realised that you didn't...didn't love me after all...'

He meshed his fingers with hers, so tightly she winced.

'When...when my mother died, I... I changed,' he told her. 'Whether, as the official verdict told us, it was because of some lethal cross-reaction of her medication with a drug she'd self-administered, or whether...' his voice became more strained '...as I feared, she had knowingly taken those pills, her death made me...withdraw.'

He took a breath, filling his lungs. He lifted her hand to his lips, his fingers meshed with hers.

'I wanted my life to be as it became—without deep emotions. But now...'

He took her hand and placed it over his heart.

'Now I will love you till I die,' he said simply.

Tears filled her eyes, spilled over. 'Oh, my darling! My dearest, dearest one!' she said softly.

She kissed his mouth gently, with all the love in her heart. All the love she was now free to give, for he was now free to receive it from her, and offer her his in exchange.

For one long, endless moment they gazed into each other's eyes, hiding nothing. Giving everything.

Then Alaina felt her son's hand patting her arm.

'I've coloured in my picture,' he announced. A plaintive look crossed his face. 'Is my burger coming? My tummy is *very* hungry…'

'Mine too,' said Rafaello.

'And mine,' said Alaina.

'We're all in complete agreement,' Rafaello laughed.

On *everything*, thought Alaina.

And all the happiness of love drenched through her, along with the wonder of it all…the joy that would always be hers—theirs—now and for ever.

EPILOGUE

JOEY WAS SPLASHING in the pool. He was squealing with glee because Giorgio, standing at the edge, was directing the garden hose fully on to him, chortling as he did so.

Alaina laughed. 'I'm not sure who's the bigger kid,' she said.

She turned to look at Rafaello, lounging beside her on the swing seat they'd had installed. Joey adored it, but had had to be warned not to make it swing too widely or it would break.

'Speaking of kids,' she said, 'what do you think? Should we try for another? Or just be glad for Joey?' She gave a laugh. 'Connie's doing her best to persuade me to go for it!'

Rafaello laughed too. 'Dante is trying with me likewise. Especially now that Connie is expecting again.' He looked at Alaina. 'What do *you* think? You're the one who'll get pregnant.' A shadow crossed his face. 'You had to cope with your pregnancy with Joey all on your own… That weighs on me.'

Alaina shook her head. 'It was my call, and I made the one I felt was right at the time. But…'

She fell silent.

'We can't change the past,' Rafaello said quietly. 'We can't change the fact that our own parents, in such similar ways, were unhappy with each other and that their unhappiness preyed on us. But we can change the future—we already have. And, however emotionally frozen our fathers were...*are*...we both know that our respective mothers would be happy for us.'

She reached for his hand. 'So very happy,' she said softly.

'And we must be happy for each other, too,' Rafaello said.

His voice was warm, and the warmth in it set a glow to Alaina's heart. The man she had thought so unreachable, so self-contained, so *apart*, was now as much a part of her as her beloved Joey was.

Her eyes went to her son...*their* son...and the glow intensified, joy welling up in her. How precious he was, her adored Joey...*their* adored Joey! How infinitely precious...

As precious as a brother or sister for him would be... A child who this time would be conceived with hope and hopefulness and above all with love. The love between her and Rafaello—flowing fully and freely and for ever...

Her gaze swept back to him, her husband and her beloved, the love of her life. No longer did she fear her mother's fate, for Rafaello returned her love, fulfilled it a thousand times, a million times, and his love was as deep as hers.

She lifted her mouth to kiss his cheek, smiling.

'I think,' she said, and her eyes were alight with longing, 'that Connie is a *wonderful* example to follow! So...' Her expression changed, and her lips moved from his cheek to graze softly and sensuously along his mouth 'How about it?'

His mouth caught hers, answering her kiss and her question.

'That, Signora Ranieri,' he said, his voice as low and as wickedly seductive as the glint in his dark eyes, 'is a very, *very* good observation. I heartily commend it.'

Alaina's hand reached to cup his cheek. 'Then let us not delay,' she said huskily. She kissed him enticingly. 'We could make a start this very night...'

Which was exactly what they did.

And for as many nights as it took.

Until one morning Alaina displayed the tiny tell-tale stick with the revealing blue lines on it and relayed the joyful tidings to Rafaello.

And then both of them reached for their phones and sent two short but highly communicative texts: Rafaello to Dante, and Alaina to Connie.

The delighted answers they received in return were exceeded only by the excitement evinced by Joey, bouncing up and down on the bed in glee as they told him that he just might be getting a baby brother or sister soon.

He eventually collapsed in a heap between them and they hugged him tightly—their wonderful, beloved son, who had brought them together not just in parenthood, not just in marriage, but in true and everlasting love.

They were a loving, devoted family—the way it should be.

Always.

Above Joey's head, Rafaello leant across to kiss Alaina, his beloved wife, and Alaina kissed him back, her beloved husband. Perfect in their happiness.

* * * * *

ENEMIES AT THE GREEK ALTAR

JACKIE ASHENDEN

MILLS & BOON

To the wonderful Caitlin Crews,
whose writing and heroes I have loved
since before I was even published.
Writing this duet with you has been the best.

CHAPTER ONE

'SO MUCH NOISE,' Dimitra Teras complained, peering out of the window of her grandson's London office. 'What is happening out there?'

Her grandson, Poseidon Teras, one half of the mighty Teras twins, lounged in his black leather chair, at his fastidiously clean and tidy desk, and regarded his grandmother with some amusement. 'Protestors, Yia Yia. Nothing exciting.'

Loud chants floated up from the square outside his office. Someone sounded as if they were in possession of a megaphone.

The protestors had been there all week and, quite frankly, Poseidon was getting tired of them. For some reason the little group had targeted him and had decided to tell the world that he was the root of all evil. That he was a misogynist, a monster. That he chewed people up and spat them out, mistreated his employees and on and on. The usual, in other words.

He was not, of course, any of those things, and nor did he do any of the things they accused him of. He liked women—no, he *loved* women—and, while his lovers were many, he never took advantage of anyone, let alone chewing them up and spitting them out. And as for his company—well. People competed for the chance to be employed by him. Hydra Shipping, the shipping and supply-chain company that he'd inherited from his father, and built up over the course of fifteen years so it now spanned the globe, was a fair and safe workplace. He'd made sure that it was. Not because he cared all that much about people, but because his business was more productive when his employees were happy. And if that made him a monster, then so be it. He didn't care what the media said about him, and he didn't care about the protestors either.

They, on the hand, clearly cared very deeply about him, and he was of the opinion that if he bothered them so very much, then perhaps they should go and do something more constructive than standing outside his building and shouting at him.

'What are they protesting about?' Dimitra continued to frown out of the window at the group.

'Oh, me. I'm the devil incarnate, apparently.'

He wasn't worried. A group of protestors shouting about how terrible he was remained at the bottom of his list of things to be concerned about. Not that he had a list. He only cared about three things in this world: his twin brother Asterion, his grandmother, and Hydra Shipping.

Dimitra turned her sharp gaze on him. 'Don't think I haven't forgotten about you.'

Ah, yes, his grandmother's edict: that he and his brother were to marry a woman of her choosing, on pain of her share of the Teras family trust being given to an outsider. A fate worse than death.

Asterion had managed to find himself a bride—an ex-nun with an interest in wildlife, much to Poseidon's amusement—and was blissfully in love. Love was something that Poseidon had managed to avoid so far and was planning on continuing to avoid for the rest of his life.

Still, his grandmother wanted grandchildren and he cared about her wishes. He wouldn't make Asterion's mistake and actually fall in love with the woman Dimitra chose for him, but the marriage and producing children wouldn't be a problem. After all, it wasn't as if that was difficult. What woman in the world would say no to him? No one had so far. It was true that was largely in the bedroom, but for the chance to wear his ring? He couldn't think of a woman who'd refuse—and that wasn't being arrogant, that was just fact. He was handsome, rich, and powerful, and he'd generally found that to be an irresistible combination.

'I know you haven't forgotten me,' he said mildly. 'I have been awaiting your choice with bated breath.'

Dimitra's gaze narrowed. 'Always so uncaring. As if nothing matters. You should have someone who cares.'

Poseidon had once cared. He'd cared very deeply. He'd loved his father, had cared about and wanted his approval, his mother's too, but then they'd both died, along with his grandfather, in a car accident when he was twelve.

After that, seeking to fill the void left by his parents' death, he'd found himself a mentor, a friend of his father's, and—

But he didn't think about that. Not any more. Just as he didn't think about caring. Caring was a weakness and not one he'd ever saddle himself with again.

'And what martyr would that be?' he asked. 'Do you have someone in mind? A virgin sacrifice, perhaps?'

Dimitra snorted and glanced out of the window again. Then she smiled.

Poseidon did not like that smile.

'Her,' Dimitra said with some certainty, pointing at the group of protestors below. 'That woman right there.'

Poseidon was aware of a certain sinking feeling, but he got up all the same and strolled over to the window.

The group outside was really only a collection of four people. He hadn't taken much notice of them earlier in the week, getting his security team to move them and the signs they were clutching along, before they started to become a nuisance. But today they'd been much louder than usual, and it wasn't until he came to the window and looked out that he saw why.

One woman had chained herself to the statue in the square in front of his building and she appeared to be wearing... Well... Nothing but body paint and a pair of very brief knickers. Her red hair was loose and wild down her back, and across her admittedly very generous chest were written the words *Poseidon Teras go to hell!*

He frowned. '*That* woman? Surely you're mistaken.'

But Dimitra had a very self-satisfied look on her face. 'Yes, Poseidon. That woman. If you can get *her* to marry you, I might not even insist on grandchildren.'

There was a note of challenge in his grandmother's voice, something that Poseidon could never resist, because he was competitive by nature and loved to win. His father used to say it was due to the minute between Asterion's birth and his own, so Poseidon was forever trying to catch up. The casual way his father had said it, as if it wasn't possible for Poseidon to match his brother in any way, had once been a source of pain to him, but he didn't care nowadays. On the contrary, now it gave him something to aim for.

'You think I couldn't get her to marry me.' He didn't make it a question.

His grandmother gave him a measuring glance. 'Not if she thinks you're the devil incarnate. Which makes her perfect. If you can get her to agree and actually bring her to the altar, then I'll consider you fully rehabilitated.'

This whole marriage farce—he couldn't think of it as anything else—was supposed to be for their own good. At least that was what Dimitra had told him and Asterion a few months earlier when she'd delivered her ultimatum. Because she wanted them to be good men, not monsters, and apparently the answer to that was marriage.

Privately he thought the whole idea ridiculous, but Dimitra had been adamant and, since Asterion had agreed, Poseidon could hardly say no.

He gazed without pleasure at his grandmother's choice of bride for him. She'd been painted to look like a mermaid, with blue, green, and gold scales covering most of lower body. Shells had been painted over her breasts to mimic a bra, and the rest of her skin was blue. The design was quite skilful, but wholly inappropriate for a public place.

She'd raised that wretched megaphone and was shouting something else through it, and there was now a small crowd gathered around the statue, staring at her. That was probably due more to her state of undress rather than what she was saying, but perhaps that was the point. She wanted attention and she was doing anything to get it.

Poseidon had no problem with women who spoke their mind and had strong opinions. What he found so distasteful was intensity, and this woman had *intense* written all over her.

'Really, Yia Yia?' he said. 'I was hoping for more of a challenge than that.'

'She will say no to you,' Dimitra pronounced. 'She will not fall at your feet like all the rest.'

Another chant rose. The mermaid was looking up at the windows now, her megaphone pointed in his direction as if she could actually see him, though he knew she wouldn't be able to. Not when he was on the top floor.

He could see her, though, and he couldn't help but notice that her body paint did nothing to hide full curves, all rounded and luscious, and that her hair was a glorious red-gold, hanging down her back in tangled ringlets, shining like a pirate's treasure. He couldn't make out her face but he was aware of a certain…frisson that moved through him as she looked in his direction, shouting through her megaphone. He knew what a frisson was. A forerunner to attraction.

Intriguing. A good thing to be attracted to the woman Dimitra had chosen. It would certainly make things easier.

'She really does not like you,' Dimitra observed. 'Good. I would not want this to be too easy.'

Poseidon didn't want it to be too easy either. Because the honest truth was that he'd become a little…bored. Hydra Shipping was doing extremely well and he was making money hand over fist. He enjoyed the competitive relationship he had with his twin, which the media made out to be much more contentious than it actually was, and he certainly enjoyed all the women who came to his bed.

Things *were* easy and, yes, he was getting tired of easy.

Perhaps his grandmother knew what she was doing after all.

'She is very…loud,' he said.

'Passionate,' Dimitra corrected. 'Not afraid to speak her mind. I think I will like her.'

'Passionate' was one word for all the chanting that was floating up to his window. But now that his grandmother had said it, Poseidon couldn't help but imagine how all that fervour would translate in the bedroom…

The woman tossed her lovely hair over one shoulder, then lowered her megaphone and raised her hand, giving him a very obvious one-finger salute.

The frisson that had chased down his spine became a very definite pulse.

Poseidon smiled.

Yes. Perhaps Dimitra was right. She was perfect.

Andromeda Lane lowered her hand. She'd been certain that someone in the huge Hydra Shipping building towering above her had been watching. She'd felt it. And, though they were too far up and the windows were slightly tinted, she was sure it had been someone important. Perhaps even that stone-cold bastard himself, Poseidon Teras. In which case she hoped he'd enjoyed her heartfelt gesture of appreciation.

Poseidon and his equally filthy-rich brother Asterion had always been fixtures in the gossip columns, but it was Poseidon's latest behaviour that had done it.

Two weeks ago he'd been photographed in a nightclub with a couple of very young women, both of them clearly intoxicated and plastering themselves all over him, and it had reminded her so forcefully of Chrissy that bile had almost choked her.

'The Sea Monster', the media called him, because of his shipping company and all the virgins he ate, or something equally ridiculous. Which should have made him anathema to all sensible people, but it seemed to have the opposite effect. People *liked* him. They thought he was a charming reprobate.

Only Andromeda knew the truth, and so something had to be done.

She'd taken action in the form of Chrissy's Hope, a drug and alcohol addiction service for women, which she'd set up a year ago and named after her older sister who'd died five years earlier. It had helped thousands of women, but it was expensive to run and it always needed money, so she spent a lot of time campaigning, trying to raise its profile in order to get more sponsors.

After seeing that photograph of Poseidon with those two women, she'd decided that she was going to use him and his notorious reputation as a way to get eyes on Chrissy's Hope.

So she'd gathered her usual coterie of friends, Tom, Ayesha, and Jo, and had organised a protest outside the Hydra Shipping offices. Yet they'd been there a week and the lack of media attention was beginning to get frustrating.

Jo was handling all the social media platforms, while Tom managed the video. Ayesha had done the signs and then—after Andie had finally got sick of the lack of movement and decided to do something a little more eye-catching—she'd got out her body paints and given Andie a mermaid paint job.

A mermaid, since Hydra Shipping was all about the sea. But Andie wouldn't be a mute Ariel. She would be a mermaid who had a voice and wasn't afraid to use it.

Hydra Shipping security guards had moved their group on a couple of times, and Tom had been at the ready with his phone, waiting to film some brutality. But while the security people had been very firm, they'd also been gentle, and sadly brutality had been thin on the ground.

Andie had been annoyed. Not that she actually wanted violence, of course, but it would have helped the cause if Poseidon Teras's security team had been more…firm, or at the very least quite rude.

They hadn't been, though, and so she'd had to settle for being half-naked in mermaid body paint in order to get some attention.

There were a few people gathered around the statue, watching her, but most seemed uninterested, which was even more infuriating. They didn't know what men like Poseidon were really like. They were predators, preying on the weak and the vulnerable. People like her older sister.

Ayesha was handing out Chrissy's Hope pamphlets and Andie couldn't help but notice that most of the by-standers had either shaken their heads as Ayesha had approached, or surreptitiously chucked the pamphlets in a nearby bin.

It was enraging. Did they think they could just ignore the issue? That the terrible situations addiction and poverty got people into would just go away? That men like Poseidon Teras would stop taking advantage?

That was never going to happen, and she wasn't going to stop speaking out until people finally listened.

'Hey, Andie,' Tom called, pointing towards the front doors of the Hydra building. 'Something's happening.'

Andie lowered her megaphone and looked, because something was indeed happening. Security guards milled around in a little huddle, then abruptly the doors opened and a man strode through them.

He was very tall, with short, inky black hair, and a face that would have shamed the angels. His chest and shoulders would have done a gladiator proud, and he moved as if he owned every inch of the ground he walked on. Confident, arrogant, and known throughout the globe for his ruthless business practices, Poseidon Teras was the very epitome of the rich, powerful billionaire—and Andie loathed him and everything he stood for.

She didn't think as he approached. Didn't pause to consider whether shouting at the very famous CEO of a powerful company was a good idea. Fury burned in her blood. Because it had been this man's yacht and the party onboard it where Chrissy had died, and Andie held him personally responsible.

If she hadn't abhorred violence she would have punched him straight in his beautiful face, but since that wasn't an option, she decided to shout at him instead.

She lifted both her chin and her megaphone and yelled a variety of expletives detailing his parentage, his general demeanour, his apparent disregard for women, and his blatant male privilege, all in very rude, bordering on obscene detail.

If he found this offensive, he didn't show it, coming to a stop before the statue she'd chained herself to and giving her a steady, half-amused look while she continued to shout. Then, when she paused for breath, he asked in a deep, velvety voice, 'Have you finished?'

'No,' Andie snapped, because she hadn't. She had five years of rage simmering inside her. Now she'd caught his attention and he'd finally come down from his ivory tower, this was too good an opportunity to miss.

Are you sure you want his attention? You're naked and he's a known man-whore.

Andie wasn't averse to using her body to get eyes on a cause, nor did she care that a cotton G-string and a thin layer of body paint were the only things separating her from total nakedness. At least she'd never cared before. Yet now, the thought of being virtually naked in front of Poseidon Teras made an odd heat go through her. Which only added to her fury.

'Do go on, by all means.' Poseidon put his hands in the pockets of his dark grey suit trousers. 'I'm all ears.'

His eyes were the most incredible blue, indigo with shades of translucent green. Like the Mediterranean itself.

Much to Andie's rage, she found that not only had she caught her breath, she was also blushing. Incensed by this feminine betrayal, she lifted her megaphone again and prepared to give him another blast.

Poseidon took one hand out of his pocket and lifted a finger. 'But before you do,' he went on in the same level tone, 'I wonder if you wouldn't be more comfortable coming up to my office. Rain is forecast and I wouldn't want your body paint to get ruined.'

For a second Andie didn't know what to say. She hadn't expected him to actually come out of his building, let alone politely request her presence in his office.

What did I tell you? He also noticed the body paint.

Another small yet unmistakable pulse of heat went through her. Infuriating. She didn't care if he looked at her body—and actually it was a good job if he did. Getting attention was the whole point.

The statue she'd chained herself to was on a plinth that gave her a bit of height, and she used it shamelessly, looking down at him with as much disdain as she could muster.

'Your office?' she asked. 'Why on earth would I want to come up to your office?'

'Because you clearly have a few things to say,' he said, as if it were obvious. 'I'll get my secretary to bring us some tea and we can have a civilised conversation that perhaps doesn't involve a megaphone.'

Andie opened her mouth to tell him that she was quite happy with the megaphone, but then Poseidon lifted another finger and abruptly a flood of security people began milling around her. One of them had some bolt cutters, which he used to cut the chain around her and the statue, while another somehow managed to nick her megaphone. Yet more were talking to Tom, Jo, and Ayesha, and leading them away.

'I don't want to come up to your office,' Andie said, pulling away from the security guard, who let her go without protest. 'And don't you dare touch me.'

'Wouldn't dream of it.' Poseidon was shrugging out of his suit jacket. 'But I'm sure you'd like some tea and your friends would like the lunch my security team is going to buy them.' He clicked his fingers. Another guard took the jacket from him and then, much to her shock, put it around her shoulders. It was still warm from his body and the dark charcoal wool smelled of some spicy scent, like amber or cedar. It was delicious, which was again enraging. She didn't want to like anything about him, including his scent.

She tried to shrug the jacket off, but soon found herself being hustled from the statue and ushered into the expensive hush of the Hydra Shipping offices.

Andie didn't mind sacrificing her pride for a cause, especially if it was for Chrissy's Hope. She debated fighting off his security and causing a scene in the lobby, since that would certainly get her attention.

Then again, he'd said he wanted to talk to her in his office and this could actually be a good thing. She could ask him about Chrissy, tell him about her and her death, and demand some justice. Financial restitution for Chrissy's Hope even. Because if they didn't find sponsorship soon, it was going to have to close.

So she said nothing, controlling her fury and letting the security guards escort her into the elevator and up to the top floor of the building. She stayed silent as they ushered her along an expensively carpeted hallway into a huge, plush office that was obviously Poseidon's.

There were big floor-to-ceiling windows along one wall that looked out over the square, and a huge wooden desk in pale wood that complemented the pale carpet. A large white leather couch plus several armchairs were arranged down one end, while sleek wooden shelves lined the wall opposite the windows.

Andie gazed around with some contempt. It was all very tasteful and reeked of money, which was as expected. She knew the Teras brothers, as everyone did— no one talked of anyone else, it seemed. Poseidon and his brother Asterion, who owned the Minotaur Group, were both of them darlings of the media.

Asterion had recently married, which had curtailed his exploits, but not so his twin. Poseidon was still as notorious as ever.

Well, she could use that. If he wanted a civilised conversation about why she was shouting outside his office, she'd tell him. She'd tell him everything. Hopefully that would shame him enough into giving her a huge donation or a sponsorship deal for Chrissy's Hope.

He hadn't come up in the elevator with her. She was just beginning to wonder if his promise of a chat had all been hot air when he entered the room, closing the door behind him and gesturing expansively to the white leather couch.

Andie didn't want to sit, since she was at a height disadvantage with him anyway, but the prospect of leaving body paint on the pristine white leather was too irresistible a chance to pass up. So she walked down to the other end of the office and sat down, keeping his jacket around her shoulders—because good luck with getting paint out of Italian merino.

Poseidon did not, as she'd expected, come to stand in front of her, looking down from his great height, intimidating her. Nor did he sit next to her on the couch, uncomfortably close. Instead, he pulled over a matching white leather armchair and sat down in it, all predatory grace, his blue gaze settling on her.

He was exquisitely dressed. His suit trousers looked handmade and tailored to fit his narrow waist and powerful thighs like a glove. He wore a black business shirt with a silk tie the same colour as his eyes. A heavy platinum watch circled one strong wrist.

She hadn't realised how unspeakably gorgeous and intensely charismatic his presence was in real life, and she hated how her mouth had gone dry in response. She hated that she was so shallow as to even notice his beauty.

She hated him, full stop.

'So,' he said, his deep voice warm, his blue gaze never dropping an inch from her face, despite the fact that all she wore was a pair of knickers, his jacket, and some blue, green, and gold paint. 'Care to tell me your name?'

It wasn't the first question she'd expected him to ask. Despite telling her he wanted a 'civilised conversation', she'd expected him to demand to know what she was doing and to cease disrupting his place of business, all while ogling her naked body. She'd even expected the police to be called, or at least some kind of threat to be issued, not a simple, 'Care to tell me your name?'

Andie folded her hands in her lap and lifted her chin. 'Guess.'

He smiled and the world just about slowed down and stopped. His mouth was just as beautiful as the rest of him, and his smile made it feel like summer.

Don't forget Chrissy. Don't forget what happened to her.

Oh, she would never forget. Their mother had been a single parent, working two jobs just to keep their heads above water. She hadn't noticed how bored seventeen-year-old Chrissy was, and how she'd wanted something more for herself, something better. Andie, too busy trying hard at school, hadn't noticed either—not then. It had only been when Chrissy had started going to nightclubs and had met Simon, the man who'd introduced her into the wrong crowd, that Andie had started to pay attention. And when Chrissy had started escorting, at Simon's suggestion, to pay for the lifestyle she'd developed a taste for, Andie had told their mother, who'd done precisely nothing.

'Why should I?' Chrissy had asked Andie, when Andie had begged her to stop escorting at least. 'It's fun and the money's good. I mean, really, Andie, do you want to be a waitress all your life?'

Her beautiful, intelligent, perfect, reckless sister. She'd got caught up in the world of the rich and famous, spirited away like a mortal into the faerie realm. And she'd ended up dying of an overdose on Poseidon's yacht during a party.

He and Simon had destroyed her and, while Simon was long gone, Andie wasn't going to let Poseidon get away with it. Certainly the very last thing she'd *ever* do was fall for him herself. So she ignored his beautiful smile and the way it made her heart beat fast, and stared at him as if he was dirt underneath her shoe instead.

Sadly this seemed to have no effect.

'You don't like me,' he said sympathetically. 'I understand. But if you don't tell me your name, I'll have to call you something like "little siren". Since you are little and have been singing a very loud song all week.'

The soft roughness of his lightly accented voice, not to mention the dry amusement in his tone, slid under Andie's skin like a burr, making her bristle.

'While you,' she said, 'are the most privileged, arrogant, misogynistic bastard I have ever had the misfortune to meet.'

His smile deepened as if she'd said something funny. 'Two of those things are absolutely true, and two are not. I am certainly privileged and arrogant, but I assure you that my parents were married. Also, I don't hate women. On the contrary, I am an ardent feminist.'

He was making fun of her, wasn't he?

'I'm glad you find taking advantage of women so amusing,' she said hotly. 'Because I don't.'

His gaze narrowed. 'Excuse me? I don't take advantage of anyone, little siren, let alone women.'

'Then how do you explain that nightclub picture?'

She hadn't meant to reveal her hand quite so quickly. Then again, why not? She was always honest about her concerns at least.

He frowned. 'What nightclub picture?'

'The one from last week.' How dared he not remember? 'With the two women who were obviously very young and highly intoxicated.'

The frown cleared. 'Oh, that. They were at the bar and causing a fuss because the barman discovered they were underage. I waited with them to make sure they didn't get themselves into trouble, while a taxi was called to take them home.'

He said it so casually that she was half inclined to believe him, though very much against her will.

'That is not what the papers said,' she snapped.

'No, because that doesn't make for good copy, does it?' He gave her a shrewd glance. 'What? Did you think I was there to debauch underage girls?'

Andie's face felt hot but she refused to look away. 'Well, were you?'

He didn't answer immediately, continuing to give her

a steady, assessing look that made her feel as if he was stripping a layer of skin away.

'You're very angry with me, aren't you?' he observed at last. 'It can't be only about those pictures. Tell me, what did I do?'

Andie was always honest and so she gave him the truth. 'You're responsible for the death of my sister, and what I want to know is what you're going to do about it.'

CHAPTER TWO

SITTING OPPOSITE THE little siren, Poseidon rapidly became aware of two things. First, it was *not* going to be as easy to get her to marry him as he'd thought. Second, Dimitra was wrong. She was *not* perfect. Not at all. And he'd known that the moment he'd come out of his building to confront her.

She'd stood on her plinth, looking down at him with furious contempt. Shouting at him through her megaphone and calling him all the names under the sun. He'd never had anyone shout at him like that before—he was a powerful man; no one would dare—and he'd been... shaken. Because she was magnificent. There was simply no other word for her. Proud in her nakedness, with his name written boldly across the curves of her full breasts, staring at him with eyes the most beautiful shade of green he'd ever seen. Light and clear, like sunshine on fresh new leaves.

There had been fire in her, and intensity, and the frisson he'd felt up in his office had turned into a kick of heat so strong it had taken him by surprise.

He hadn't liked it. He hadn't liked it at all. Any feeling with the power to grip him by the throat like that was suspect, and that included physical desire.

Sex he indulged in whenever he felt like it, and with anyone he wanted who also wanted him. He never had to work for it. He never *wanted* to work for it. But this woman had *work* written all over her—which made her instantly off-limits to him. The strength of his physical attraction also made her off-limits.

He never wanted to desire someone so badly he lost all sense. Desire was manageable, controllable, and so he controlled it ruthlessly.

But he'd also known pretty much straight away that this woman was *not* going to mindlessly accept a marriage proposal from him.

Dimitra had wanted both him and Asterion to court the women she'd chosen for them and then to marry them, as proof they weren't complete monsters. Asterion had once been dubbed the Monster of the Mediterranean, and he was certainly a monster no longer—not now his Brita had tamed him.

Poseidon had no intention of being tamed, and nor did he want to change his already very comfortable life. He liked things the way they were, and he certainly wasn't going to alter his behaviour just because he had a wife.

So while Dimitra might have insisted on a courtship, as he'd ushered the little siren up to his office he'd had a better idea—one that gave him more certainty and might make her more open to at least listening to him.

Except then she'd sat on the couch in his office, draped in the jacket he'd given her, partly for her own modesty and partly because he'd had to cover at least some of those luscious curves, and he'd found himself...transfixed.

Go to hell Poseidon Teras was staring him in the face,

sparks of anger in her green eyes, her chin jutting. And the uncompromising and blunt way she spoke, looking at him as if he was nothing more than dirt beneath her shoe…

All of her was fascinating and he'd let himself become distracted.

His lovers were all women who were as jaded as he was…as bored and as cynical. They never required anything of him but pleasure, so that was what he gave them. He could make them come, but whether they liked him or otherwise he didn't know and didn't care.

But not this woman. She was actively furious with him and now he knew why. However, while he was a certified playboy, who'd spent many nights with many women and sometimes more than one, he'd never been directly involved with anyone's death before.

He frowned. 'Your sister? Please explain.'

'You own a yacht called *Thetis*,' she said, in her light, clear voice. 'And you often use it for parties.'

He did have a yacht called *Thetis*—it was one of many he owned—and he sometimes used it for parties. 'Yes,' he said slowly. 'That is correct.'

'Five years ago there was a party on board the *Thetis* and a woman died.'

The siren's green eyes glittered with anger and a few other deep, passionate emotions he didn't recognise.

'That woman was my sister.'

A pulse of shock went through him. There had been an incident, he recalled now, when he'd loaned *Thetis* to an acquaintance, who'd then had a different friend organise a party on board. Poseidon hadn't been involved with the organisation, though he'd briefly considered attending. He'd decided not to in the end, because he'd had an upcoming business trip. It hadn't been until he'd returned to London that he'd been notified about the death of a woman at that party. An investigation had been conducted, which he'd fully co-operated with, and in the end the organiser of the party had been prosecuted. He'd sent some money to the woman's family to help with funeral expenses, and he'd never loaned out his yachts to anyone ever again.

He hadn't thought of the incident since.

Now, it was clear why the woman sitting opposite him, straight-backed and defiant, her gaze unwavering, was so full of righteous anger towards him.

'I'm so very sorry,' he said, and meant it, because he knew what it was to lose people you loved. 'I hope you received the money I sent for her funeral.'

The siren's pointed chin lifted higher, the green sparks in her gaze becoming flames. 'Money. That's all you care about,' she spat. 'As if that could make up for losing Chrissy.'

Grief—that was the other emotion in her eyes. It was grief.

He knew about grief. He knew how it could hollow you out and turn you into a shell. How it could make you desperate, a target for anyone to manipulate. Well, she was safe from him in that respect at least. He'd had his own grief for his parents used against him and he wouldn't wish that on anyone else.

So he was going to need to be careful, since he had no desire to make it worse for her. But she did have to know that he had nothing to do with her sister's death.

'As I said, I'm very sorry for the loss of your sister,'

he said gently. 'But I was not on the boat at the time, nor did I have anything to do with that party.'

This didn't seem to mollify her, because her expression didn't change. She still looked furious. 'Whether you were on it or not, you owned the boat and it was your responsibility.'

Clearly she was looking for someone to blame, which was fair. And he supposed his response might have sounded a little like an excuse. He couldn't remember exactly what the organiser of that party had received in the way of justice, but it had been a jail term. Though, of course, as she'd said, none of that would bring her sister back.

He gave her an assessing glance. 'What would you like me to do in that case?'

There was an uncompromising slant to her jaw, and she answered without the slightest hesitation. 'You can sponsor the drug and alcohol addiction service I've named after my sister. For the next five years.'

Poseidon was aware of deep surprise, since he'd been expecting a demand for personal recompense, which was what most people wanted in these situations. He hadn't expected a sponsorship request for a charitable service.

'*You* don't want money?' he clarified, just to be sure.

'*I* don't need money.' She gave him a look as if he'd personally offended her. 'But Chrissy's Hope does.'

He was still surprised, but it did seem a reasonable request. He had more money than he knew what to do with, quite honestly, and he could spare it. But he also wasn't a master of business for nothing, and here was an opportunity. A way for them to both get what they wanted.

You weren't going to use her anger and grief against her, remember?

And he wouldn't. This was a...business proposition, that was all. He required her to marry him and she needed money for her service. All he needed was her presence at the altar, an appearance of willingness enough to satisfy Dimitra, and her signature on their marriage certificate. He didn't need to sleep with her or, indeed, anything else. And in return he'd offer to sponsor her service for as long as she needed. Easy.

She was sitting up very straight on his couch, not making even one attempt to cover herself, her opinion of him written loud and clear on her skin. Her gaze was very direct and almost searing in its honesty, and he felt that heat kick inside him again. She had the delicate, pale skin of a redhead beneath all the paint, and he found himself wishing he had a damp cloth so he could wipe the paint away, discover the texture of her skin and the shape of her beneath it.

But no, he wasn't going to give in to that heat, not with her, and certainly not now he knew about her sister. He didn't care about people's feelings as a rule, because once you cared that was a slippery slope. You could be manipulated...you could be used. Feelings were a vulnerability, a weakness, and caring was a chink in your armour.

The easiest answer was simply not to care and so he didn't. However, he had his own personal lines that he would not cross. He did not manipulate people and he did not take advantage of them. Not in business and not in anything else. That didn't mean he wasn't ruthless— he was just honest about it.

He could flirt with this siren. He could probably bring her around to his way of thinking at some point, using either his charm or his looks to get her to give him what he wanted. But she was furious and grieving, and to do that would be wrong.

He would, however, use her need for money to his advantage. He had no qualms at all about that.

'Well?' she said when he didn't speak.

So it seemed that not only did she have a temper, she was impatient too. She had her hands folded in her lap and one finger was tapping the back of her other hand. The rest of her was very still, but it felt forced. As if she was containing herself, directing all that passion and fire into the blaze of her green eyes.

Pull yourself together and stop staring at her.

Annoyed with himself, Poseidon ignored the pull of his fascination and leaned forward, elbows on his knees, hands clasped between them. 'Very well,' he said. 'I will sponsor your service. But only on one condition.'

Somehow she managed to look down her nose at him, though even sitting down he was taller than she was. 'Of course there's a condition. God forbid you actually donate money to a worthy cause.'

'I'm a businessman, little siren, and I don't much care about your opinion of me, or indeed anyone else's opinion of me. And I need something from you.'

He didn't miss how she tensed, and it was clear she was expecting him to ask her for something distasteful, and, given her view of him, no doubt she was expecting it to be sexual.

'Naturally,' she said. 'Men like you never do anything for free, do you?'

'I don't know about other men like me, but no, I don't,' he agreed. 'And certainly in this instance I don't.'

'I suppose your condition is that I have to sleep with you.' She somehow made the statement defiant, challenging, and contemptuous all at the same time. 'In which case the answer is no, and if you dare touch me I'll call the police.'

His fascination tugged at the leash he'd put on it. She was small, very naked, and in the presence of one of the most powerful men in Europe. Yet she acted as if she was encased in a full suit of armour, carrying a sword, and leading a whole army into battle.

She was either very brave or very foolish, and he couldn't decide which.

'What would you call the police with?' he asked, momentarily diverted. 'You're clearly not carrying a phone—unless you're very clever at hiding it.'

She sniffed, as if he'd said something unbearably stupid. 'There's a phone on your desk.'

'True. But you'd have to go past me to get it.'

Her eyes narrowed. 'I know self-defence. I'd break your nose.'

That made him want to smile, because she was so very fierce. 'No doubt,' he murmured. 'Rest assured, though, you're safe from me. I don't touch women who don't want to be touched.'

She eyed him, doubt clear on her face, while he stared blandly back. 'Perhaps you should ask me what my condition is instead of assuming,' he suggested.

'Perhaps you should tell me instead of playing stupid games.'

Oh, she is delicious.

The heat inside him kicked harder, bringing with it a sensation he hadn't felt for years, almost like…anticipation. But no, he couldn't start thinking like that. What he was proposing was a business deal, nothing more.

'Fine,' he said. 'I'll sponsor your service indefinitely. On the condition that you marry me.'

At first Andie didn't quite understand, because what he'd said didn't make any sense. 'Marry you?' she said blankly. 'Why?'

Poseidon was sitting forward with his hands clasped loosely between his knees, an almost apologetic look on his beautiful face. She was sure that wasn't real—that he wasn't actually apologetic. In fact, she was positive most things about him weren't real, including the fact that he *wasn't* responsible for Chrissy's death.

He *had* sent money for her funeral, along with an apology. She remembered that. But Miranda, Andie's mother, hadn't given Andie any details of the apology or the amount of money he'd given her. And Andie hadn't asked. The pair of them had been too mired in grief at the loss of their perfect, beautiful daughter and sister, crushed by the hole in their lives Chrissy's loss had left.

She'd died on this man's yacht and, despite what he'd said about not being responsible, the fact remained that if he hadn't loaned the yacht to a friend, there wouldn't even have been a party for Chrissy to go to.

And of course there would be a condition in return for his sponsorship of Chrissy's Hope. He wouldn't do it out of the goodness of his heart—that kind of man never did. He probably didn't even have a heart. He was, as he'd said, a businessman, and Andie knew all about businessmen. Simon had been a businessman, and so had all his friends. Chrissy had told her many stories about them when she'd started escorting—about their arrogance, their money, and their privilege. Chrissy had found them exciting. Certainly more exciting than the boys at school or on the council estate where they'd both grown up.

And Andie had agreed.

It hadn't been until after Chrissy had died that the truth had come out.

They weren't exciting. They were predators. And Poseidon Teras was one of them—which meant she needed to be on her guard around him.

Now, he gave a theatrical sigh and said, 'Why? Because my grandmother is an old dragon and has decided, in her wisdom, that my brother and I should marry women of her choosing. And, sadly for you and I, your little performance with the megaphone attracted her attention, and she decided that the woman for me would apparently be you.'

Despite her best intentions, she felt the shock return, and for a moment it even made her forget her anger. 'Me?' she squeaked. 'Why me?'

'I think she was taken with your varied curses,' Poseidon said. 'I've been called many things in my time, but I have to admit you put them all together in a very creative way.'

Andie stared at him, nonplussed. 'I still don't understand.'

He lifted one powerful shoulder. 'The ways of my grandmother are varied and mysterious. Who can say why you? Possibly because you don't like me and were vocal about it.'

'She chose me because I don't like you?'

'Yes.' Poseidon smiled that devastating smile again. 'She likes a game.'

Andie struggled to hide her shock, because she really didn't want him to know how badly he'd surprised her. Anger was her go-to, her fuel, her engine. Anger was easy and familiar. While shock felt like…helplessness. Like standing in the hallway of the council flat where she'd lived with her mother, listening to a policeman tell her that her beloved older sister had died.

She went for anger now. 'You can't possibly think I'm going to agree,' she said hotly. 'What a stupid idea.'

'I heartily concur,' he replied, much to her annoyance. 'It is a stupid idea. But my grandmother is very insistent.'

Marry him. Marry Poseidon Teras—the man who wasn't quite as responsible for her sister's death as she'd thought, but who'd still had a hand in it. A man who was the epitome of everything she'd spent years fighting against.

It was impossible. Insanity.

A sudden suspicion gripped her. 'Is this some kind of elaborate joke? Because if so, I'm not—'

'It's not a joke, believe me.' His smile had become a little sharp, like a shark's, and it came to her suddenly that perhaps he didn't like the idea any more than she did.

'You don't actually want to marry me, do you?' she asked.

'I don't want to marry anyone, but what can you do?' He opened his hands. 'Dimitra is a force of nature and will not be denied.'

'That's ridiculous.'

'You've never met a Greek grandmother, I see.'

'So, what? You do everything she says?'

'No, but in this instance, if we don't marry, she's made it clear that her share of the family trust will go to someone who isn't family.' Again, he looked apologetic. 'It's important to my brother and I that her share does not go to outside hands.'

He said it so reasonably, Andie almost found herself nodding in agreement.

'Don't worry,' he continued. 'I won't be requiring sex, if that's what you're worried about. It'll be a paper marriage to fulfil her wishes, nothing more.'

At the word 'sex' a little spark of heat streaked through Andie, making her aware once more of her nakedness, of how his blue gaze hadn't dipped once to look at her body, and she found herself wondering why. Because when she used it as a weapon of protest it certainly got her attention, and usually from men.

Poseidon Teras was a well-known womaniser, so why wasn't he ogling her as she'd expected him to? Why hadn't he made a pass at her or even dropped a double entendre? Surely he'd be the first man to insist on sex along with this ridiculous marriage proposal.

'No sex?' she said, before she could think better of it. 'So you're going to stay celibate?'

'I did not say that.'

For a moment something glittered in those blue eyes... something hot and wicked. And the spark inside Andie ignited into a small flame, her brain taking the image of Poseidon Teras not staying celibate and running with it. He'd had a lot of lovers—the media was constantly full of pictures of him and his latest conquests, all of them as beautiful as he was. In the course of reading about him before the protest, she'd discovered he was reputed to be an excellent and generous lover, with all his exes going into raptures about his bedroom skills. And now she couldn't help but picture exactly what those skills were and what they would feel like…

No. What was she thinking? She'd specifically avoided men and their complications after what had happened to Chrissy, and she'd certainly never met anyone since then who'd made her change her mind.

This man would definitely *not* be the first—especially if his attitude to marriage was 'pay someone to marry me'.

'You wouldn't be faithful?' she asked. 'At all?'

He tilted his head slightly to the side, that faintly wicked gleam in his eyes becoming more pronounced. 'Why? Would you like me to be?'

Her cheeks warmed, which was irritating, but she didn't look away. A part of her wanted to, but it would feel too much as if she was giving ground. 'No,' she said. 'I don't care what you do. Except you mentioned sponsoring Chrissy's Hope indefinitely, right?'

'Yes,' he said. 'That's correct.'

You can't be seriously considering this.

She wasn't. Not at all. It was completely out of the question, not to mention insane. Then again, Chrissy's Hope was very important, and if there was even a chance it could be sponsored indefinitely she had to at least explore the offer. Even if he wasn't serious about it.

'And this would be regardless of how long we stay married?'

'Yes,' he repeated. 'Irrespective of a later divorce, Hydra Shipping will commit to the deal until you decide to end it.'

It would mean she'd never have to go scraping around for funds again. All those desperate people who needed help would be given it, and she'd never have to turn anyone away.

It had been such a struggle, keeping the service going, and demand was increasing by the day. It needed money—a lot of money—in order to operate even the most basic services, let alone provide the support she wanted it to.

'How much are you offering?' she asked bluntly, and then told him how much it took to operate on a daily basis.

He didn't even blink. 'I'll double it.'

Andie's stomach dropped away. Double? God, there were so many things she could do with that...so much she could offer. Perhaps widening the scope of the service so that it would provide support for general health as well as for addiction. Better facilities too...

She became conscious that she was staring at him and that her shock was probably obvious. That wouldn't do. He couldn't be allowed to see how desperate she was, because she certainly wasn't going to beg. She was owed this. *Chrissy* was owed this.

'Okay,' she said, keeping a fixed expression on her face. 'And all that for simply agreeing to marry you? Which would be...what? My name on a piece of paper?'

She wasn't precious about the institution of marriage itself. Chrissy had told her enough hair-raising stories about the men she'd gone out with, who'd cheated on their wives and girlfriends, to make Andie highly sceptical over it. Her mother had separated from Andie's father when Andie had been a baby, and she'd never had a good word to say about it either.

However, Andie wasn't naive enough to think it would be as simple as her name on a piece of paper. There had to be more to it than that.

Poseidon nodded. as if he was pleased with the question. 'It will be a legal marriage, with a ceremony. Dimitra does love a wedding. Also, you'll have to pretend as if you're madly in love with me, otherwise she'll start to get suspicious.'

Andie frowned. He hadn't mentioned *that*. She wasn't very good at pretending. She prided herself on her honesty, and she lived her truth every single day. Pretence was anathema to her.

'You want me to pretend I'm in love with you?' She had to ask, just to be clear.

Again, he gave her an almost apologetic look. 'A little, perhaps. Dimitra wanted Asterion and I to court our respective wives, not pay them to be with us, and she'll be very unhappy if she discovers that that is indeed what I've done. Also,' he went on, before she could respond, 'we'll have to have a honeymoon. I hope that won't be a problem?'

So a wedding ceremony, acting as if she was in love with him, and now a honeymoon? Was he mad?

'It's a problem,' she snapped.

He held up a hand. 'Don't worry, we'll have separate rooms. And there will be no obligation for you to provide any…wifely duties, so to speak. The honeymoon will be entirely for show. You could even think of it as a well-earned holiday.'

A holiday? With him?

It certainly wasn't anything she'd want to do herself, that was true. But she couldn't ignore the sponsorship for

Chrissy's Hope. There was so much good she could do with that money. Surely she had to consider it at least?

She gave him a narrow look. 'If I agree, I'm not living with you. And I'm not giving up any part of my life for you.'

'Of course not,' he said smoothly. 'I wouldn't ask you to. We can deal with the living arrangements later.'

'And I want the sponsorship deal in writing and all the paperwork done before any kind of wedding ceremony. I want the terms of the marriage agreement in writing too, and signed.'

He nodded. 'I can arrange that.'

Andie waited, expecting some kind of counter offer in return, but he remained silent. Which was suspicious. He'd agreed to everything so quickly and hadn't protested. Was she missing something?

'How long would we have to stay married?' she asked after a moment's thought.

'Legally? Until Dimitra passes away, I would think. But she's very old, so I'm sure that won't be too long.'

Andie did not like his casual tone one bit. 'That's a terrible way to talk about your grandmother,' she said.

His eyes widened at that and it hit her, very belatedly, that he wasn't just some guy. He was Poseidon Teras, a powerful billionaire, and not only had she called him all the names under the sun earlier, and accused him of being complicit in Chrissy's death, she'd also just pulled him up sharp about his grandmother. As if she had a right to it.

Andie could apologise when she was wrong—she had no problem with that. But she didn't like apologising to men who didn't deserve it. And he didn't deserve it. So she only stared at him belligerently, despite her cheeks being hot yet again, daring him to call her on it.

But all he did was study her in a way that made her want to shift around on the couch. He wasn't leering and he wasn't ogling. He only looked at her as if she was… interesting to him.

Which hadn't been her intention.

She didn't want to attract his interest, only his attention.

'You're very forthright, aren't you?' he observed at last, almost sounding admiring.

Disconcerted, she shrugged it off. 'I call it like I see it.'

'Indeed you do.' Then, rather to her surprise, he smiled again, and this time it was warm and natural, and, quite frankly, even more devastating than his previous smiles. 'I like that.'

Another thing she didn't want. Him to like anything about her. Him to…surprise her. She hated it…just as she hated that beautiful smile of his.

'Good for you,' she said. 'But I don't care about your opinion.'

'Oh, I think you do,' he murmured. 'If you didn't, you wouldn't have spoken to me so sharply about Dimitra. And you're right, by the way, it *is* a terrible way to speak about her.'

For a second she couldn't think what to say to that, but he didn't give her a chance to think, because then he went on. 'So? What's it to be, little siren? Is it a no? Or would you like to think about it?'

She eyed him. 'What happens if I say no?'

'Nothing happens if you say no,' he said. 'Except I will not be sponsoring your service and, perhaps worse, you'll disappoint Dimitra.'

'And if I say yes?'

'Then we'll get married, you'll enjoy lots of money and the warm approval of my very Greek grandmother, and her share of the trust will remain in family hands— as it should be.'

Are you really going to go through with it?

Probably not. But, again, she had to consider it. The opportunity for Chrissy's Hope was too good to pass up.

'I'll think about it,' she said finally.

He had the grace not to look too satisfied. 'Excellent.' Reaching into his pocket, he pulled out a plain white card and held it out. 'Here is the number for my private cell phone. I'd like an answer in a week, if possible. Though if you need more time, let me know.'

Andie reached for it, startled as her fingers brushed his and a ripple of electricity crackled through her. It nearly made her drop the card, and she was surprised enough to look into his blue gaze to see if he felt it too.

A mistake.

Because she could see it, glowing in the blue depths of his eyes. Attraction. Interest. Chemistry.

She blushed like a rose and jerked her hand back before she knew what she was doing.

Now you've given yourself away.

Andie ignored the whisper in her head. It had been static, nothing else. Because she hated him. She certainly *wasn't* attracted to him—not on any level.

Deciding that she was done with being here in his presence, Andie slid off the couch. 'A week should be fine,' she said crisply, and then, without another word, she turned to the doors and headed towards them.

She was halfway across the room when she remembered his jacket was still around her shoulders. So she stopped and shrugged, allowing the jacket to slip onto the floor. Then she turned her head and glanced at him over her shoulder. 'Oh, and by the way, my name is An-dromeda.'

Leaving him with that, she turned back to the doors again and went out.

CHAPTER THREE

THAT NIGHT POSEIDON had his promised dinner with Dimitra, since she was flying back the next morning to the Mediterranean island kingdom that was the Teras family seat, and was suitably vague when she questioned him about Andromeda. He didn't want to give anything away about his plans, but she was naturally suspicious, so he had to walk a fine line.

However, when he got back to his London residence—a penthouse near the Hydra Shipping office that gave a perfect view over the Thames—he called his brother to discuss it.

'Did you tell her she'll need to come to the island?' Asterion asked, after Poseidon had related what had happened with Andromeda.

He sounded vaguely disapproving, which annoyed Poseidon irrationally.

Then again, he was already annoyed by how his thoughts kept returning to the siren as she'd left his office. How her fingers had brushed his as she'd taken his card—it hadn't been intentional on either part, he was sure—and the pulse of electricity that had followed. It had been deep, strong, a gut-punch of attraction. But nothing he couldn't have handled if he hadn't seen the flare of response in her eyes.

She might not like him, and she might be furious with him, but she'd felt the pull of their chemistry as deeply as he had—he was certain.

That's not going to make things easier.

It would certainly make things more…challenging. A beautiful woman whom he wanted and who wanted him had always been a temptation he could never resist. But this was a business proposal, not an actual marriage, and he'd decided he wasn't going to touch her. So he wouldn't. It was as simple as that.

He'd also been clear about what he expected from their potential wedding agreement. Or, at least, mostly clear. He'd neglected to mention a couple of things, as Asterion had pointed out. Such as the wedding ceremony in the ancient church that Dimitra so loved. But, again, it might not be an issue.

The island kingdom was where the Teras family had lived for generations, and where the Minotaur Group, Asterion's half of the family holdings, and Hydra Shipping, his half, had had their start.

It was beautiful, the island, a jewel in the middle of the deep blue of the Mediterranean, just off the coast of Greece. Tourists flocked to it every year and he was sure Andromeda would love it.

Will she, though? She's clearly not enamoured of anything about you.

That didn't matter. He didn't need her to be enamoured of him. He only needed her to agree to be his wife, that was all.

'No,' he said to his brother. 'I haven't told her. She hasn't agreed to marry me yet.'

Asterion made another disapproving sound, and started in with one of his lectures about how paying for a bride wasn't what Dimitra had intended, and how taking shortcuts wasn't a good idea, but Poseidon tuned him out, as he always did when Asterion decided to instruct him on something. His brother sometimes acted as if he was a full ten years older than Poseidon rather than only a minute.

Mainly, though, he tuned out Asterion because his thoughts had once again turned to Andromeda. How she'd paused on her walk out of his office and shrugged, letting his jacket slip from her shoulders and fall to the floor. How she'd glanced at him over her shoulder, gloriously naked apart from that tiny pair of knickers and her body paint, her clear green eyes meeting his.

'My name is Andromeda,' she'd said grandly, as if giving him a gift.

And the curious thing was that it *had* felt like a gift.

Asterion kept talking, while Poseidon again went over the questions she'd asked him about the marriage proposal, and how she'd narrowed her gaze as she'd demanded everything in writing and signed.

She was an excellent businesswoman, he couldn't help thinking. But Asterion was right about one thing: Dimitra wouldn't like it if she found out his marriage was basically a business deal. The whole point was for him to 'woo' the woman Dimitra had chosen, not pay her to be his bride.

In which case, he needed to be seen to be 'wooing'. It wasn't something he was used to doing, since women came to him, not the other way around. Besides, he certainly knew how to get a woman screaming his name. But a) while Andromeda might want him, she certainly wasn't going to admit it to him, and b) he'd already decided he wasn't going to use sex to get what he wanted.

Which meant he was going to have to do things differently. Except how to court a woman he knew nothing about and make it look sincere? At least from the outside?

He couldn't use the obvious gifts—jewellery et cetera—because this woman who could have demanded anything from him in return for her name on the marriage certificate only wanted a donation for her addiction service. It seemed unlikely she'd be happy with, say, an expensive necklace or earrings, or a couture gown. It had to be something that would satisfy Dimitra's nosey tendencies too.

Aren't you jumping the gun? Andromeda hasn't even agreed to do it yet.

That was, alas, true. He'd given her a week to decide, and she could very well refuse, no matter what he offered her, which meant he had to do something that would ensure she didn't. Choice was important to him, but that didn't mean he couldn't influence things a little.

'This is not one of your games, Poseidon,' Asterion growled in his ear, obviously coming to the end of his lecture. 'And you cannot treat it as such.'

With some effort, Poseidon dragged his thoughts back to the conversation at hand. 'Is that disapproval I hear, brother mine? Surely not.'

'You're supposed to *woo* her, not pay her to stand at the altar.'

'Dimitra won't find out that I've paid her,' he said

calmly. 'And I've already told Andromeda that she'll have to act as though she's in love with me. She was fine with it.'

She had *not* been fine with it, of course, but Poseidon could offer her some assistance with that before the actual wedding. Perhaps some practice would be in order. She'd have to get used to him touching her, for example. An arm around her waist, her hand in his, standing close...

You might even have to kiss her.

A burst of unwelcome heat went through him at the thought of that lush mouth under his. Would her taste be tart and sharp like citrus? Or would it be sweet and sugary? It would be hot, that was certain, and her curves under his hands would feel like—

But no. He wasn't going to be doing anything more than giving a brief touch here and there, and maybe a kiss. He wouldn't let himself get carried away. If he was really so worked up that a prickly little siren could get him hard, then he should go and find another woman— someone warm and soft and willing, not spiky and angry. Then again, finding himself a woman now, after Dimitra had chosen Andromeda for him, would risk undermining the illusion of romance he was trying to build. Better to wait until after he'd done his duty.

'I'm sure Andromeda was fine with that,' Asterion said dryly. 'And I'm also sure it'll work out exactly as you expect.'

Poseidon decided to ignore the blatant scepticism in his twin's tone. 'I need to at least make it look like I'm courting her. But she's not the kind of woman who likes jewels, which means I have to do something else.'

There was a silence.

'Wait…' There was a suggestion of amusement in Asterion's deep voice. 'Are you asking me for seduction tips?'

'*Courting* tips,' Poseidon corrected. 'I have to look as if I'm madly in love, and, as you know, I have no experience of that nonsense.'

'Take her to bed,' Asterion said. 'Isn't that what you normally do?'

Another of those unwelcome bolts of heat went through him. All those pretty curves, that smooth skin and passion… She would be fire in his hands, but he could direct it. He could turn all that glory on him and—

'No,' Poseidon said, both to his own thoughts and yet again to his brother, conscious that he was sounding too emphatic about it. 'It's a business deal.'

Another silence fell.

'I see,' Asterion murmured, his tone very neutral. 'Well, if it's a business deal, then I take it you have her agreement? Because you know that as soon as you make any kind of move the media will be onto it.'

Poseidon stilled. 'No,' he said slowly, because Asterion had just given him a very good idea. 'She hasn't agreed…' he paused '…yet.'

'You have a plan.'

It wasn't a question.

'Oh, yes.' Poseidon smiled. 'I have a very good plan indeed.'

Andromeda stared around the rundown waiting room of Chrissy's Hope at the end of the day, a deep feeling of discomfort sitting inside her.

She'd tried to make the place look welcoming, but it was difficult when the only rooms she'd been able to afford for the service were situated in a shabby office block, and there was no money left over for anything resembling decor.

She'd put up a couple of nice pictures of scenery cut from some travel magazines, and there was a small vase of freesias on the rickety table, which she'd nicked from someone's garden. But the plastic chairs she'd rescued from the side of the road, so clients could have somewhere to sit, were scratched, the worn grey paint on the walls drained the pictures of life, and the freesias were drooping.

It was depressing. Hardly living up to the 'hope' in Chrissy's Hope.

Money. You need money. You need Poseidon Teras.

Andromeda scowled harder, then turned and went back behind the second-hand reception desk she'd managed to source for free from a recycled furniture website.

She'd deliberately forgotten about Poseidon Teras for the past few days and she didn't want to remember him now.

You haven't forgotten. Not even deliberately.

She didn't want to admit it. She didn't want to admit that the man had been lurking in her brain, like the monster he was, ever since she'd walked out of his office. His astonishing blue eyes, and the electricity she'd felt when she'd brushed his hand, had seared themselves into her memory...a burn so deep that no amount of running mental cold water on it seemed to get rid of the heat.

Perhaps she hated him a little less than she had, knowing he wasn't ultimately responsible for Chrissy's death and that he'd paid for the funeral, but she still hated him and everything he stood for. And as for this marriage proposal... It was preposterous. How could she even think about taking it seriously?

Men like him never kept their word, and they never did what they promised. Simon, the man Chrissy had met in the VIP area of one of London's more exclusive nightclubs, had promised her the world, yet he'd given her drugs and led her to her doom. Men lied. All the time. And Poseidon was surely no different.

Except he agreed to all your demands, including that he put it all in writing.

True...he had.

Not forgetting his offer of sponsorship indefinitely, not dependent on the marriage...

Andromeda scowled harder. He was using Chrissy's Hope against her to get what he wanted. It was manipulation, pure and simple.

He's not manipulating you into anything but your name on a piece of paper and a bit of theatre. Calm down.

She rearranged the pens beside the pad on the desk, irritated, because that *was* actually true—as much as she hated to admit it. He was a businessman, he'd told her, and he didn't do anything for free. But...well, was what he'd done any different from what she would have done in his shoes? For Chrissy's Hope? He was doing it for his own selfish interests, while her motivations were more altruistic, but she'd have done anything if it meant saving her service. Including manipulating people.

Are your motivations really that altruistic? Aren't you

doing this for you? Because you were silent when you should have spoken up? Because you let Chrissy die?

Andie shoved that thought from her head. She hadn't 'let' Chrissy die. And she *had* spoken up. It hadn't been her fault that their mother hadn't wanted to listen. Miranda had been thrilled for Chrissy, who had been mixing with 'the stars and all the famous people'. Chrissy was 'going places', Miranda had kept insisting, and Andie shouldn't complain about it because that looked like jealousy.

So Andie, fifteen and not knowing where else to turn, had stopped complaining and hoped that her sister would be fine.

Except she hadn't been fine.

It was too late for Chrissy now, but Andie was making up for what she hadn't done back then. All of this was for her sister's sake, not hers. It really was. To stop others from falling down the same addiction hole Chrissy had.

At that moment the waiting room door opened and a couple of men in black suits, with earpieces in their ears, came in. They both scanned the waiting room with professional eyes, then one held the door open, while the other stood at the ready beside it.

Andie stared at them in surprise, only to have the surprise turn to shock when Poseidon Teras strode through the open door.

Instantly a wave of heat washed over her, closely followed by an inevitable wave of anger. Because what on earth was *he* doing here? It hadn't been a week yet, and she still hadn't decided what she was going to do. He had no call to be coming into her place of business as if he owned it.

She shot to her feet, ready to demand the reason for his presence, when he stopped in front of the reception desk, his intense blue gaze fixed on her. With a flourish, he produced the biggest bunch of dark red roses she'd ever seen in her life.

'For you, my lady,' he said, in his deep, warm voice.

Andie blinked, shaken for a second. Flowers. He'd brought her flowers. No one had ever done that before. They were beautiful too, the velvety petals a deep red and with the most gorgeous scent.

'What are these for?' she asked, momentarily taken by surprise.

The beginnings of a smile curled his beautiful mouth. 'Because when a gentleman is courting a lady, he always brings her flowers. Also, I thought it might help your decision along.'

She found herself bristling, though she didn't quite know why. Perhaps because he'd surprised her and she didn't want to be surprised by him. She didn't want him to know he'd surprised her either.

Ignoring the flowers, she said, 'A week. You were going to give me a week to decide.'

'I am,' he agreed. 'I'm not here for an answer, Andromeda. I'm here to give you a token of my appreciation.'

She folded her arms, eyeing him, very conscious once again of how tall he was, how broad. How the force of his charisma was like a storm front blowing in, making everything inside her lift up and get whirled around in utter chaos.

He's like Simon, and you know it.

Simon, who'd led Chrissy down the path she'd followed with such abandon. He'd been rich, charismatic, and one night, after Chrissy had been dropped off home, Andie had peeked out through the curtains of her bedroom window and caught a glimpse of him. He'd been the most beautiful man Andie had ever seen. Chrissy had fallen for him and fallen hard, and that night Andie had fallen for him too. But she'd only been fifteen…a girl… while Chrissy had been twenty and a woman.

She hadn't been jealous—no matter what Miranda had said. She'd known she was too young and that Chrissy was more beautiful, more fascinating than she'd ever be. But she'd been envious. Simon had taken Chrissy into his world of high-society parties, of beautiful gowns and champagne and trips to Monte Carlo, to Paris, to Cannes. And Andie hadn't been able to help wanting that too. To be taken away from the stifling confines of the council flat and the drudgery of school, and her part-time job in the supermarket. Swept off her feet by a handsome man and taken into a bigger, more exciting life.

Until it had all gone to hell.

Poseidon Teras was that kind of hell. He was even richer and more charismatic and more beautiful than Simon had been, and Andie was now a woman. A woman with the same hunger inside her that her sister had had. But, unlike Chrissy, Andie knew what happened when you indulged that hunger. She knew where following men like Poseidon led, and she wasn't going down that path. No matter how beautiful and rich he was.

He was in a dark charcoal suit today, with a white shirt and a tie of emerald silk that caught the green glints in his sea-blue eyes, and it was galling to realise how much she'd been playing down his attractiveness over the past couple of days. Telling herself that surely he hadn't been as beautiful as she'd thought, that it had been merely her fevered imagination.

But, no, he really was as handsome, and his presence made the waiting room seem even more dingy and depressing than it had been a few moments ago.

It was infuriating. She'd tried very hard, and with very limited resources, to get Chrissy's Hope up and running, and naturally all he had to do was step through the doors and it was as if a spell had been broken, revealing the truth that her efforts had been in vain. Nothing she could do with the funds she had was ever going to make this place a success.

She glared at him with open dislike. 'Thank you, but your appreciation isn't necessary. So please take your... token and leave.'

He made no move to do so, leaning against the reception desk instead, as if he was going to stand there all day. 'I allowed my PR department to let slip to the media that I was making a little trip, and I couldn't help but notice that several paparazzi followed me.' He glanced casually towards the front doors. 'I'm sure they'll be curious about why I'm here. I'm sure they'll want to investigate thoroughly and report.' He turned his gaze to the rest of the waiting room. 'They'll also note that I'm carrying a bunch of roses and will assume certain things based on that, since I'm not often seen carrying flowers. There'll be lots of speculation about who they're for and why.' Finally his blue gaze came back to hers. 'All of which adds up to the kind of publicity that thousands of companies pay millions for, wouldn't you say?'

Andie wanted desperately to refute every single one of

his points. But she knew how the media worked as well as he did—she wasn't exactly a novice when it came to getting attention for a cause, after all—and he was right. He was infamous. The press loved him and followed him wherever he went. His presence here would cause a small sensation. The kind of sensation that could be very good for Chrissy's Hope indeed.

'Aren't you afraid they'll think you're an addict?' she asked, since it was all she could think of to say.

'No,' he said dismissively. 'And speculation is part of the point.' He glanced around the room once again and frowned. Then, before she could say anything, he crossed to the rickety table by the plastic chairs, still carrying the roses. 'Look,' he murmured. 'Your poor freesias are a bit the worse for wear.' He took the drooping freesias out of the vase and replaced them with the roses, arranging them in a few quick, deft motions. 'There,' he said. 'Much better.'

Gathering the freesias, he paused a minute, staring critically at the vase, then he plucked out a single rose stem. He glanced at one of his security guards, who was still standing at attention by the door, and the man instantly came over to him.

Poseidon handed him the freesias. 'Dispose of these, please,' he instructed, before strolling leisurely back to the reception desk, holding out the single rose to Andie.

There was a slightly wicked glint in his eyes...the same glint that she'd seen back in his office when they'd first met. It made her heart beat suddenly fast.

'You can surely allow yourself one,' he murmured.

That voice of his...so seductive. The devil himself surely had a voice like that, tempting mortals into sin.

The way Chrissy was tempted. And she gave in.

Her poor sister. But Andie wouldn't make that same mistake. She would resist.

Ignoring the rose, she stared at him. 'What is the point of this? Is it to manipulate me into agreeing to your stupid marriage idea?'

'If by "this" you mean the roses and my visit, then yes,' he agreed calmly, which took the wind out of her sails. 'But, as I said, it's also to generate some media interest in your service. A demonstration, if you will, of what I can do for you. After all, I merely need your presence at the altar and a bit of pretence. While you get...' He paused, looked around the sad waiting room once again, then back at her. 'You get the money and exposure that your very worthy service could use.'

He was correct and she didn't like it that he was. But her not liking it didn't make him any less right. She *could* use the money, and needed it badly. And if it was true, what he said about the publicity his visit here today would bring, then...well. She needed that too.

This is an opportunity. Don't waste it.

It *was* an opportunity—and one she couldn't allow to slip through her fingers. Yes, he was far too attractive for his own good, but that shouldn't get in the way of doing what was right for Chrissy's Hope. Also, he wasn't Simon and she wasn't Chrissy. She wouldn't make the same mistakes.

She would accept his proposal, get the sponsorship deal he'd promised and, with the money, turn Chrissy's Hope into a service that would save lives.

Decision made, Andie took a breath and then reached for the rose Poseidon held out. And once again, even though she hadn't meant them to, her fingers brushed his, a surge of electricity arrowing down her spine, making her breath catch. Sparks of an answering heat glowed suddenly brilliant in his eyes, and for a second every thought in her head vanished.

He wants you, too.

'No,' he murmured, seemingly to himself, so low and quiet she barely heard.

'What did you say?' she asked, her own voice oddly husky.

'I said, are you going to agree, little siren?'

That wasn't at all what he'd said, but she suspected she knew why he'd said 'no' so emphatically. Since it wasn't a subject she wanted to talk about, or even think about, she let it go.

Instead, she put the rose carefully down on the reception desk and met his gaze. 'I'll need what you promised for Chrissy's Hope put into a contract and signed.'

Poseidon smiled, and instantly all her threat senses sprang into high alert. He reached inside his jacket, brought out an envelope, and handed it to her.

'Already done,' he said with some satisfaction. 'I had your lawyers okay it this morning.'

Of course he had. The man was arrogance personified, and then some.

Furious, she snatched the envelope from him—making very sure that this time their fingers didn't touch—and ripped it open. Sure enough, it was a full legal contract detailing her terms, and it had been signed by him.

'Check your email,' he added. 'Your lawyers have sent you their advice.'

'How did you even know who my lawyers were?' Andie demanded.

He lifted one powerful shoulder. 'I have excellent staff who easily found out which firm Chrissy's Hope uses. You can call them if you like, just to be certain.'

She wanted to change her mind, to refuse. She wanted to tell him to take his contract and leave and never come back, because this felt as if he'd somehow outmanoeuvred her and she hated that.

But she couldn't. She'd decided she was going to accept his marriage proposal and she couldn't keep letting her feelings get in the way.

'You're the most arrogant bastard I've ever had the misfortune to meet,' she said at last, because she had to vent those feelings somehow.

He kept right on smiling that devastating smile of his. 'What can I say? It's a gift.' He turned to the door. 'Call me when you've made your decision.'

She wanted to let him walk—she very much did. Because if what he'd said about his grandmother was correct, that he had to marry a woman of her choosing, then she was the woman who'd been chosen. He couldn't just find someone else if she refused. She had the power here, not him.

But it was pointless to wait when she already knew what she was going to do. What she'd been going to do the moment he'd suggested sponsoring Chrissy's Hope back in his office.

'Wait,' Andie said.

He stopped, his back to her, a tall, powerful figure in the shabby waiting room. His head turned slightly. 'Yes?'

'Okay,' she said. 'Yes. I'll marry you.'

He nodded, with his head half turned away. She couldn't see his face. 'I'll send a car for you tomorrow,' he said. 'We can go over the details then.'

Then, before she could make any further comment, he walked out.

CHAPTER FOUR

POSEIDON SAT AT the table on the terrace of his penthouse apartment in the warm summer sun, studying the media reports his PR department had forwarded to him of yesterday's little visit to Andromeda.

There were pictures of him exiting his limo and going into the shabby offices of her addiction service, carrying the big bunch of roses, along with gossipy articles about what the roses meant and who they were for, and what Chrissy's Hope was, and why he was there.

It had been a relatively small performance in the greater scheme of things—a demonstration, as he'd told her, of the kind of attention he could command and what that could potentially mean for her service. Yet it seemed to have had the desired effect, both with the media and with Andromeda.

She'd been hostile initially, as he'd known she would be, standing behind her clearly second-hand reception desk, back straight, chin lifted, as if she was the empress of all she surveyed.

It had been sexy, he had to admit, even though she was fully clothed this time. A pity. Then again, the jeans and T-shirt she'd worn had outlined her curves just as effectively as the body paint, and those curves had been just as delicious as he'd remembered. Her riot of red-gold curls had been gathered in a loose ponytail at her nape, and there'd been the sweetest little scattering of freckles across her nose.

But her eyes had been as sharp as green glass, and just as full of dislike as they had been a few days earlier, and he'd known a second's doubt as he'd handed her the roses. Which was strange. He'd never doubted himself before with a woman—never.

The doubt had only deepened when she'd taken the rose from him and her fingers had once again brushed his. And he'd felt heat surge between them—the same heat that had seared him in that moment in his office a few days earlier. A gut-punch of attraction that he'd found impossible to ignore.

The 'no' had escaped him before he'd been able to think better of it, a reminder to himself that he'd made the decision not to touch her. But she'd heard him. Had she known what he'd meant? He hadn't been sure, but he hadn't bothered to explain. People could use desire to get anything they wanted out of you if you weren't careful, so she didn't need to know he found her beautiful or in any way desirable. That was a power he didn't want to give her. Especially a woman like her, a woman who cared deeply and passionately for her cause, and who would no doubt be willing to do anything for its benefit.

You're manipulating her the way Michel manipulated you. You do realise that, don't you?

No, he'd already told himself that wasn't what he was doing. He'd merely put together a proposal for their mutual benefit, that was all. He wasn't forcing her to sign anything if she didn't want to.

The memory of that dingy, shabby waiting room drifted through his consciousness, with its plastic chairs and the drooping flowers, and the pathetic pictures on the walls, obviously torn from a magazine. She'd clearly tried to make it welcoming, but had only succeeded in making it depressing—and, honestly, the real question was why it had taken her so long to agree to his marriage proposal, given how desperately she needed the money.

Yet she had agreed, finally, and he could still feel the thrill of satisfaction that had gone through him in that moment. A hungry kind of satisfaction, which had disturbed him so much he'd thought it better to leave rather than hash out the details there and then. Satisfaction was allowable, but he had not liked that hunger. It spoke of need, of that void inside him that his father's death had left and that Michel had stepped into.

He wouldn't ever let himself feel that again.

'Mr Teras?'

He looked up from his laptop to see his housekeeper standing in the doorway to the terrace. 'Has Miss Lane arrived, Molly?'

'Yes.'

'Good. Show her out here, if you would.'

Molly nodded, then disappeared back into the penthouse interior.

Andromeda had arrived, as he'd instructed.

He felt an odd leap of something that couldn't possibly be anticipation—because why? He should feel satisfied, yes, as once this marriage issue was over and done with, and the issue of Dimitra's shares settled, he could return to what really mattered, which was his shipping empire. Yet he couldn't deny he was looking forward to seeing Andromeda again.

He wasn't sure why, since she was nothing but sharp edges, and too much dislike could get tiresome, yet there was something about her that fascinated him. Sexual attraction, of course, but also the fire in her that seemed to burn so hotly and so bright. She didn't strike him as being a woman who was afraid of anything. She certainly wasn't afraid of him, and why that was so damn attractive he couldn't say.

He glanced around the terrace to make sure all was in order. Molly had prepared a wonderful morning tea with scones and jam and some clotted cream. The day was warm, too. The scent of lavender from the large pots lining the terrace reminded him of the Teras estate on the island kingdom where he'd grown up.

After Michel he'd left the island, and had avoided it like the plague ever since, only returning once when Dimitra had demanded his presence to lay down her marriage challenge. It wasn't the memories that bothered him—not at all. He never thought of that time. It was only that he'd outgrown the place, that was all. Michel had died a decade ago, and he had no hold on Poseidon—not any more.

'Mr Teras,' Molly said from the doorway. 'Miss Lane is here.'

Poseidon dragged his thoughts away from the past and looked up. Andromeda stood beside his housekeeper wearing a light, airy, flowing dress the colour of spring leaves. Her hair was loose, her red-gold curls a riot down her back, and she wore a quantity of thin silver bracelets around one wrist. Her green eyes, echoing the colour of her dress, met his, and he felt it yet again, that punch of desire, so strong it stole his breath.

She was so beautiful. Had she worn that dress for his benefit? Surely she had. The colour made her skin look pearlescent and her eyes glow. While the loose fit hid her curves, the fabric was so filmy he could see the delicate lines of the pretty lace bra and knickers she wore underneath it.

'Thank you, Molly,' he said, struggling to keep his voice even as he rose from his seat. 'Welcome, Andromeda.' He moved around the table and pulled out the chair opposite his, gesturing to it. 'Please, join me for some tea.'

Molly withdrew, while Andromeda eyed him with her usual suspicion.

He was going to need to do something about that suspicion, because Dimitra would certainly pick up on it—she was sharp like that—and that would expose his little charade.

He smiled. 'There's no need to look at me with such distrust, little siren. I'm only offering tea and scones, not heroin.'

'Don't call me that. I gave you my name.'

He lifted a brow. 'You'd rather not be called after a beautiful woman with a seductive voice?'

Andromeda's gaze narrowed even further. 'I suppose it's better than being called Poseidon.'

He laughed—because, really, no one had made fun of his name since he was a child. No one would dare. Yet of course *she* would.

'There's nothing wrong with being named after the god of the sea,' he said. 'Especially when one owns a highly successful shipping company. A bit disconcerting, I suppose, given your name is Androm—'

'Yes, yes, I know,' she snapped.

Her cheeks had gone pink, which intrigued him. What was she embarrassed about? Or was she angry? Perhaps both?

'But I'm not a helpless princess. And you're not a god.'

'Am I not? The women who scream my name in bed might disagree with you.'

Her flush deepened even more. 'You're the most arrogant—'

'Bastard you've ever met,' he interrupted. 'Yes, so you've said.' He gestured to the chair again. 'Come and sit down. It's perfectly safe to step onto the terrace. Both the floor and this chair are very sturdy.'

She rolled her eyes, but stepped onto the terrace and came over to where he stood behind the chair, stopping next to it. 'You don't have to stand there,' she said. 'I can push my own chair in.'

He looked down at her, since she was shorter than he was by nearly a head, very conscious of how close she was and of her delicate scent...unexpectedly sweet, like vanilla.

You should not let her get this near to you.

No, he should not. Especially when he could now see her bra and knickers even more clearly through the fabric of her dress. He'd thought that perhaps it had been deliberate, but now he'd changed his mind. She'd flushed so deeply when he'd mentioned women screaming his name, maybe she wasn't aware.

'And you can stop looking at my underwear too,' she said, plucking the thought right out of his head.

It took him off-guard so completely that he actually found himself protesting. 'I wasn't looking at your underwear.'

'Of course you were. This dress is a bit see-through, but I had to wear it because all my other clothes were in the wash.' She gave him a very penetrating look. 'And you're a man. You can't help yourself.'

For a long moment Poseidon was so confounded by this bit of truth that he couldn't think of a word to say. Her green gaze was steady, disapproving, as if she didn't care about the fact that her dress was see-through. As if it didn't bother her at all. As if *he* didn't bother her, despite the way she was blushing like a sunset. And suddenly he was seized with an urge to make her bothered, to shake her the way she'd shaken him.

'Were your other clothes really in the wash?' he drawled. 'Or is that dress and the pretty little bra and knicker set for my benefit?'

Instantly emerald sparks glittered in her eyes and her chin lifted. 'Hardly. Why would they be?'

He found he'd taken a step towards her, closing what little distance there was between them, even though he knew it was a stupid idea.

'Because you want my attention, little siren,' he said. 'Why else?'

'I do not.' The pink in her cheeks had deepened still further, bringing out the brilliant clear green of her eyes. She didn't step back, didn't give an inch of ground. 'I can't think of anything worse.'

'Really?' He lifted his hand and cupped her cheek, her skin soft beneath his fingers. 'My attention is the worst thing you can think of?'

She went very still as he touched her, and he heard her breath catch. Her eyes had gone wide, staring up into his, and he thought she'd pull away, but she didn't.

She only stood there, looking up at him as her leaf-green eyes slowly darkened into deep emerald. Time seemed to slow, the air around them becoming thick and crackling with static. Her skin was warm and smooth, like satin pressing against his palm, and he couldn't help sliding his hand along her jaw, into the silky softness of her glorious hair, tilting her head back slightly.

Again, she made no move to pull away, only staring up at him as if mesmerised. Then, suddenly, she rose up on her toes and pressed her mouth to his.

Andie didn't know what had come over her. She'd arrived at his ludicrously expensive city penthouse, her loins girded for battle over this marriage deal, only to find him lounging at a table on the terrace, looking so ridiculously sexy she almost couldn't tear her gaze away.

He looked more casual today, in a plain black business shirt and grey suit trousers, no tie. His shirt was open at the neck and she'd immediately fixated on the smooth, olive skin of his throat and the pulse that beat there, strong and regular. His hypnotic gaze had met hers, and the same heat that had gripped her the day before, when he'd handed her the contract and their fingers had brushed, had gripped her again.

It wasn't fair that he should be so fiercely attractive and it wasn't fair that she should notice. It wasn't fair that she'd found it so hard to resist the draw of him and she had to. She was furious with herself and her physical reaction to him. Furious with him, too, for calling her 'little siren' and looking at her with that knowing blue gaze. Her dress was slightly see-through—yes, she knew that—but it was hot, and she'd wanted to wear something light, and her only clean underwear had been dark.

He shouldn't have been looking at her that way and she shouldn't have liked it. She shouldn't have let slip that she knew he'd been looking. She shouldn't have snapped at him...shouldn't have reacted when he'd taunted her about his attention being the worst thing that she could think of.

She shouldn't have allowed her anger to get the better of her.

Because if she'd controlled it...if she hadn't risen to his bait...he wouldn't have laid his large, warm palm against her cheek, and all the breath wouldn't have left her body. She wouldn't have felt his touch like a lightning bolt, igniting something inside her and making it roar into life, like dry grass to a lit match.

She wouldn't have completely lost her head, wanting to shock him the way he'd shocked her, and risen up on her toes to kiss his beautiful mouth.

But she'd done all of those things. And now it was too late.

Because after a moment of stillness, when she could sense that she'd surprised him, that mouth of his opened, and his fingers tightened in her hair, and he was kissing her, and she was lost.

He tasted of everything dark and sinful and delicious...everything that she knew was bad for her...everything she'd been running from since Chrissy had died. The hunger that she'd always known was inside her, that somehow he'd brought into full, aching life, had her in its grip, and she had her hands on his chest, her palms pressed to his shirt, feeling the hard muscle and heat beneath it before she could think straight.

He made a rough sound and his fingers tightened in her hair, his mouth opening, his tongue exploring her, hot and demanding. She hadn't kissed anyone before, had no idea what she was doing, but she followed his lead, kissing him back as hungrily as he was kissing her.

She felt desperate, taken out of herself, and the only things that mattered were the pulsing ache that had started up between her thighs and the frantic need to touch his bare skin, feel his warmth.

Her fingers curled into his shirt as she pressed herself against him. The heat of his rock-hard body was like a furnace. Some part of her was screaming that this was a terrible idea, that this was the same trap Chrissy had fallen into, but she ignored it. It felt as if her every thought was fracturing under the pressure of her hunger, and she wouldn't be able to think clearly until she'd sated it.

He slid one arm around her waist, holding her to him, and the fingers in her hair opened, so he was cradling the back of her head. He'd gentled the kiss, which was not what she wanted, and she clutched at him, trying to follow his mouth as he lifted it from hers.

'Little siren,' he murmured against her lips. His deep voice had gone rough, as if he too felt the same hunger she did. 'Keep kissing me like that and we're going to end up in my bed, and I need you to be very sure that's where you want to be before that happens.'

Someone was breathing fast and hard and Andie was suddenly aware that it was her, and also that she was shaking. Her mouth felt hot and sensitive, and the rich, woody, spicy scent of him had lodged somewhere deep inside her.

In his bed. Did she want that?

Of course you do. You're just like Chrissy...too hungry...and if you're not careful you'll get into the same spiral she did.

Poseidon Teras was everything she was supposed to avoid, not throw herself at. How could she have forgotten that so completely?

Andie pushed herself away from him, turning so he wouldn't see how hard it was to pull herself together. He was silent, making no move to touch her as she took a couple of deep breaths, struggling for control.

'I'm sorry,' she said. 'That was my fault. I shouldn't have kissed you.'

Because it *was* her fault. She'd let herself get too angry and it had backfired spectacularly.

Bracing herself for him to say something insufferably smug and arrogant, she was surprised when he said, 'No, you shouldn't have.'

She glanced at him, because she'd clearly offended him—which was strange, because surely women throwing themselves at him wasn't anything new.

Yet it wasn't offence burning in his eyes, but fire. An intense blue flame that made the hunger inside her pull on its leash.

'We have chemistry, Andromeda.' His voice was flat, with no humour in it, no trace of his usual charming smile or dry tone. 'And it's volatile. So if you don't want to end up flat on your back with me inside you, perhaps it would be best if you kept your distance.'

She shivered, the image his blunt words had conjured up making her dry-mouthed with want, but she forced the feeling aside and nodded. He didn't say anything else, moving past her to sit down at the other end of the table as if nothing untoward had happened.

Yet she felt as if the world had shifted on its axis... as if the ground under her feet wasn't as steady as she'd thought and now every step was suspect.

What had she done? Why? What was so special about him that made her forget every rule she'd given herself since Chrissy had died?

That kiss... She'd tasted something in him, something passionate and raw that had been the same hunger she'd felt herself. It was as if some part of her had recognised a part of him and seen a kindred spirit. Except that made no sense. He was nothing like her—nothing at all. He cared about nothing and no one, and the kiss had probably been a cynical way to—

You *kissed him. And he was the one who stopped it.*

He hadn't taken advantage of the moment by using her hunger against her in some way. Unlike Simon, who'd used Chrissy's infatuation with him to draw her deeper and deeper into his world.

Still, that didn't make Poseidon a good man—though he was right about one thing. They did have chemistry, and she really did need to keep her distance from him.

Unless you want to end up in his bed?

No, she *didn't* want that. Not at all.

Slowly, she moved over to the chair he'd been standing behind and sat down.

His beautiful face was drawn in hard lines, his finely carved mouth—that beautiful mouth she'd just kissed—was unsmiling. He looked stern. And there was a definite chill in his blue eyes...a stormy blue with no green at all.

That kiss had been a mistake and they both knew it.

'Tea?' he asked, his voice very neutral. 'A scone, perhaps?'

'No, thank you.' She wished her own voice didn't sound quite so husky, but there was nothing she could do about it.

He didn't insist, pouring himself tea and adding a touch of milk. Then he picked up one of the fluffy-looking scones in a long-fingered hand and put it on a plate, deftly cutting it in half.

'So,' he said, as he began to butter it in a leisurely fashion. 'You understand that before our marriage a period of courtship will need to take place? In order to convince my darling grandmother that this is a real marriage.'

It was clear they weren't going to talk about that kiss again, which was good, since she definitely didn't want to talk about it. But, still, it was difficult to get her mind back on track when her mouth still felt sensitised, and her heartbeat was going like a drum, and the ache between her thighs was insistent.

She wanted to get angry, because anger was familiar, but she couldn't seem to grab hold of it.

A good thing. That's not useful to you now.

It was true. Letting it control her around him was not a good idea, and, besides, they needed to talk about this whole marriage deal. No point starting off negotiations with fury.

'Yes,' she said. 'I understand.'

'Good.' He picked up a silver bowl and proceeded to spread jam on the scone. 'So, I propose a few public appearances, so the media are clear we are an item. Two should do it, I would think. Then I'll have my PR people issue a press release about our upcoming wedding.'

Andromeda felt something inside her tense. *Public appearances.* She supposed it made sense, since they were supposed to be actually in love, but she didn't like it. What would it mean for Chrissy's Hope if she was seen with him? Exposure, yes, but for an addiction service, and he was a notorious playboy. How would that look?

'Can we not just get married?' she asked, trying not to sound reluctant. 'Do we need to have any public appearances?'

'Dimitra is by nature suspicious,' he said. 'And I fear that me marrying you a week after she chose you for me won't be a convincing enough love story for her.'

He'd finished with the jam and now picked up another bowl full of delicious-looking clotted cream.

'She will also insist on us marrying in the church on the island kingdom where I grew up, by the way. It's in the Mediterranean...not too far by plane.'

Andromeda's vision of a quickie wedding at a register office quickly vanished. 'So, you're talking about...?'

'A white gown, walking down the aisle, vicars, heavenly choirs—yes, the whole nine yards.' He gently laid a scoop of cream on his scone. 'Necessary theatre in this instance.'

Andie had never envisaged herself as a bride, never had dreams of a white wedding, never thought she'd walk down the aisle. Not after her sister had died. Simon had given Chrissy vague hints about taking their relationship to 'the next level', or so she'd told Andie, and Chrissy had been starry-eyed about it. She'd been the one with the white wedding dreams, thinking Simon was the love of her life.

Except he hadn't been. He'd taken her to parties, given

her drugs, and then suggested that sleeping with his friends would be an easy and quick way for her to earn money. And that had been the end of Chrissy's dreams.

The fury inside Andie at the injustice of it all, which had been burning sullenly for years, flickered back into life again. But this time, instead of reaching for it, she tried to ignore it.

Chrissy wouldn't get a white wedding, but if Andie did what Poseidon wanted, and participated in his 'necessary theatre', then she could help other women like Chrissy—women in desperate situations. That was more important than her rage.

So all she said was, 'Okay. I can do that. So what kind of appearances are we talking about here?'

'Probably a couple of events. Hopefully the exposure will have some positive implications for your service.'

'Yes, I'm sure being seen with a notorious playboy billionaire will help my service,' she couldn't help saying tartly.

He gave her a cool look. 'I'm not an addict.'

'But you're also not known for your abstemious lifestyle.'

'Does it matter? There's no such thing as bad publicity, Andromeda, or haven't you heard?'

He was right. Chrissy's Hope needed the exposure, regardless of who he was, and without him being who he was she'd be back at square one.

She let out a breath. 'I don't want it to look like I'm selling out.'

He'd gone back to his scone, but now he looked up from it, and for a second amusement lit his blue eyes. 'Oh, dear. Have I become "the man"?'

He'd been so serious just before that his sudden amusement now caught her off-guard, almost coaxing a brief smile of her own out of her. It felt unfamiliar to smile. To find something even mildly funny. In fact, she couldn't remember the last time she had. Everything had been so very serious since Chrissy had died, and so desperate. It still felt that way—mainly because it *was* desperate. Other lives were at stake here and she couldn't joke about it.

Except she couldn't resist saying, 'If I was working for you, then you would indeed be "the man". But since I'm not, you're just "a" man.'

His expression relaxed, his mouth curving into a suggestion of that devastating smile, hints of fascinating green glinting in his eyes, and she felt something shift inside her. Because it was a natural smile, as if she'd surprised it out of him, and for some reason that made her feel a little less desperate and a little less angry.

'I'm not just *a* man, little siren,' he said. 'I'm the god of the sea.' He pushed the plate with the scone on it in her direction. 'Here, have a scone.'

The god of the sea indeed. She wanted to tell him he was being ridiculous, and that she didn't want a scone, but for some reason she reached out and pulled the plate closer. She hadn't had any lunch and the scone did look delicious.

'So how will you be at acting as if you're madly in love with me?' he asked, leaning back in his chair and watching her. 'As opposed to, say, acting as if you want to bury my body where no one will ever find it.'

She eyed him. 'I don't look at you like that.'

'Perhaps not,' he murmured. 'At least not all the time.'

Just for a moment the reminder of that kiss burned between them, hot and hungry and desperate. And, no, she hadn't looked at him as if she wanted to kill him then. She'd looked at him as if she wanted to eat him alive.

Her cheeks felt hot, but she wasn't going to look away or act as if it hadn't happened. 'If you're referring to the kiss, that was a one-off thing.'

He shrugged. 'Then you'll have to pretend.'

Andie let out an irritated breath. This was going to be even more annoying than she'd thought. She wasn't good at pretending, because it felt dishonest, and she hated dishonesty.

Is it pretending, though? You do *want him.*

She wished she could deny it, but that would be lying to herself, and that was dishonest too. So, yes, she did want him. But that wasn't love, and pretending to be in love with Poseidon felt wrong. It was a deception, and it wasn't just the media they were deceiving, but also his grandmother.

'I don't like lying to people,' she said, just so he was clear. 'And this is one big lie.'

'Yes,' he agreed. 'It is. But in this instance it's a small lie for the greater good. No one will be hurt by it, for example, and certainly for you lives could be saved.'

This was all very true and, loath as she was to admit it, he did have a point. 'Your grandmother will be hurt if she finds out,' she said.

'But she won't find out if we're careful.' He nodded to the scone. 'You're hungry. I can tell. And that scone is looking very good to you right now, isn't it?'

'Yes, I suppose so.'

'So…' He smiled 'Look at me as if I'm that scone.'

Andie blinked. 'What?'

'You're eyeing that scone as if you can't wait to eat it. That's the way a woman should look at the man she loves, hmm?' He tilted his head, and the blue of his eyes intensified. 'Alternatively, you could look at me the way you did just before you kissed me.'

And it was back—the hot, bright crackling energy that arced between them, making her breath catch, her heart beat far too fast, and the pressure between her thighs ache.

'Yes,' he breathed, his gaze holding her captive. 'Just like that.'

She should look away, and yet she couldn't bring herself to. It felt like a concession, and she wasn't prepared to give him one, not when he was so powerful already.

So she held his gaze and kept on holding it, daring him to look away first.

'Andromeda,' he murmured, her name sounding deep and rough. 'You are playing with fire.'

'Why? Is it yourself you don't trust or me?'

'Do you want to be in my bed?'

His voice wound around her, the rough heat in it making her shiver.

'I warn you that's where you're going to end up if you keep looking at me like that.'

A dark shiver went through her, and a kind of recklessness followed on behind it. He was so sure of himself, and so certain about what she wanted and what she didn't. But what did he know? He knew nothing about her.

'Is that a promise or a threat?' she asked.

The look in his eyes became focused, intent. 'What do you want it to be?'

You are *playing with fire.*

Maybe she was, but that wild recklessness was deepening its claws in her, making her want to push and keep pushing, prove her power over him. And she did have power over him—she could see that. His knuckles were white where he gripped the arms of his chair, and a muscle jumped in the side of his strong jaw. He looked as if he was struggling to hold himself back, and he was so unbearably sexy like this she could hardly stand it.

His intensity drew her like a moth to a flame.

The same way Simon drew you. The same way he drew Chrissy.

She tore her gaze from his as the thought hit her, her heart thumping uncomfortably loud in her ears. By looking away she'd conceded ground, she knew. She'd given up a piece of her power. But continuing to stare at him was madness.

She needed to get out—leave. Get some space. Figure out how to deal with him. Because getting angry wasn't it. It only led her further into the trap.

She risked a brief glance across the table at him, and once again she found him looking back. Their gazes clashed, held.

'I think you should probably leave,' Poseidon said, in a voice that was deeper and rougher than she remembered.

'Yes,' she said hoarsely. 'I think you're probably right.'

So she thrust her chair back, got to her feet, turned around and left.

Before she did something stupid.

CHAPTER FIVE

POSEIDON STOOD OUTSIDE the front door of the rundown flat where Andromeda lived, his limo waiting at the kerb. Normally he'd have sent his driver to announce his arrival, but tonight he wanted to meet Andromeda at the door himself.

He was here to collect her for their first appearance together—a child poverty fundraiser at the Natural History Museum—and they'd already had a fraught phone call a couple of days earlier, when he'd given her the details of the event, and she'd argued with him about the outfit he'd sent her, since he was sure she didn't have a wardrobe full of event wear at the ready.

He'd known she'd argue with him and he'd relished it, even though he knew he shouldn't. Even though he knew encouraging the sparks they drew from each other was a mistake. She'd agreed at last that a dress from a high street chain store wasn't going to cut it at a glittering, star-studded event, but then tried to insist on choosing her own dress. He'd offered her an alternative, her modelling a selection for him, which she'd declined. It had only been after a good fifteen minutes of back and forth that she'd accepted that, since he attended these events all the time, he had a better idea of what kind of dress was appropriate than she did.

He'd taken his time choosing the perfect gown. Green, naturally, for her eyes, and simple—nothing that would detract from her glorious figure or her hair. Silk, of course, with a drape, and a sheen that would complement her skin and feel nice to wear.

Eventually he'd settled on something beautiful and had it sent to her, and had braced himself for yet more argument. But the only reply he'd received was that it had arrived and it fitted. That was all.

Now, he stood on the doorstep, every muscle in his body drawn so tight with anticipation it was almost painful. Though, to be fair, he'd felt that way ever since the glory that had been her kiss a week earlier. He'd never had a woman tie him up in such knots before, and with only a kiss. Quite honestly, he couldn't understand it. Her kiss had been unpractised and uncertain, a little hesitant. Yet after that first moment it had blossomed into something so hot and sweet he hadn't been able to resist her. She hadn't tasted like citrus, but strawberries, and then she'd pressed all those delectable curves against him, and he'd felt the flame of her burn bright between his hands—

No. He had to stop going over it. He'd been doing so for days, the memory catching him at the most inappropriate times, in meetings with shareholders, while he was trying to concentrate on reports, or troubleshooting staffing issues. It was getting tiresome, especially when he knew he had only himself to blame. He hadn't been going to touch her, yet he'd cupped her cheek in his hand, unable to resist the temptation, and her skin had been so warm. Then her eyes had darkened. He'd been going to pull away, put some distance between them, but then she'd risen on her toes and pressed her mouth to his before he'd even known what she was doing.

It had shocked him. Then he'd been shocked again as the most intense heat had risen inside him, a hunger he'd had no name for, which had reminded him of long ago. It should have been enough for him to step away, but he hadn't. There had been something between them more than physical attraction, something deeper, and he hadn't be able to resist.

A mistake.

And a hell of a mistake. Because now he couldn't stop thinking about it, about her, and about that kiss and how he wanted more.

You weren't going to sleep with her, remember?

Poseidon bit off a curse and pressed her doorbell again, impatient. He definitely *wasn't* going to sleep with her, and that was all there was to it. Her kiss might have set him on fire, and he might still be burning even a week later, but those flames weren't going anywhere. He'd bank the embers until he could let them burn at a later date, with someone more appropriate. Someone who wasn't her.

Finally, the door was pulled open and Andromeda stood in the doorway. All the breath left his body.

He'd known she'd look beautiful in the gown he'd picked, but he hadn't known she'd look *quite* so beautiful.

The gown was simple, cut on the bias so it hugged her figure, curving around her breasts, hips, and thighs before swirling out into full skirts just above her knee. Tiny straps over her pale shoulders held it up, and the neckline draped beautifully over her breasts. The rich silk was the same clear leaf-green as her eyes and, as he'd thought, she looked like a wood nymph or the goddess of spring personified. Her hair was loose in artfully styled curls down her back, framing her angular face in the most flattering way.

Poseidon couldn't think of a woman he'd escorted anywhere who was lovelier.

She gave him a challenging stare, as if daring him to make some comment, her sharp chin lifted, but even the expression on her face couldn't detract from the overall effect of the gown.

'You're beautiful,' he said simply. 'You take my breath away.'

Her lush mouth parted and her eyes widened, a blush rising to her cheeks.

He was a practised flirt, and yet he was aware that there had been nothing practised about what he'd just said. And he meant it. She *had* taken his breath away. And that was a dangerous thing to admit. It was honest. Perhaps it was too honest.

'Thank you,' she said, and glanced down at the clutch in her hand, fussing with it a moment, before looking up at him again. 'Well? Shall we go?'

He'd flustered her, he could see. Good. If he'd slipped up with an honesty he hadn't meant to reveal, she could be bothered by it in a way she hadn't expected.

Wordlessly, he held out an arm and, to his surprise, she laid one small hand on it without protest, letting him escort her to the limo. He opened the door and she got in, then he followed, shutting it behind him and enclosing them both in the warm interior.

He was almost unbearably conscious of her sitting next to him, not touching, but close, one silk-covered

thigh next to his. He could feel her warmth, the light vanilla scent of her perfume wrapping sweetly around him.

He forced himself to ignore it. Bringing her to the
gala was for show and for show only. Nothing would be
happening between them.

*And when she looks at you the way she looked at you
on the terrace last week? Just before she kissed you?
How are you going to resist then?*

He just would. He wasn't a teenage boy at the mercy
of his hormones. He was a grown man who'd been controlling himself easily for years, and one pretty activist
wasn't going to change that.

'I meant what I said,' he murmured into the heavy silence. 'You *do* look beautiful in the gown.'

She pulled a face. 'It's too tight, and the fabric pulls
weirdly, and it's also far too expensive. You could have
let me choose the dress myself.'

'It's true, I could,' he agreed. 'But in the end I decided on the more irritating path and chose it for you.
You're welcome.'

She snorted and looked away out of the window. 'I'm
not keeping it. I'm going to donate it.'

Poseidon stared at her, thinking about the shabby waiting room of Chrissy's Hope and the rundown exterior of
her flat. The dress she'd worn the last time he'd seen her
because all her other clothes were in the wash.

She didn't have much, he suspected, and yet instead of
being concerned about herself, she expended all her energy crusading on behalf of others. He wondered why. He
wondered why she was so angry, so full of fury and sharp
edges and ferocity. It was for her sister, he was sure.

Don't get interested. You're not supposed to care.

He didn't. He was just…curious, and their time together would go easier if they weren't at each other's throats all the time.

'You're allowed to have nice things, you know,' he murmured.

She turned her head. 'What do you mean? What nice things?'

'The dress. It's yours. If you like it, keep it.'

'Why would I want to?' There was a belligerent look on her face. 'It's completely inappropriate. Also, I have nowhere to wear it, and I—'

'You like it, don't you?' Poseidon interrupted as the realisation caught him.

A wild rush of colour stained her cheeks. 'No, I don't. Why would you say that?'

'Because you're expending so much effort denying it.' He was conscious of a certain satisfaction rolling through him, that she liked what he'd chosen for her after all. 'It does make me want to know why, though. After all, the entire world won't collapse if you like wearing a pretty silk gown. Is it because it's expensive or because I bought it for you?'

A shadow moved across her face, gone so fast he wasn't sure he'd seen it at all.

She looked down at the green silk clutch in her hands. 'You wouldn't understand.'

It wasn't a denial this time. Interesting…

'Try me,' he said.

She was silent a moment, still staring down at the clutch in her hands. Then she said, 'My sister and I came from nothing. Our mother was a single parent and we never had much money. Chrissy hated being poor. She wanted more—something better, something that wasn't a council flat and a life spent slaving away in a dead-end job. So when she met a man—Simon—who showered her with expensive presents, who partied with celebrities, who showed her a world she wanted to be part of... Well, she fell for him.' Slowly, Andromeda's lashes lifted and she looked at him. 'And in the end it killed her.'

The words were a shock, as she'd no doubt intended them to be. He also didn't miss the accusatory note in her voice.

'I had nothing to do with your sister's death,' he said. 'I told you that.'

'It was still your yacht. And how are you any different from Simon? He bought her pretty dresses, jewellery, holidays in Paris and Rome. Took her on private planes and to exclusive nightclubs where they only drank the best champagne. Then he introduced her to the best drugs and got her hooked, before pimping her out to all his friends.'

She threw the words like stones, as if he was a glasshouse and she was trying to break each and every one of his windows. He could understand why. He'd somehow become emblematic of the man who'd hurt Chrissy, who'd led her to her death, hadn't he? And now Andromeda was taking her anger out on him.

'You think I'm the same kind of man?' he asked, just to be clear. 'Because I'm rich and I bought you a gown?'

She was sitting rigid in the seat, green eyes sharp, and she didn't flinch. 'They were all like that—all his rich, powerful friends. None of them helped her on that yacht when she took that overdose. And none of them cared.'

He shouldn't want to prove to her that he wasn't like

them. What did her opinion matter? Yet somehow it was important to him that she understood that he *was* different. But also...was this really about the gown? Or did it have more to do with the fact that she liked it and didn't want to admit it? Was she afraid? Was that it? And, if so, what was she afraid of?

He studied her a moment. 'Liking the gown I bought you doesn't automatically lead directly to an overdose on my yacht—you know that, don't you?'

Her colour deepened and he knew that he'd got it right. She *was* afraid, and not of him.

'Firstly,' he went on, not waiting for her to waste time denying it, 'while it's true I am rich, and fairly powerful, and I do like to buy women pretty dresses and jewellery, I don't do drugs. Nor have I ever bought drugs for anyone else. Secondly, I have never pimped anyone out to my friends, and if I knew of anyone who had I'd take him out into a dark alleyway and show him the error of his ways in painful detail.'

She took a little breath, her jaw tight. 'I've only got your word for that.'

He still couldn't understand why it was important that she believe him. Perhaps it was only that she had to stop thinking he was the devil incarnate every time he opened his mouth so that this little game they were playing for Dimitra's benefit would work.

'I know. Nevertheless, it's true. I'm not Simon, Andromeda. And you're not your sister either.'

She kept on staring at him. The atmosphere in the limo was taut and crackling with a familiar electricity. Then she tore her gaze away and looked down at her hands again.

'I'm still going to donate the dress.'

Did that mean she believed him? The fact that she'd changed the subject was proof enough, he supposed. She didn't like giving in, that was clear.

'You can send the dress on a rocket ship to the moon for all I care,' he said. 'But I suggest not biting my head off every time we meet. Why make this harder than it needs to be?'

She was silent for a long moment and then, slowly, the tension began to bleed out of her. 'You're right,' she said at last. 'I'll try.' She lifted her gaze to his again. 'So. What do I have to do at this event?'

He was tempted to ask her more about her sister, though again he wasn't sure why, when getting to know her wasn't part of this deal. He only needed her presence, not her history, so he let it go.

'You don't have to do anything but stand next to me and look adoring.'

She rolled her eyes. 'Really?'

'We do have to look as if we're in love, little siren. And generally people who are in love look at each other with some degree of adoration...' He hesitated, and then added, 'They don't tend to stand apart from each other either.'

Another blush stole across her cheeks. 'What are you saying?'

The strange intensity that had been gripping him all week coiled through him once again at the thought of getting close to her. Of touching her. Because of course he'd have to touch her. They were supposed to look as if they were in love, after all.

'You'll probably have to stand close to me.' He tried to

keep the intensity out of his voice. 'And I'll have to put my arm around you, hold your hand, et cetera.'

They were only stage directions, not promises. Because that's all it was, a performance for the media and Dimitra, nothing more. Yet…the anticipation that gripped him at the thought of her touch, and of him touching her, was making all the blood in his body rush below his belt.

Her eyes glittered like jewels in the dim interior of the limo. 'Will I have to kiss you?'

A shock went through him. He hadn't expected her to bring up that subject, especially given how flustered she'd been by the kiss she'd given him on the terrace. And she *had* been flustered. After all, he'd been the one to stop it, not her.

You could have had her in your bed and you both know it.

She wouldn't have objected if he'd picked her up and carried her inside—not given how she'd followed his mouth as he'd tried to break it off, her fingers curling into his shirt. It had only been when he'd given her time to think that she'd pushed herself away from him.

He should do the same thing now. Look away, break the hold this chemistry had on them both. Yet he didn't.

'I should think so,' he murmured. 'The media will probably insist.' He lifted one brow. 'Is that going to be a problem for you?

Of course it was going to be a problem for her, but Andie wasn't going to admit that to him. Not when he sat next to her with all the casual arrogance that was a part of him, looking particularly devastating in black evening clothes that suited his dark, fallen angel looks to perfection.

Her heart was beating so loudly she could hardly hear anything else, and the warmth of his body and the scent of his aftershave was making her dizzy and dry-mouthed with want.

She shouldn't have been so prickly with him. He was right about not biting his head off every time they met— not if they were supposed to look as if they were in love. But she'd been on edge the whole week, and seeing him again hadn't done anything to make it easier.

She hadn't been able to stop thinking about the kiss, no matter what she'd been doing, and the calls she'd been getting from the media with questions about her 'relationship' with Poseidon Teras hadn't helped. She'd been issuing a steady stream of 'no comments' to each one, except when they asked about Chrissy's Hope, and she was tired of it. She was tired of thinking about how his mouth had tasted and how his body had felt when she'd pressed herself against him, and how much she'd wanted to bury her face in his neck and inhale him.

Their argument on the phone about the event, and his high-handedness in buying her a dress, had helped let off a bit of steam—until the dress had arrived, that was, and had been the most beautiful thing she'd ever seen in her entire life.

She remembered watching Chrissy dress in the pretty things that Simon had bought for her, secretly burning with envy, wishing she had someone who would buy her such lovely things too. She'd cut that envy out of her heart after Chrissy had died. She had told herself that she didn't need any expensive, pretty items, that she could get a perfectly lovely dress from the charity shop down the road. But as soon as the gown had been delivered all those firm instructions to herself had gone out of the window.

The silk had felt so soft, and the sheen of it had caught the light, making her chest ache. She'd punished herself by not taking it out of the dustcover for a few days, and then told herself not to be so stupid, that she had to try it on to see if it fitted. And of course it did. Like a glove. It flattered her, too, and the teenager she'd once been, who'd been so envious of her sister, had gloried in its beauty, feeling like a princess.

She hadn't indulged that, putting the gown away until the day of the gala had come around, and she'd told herself she was forcing herself to wear it. That she didn't like it and she'd tell him so too, so he knew he shouldn't buy her anything else.

Then, of course, he'd looked so devastatingly handsome, and had first of all unsettled her by telling her how stunning she looked, then by somehow seeing that, no matter what she told herself, she *did* like the dress and didn't want to admit it.

God, he was so annoyingly perceptive. She shouldn't have told him all those details about Chrissy, but she'd wanted him to stop asking questions and shock him into silence. But if he'd been shocked, he hadn't shown it. He'd only told her that he wasn't like Simon in any way. She hadn't wanted to believe him, but there had been nothing but truth in his blue gaze. He might be a notorious playboy, but he hadn't done any of the things that Simon had done to Chrissy, and something inside her was telling her that he wouldn't either.

He *wasn't* Simon, as he'd said, and she wasn't Chrissy, and whatever was between them, it didn't mean she'd end up going the same way as her sister. She had to stop snapping at him too, no matter how much he got under her skin. And he *was* getting under her skin—she could admit that now. Sitting next to her with that intense blue gaze on hers, the full force of his charisma directed at her. Everything about him unsettled her, including her own response to him.

Because she could feel it even now, after a week of trying to forget that kiss. All she had to do was look at him to feel his beautiful mouth on hers, the hard length of his body pressed against her curves, and the relentless, driving ache between her thighs that left her restless at night.

You're not the only one, though, remember? He feels it too.

He'd told her if she didn't stop looking at him she'd end up flat on her back with him inside her.

So she wasn't sure why she'd mentioned the kiss again—not when she knew what a Pandora's box that would open up. Then again, he was the one who'd mentioned having to touch one another, which he wasn't wrong about, since they were pretending they were in love.

You wanted to shake him, though. Don't lie. Like you did on the terrace.

Sadly, that was true. Yet she shouldn't give in to the temptation to do so, especially when she knew what had happened last time. Still, they weren't alone in his penthouse now. They were in a limo on the way to an event. So what did it matter if she pushed him just a little? Men used sex to manipulate women all the time, so why shouldn't she give him a taste of his own medicine?

'No, kissing you won't be a problem.' She raised a brow in deliberate imitation of him. 'Did you think it would be?'

A blue flame ignited in his eyes. 'Well, you barely held yourself back from ravishing me on the terrace last week,' he murmured, his voice low and velvety. 'And *that* would not be appropriate at a gala fundraiser for child poverty.'

He might be rich and powerful, but he wants you. You could use that.

No, she wouldn't use that. Chrissy had used the power of her beauty, her sexuality, to earn herself the money she'd craved, and it had ended up backfiring on her. She'd become the one being used instead of vice versa. Yet another mistake Andie wasn't going to make.

'Are you ever serious about anything?' she snapped, forgetting that she wasn't supposed to snap at him for a moment. 'Not everything is a joke.'

Something shifted in his gaze, though she couldn't tell what it was. 'Of course it is, little siren. Life itself is just one big joke. Didn't you know that?'

'Why? Has everything in your life been so easy that child poverty is funny to you? Is that what it is?'

The flame in his eyes glittered. 'Easy...' he murmured, as if tasting the word. 'Everything in my life has been easy? Interesting word, that.'

'Of course it's been easy for you,' she said heedlessly. 'You're rich, powerful. You're drowning in privilege and you're—'

'My parents and my grandfather were killed in a car accident when I was twelve,' he interrupted flatly. 'My brother and I were in the car when it happened and we barely made it out alive. So, yes, you might very well say I'm drowning in privilege. The Teras family isn't exactly without means. But nothing about my life has been *easy*.'

She knew that about his family of course—most people did. But that he'd lost his parents at such a terrible age had only been a fact to her. Something she'd read in a bio. Not an actual event that had happened to a young boy. Yet it had. She could see the shadows of it in his blue eyes, and in the sudden burning anger beneath it.

Instantly, she felt awful. 'I didn't mean—'

'Then what *did* you mean? Perhaps you'd also like to know the details about the friend of my father who—' He broke off suddenly and, much to her surprise, looked away. 'What does it matter? You see what you want to see. Anyway, yes, life is one big joke. That's why Hydra Shipping donates to charities and why I attend so many fundraising galas. Because it's amusing to me, that's all.'

She stared at the pure line of his profile, seeing the tension in his jaw and shoulders. His voice had lost its harshness, but there was no warmth or amusement in it, no matter what he said about jokes, and for some reason she felt chastened.

She'd judged him, and harshly, and while part of her felt defensive about it, another kept whispering that maybe she'd been unfair. That he might be many things, but she couldn't keep sniping at him just because she was attracted to him and didn't like it.

He has lost people too, don't forget.

His parents and his grandfather. And she knew what it was like to lose a family member. The pain never left you.

Impulsively, she reached out and touched his thigh. 'I'm sorry,' she said. 'I'm too quick to judge sometimes.'

He went very still. 'Are you, indeed? I never would have guessed.'

Had she hurt him? She'd definitely offended him. Which shouldn't matter to her, because offending the privileged and shocking them was part of what she'd set out to do after Chrissy had died. But she didn't like the thought that she'd hurt him.

'I shouldn't be, I know,' she said, forcing herself to hold his gaze. 'I just…don't trust men in general. And so far I haven't met any who've made me change my mind.'

'Don't go pinning your hopes on me, little siren. I'm no better than the rest.'

Except she couldn't help thinking back to when he'd called her up to his office the day they'd met, when she'd only been wearing body paint. He'd put his jacket around her and hadn't looked at her body. Plenty of other men would have, and they wouldn't have cared if she'd noticed. But he hadn't. And when she'd kissed him, instead of taking advantage of her, he'd been the one to stop it, to warn her that it wasn't a good idea.

'Maybe not,' she said. 'But you're certainly not any worse—and, believe me, I've seen the worst.'

He stared at her, that flame still flickering in his gaze. 'I am sorry about your sister, Andromeda,' he said abruptly. 'Losing someone you love is very painful.'

For half a second a moment of understanding flowed between them, a shared acknowledgment of loss that eased something tight inside her. Then she became aware that her fingertips were still resting on his thigh, and beneath the expensive wool of his trousers she could feel the hard muscle and power of him. He was very warm. She was filled with the urge to slide her hand across that hard thigh of his and touch that other, very male part of him. To feel if he was as hard there as he was everywhere else.

His gaze gleamed brighter, as if he knew exactly what she was thinking. 'Yes,' he murmured. 'You can touch me. I won't bite.'

Insanity, of course. Utter madness. She should take her hand away immediately. Except...she couldn't quite bring herself to.

Then, when he gently picked up her hand and moved it to where she wanted it to be, so that her palm was pressed against his fly, she kept it there. And he *was* hard beneath her hand...so very, *very* hard...and he watched her, his blue gaze full of flames.

What would it be like to burn with him?

'We are here, Mr Teras,' the driver said.

Heat flooded through her as she realised that the limo had stopped and there were cameras going off outside. The driver was looking in his rear-view mirror and she still had her hand over Poseidon Teras's fly.

Andie made to pull her hand away, but he simply shifted her palm off him without fuss, as if it had been some innocuous touch and not her feeling how badly he wanted her.

'Well, little siren?' His gaze glittered in the lights coming through the window. 'Are you ready to show the world how in love with me you are?'

CHAPTER SIX

POSEIDON WAS FAIRLY sure Andromeda Lane was going to kill him at some point, and he had no one to blame but himself. He was the one who'd looked into her eyes and known exactly what she wanted—because he knew when a woman wanted him. So he'd told her that she could touch him. And when she'd blushed fiercely, he'd taken her hand and put it where they'd both wanted it to be.

She hadn't pulled away. She'd kept her palm there, resting lightly, a warm pressure that had made it almost impossible for him to breathe.

He shouldn't have done it. It had been a temptation too far. Yet he'd been caught in the moment, tangled up in the want and the heat he'd seen in her eyes.

Now he was going to have to get out of this limo with a hard-on in full view of the press. Not that he hadn't done such things before, though it was usually in the context of a night out at a nightclub or a celebrity party, rather than a gala fundraiser for children. Then again, maybe it wouldn't be the end of the world if people noticed. They'd assume certain things about Andromeda and his feelings for her, which would all work in nicely for their little game of pretence.

Your physical reaction to her isn't pretence.

Oh, *that* wasn't. He wanted her. He'd wanted her from the moment he'd first seen her, wearing nothing but body paint and holding a megaphone. That had been a purely physical attraction, it was true, yet now he was starting to find other things about her attractive as well—things that weren't to do with her beauty. Which was dangerous.

For example, not only was she beautiful and fierce, with a passionate heart, she'd also been quick to apologise when he'd let her judgement matter a little too much for comfort. He shouldn't have let it get under his skin in the first place, of course, but her assumptions about him had a hit a nerve he hadn't realised was there.

And she'd been apologetic. He might not have deserved the apology—she'd been right, despite his losing his parents so young, his background had been pretty privileged—but the fact that she'd given it without any prompting had eased some of his own temper.

Then there had been that moment when he'd offered his genuine sympathies for her sister's death, and they'd shared a few seconds of connection, a mutual understanding of grief.

He hadn't meant for that to happen. He hadn't meant to nearly give away the existence of Michel either, even though he hadn't thought of it for years and shouldn't be thinking about it now.

It had been good at first. An old friend of his father's, Michel had been more than willing to give Poseidon the help he'd needed when he'd taken over Hydra Shipping, filling the void left by Poseidon's father's death. Until Michel had made it clear that in return for his support Poseidon needed to give him other things…such as his body, for example.

Poseidon had been young, desperate for Michel's support and approval, and so he'd given Michel what he'd asked for. And once Michel had taken it, he'd cut off all contact.

Poseidon had never heard from him again.

Poseidon had felt used after that, and stupid for letting it happen. Stupid for letting his grief over his father make him so open to manipulation. Stupid for letting Michel's betrayal be such a big deal.

Stupid for caring.

So, that had been the end of caring. For good.

He never thought of it these days. He'd dismissed it from his mind as a youthful mistake, now long forgotten. And he didn't know why he'd almost told Andromeda when he'd never told anyone else—not even Asterion. It certainly hadn't been on a par with losing his parents in terms of trauma, so it shouldn't have even crossed his mind. The only mercy was that he'd stopped himself before he'd said anything else.

Cameras flashed as he got out of the limo and then turned to help Andromeda. The flush that had washed through her lovely face as he'd put her hand on him was still there, and when her gaze met his she went even pinker.

The blood hammered in his veins, a rushing pulse of desire, but they were in full view of the press, so all he did was offer his arm, and she took it, smiling for the cameras as they went up the stairs together.

He couldn't stop looking at her. The cameras kept flashing, and people called his name, but he ignored them. She was so beautiful in that gown, and even though the smiles she gave were fake, they lit her face like sunlight. It made him desperate to know what one of her real smiles would look like and whether he might ever be the cause. He wanted to be the cause.

At the top of the stairs he slid an arm around her waist and pulled her in close—because he could. Because they were supposed to be pretending to be in love and he was going to take full advantage of being close to her while he could.

She stiffened and then, as if she'd remembered what they were supposed to do, relaxed, allowing his arm to settle around her. He put a possessive hand on her hip, feeling the warmth of her body beneath the thin silk of her gown. It was intoxicating.

That is not going to make things easier.

No, but he could handle himself. Nothing would happen. But Dimitra was sharp-eyed and wise to his ways, so it had to look believable.

The Hintze Hall, where the gala was being held, looked magnificent. The dramatic Romanesque arches lining it were lit up in blue and pink, as was the huge skeleton of a blue whale that hung suspended in the air above the hall itself. There was a dramatic central staircase that looked like a cascade of flowers, and more tubs of flowers and trees dotted here and there.

Delicate music floated in the air, along with the buzz of conversation, while wait staff in formal black and white threaded through the bejewelled crowd with trays of expensive French champagne.

Andromeda's eyes were wide and her mouth was open slightly, as if she'd never seen anything like it in her entire life. It was such a different expression from her normal look of distrust, suspicion, and challenge that he almost stopped dead in his tracks.

She should look at you like that.

Like her smiles. They should be for him too.

The air had gone out of him and he couldn't understand why. She was just a woman, and no different from any other, yet he hadn't been obsessed with another woman's smiles the way he was with hers. And he'd never wanted another woman to look at him with that same intriguing combination of awe and wonder. But all the lack of understanding in the world didn't change the intensity of the desire inside him.

She should look at him like that in bed, with her wide green eyes gazing up into his, awestruck at the pleasure he was giving her...

The thought stuck in his head like a splinter and he couldn't get it out. He'd slip those silky straps from her pale shoulders and the silk would fall slowly down, revealing her full breasts. She wasn't wearing a bra and they would—

Someone said his name and he forced himself back to reality, reluctantly tearing his gaze from Andromeda's face as people greeted him.

It was a struggle, but he managed it, introducing her around and purposely singling out the people he thought she and her addiction service would find useful—because, after all, that was what he'd promised her. It was interesting to watch her speak to them. She was friendly and warm, almost the opposite of the shouting termagant she'd been outside his office that day, and he wanted that warmth of hers too. He wanted it directed at him. He'd had a taste of it in the limo earlier, in that moment of shared understanding, and he wanted more.

'Why do you keep staring at me?' she murmured,

as they finished chatting with one group of people and Poseidon steered her in the direction of another.

'Because I didn't know you even knew what a smile was.' His hand was on her hip again, as if her curves had been made to fit in his palm, so he kept it there.

'I feel that's getting perilously close to saying *You should smile more.*'

Amusement curled through him. 'I would never say that, little siren. If anything, I think you should smile less. You're even more magnificent when you're angry.'

She gave him a sidelong glance, which amused him still further, but then they reached the group he was aiming for and the round of introductions began again.

He couldn't still the beat of his heart. Couldn't slow the pounding rush of blood in his veins. She was so close to him, her sweet vanilla scent all around him, the warmth of her skin against his, and he couldn't concentrate on a single thing. It was maddening.

He'd always thought that he was in perfect control of himself, but ever since that kiss that control had felt as if it was slipping through his fingers, and he knew there was only one answer for it. He either put some distance between them or—

Took her to bed?

No. He'd told himself sex was off the table and he wasn't changing his mind. Yet he couldn't do distance either—not with the game of pretence they were playing. Which meant he was going to have to get himself in hand if he was to survive the night.

Eventually, about an hour and a half after they'd arrived, his control in tatters, Poseidon guided her to an empty couch positioned behind some tubs of flowers.

'Sit,' he said, gesturing to the couch. 'I'll go and get you a drink.' And get himself a well-earned break from the constant pull of need she'd set up inside him.

She glanced at the couch, and as she did so he became aware that one of the photographers for the evening had his camera pointed in their direction. *Damn.* A picture of her standing alone in the hall wasn't exactly what they'd been going for, so he pulled her in close instead.

'There's a photographer not far away and he's looking in our direction,' he murmured in her ear. 'We should take advantage of it.'

Her cheeks were flushed, her eyes darkening as she glanced up at him. 'So, I should look at you like this?'

'Yes. Just like that.'

He felt caught by that gaze of hers, held hostage by it, and he found himself lifting a hand and cupping her cheek the way he had done that day on the terrace of his penthouse. Her skin was warm beneath his palm and felt like silk, and she didn't move.

'Lean into my hand, little siren,' he said quietly. 'Look at me as if you want to devour me whole.'

She didn't hesitate, leaning into his palm as he'd instructed, her gaze darkening still further. 'Are you going to kiss me?'

Her voice was low and husky and she didn't sound at all upset by that.

'Yes.' He didn't think he'd be able *not* to. 'The opportunity is too good to miss, no?'

This is a mistake.

It wasn't. As he'd said, this was the perfect opportunity to leave no doubt in the public's mind about the nature of their relationship. A shared secret kiss at a gala.

But you want it too much.

He ignored the thought, lowering his head instead and brushing his mouth lightly over hers. At least, that was what it was supposed to be—a moment of light contact, a brief opportunity for the photographer to get a picture.

Yet as soon as their lips touched it felt as if the air around them had ignited, heat exploding like petrol thrown over an open fire.

She made a sighing sound, her hands pressing against his chest, her mouth opening beneath his like a flower, so sweet, and he was utterly unable to stop himself from taking advantage. He swept his tongue into her mouth, deepening the kiss, tasting her, exploring her, and her head went back allowing him greater access. He slid his fingers into her hair and curled them into the soft silken mass, suddenly ravenous for her in a way he'd never experienced with anyone before.

You can't get this desperate.

The thought was loud in his head before becoming lost under a wave of desire as she pressed herself against him, leaning into him as if she was as desperate to be as close to him as he was to her.

He slid his other hand from her hip to curve over her rear, cupping her, urging her hips against his, so he could press his hard, aching shaft against the softness and heat between her thighs. She felt unbelievably good, and she smelled of sweet musk and vanilla. Good God, he wanted to eat her alive.

He kissed her deeper, hotter, oblivious to the fact that the hall was full of people and he'd only meant the initial kiss to be pretend. There was nothing pretend about this kiss. He felt hungry, demanding. He wanted to push her up against a wall somewhere, haul her gown up, slide his hand between her thighs and stroke the softness there, then bury himself inside her and satisfy this insatiable hunger once and for all.

And why not? Perhaps the reason for this desperation was because he'd been denying himself. Perhaps if he stopped, if he allowed himself to have what he wanted, then it would burn itself out.

He squeezed her rear gently, feeling her shiver and arch against him, and somewhere a camera flashed, bringing him back to reality.

Forcing himself to let go of her hair, he lifted his head and looked down into the endless green darkness of her eyes. There was heat there, and desperation, and hunger. The same hunger he felt.

'I want you,' he said starkly, unable to be anything but blatantly honest. 'I want you now. Here.'

She was trembling, her breathing fast and hard. 'Yes,' she whispered, her gaze dropping to his mouth. 'Yes. Please.'

He couldn't think. Part of him was trying to remind him that he wasn't supposed to be touching her, that this was wrong—but, as he'd already thought, perhaps it was the denial that was wrong. Perhaps the only way out of this was to satisfy the hunger, get rid of this desperation once and for all.

He stepped away from her, then took her hand. 'Come with me,' he said.

Andie's heart was beating far too hard and far too fast, and the ache between her thighs was a steady pressure that she knew only one thing would ease.

Him.

She knew it wasn't a good idea. In fact, it was the last thing she should want, and especially with him. But ever since she'd laid her hand on him in the limo she hadn't been able to think of anything else.

Sex was something she'd avoided so far, and deliberately. Chrissy had ruined herself over it and Andie never wanted to allow a man that much power over her. So far, she hadn't regretted her decision, but now... Now she couldn't help wondering if that had been a bad idea. Because maybe if she'd had a relationship, or even a one-night stand, then she wouldn't now be so at the mercy of her own body's demands.

Poseidon had had his arm around her all evening, his large palm resting on her hip, his warmth soaking through the fine silk of her gown. She'd been so insanely aware of both that hand and his body next to hers she'd barely been able to concentrate on anything else. She'd smiled at people, shaken their hands, had conversations of some kind, but she couldn't remember what they'd talked about or recall their names.

The only thing that felt real in this whole dream of an evening was him. Strange, when wearing a beautiful gown at a star-studded gala should have been a high point in her life, giving her, as it did, a taste of what her sister had had.

Then he'd kissed her. She shouldn't have agreed to it—she should have pushed him away after that first second of contact. Yet she hadn't. No, she'd stepped in even closer, opened her mouth beneath his and let him kiss her. Let his rich flavour turn her inside out. Let herself get dizzy with his scent, and the heat of his body, and the hard evidence of his desire pressing between her thighs.

She might have refused if he hadn't told her that he wanted her in that voice raw with need. As if he was desperate. As if she'd pushed him, a notorious playboy, to the end of his control.

Taking his hand and letting him lead her out of the hall was the height of stupidity, but she didn't pull away. Because she wanted him too, as desperately as he wanted her. And she also wanted to know the nature of the thing that had led Chrissy down the path to ruin. Some part of her needed to know, to experience it for herself, to understand.

So she followed him into a short, darkened hallway not far from the hall's main entrance. And when he pulled her into it, and pushed her up against the wall, she didn't protest.

His blue gaze was all fire as he put his hands on the wall on either side of her head, caging her against it.

'Can you be quiet?' he asked. 'Very, *very* quiet?'

Her whole body trembled with anticipation and need. 'Yes,' she said breathlessly, and then she added, because it was only fair that he should know, 'I… I haven't done this before.'

He frowned. 'What do you mean? Had sex in a public place?'

Perhaps she shouldn't have said anything. Then again, it was too late now. 'No. Sex, full stop.'

Shock flared in his eyes and he stiffened. 'Oh, Andromeda…'

But she didn't want him to pull away, so she reached

for him, sliding her hands up and over the hard wall of his chest.

'Show me,' she whispered. 'I want to know why my sister followed a man who ruined her. I want to know what's so great about sex that people destroy themselves for it.'

He let out a breath. 'It shouldn't be like this...not your first time.'

'Why not?' She looked up into the vivid blue of his eyes, seeing the flames still blazing bright in them. 'Shouldn't I be the one to choose when and where?'

'It's true. You should.'

He lifted a hand and pushed a curl behind her ear, his fingertips brushing her skin and making her shiver. Then his fingers dropped to the strap of her gown on her left shoulder.

'In which case, tell me if you want me to stop.'

Slowly, he eased the strap down, keeping his gaze on hers, and she felt the fabric fall, leaving her breast bare.

She shivered, her skin tight and hot, and when he looked down she shivered again.

'So beautiful,' he breathed, tracing the delicate curve of her breast with light fingertips, before brushing them lightly across her nipple.

His touch was electric, a sharp jolt of sensation that made her gasp and arch her back against the wall, and the sound echoed softly around them.

'Hush,' Poseidon murmured, his wicked fingertips continuing to caress her sensitive breast. 'There are people in the hallway.'

She could hear them, too...the buzz of light chatter and the sound of laughter. So close. They could be found at any moment. That should have made her embarrassed, but it didn't. If anything, the thought of discovery only added to the wild excitement coursing through her, making her heart beat hard and the pulsing ache between her thighs get worse.

'Please,' she whispered, her fingers curling into his shirt to bring him closer. 'Poseidon...'

He leaned in, giving her what she wanted, which was his mouth on hers, kissing her deeply, and with so much heat she thought she might actually catch on fire. Then his hand was smoothing down her hip to her thigh, fingers curling in the silk of her gown and lifting it.

This is a mistake. Are you really going to let him take you up against a wall at a gala?

The thought spun through her fevered brain for a moment, then disappeared as quickly as it had come. She didn't care. She'd never wanted anything as badly as she wanted him right now. So she didn't stop him as he lifted her gown and slid his hand between her thighs, his fingers slipping beneath the damp fabric of her knickers and stroking her. She was aching, and slick, and, when he touched her the pleasure was so intense she had to bite her lip hard to stop from crying out.

'No,' he whispered. 'Give me your cries, little siren. Scream if you need to.' Then he bent and kissed her, his fingers exploring her, stroking her soft, wet flesh, then sliding wickedly inside her.

She moaned into his mouth as the aching pressure built and built—and then he did something with his fingers that released it in a burst of wild pleasure that had her crying out against his lips and writhing in his arms.

He leaned in, pressing her body harder against the

wall, containing her with his warmth and strength as the pleasure cascaded through her, making her shake and shake. After the trembles had eased, he got out his wallet and extracted a condom, dealing with the issue of protection swiftly and with minimal fuss. Then he slid one hand behind her knee and lifted her leg up, hooking it around his hip.

His eyes were blazing blue and she stared up into them, her whole body drawn tight with anticipation. Then he was pressing forward, pushing inside her, gently and slowly, and she could feel herself stretching around him in the most exquisite way. It was supposed to be painful—that was what Chrissy had told her—but she didn't feel any pain, only a sense of wonder.

She'd never thought she'd want a man to get so close, to allow him into her body, yet it was different with Poseidon. He wasn't just any man and he felt...amazing. There was so much intensity in his face as he looked at her, as if he felt the same wonder she did at this closeness, this intimacy. No one had ever looked at her that way...not one single person.

'Poseidon,' she whispered, simply for the sheer pleasure of saying his name.

He murmured something raw in what she thought must be Greek, and then he lifted her leg a bit higher, sliding even deeper, making a connection so intimate it took her breath away. He didn't move—not immediately—and the two of them pressed together.

She was amazed at the beauty of him like this. There was no artifice to him now, no dryly amused playboy. Only a man looking at her with such hunger and such passion. He hid it well, but she could see it now, laid bare before her. He'd lied when he'd said he didn't care about anything, that life was just a big joke, because how could a man who burned this intensely not care? How could he not feel when all evidence to the contrary blazed so brightly in his eyes?

He began to move, slowly at first, his hips setting a rhythm that had her shaking. Her hands were gripping his shoulders, her nails digging into his jacket, as the pleasure began to coil tighter and tighter, breaking her open, breaking her apart.

'Andromeda,' he said in a low, ragged voice. *'Asteri mou.'*

He began to move faster, his gaze holding hers, and she felt as if she was falling into the endless blue of his eyes. Into the endless pleasure of him inside her. The driving thrust of his hips and the heat of his hard body moving against her.

The pleasure became frantic, and she was desperate, the effort not to cry out almost too much for her. As if he knew exactly what she needed, he bent again and covered her mouth, at the same time slipping a hand between her thighs, to where they were joined. He stroked her once, twice. Then that aching pressure inside her sprang apart, exploding in a wild shower of sparks. Pleasure expanded inside her, and she screamed into his mouth as it took her.

Then it was his turn, his rhythm hard and fast, until he turned his face into her hair and climax took him as well.

For a long moment all she could do was stand there, pressed against his heat, listening to the sounds of people talking in the hallway, the echoes of pleasure still crashing inside her.

She was aware, too, that a part of her was growing a

little panicky. Because Chrissy had been very clear about men, and what they expected, and how, after you'd given them what they wanted, you were disposable.

Ridiculous to panic—because why did she care if Poseidon pushed himself away from her and never spoke to her again? No, of course she didn't. If anything, *she* had been the one to take what she wanted from *him*, and now she'd had it, what did she even need him for?

She readied herself to push him away, before he could do the same to her, only to be shocked when abruptly his hand cupped her cheek, lifting her face so he could look in her eyes.

'Are you okay?' he asked, his gaze searching. 'Did I hurt you?'

A strange lump of emotion sat in her throat and she wasn't sure where it had come from. It made her feel raw and vulnerable, and she didn't like it.

'No,' she forced out, trying to sound casual. 'I'm fine.'

Yet the look in his eyes intensified, and his thumb passed over her cheekbone in a gentle caress. 'Come home with me. I want you in my bed.'

She swallowed, her mouth dry. This was not what Chrissy had said about men. Once they'd had what they wanted from you they discarded you—that was what she'd said. Unless they were Simon, of course. Then again, Simon had wanted other things from Chrissy.

Poseidon's fingers gripped her chin, and the look in his eyes turned even hotter. 'I only want a night, little siren,' he said, low and insistent. 'That's all. You've been killing me for a week now, and five minutes up against a wall isn't going to cut it.'

The honesty in his voice and the intensity in his eyes

echoed inside her, striking a chord in her soul. He wanted her. He *wanted* her. The girl who hadn't been able to save her sister. He wanted her very badly indeed.

'I thought we weren't going to do this,' she said.

'We weren't. But give me one night, Andromeda. Just one.'

'Why? Why me?'

He was silent a moment, but his gaze was devouring. 'I'd love to say it's only chemistry, but… You're the most passionate woman I've ever met and I want a night when all that passion is mine.'

Again, his honesty left her speechless, almost stripped bare. She hadn't expected that from him, and it made her want to be equally honest back.

But you have to be careful. You don't want to end up like Chrissy.

She wouldn't. She knew the dangers, and it would be only one night and no more. What harm could it do? Once she'd had that night, and fully explored what it was that had addicted her sister, she'd walk away. It would be a good test for herself.

'Yes,' she said, giving up on her resistance and leaning into the heat of his body. 'I want that too. Take me home, Poseidon.'

CHAPTER SEVEN

THE CHANDELIERS OF La Salle de Europe in the Casino de Monte Carlo lit up the opulent gilt ceiling and the frescos on the gilt-covered walls, before glittering off the jewels of the couture-clad crowd milling below.

The room was full of the buzz of conversation and the clatter of the roulette wheel, croupiers calling, and cheers coming from those gathered to play at the tables.

Poseidon, leaning against the wall near one of the blackjack tables, surveyed his party with some satisfaction, before glancing at the woman standing next to him.

Tonight, Andromeda wore a Grecian gown of pale gold silk—another dress he'd taken great pleasure in picking especially for her. As he'd thought, the colour complemented her skin and brought out the fire in her red-gold curls. She wore her hair piled on top of her head, with a few artful ringlets allowed to dangle here and there, and she looked like the goddess she was.

Fierce need gripped him, the way it had been gripping him the whole two weeks since their one night together, at the most inopportune times.

He couldn't stop thinking about it. About her and what a revelation she'd been. Fire in his hands, just as he'd thought. Passionate, hungry, curious too. And he'd known the second he'd kissed her goodbye the next morning that one night wasn't going to be enough.

Not nearly enough.

He wanted more.

Perhaps he shouldn't have taken her the way he had, the night of their first public appearance, in a dark hallway up against a wall, with people nearby. Especially considering she'd been a virgin. But he'd wanted her too much to stop. He'd appreciated her telling him, though, just as he'd appreciated her telling him that she was very sure she wanted him and that she was the one who should get to choose where her first time was.

Choice was important to him, for very good reasons.

But, whether it was wrong or not, he hadn't regretted it. Watching her green eyes widen with shocked pleasure as he'd pushed inside her had been a glory, as had feeling the slick heat of her sex grip him tight. And when he'd kissed her, taking her cries of ecstasy into his mouth as she'd climaxed, he'd been so pushed to the edge of his control he'd barely been able to hold on.

It had never been like that for him. *Never.*

He had to have another night.

Of course, he shouldn't want more. One night, they'd agreed, just one. But denial only made the fire burn hotter, and the most logical thing was to feed it until there was nothing left to burn.

So the following day, after she'd gone, he'd decided their next public appearance would be something special, that he'd pull out all the stops. He thought she might want another night too, but he didn't want to assume and so wouldn't leave anything to chance.

He was going to seduce her, and thoroughly, and to do

that he was going to organise his own event. An event especially for her, which would incorporate Chrissy's Hope and yet more donations. The cause was worthy, naturally, but his main focus would be on pleasing Andromeda.

It was very short notice to organise such an event, but his PR team were excellent and he had a couple of contacts in Monte Carlo who owed him a favour or two. As for getting enough guests, there was no one in the rich, moneyed, and powerful circles he moved in who'd refuse one of his invitations—especially if it involved a party for a good cause. A party such as an exclusive fundraising night at a luxury casino in Monte Carlo with all the winnings going to Chrissy's Hope.

Andromeda had been wary at first, when he'd called her to discuss it, and had pointed out to him that perhaps having a gambling event to raise funds for an addiction service would be sending out mixed messages. Which was fair. But he'd countered with the idea that rich people liked to gamble and, if it involved an exclusive party, free alcohol, celebrity guests, plus all the money going to a good cause, not only would they come in droves, they'd also probably end up giving more as a sop to their conscience.

Cynical of him, as she'd said, but also true.

He'd thought she might protest at the gown, or at the very least insist on staying somewhere downmarket and not the luxury hotel he had them booked at—separate rooms, of course, since he wasn't assuming—yet she hadn't.

She *had* declined a seat on his private jet, telling him she had some other business to attend to first and would join him in Monaco in time for the event. He'd paid for her flights, though she insisted on economy and he hadn't argued. If she wanted to travel in discomfort that was her choice.

He'd told her to meet him in the lobby of their hotel, so they could travel to the event together, and when she had, resplendent in that gown, all the breath had left his body. She'd looked exquisite. And she'd smiled at him, as if she was as pleased to see him as he was to see her, and it had been as if his whole world had slowed down and stopped.

It was still stopped now.

She was gazing out over the crowd, a glass of champagne in her hand, her pretty face still flushed with excitement. They'd just come from the roulette table, where he'd showed her how to play, and she'd ended up winning a large amount of money for Chrissy's Hope. She might not want to admit it, but she'd enjoyed the game as much as she had the winning, he was sure. In fact, he was beginning to suspect that she liked games rather more than she was letting on.

'Are you having a good time?' he asked, watching her face.

She glanced at him, her green eyes alight. 'Yes. I know I was dubious about this, but it's a lot more fun than I thought it would be. And all the money is going to Chrissy's Hope…' Another of her beautiful smiles curved her mouth. 'Thank you, Poseidon.'

A feeling he didn't recognise shifted in his chest… a kind of tightness. But then a couple of photographers passed by, taking pictures, so he ignored the sensation, reaching for her and pulling her in close. Only to feel her go rigid in his arms.

He glanced down at her in concern, but she wasn't looking at him. Her gaze was on the crowd by the black-jack table. Her face had gone white, her smile vanishing.

The tightness in his chest tightened still further. 'What is it?' he asked. 'You've gone pale.'

She looked down at the glass in her hand. 'Nothing.'

'It's not nothing, Andromeda. You look like you've seen a ghost.'

She shook her head, but he drew her closer and at the same time turned them both slightly, shielding her with his body from the rest of the room and the photographers.

'Tell me,' he murmured quietly. 'You look upset.'

She was silent a moment, then she glanced up at him. 'Why did you do this? The party, I mean? You must have had a hundred other events we could have gone to. You didn't have to organise one especially for me.'

This wasn't what was bothering her, he was certain. She'd seen something, or maybe someone, who'd upset her. But if she didn't want to tell him he wouldn't push.

'I thought you were enjoying yourself,' he pointed out mildly.

'I am, but… You've already agreed to sponsor Chrissy's Hope in return for me marrying you.' She gestured to the room. 'You didn't need to do all this as well.'

'I didn't, it's true.' He settled her more firmly against him. 'But I can't lie and say I don't have any ulterior motives.'

She regained a bit of colour, which was good, and a flash of her fiery spirit was showing in her eyes. 'Of course you have ulterior motives. I presume you're going to share them with me?'

He gazed down at her, very conscious of what her

proximity was doing to him. Her warmth and sweet scent were making him hard, and all he could think about was taking her back to their hotel and getting rid of that gown, sating himself on her beautiful body again. It had been two weeks since he'd touched her and, right now, every second of those weeks were weighing on him.

Abruptly, he was tired of his own games. 'My ulterior motive is you,' he said bluntly. 'I want another night, Andromeda.'

More colour flushed her cheeks, pink and pretty. 'So all of this is…what? To get me into bed again?'

He lifted a brow. 'Is it too much?'

She gazed at him for a second, then her mouth softened and curved slightly. 'You could have just asked me, you know. You didn't need to make it an entire production.'

A savage kick of satisfaction caught at him. So, she *did* want more. He'd known she would. 'You don't think you're worth an entire production, little siren?'

She let out a breath. 'But you've gone to so much trouble.'

'You like a pretty dress and a glitzy event.' He smoothed his hand over her hips. 'And don't bother denying it. I know you do.'

'Poseidon…'

'It's okay to enjoy it, Andromeda,' he said, a bit more insistently. 'It doesn't mean you're going to suddenly turn into your sister.'

Because of course that was what she was worried about, wasn't it?

She opened her mouth, probably to protest, but he held up a hand.

'So,' he went on, 'you should relax and enjoy yourself,

because it's for a good cause. Plus, it's going to look even better for our little bit of relationship theatre, don't you think? Me doing something thoughtful for my beautiful new girlfriend.'

An expression flickered over her face that he couldn't read, but then finally the tension left her and she gave him another one of her beautiful smiles.

'I suppose when you put it like that, I can't really refuse.'

Another surge of satisfaction filled him. 'I hope that means *Yes, Poseidon, I'd love to have another night with you.*'

Her smile turned into something that was a little wicked, yet also shy at the same time, and it made the desire inside him burn even hotter.

'You said only one night,' she murmured.

'I did,' he agreed. 'But you were such a glory, little siren, that I can't resist another. Would that really be so bad?'

She lifted her champagne and took a slow, meditative sip, staring at him over the rim of her glass. 'No,' she said at last. 'No, it really wouldn't.'

'In that case, let's—'

'Excuse me,' a voice interrupted from behind him. 'Andie? Is that you?'

Poseidon saw the moment the colour left Andromeda's face again, fury igniting in her green eyes.

'Simon,' she said flatly. 'What the hell are you doing here?'

Andie fought to get a handle on her fury and shock. She'd thought she'd seen Simon in the crowd near the blackjack table just before, but had convinced herself that she was seeing things. He'd pretty much vanished after Chrissy had died—he hadn't even come to the funeral—and she'd been too angry to keep track of him. Yes, he was rich and well-connected, and he liked a party, but he surely couldn't be *here*.

Then again, he must have links to Poseidon since he'd been the one to take Chrissy to the party on that yacht. Poseidon's yacht.

He was standing behind Poseidon, all smooth and handsome in his tux, smiling the smile that Andie had once thought so dreamy. He'd dazzled her once, the way he'd dazzled Chrissy, but now, looking at him, she couldn't understand what she'd seen in him.

His smile was more of a smirk than anything sexy, and he'd used too much hair product, making his hair look oily instead of glossy. There were creases in his tux jacket, and lines of dissipation around his eyes and mouth. He looked…sleazy. A man who'd indulged himself far too much and far too often.

Anger was burning a hole in her chest, and the urge to scream at him, then throw her drink in his face for what he'd done to her sister, was almost overwhelming. But she couldn't do that here—not in this room full of people having fun and donating large sums of money for Chrissy's Hope.

Instead, much to her horror, she felt her eyes prick with ridiculous tears of fury.

Simon was smirking at her as if nothing was wrong. 'Wow, you look fantastic, sweetheart. I've been wondering how you were doing. You should join me for a—'

'She will not be going anywhere with you,' Poseidon said with utter finality, stepping in front of her as if to shield her. 'So you're Simon. You're the one who invited Chrissy to that party onboard *Thetis*. Andromeda tells me you're also the one who provided the drugs that night.'

Simon had gone white, making the blue eyes she'd always thought an amazing colour look washed out. 'Teras, right?' He gave Poseidon an ingratiating smile. 'Good to meet you at last. I'm Simon Winchester.' He held out a hand.

Poseidon ignored it, and it struck Andie, all at once, how different the two men were. On the surface, they were both rich and handsome—the same, almost. Yet one man was the most intrinsically selfish man she'd ever met, while the other was...protective. More caring that he'd ever admit. And kinder too.

Poseidon was a man who'd told her he didn't care about anything, and yet he cared enough about his grandmother that he was marrying a complete stranger without a word of protest, simply because she'd asked him to. He'd been up-front with her from the start about what he wanted, including all his ulterior motives, and he cared enough about her to respect her choices.

Simon respected no one's choices and didn't care about anyone but himself. And what she'd once thought of as charm had turned out to be only sleaze.

Now, looking at the two of them, she couldn't understand how she'd ever thought Poseidon was in any way, shape or form like Simon.

Poseidon had returned Simon's smile, but his was white and sharp and terrifying. 'Tell me, who let you into my party?'

Simon bristled. 'I was invited. A friend of mine—'

'I'm rescinding the invitation.' Poseidon lifted a finger and abruptly a number of security guards appeared. 'You can leave under your own steam or I'll have security carry you out.' His smile widened. 'And if you ever approach Andromeda again, including by phone or text or email, I'll have your hide.'

A little shock went down Andromeda's spine. He was protecting her, wasn't he? Defending her. Of course she didn't need defending, but rage was still twisting in her gut, along with a healthy amount of grief, and she didn't want to have a confrontation with Simon. Not here.

'Are you threatening me, Teras?' Simon blustered.

'Of course I'm threatening you, you idiot,' Poseidon said pleasantly. 'If you have a problem with it, feel free to take it up with the police. I'm sure they'll be very interested to hear about a few nasty little habits of yours.'

Simon started to say something else, but by that stage, clearly losing patience with him, Poseidon had lifted another finger and, with relatively little fuss, Simon was escorted from the casino by security guards.

Then Poseidon turned, slid a steadying hand beneath Andie's elbow. Somehow she found herself being ushered from the main gaming room and into another smaller but no less opulent room, with a lounge area, where there were mercifully no people.

'Are you all right?' he asked as he steered her towards one of the velvet-covered couches. 'If I'd known he was coming I would have had Security watch out for him at the door.'

Andie put her champagne glass down on the small

table beside the couch and took a shaky breath. 'I'm okay. It was just a shock. I didn't expect him to turn up.'

'Was that why you went pale earlier?'

So he'd noticed that. Well, that wasn't a surprise. He noticed a lot of things about her.

'Yes.'

There wasn't any point in denying that, nor the echoes of grief that were now resounding inside her as her anger dissipated.

'I haven't seen him for years. Not since Chrissy died. He didn't come to her funeral…didn't send any form of condolences. Basically he vanished. I used to think he was so handsome.'

Her throat was tight. She hadn't told anyone any of this before, yet now the words kept on spilling out.

'I used to be so envious of Chrissy. Because she had this amazing guy interested in her, who showered her with gifts and all his attention. And she got to go to the most amazing parties, travel to wonderful places, have all these exciting experiences.'

She looked down at her hands twisted in her lap.

'Then I found out the truth. How Simon had been using her, giving her drugs and passing her around his friends.'

'I lied,' Poseidon said flatly. 'When I told him I'd get the police involved, that wasn't a threat. That was a promise.'

But a lead weight was sitting in the pit of Andie's stomach all of a sudden.

'He was only part of the problem. The real issue was that she thought she was in love with him and so she did everything he told her to do. I tried to tell her that maybe taking drugs in nightclubs wasn't a good idea, that maybe she should lay off going to parties every night, but…she didn't listen.'

Andie swallowed, grief constricting her throat.

'She told me that she was fine, that she was having a great time and that I was just jealous.'

Unexpectedly, Poseidon reached out and took her cold hands in his large ones, and she felt the shock of his touch echo through her entire body. His grip was so warm, easing the tension inside her.

'How old were you when Chrissy died?' Poseidon asked.

'Fifteen.'

His fingers around hers were so warm. 'And did you think you should have saved her?'

Andie closed her eyes.

You should have saved her. If you'd only tried harder.

'I tried talking to Mum about her,' she said hoarsely. 'But Mum wouldn't listen either. She thought Chrissy was doing well for herself and didn't need saving.'

'You did what you could.' He sounded so reasonable. 'Chrissy was older than you and she made her own choices. No, they weren't good ones, but you can't take responsibility for them. You can't take responsibility for anyone's choices—not as an adult, and certainly not at fifteen.'

She'd gone beyond trying to keep everything contained. Now she couldn't help but let it spill out—all the doubts and worries she'd had, all her fears.

'But I was the only one who could see the path she was heading down, Poseidon. No one else did. And no one else would listen.' Tears pricked at the backs of her eyes, but she refused to let them fall. 'I'm sure there was more I could have done, but I just…gave up in the end. I didn't know what else to do.'

He let her hands go then, and she found herself pulled into his arms. She didn't fight, though. Instead, an odd feeling of security filled her, as if there could be a hurricane or a tidal wave, but as long as he held her she'd remain safe. Anchored.

'You did what you could,' he said, with such certainty that she almost believed him. 'But you were only fifteen. You tried, Andromeda. That's all anyone can do. Chrissy's choices were her own and they're not yours to bear. The only control you have is over the ones you make yourself.'

He's right. And you have to accept that, because what's the alternative?

The alternative was to continually beat herself up for all the things she hadn't done.

'I suppose so,' she said at last.

Poseidon eased a curl behind her ear, his blue gaze intense. 'Is that why you deny yourself the things you enjoy? Is it really because you think you're too like Chrissy? Or are you just punishing yourself?'

He's right about that, too.

That vulnerable feeling crept through her again, making her want to turn away from him, but his fingers caught her chin before she could, holding her firmly.

'You loved your sister, *asteri mou*, and you did what you could for her. But you can't change what happened to her, so why keep going over it?' His blue eyes were full of concern. 'Stop torturing yourself, little siren. It doesn't do you any good. Let yourself enjoy life's pleasures while you can, hmm?'

And somehow the weight inside her eased, and the tightness in her chest was released. He was right. There *was* no point going over things she couldn't change. And, to a certain extent, punishing herself was exactly what she was doing.

Denying yourself him is part of the punishment.

That was true too. Though it wasn't only punishment—there was a certain amount of fear too. Because now she'd had a taste of what had led Chrissy to her doom. Now, finally, she understood the breathless grip of chemistry, the dizzying rush of pleasure. The intensity of their connection was addictive, so she'd tried to push the night she and Poseidon had had out of her mind, not go back over it again and again.

But she hadn't been able to. Memories of that night had continued to plague her. The feel of his hands on her, the taste of him, the unbelievable pleasure he'd given her. And it had been *so* much pleasure.

The depth of her need had frightened her, so while she'd allowed herself the dress, she'd denied herself the pleasure of being on his private jet, the pleasure of his company, delaying it as much as she could.

But then, at that overly lavish hotel, as she'd come into the lobby to meet him, breathless at the thought despite herself, he'd started towards her, magnificent in his black evening clothes, and her heart had leaped inside her chest. And her feminine awareness had been a pulse between her thighs, deep and strong.

She wished he wasn't right about her liking a glitzy event, but she did. It put distance between her and the council flat and the suffocating grief that had enveloped her after Chrissy had died and her mother retreating into depression. Here there were glittering lights and people laughing, wonderful clothes and fine champagne, and the most beautiful man at her side.

Chrissy would want you to have it. She'd approve.

Maybe she would...maybe she wouldn't. Either way, she wasn't here now. But Poseidon was. And he wasn't Simon. He'd never do the things Simon had done, and she wasn't Chrissy.

Taking what he was offering wasn't going to lead to her doom—and, besides, life was short. Why deny herself?

Andromeda lifted her hands, threading her fingers through the thick black silk of his hair. 'Another night,' she murmured. 'Let's take it now.'

And she drew his mouth down on hers.

CHAPTER EIGHT

THE LITTLE ISLAND kingdom glowed like a jewel in the middle of the deep blue of the sea as the plane came in to land. It was one of the world's prettiest airports, apparently, but Poseidon had never paid much attention to its beauty—not when every time he landed dread sat heavy in his gut.

It had been that way when Asterion had married his little ex-nun and Poseidon had forced himself to attend the wedding, as he was supposed to. But he'd left the next day, escaping to New York and the endless round of business and parties that he'd thrown himself into.

Ridiculous to be so full of dread when the only thing waiting for him was Dimitra and her gimlet eye, and Asterion's blissful state of holy matrimony. Oh, yes, and a wedding, of course.

As the jet taxied towards the terminal Poseidon glanced at Andromeda, sitting opposite him. She was currently peering out of the window with wide eyes. On her hand glittered the massive sapphire he'd given her after a very public proposal while in Milan.

That had been the culmination of the perfectly orchestrated media campaign that he'd planned following the party in Monaco, consisting of a few other charity events in various European cities, a couple of 'private' dinners, and one midnight stroll along the Seine in Paris.

The media were in raptures over his courtship of a 'previously unknown redhead' and how romantic it was. And Dimitra had been grudgingly pleased with him— which was just as well because, when he'd thought Andromeda might kill him, he hadn't been far off.

That night in Monaco, after he'd dealt with scum in the shape of Simon Winchester, had proved to him that even a second night wouldn't be enough. That he had to have more. She'd agreed the moment he suggested it, and in the end she'd spent more nights in his penthouse than she had on his arm at the various events he'd taken her to.

By now he should be well-satisfied. But he wasn't.

It was as if the more he had of her, the more he wanted—which hadn't been his intent at all. His hunger for her was supposed to get easier to deal with, not more intense, and he was at a loss to explain why.

Every time he touched her he went up in flames, and he couldn't stop it. Really, the sooner they got this marriage over and done with and went their separate ways the better.

Andromeda straightened in her seat and glanced at him, her eyes shining. 'This place is beautiful, Poseidon. I had no idea.'

'There's a reason all the tourists flock here,' he said casually, shifting in his seat as the plane came to a halt.

Her gaze sharpened. 'You're very tense. Why?'

She was like this, he'd learned. Perceptive, picking up on his moods with almost insulting ease and asking him direct questions he'd rather not answer. She wouldn't ask her questions while they were in bed—they never talked there, too caught up in mutual pleasure—but when they were out of it, it was an entirely different matter. She ignored his idle flirting and insisted on serious conversation, which he didn't want to have. It was aggravating.

'Pre-wedding jitters,' he said, dismissive. 'I have a nervous temperament.'

'No, you don't.' Her red brows drew together. 'Are you worried about Dimitra?'

'I'm always worried about Dimitra.' He pushed himself up from the seat, unable to stay in it a second longer. 'Come, little siren. Time to disembark.'

She didn't say anything more, but the look she gave him told him that she wasn't letting it go.

He'd be fine. By tonight, the dread would be gone—he'd make certain of it. And if it hadn't, then he'd take Andromeda to bed and get rid of it that way.

The weather was beautiful, the air warm, and the drive from the airport to his residence, along the cliffs near Asterion's architecturally designed wonder of a house, was a pretty, winding journey.

He busied himself with phone calls to various people to see how the wedding arrangements were progressing, while Andromeda stared out of the window at the stunning beauty of the blue-green Mediterranean washing itself against the cliffs below.

His home was a more traditional affair than Asterion's, in whitewashed stone and red tile, with terraces stepped down the sides of the cliff, as well as a swimming pool. He also had an olive grove and grapevines, and staff that took care of both as well as the house while he was away.

Which was all the time.

The place held no memories. He'd bought it after Michel. Yet that cold, hard lump of dread sat heavier inside him as the car drew up to the house and his staff came out to greet him.

Settling in took a certain amount of time, as did receiving the various complaints and problems that had come up over the course of his absence. He took shameless advantage, sending one of his staff members to show Andromeda around. It wouldn't matter to her if he didn't do it himself, and besides, he *did* have a lot to do to get the wedding arranged.

Dimitra had wanted a vast affair, with many guests, as befitted a member of the Teras family, but since that would have involved more time than he wanted to spend, Poseidon had argued for a quick wedding, and the sooner the better. Dimitra had grudgingly agreed, muttering something about him having wedding night urgency. He hadn't argued. His grandmother didn't need to know that his fiancée had been spending every night in his bed already.

Later that evening, when there were no more urgent tasks he could reasonably use to distract himself with, Poseidon stepped out of the house and strolled over the white terrace to the pool, where Andromeda lay floating on her back with her eyes closed.

The sun was going down, painting her in tones of pink and gold, and her hair a swirling mass around her head. All she needed was more body paint and a tail and she would indeed be the mermaid he'd seen when he'd first met her.

Instead all she had on was a tiny green bikini. All he could think about was diving into the water and tearing it off her before carrying her over to one of the sun loungers and burying himself inside her.

Maybe that was exactly what he'd do.

'You're avoiding me,' Andromeda said as he began to take off his clothes. 'You've spent all day doing lots of things, and I bet they're all very important, but you're still avoiding me.'

A small shock went through him. Had it really been that obvious?

'Why on earth would I be avoiding you?' He began to undo the buttons of his shirt. 'Especially when all I've been able to think about all day is ravishing you on one of these sun loungers.'

'You're tense about something, and I know you don't want me to ask about it.'

He discarded his shirt and then his shoes, trousers and underwear. And then, finally, naked, he dived into the pool, relishing the cold shock of the water. Andromeda was still floating on her back, so he swam over to her.

'I can think of many better things to do than talk,' he murmured, tugging her into his arms.

She didn't protest, only slid her arms around his neck and leaned into him. Her skin was hot on his, in delicious contrast to the cool of the water, but her gaze was sharp as knives.

'You're very casual and dismissive when you don't want to talk about something,' she said. 'You turn it into a joke. And now you're trying to distract me with sex. Why is that?'

'Perhaps because I like jokes?' He slid one hand up her back and pulled at the tie of her bikini top, undoing it. 'And sex is more pleasurable than talking.'

'Ah, yes,' she murmured, letting him pull away her top so her breasts were free. 'Life is one big joke, isn't it? That's what you said.'

He had, that day of the gala at the Museum of Natural History, in the limo. When he'd also nearly told her about Michel.

'But,' she went on, pressing her bare breasts against his chest, so the softness of them made all the blood in his body rush south, 'I don't think that's true, is it?'

He didn't like the direct look in her eyes. He didn't like it at all. 'Not everything is a joke,' he said. 'Your naked body, for example, is—'

'Poseidon...' Her voice was very quiet, her gaze very steady.

All his muscles tensed—he could feel them—and it didn't seem to matter how hard he tried to relax, he couldn't get rid of the tightness.

'Why do you want to know?'

'Because you don't want to tell me—why else?'

Her warmth and her softness were too much...too distracting. If he wasn't careful he might let something slip, and he didn't want to. Michel and everything associated with him were in the past, and there was no reason to revisit it.

He let her go, leaving her floating, her glorious hair like kelp, the lights from the villa shining on her satiny wet skin.

'This isn't real, Andromeda,' he said, his voice hard, so that she would know this was crossing a line. 'This relationship of ours isn't an actual relationship. We're not together except in bed. And I don't have to tell you a damn thing.'

She only stared at him in the way he was starting to hate, as if she could see past all his walls, all his defences. As if she could see the idiot boy he'd once been, who'd let himself be broken for absolutely no reason at all.

'What are you so afraid of?' she asked.

The tension inside him got worse. He should leave. He should swim to the side, get out, get dressed, and go inside. Go to his gym and work himself into physical exhaustion. Because that would get rid of it. It always did.

Yet he stayed where he was. 'I'm afraid of nothing,' he said flatly, but they both heard the hollow note in his voice.

'Do you have anyone to confide in, Poseidon Teras?'

The look in her eyes had turned soft, which made him even more tense.

'Do you have anyone to talk to? Anyone at all?'

He didn't know why he was still in the pool, why he was still there when he should deal with this in his gym.

'I have my brother. What has that got to do with anything?'

'Everyone needs someone to talk to. Someone they trust. And you can trust me. I won't tell anyone.'

'Why?' he demanded. 'Why should I talk to you? Why does it even matter?'

She was silent for a moment, then she said, 'I knew Chrissy was unhappy at the end, no matter how much she kept insisting she was fine, but she refused to discuss it. And I couldn't talk to Mum, because she didn't want to hear that Chrissy was unhappy. God, I'd have given my eye teeth for someone to talk to…someone who'd listen.'

She paused, her gaze full of something that made his chest ache suddenly.

'Every life matters, Poseidon. Including yours.'

He wanted to deny it. He wanted to tell her that his life was no more important than anyone else's, and that also he wasn't her sister.

Her sister, who had been taken advantage of by an older man.

It wasn't the same. It *wasn't*.

In which case what does it matter if she knows? Who are you trying to protect?

Surely not himself. He didn't need to protect himself from anyone, because he wasn't vulnerable. Not any more. So why shouldn't he tell her? After all, it wasn't a big deal. It never had been.

'It's nothing,' he said, trying to sound casual. 'But if I tell you, I want you on that sun lounger.'

Because he might as well get something good out of this nonsense.

'I want you naked and I want you screaming my name.'

She stared at him for a moment, and then she reached down into the water. When she lifted her hands, she was holding her bikini bottoms in them. She tossed them negligently onto the side of the pool, then stood in the water with her arms folded, waiting.

'It was a long time ago,' he said. 'I barely remember. I think I was twenty. A close friend of my father's had become my mentor. He helped me deal with Hydra Shipping when I took it over, gave me support and advice, and I... I valued it greatly.'

It shouldn't have been so hard to say the words, yet he found he had to force them out.

'He was like a father to me, but he didn't see me as a son. He wanted...more.'

Andromeda's expression betrayed nothing, which was good, because the last thing he wanted was her sympathy.

'He told me he'd cut off all contact with me if I didn't give him what he wanted,' he went on, keeping everything very light and casual. 'So I did. Because I needed him. And afterwards he cut off all contact with me anyway.' He made himself smile. 'It was years ago, and I was very young and very stupid, and I let it matter. It doesn't now.'

A ripple of emotion passed over her face, though what it was he didn't know.

'If it doesn't matter then why are you so tense?' she asked.

But he'd had enough. He moved over to where she stood and pulled her into his arms, easing her naked body against his.

'I'm tense because you're naked and I want you.'

Her hands rested on his chest, not pushing, but definitely holding him at bay. She looked up at him. 'I think I can guess what he wanted from you. But…did *you* want it? Did you want him?'

A narrow flame of anger lit inside him—hot, burning. He'd never thought about that…never let himself think about it. Michel had been warm and kind at first, his fatherly approval balm to Poseidon's grief-stricken soul. And Michel had been proud of him, encouraging him to extend Hydra's operations and supportive of his ideas. He'd often told Poseidon that he was the son he had never had, and Poseidon had loved him like a father.

So when the suggestions had come—that Poseidon could perhaps give back the love Michel had given him—Poseidon hadn't understood. Not at first. Then, when he had, he'd tried to be kind, refusing Michel gently. He hadn't been inclined that way sexually, and had never expected the man he'd thought of as a father to see him as anything more than a son.

But then Michel had become insistent. Poseidon was beautiful, he'd said, so was it any wonder that he wanted him? Just once, he'd promised. That was all it would be. Poseidon had tried to be firm, but then Michel had wept and pleaded, telling him that he loved him, that surely Poseidon could give him just one night. That wasn't much in return for everything Michel had given him. And Poseidon, who'd always felt too deeply and cared too much, hadn't wanted to hurt him.

Nothing would change between them, Michel had promised. *'Indulge an old man,'* he'd said. *'It's only sex... no big deal.'*

You didn't want it.

No, he hadn't.

But he'd given Michel what he'd wanted, and he'd told himself that it *wasn't* a big deal, and had forced himself to believe it. Afterwards he'd expected their relationship to go back to what it had been, just the way Michel had told him it would.

But it hadn't. Because Michel had never spoken to him again.

'What does it matter if I wanted it or not?' Poseidon snapped, the steady anger burning inside him even though it shouldn't. Even though it had been years. 'It made no difference in the end.'

A flame leaped in her eyes, fierce and hot. 'It *does* matter. If you didn't want it then it was sexual assault,

Poseidon. It was rape. No matter if you said yes. You didn't want it. He assaulted you.'

The words felt too sharp, like knives cutting away parts of him. How could it be assault? He'd agreed to it and he hadn't fought it. Michel hadn't hurt him. He hadn't enjoyed it—even if he had been that way inclined, he wouldn't have enjoyed it, because he simply hadn't ever seen Michel in that light—but his enjoyment or otherwise hadn't mattered.

So you didn't feel dirty afterwards? You didn't feel used? You told yourself you were fine, that it wasn't a big deal, but you lied. You've been lying to yourself for years.

He ignored the thought. 'Don't.' He gripped her, hard. 'It's over. It's in the past. Leave it there.'

But of course she didn't.

'My sister was assaulted. Simon was older than she was and he showered her with gifts. He used her, manipulated her. He gave her drugs and then used her addiction to share her with his friends. She didn't say no to him. She loved him. But I know she didn't want what he did to her either.'

'I'm not your sister,' he said roughly. 'It was different.'

'How? He was older than you. A powerful businessman. He manipulated you in the same way Simon manipulated Chrissy.'

There was something cold inside him that his anger hadn't melted and probably never would. A shard of ice that he'd ignored, telling himself it wasn't there. The ice that had settled inside him the morning after he'd got home from Michel's, when he'd got into the shower and had stayed there an entire hour, scrubbing and scrubbing. He didn't know what exactly he'd been trying to wash off. All he knew was that no amount of scrubbing had made him feel clean.

And then, when he'd called Michel the day after that, assuming their relationship would go back to the way it had been, the call had gone straight to voicemail. Michel had never called him back. Never emailed him, never texted. And when Poseidon had visited him he hadn't answered the door.

He'd cut him off cold and Poseidon had never known why.

You do *know why. He never wanted you. Only your body.*

It was a mistake he would never make again.

'I think this conversation is at an end,' he said, gripping her harder. 'Time to give me what you promised, little siren.'

His grip was punishing, the glittering blue of his eyes hard and sharp as sapphires. Everything about him was hard, and Andie hadn't fully comprehended that until now. His body, obviously, and his sex, long and hot, pressing against her stomach. But there was a hardness in his smile, in his laugh, in his voice, when he made everything sound casual and unimportant.

He'd armoured himself—she could see that now. He'd armoured himself with his looks and that smile, that laugh, hiding his true nature away. But she suspected she knew what his true nature was. She saw it whenever he took her in his arms, when he burned like a flame with passion and intensity.

And now she understood why he needed his armour. He'd been taken advantage of. He'd been groomed.

He'd been manipulated and used, his trust betrayed, and it was obvious that he blamed himself.

Stupid, he'd told her. He'd been stupid.

Yet he wasn't to blame, and now she was burning with helpless fury. Not at him, but at the man who'd hurt him.

'Is he dead?' she demanded. 'The man who hurt you? Or is he still alive? Tell me where he lives. I'll call the police.'

A muscle jumped in Poseidon's jaw. 'Andromeda—'

'He hurt you. I can't let that stand—I can't.'

Rage burned through her like wildfire. This was what Chrissy had had happen to her. A powerful, older man manipulating someone younger, more naive, using their own desires against them.

'You didn't deserve the hurt he caused and he deserves to pay.'

Poseidon shook his head. 'He's dead. He doesn't matter any more.'

But he did matter. She could see it in the tension in Poseidon's shoulders, in the tightness in his jaw, in the hard glitter of his eyes.

She'd seen it the moment the plane had landed. Because when she'd looked at him sitting opposite her, his gaze fixed out of the window of the jet, every line in his beautiful face drawn tight, she'd realised, with a kind of shock, that he'd come to matter to her.

It had happened slowly, over the weeks after that night in Monaco, as she'd attended events with him and spent nights in his arms, and she wasn't even sure how. They hadn't talked about anything meaningful or serious, only about movies and books, or occasionally a rousing argument about politics. After which he'd take her to bed, and there was definitely no talking then.

Still, she'd come to learn more about him than she'd intended. He was incisive and perceptive when it came to political arguments, and also well-read. He had an interest in technology, which didn't surprise her, and in philosophy, which did. He thought deeply about things, and he was far more considerate than she'd ever have guessed, and it had come as a shock to find that she liked him.

It had come as a shock to find that his feelings mattered to her, too. That she didn't like him being tense because it meant something was bothering him, and she wanted to know what it was so she could help.

She'd never expected the reason for his tension to be the fact that he'd been assaulted by an older man—and it *had* been an assault. Poseidon didn't want to accept that, it was clear, but that was what it had been. Why else would there still be so much anger in his eyes? He'd told her it didn't matter now, that it was in the past. And, sure, it *was* in the past. But it certainly still mattered. Because it was obviously still hurting him.

His hands were nearly painful, digging into the soft flesh of her hips, but she didn't tell him to let her go. She was so angry for him, and she wanted to do something, but she didn't know what. He didn't want to talk about it, and she knew she couldn't push him—that wouldn't be right. Nor would putting her own anger onto him.

She hated not being able to do anything. *Hated* it. She hadn't known what to do with Chrissy either. All she'd been able to do was be there on the end of the phone, listening to Chrissy as she told Andie about the latest party she'd attended, hearing the hollow sound of her sister's voice. There had been despair in it too, but Chrissy hadn't wanted to talk about what was wrong, and Andie hadn't pushed. She'd been forced to stand silently by as Chrissy slipped further and further away.

Tears of frustration pricked at her eyes, but she knew he wouldn't want her crying over him either, so she blinked them fiercely away. 'Tell me what you need,' she said. 'Anything at all. I'll give it to you.'

He didn't say a word, only bent his head and took her mouth. She let him in. He was so hot, and she could taste the desperation in his kiss. He was running from it, she suspected. Trying to put what had happened with his mentor behind him—to minimise it, pretend it didn't exist. But she knew how the past wouldn't stay where you put it. How it kept creeping in, no matter how hard you tried to push it away.

She'd embraced hers in the end, since her sister seemed so set on haunting her, and had turned her life into a crusade. Yet she could understand why he didn't want to do the same. He'd trusted the man who'd used him...who'd manipulated him. Who'd made him do something he hadn't wanted to do. No wonder he didn't want to come back to this island. What memories must there be here for him?

His mouth became hotter, more demanding, and then abruptly he broke away, pulling her over to the edge of the pool. He got out, then tugged her after him, carrying her, still wet, over to a sun lounger and laying her on it. Then he followed her down, his hot, slick skin sliding over hers, his weight pinning her to the cushions. She reached up and ran her hands over his powerful muscled shoulders and down his strong back, glorying in the feel of his skin.

'I'm sorry,' she said, meeting his gaze. 'I shouldn't have pushed you into telling me. I just…wanted to help you if I could.'

'You can't help everyone, Andromeda. Some people don't need it.'

'You don't?'

'No.' His gaze had darkened, and it was sharp as it looked into hers. 'And I don't need saving.'

It felt as if he'd ripped some kind of protective layer off her. 'I'm not trying to—'

'Aren't you?' Gently he took her hands from where they rested on him and put them down on either side of her head. He held them there. 'Isn't that what you're doing with your cause? With your addiction service? You're trying to make up for the fact that you didn't save her.'

She took a breath, feeling almost winded. 'You think I don't know that? That I don't think about that failure every day?'

'You didn't fail, Andromeda. I told you that.' His gaze was merciless. 'And I'm not a new cause for you to champion, understand? We're sleeping together, and in a couple of days you'll be my wife, but that's where our story ends.'

They hadn't talked about how long they would continue sleeping together, and they hadn't talked about what would happen after the wedding. She'd assumed that they'd go their separate ways, since that was what their agreement had been about, and she'd thought she'd be fine with it.

But hearing him say it so bluntly made her feel… bruised.

He's got under your skin and you weren't supposed to let him.

She shoved the thought aside. She was fine—she wasn't hurt. She knew this wasn't supposed to go on longer than the wedding, that it was just sex and nothing more, so why the thought of it ending should be painful, she had no idea.

'You're *not* a cause,' she said. 'I was only asking if you were okay.'

There was anger in his eyes—she could see it glittering there. This thing with his mentor was an unhealed wound and she'd jolted it. Now he was lashing out.

The realisation made her own anger drain away.

This wasn't about her. This was about what had happened to him, and the fact that no matter how many times he said it didn't matter, it still did.

Like Chrissy did.

'Look,' she said in a quieter tone. 'I know you're not a cause, and I'm not trying to turn you into one. I only wanted to help.'

He said nothing for a long moment, just staring at her, and she couldn't tell what was in his eyes now.

'I meant what I said,' he murmured. 'This *will* end, Andromeda. I don't do relationships—not with anyone.'

Had she given herself away somehow? Made him think that she'd been hurt when he'd told her that? Because she wasn't. Not at all. In fact, that was what she meant to say.

But what came out was, 'Why not? Is it because of what happened with *him*?'

He smiled, but it was hard and brittle. She could see that now. Practised.

'No, why would it be? Michel did teach me one lesson, though. Caring about anything is a mistake. Wanting anything too deeply is a mistake. Feelings in general are a mistake. And they're not a mistake I'm willing to make again.'

She should have left it there, but she couldn't stop herself from asking, 'Why are feelings a mistake? I thought you didn't want him.'

'I didn't. What I wanted was my father back. Now, this conversation is definitely over.'

She could see that he meant it and knew she'd have to let it go. But her heart ached for some mysterious reason known only to itself.

It seemed too bleak not to care. Bleak and lonely. Also, you *had* to care at some point, didn't you? How else could things change? How else could you save people?

Yet it wasn't the time to debate that now. They weren't going to be together much longer anyway, and she didn't want to waste any more moments with him arguing.

All she could do was reach up and pull his head down, taking his mouth, kissing him deeply, passionately, letting him know that while they weren't in a relationship she still wanted him, and he could do with that what he wanted.

And what he wanted appeared to be escape. So she let him spread her thighs, and when he thrust inside her she lifted her hips to meet his. Then she wound her legs around his waist, giving herself up to him and to the pleasure that he was giving her.

He took her hard, driving himself deep into her body,

his mouth on hers, ravaging. He bit her lower lip and then nuzzled down her throat, licking her skin, biting the sensitive cords at the side of her neck. There was a desperation to him, a rawness that he only ever let out when she was in his arms, and she took it, letting her hands caress the strong muscles of his back.

When he put a hand down between her thighs, to touch and caress her there, making her gasp and arch against him, her gaze took in the storms in his deep blue eyes and she knew she was losing something.

She wasn't sure what it was, but it scared her. And when the orgasm came for her, barrelling over her like a freight train and causing the world to explode into flame, she had a horrible feeling that what she was losing was her heart.

CHAPTER NINE

ANDROMEDA STOOD IN the living area of the villa, her glorious figure swathed in the simple gown of white silk that was to be her wedding dress.

Poseidon had made it clear that he wanted to choose the gown himself, though obviously she'd have to like it too, and she'd let him. He didn't ask himself why that was important—just as he didn't ask himself why an unfamiliar possessiveness crept through him whenever he looked at her.

He didn't ask himself why he couldn't settle to anything, either, when surely, after telling Andromeda about Michel the night before, he should feel calmer. Yet he didn't.

Both her questions and her fury had bothered him, making him feel as if she'd ripped a bandage off a wound he hadn't realised was only half-healed, and no amount of putting that bandage back on would help.

He didn't want to think about the night he'd spent with Michel and he never thought about the morning after. Never thought about the days following, when he'd tried to get in touch with him, to resume their friendship, hoping it would go on as if nothing had happened, the way Michel had promised him.

Only to get back silence.

He'd never told anyone what had happened with Michel—not Dimitra, not Asterion—because it didn't concern them. And not because he felt shame or worthlessness. Yes, he'd made a mistake in giving Michel what he'd asked for, but that was all it had been. An error of judgement. It really wasn't worth getting so furious about.

You know it wasn't just an error of judgement.

That cold feeling crawled through him again, but he ignored it. He was good at ignoring it. He'd spend fifteen years doing so, after all. The main thing was that now he'd told her she'd stop asking questions and leave the past to lie where it was.

He didn't want their last few days together marred by more arguments over something that had happened a long time ago.

Only a few more days and yet you're dressing her up in a wedding gown of your choosing and wanting to get all the details right.

But he was tired of listening to his thoughts, so he ignored that one too and stared at her instead.

'Hmm,' she said, studying herself in the full-length mirror, fiddling with a fold of fabric at her hip. 'Do you think this needs adjusting?'

It didn't. Nothing needed adjusting. The dress was perfect, as he had known it would be, the silk wrapping around her curves, the strapless style cupping her luscious breasts. The frothing skirts had been sewn with crystals, making it look as if she'd been dipped in diamonds, and there were more crystals sewn into the bodice. She glittered and, with her red-gold hair loose, she looked like a goddess.

His goddess.

She's not yours, though. Remember?

Everything in him tightened, as if with denial—which was pointless. Because of course she wasn't his and never would be. Perhaps he'd claim a wedding night, but after that they would be going their separate ways.

He strolled over to where Andromeda stood and gave her an outrageously appreciative look in the mirror. 'It's perfect,' he said. 'Change nothing.'

Colour rose in her cheeks, but her gaze when it met his in the mirror was challenging. 'You shouldn't be seeing me in my gown before the big day.'

'If it was a real wedding then, no, I shouldn't.' He circled her, running his eyes over her just to be sure everything was perfect. 'But since it's not a real wedding it doesn't matter.'

'And what happens after the wedding? We haven't talked about it.'

He came to a stop behind her and shrugged. 'We'll have our honeymoon and then we'll go our separate ways.' He lifted his hands and put them on her silk-clad hips. He really couldn't get enough of touching her. 'If you don't want to continue sleeping together for our honeymoon, that's fine. But you should know that I have plans for a wedding night.'

'Oh?' she murmured. 'You have, have you? Well, you might get one. If I decide to give you one.'

A strange jolt of electricity went through him, as if a part of him wasn't happy at the thought of her refusal. Strange… He'd admit to feeling a little possessive of her in that gown, but when it came to sex it shouldn't matter to him if she refused him. It wasn't as if he hadn't had her before, many times over.

He turned his head, brushed his mouth over the side of her neck, making her shiver. 'Are you really going to say no to me? *Can* you say no to me?'

She leaned back against him, relaxing into his body, and sighed. 'You know very well that I can't, Poseidon Teras.'

Satisfaction closed like a fist inside him and he wanted to growl with the pleasure of it. 'Good. I'll have you know I'm going to take shameless advantage of that.'

He brushed another kiss over the side of her neck, then lifted his head to find her gaze meeting his in the mirror once again.

There was something open in it…a vulnerability that stole his breath away.

'Chrissy was always the special one,' she said. 'She had the beauty and she was smart. She got fantastic marks at school. She was supposed to go to university, be successful. While I… I worked hard, but I wasn't a straight-A student like she was. I wasn't as good with people, and I wasn't as beautiful. She said I was jealous, like I told you, but… I guess I wanted what she had. I wanted the beautiful man and the expensive gifts. I wanted to be special.'

She glanced at herself in the mirror, at the crystals sparkling along the bodice of her gown, glittering like stars, then at him again.

'And I feel special, Poseidon. *You* made me feel special.'

He found himself rooted to the spot, as if she'd struck him with a lightning bolt, searing him all the way through. Women told him that they wanted him all the time, told him that they loved the pleasure he gave them, but no one had ever told him that he made them feel special.

'It's just a couple of gowns,' he said, his voice unaccountably rough. 'And a few parties. It's nothing.'

'No,' she said. 'No, I'm not talking about the gowns. I'm not talking about the parties, either. I'm not even talking about the sex—though that's part of it.' She turned around suddenly and looked up at him. 'It's you. You listen to me. Oh, you make it seem as if you don't, with your smiles and your jokes and your casual asides. But you listen. You know what's important to me. Any man could have offered me money in return for being his bride, but you offered me more than that. Ongoing sponsorship. Publicity. Exposure. You introduced me to people who could help. And you planned a special event just for me and Chrissy's Hope because you knew it was important to me.'

The intensity in her eyes made him uncomfortable. Made him want to deny it. Because it had been nothing. A few words in the right ears and money he wouldn't ever use himself.

'I was being a businessman. It wasn't for you, Andromeda. It was all for me, and for Dimitra.'

'Perhaps. But, like I said, another man would have offered me just the money, or maybe even threatened me. They wouldn't have kicked Simon out of that casino, and they certainly wouldn't have sat down and held my hand and listened as I spilled my guts about Chrissy.'

He remembered that night in Monaco and the feel of her cold hands in his, the grief in her green eyes. A grief he'd wanted so badly to ease, not knowing how. The only thing he had thought to offer her was the comfort of his touch and hope that was enough.

'That was only because I wanted to get you into bed,' he said—because surely it had only been that. 'Nothing more.'

But she shook her head. 'You're wrong. You know, I was expecting you to be just like Simon, but you're not. Not in any way. You're more of a decent man than he is or ever will be.'

'You make me sound like a paragon.' He tried to smile. 'I don't like pedestals, little siren. I'm not suited to them.'

She didn't answer that, only giving him the most direct stare and making his breath catch. 'You do know it wasn't your fault, don't you?'

Another shock went through him, shaking him to his foundations. 'What?' His smile felt pasted on. 'I'm not sure what you're talking about.'

But he did know. They both did.

'You're a good person, Poseidon,' Andromeda said. 'It wasn't your fault.'

She stepped close to him and laid a hand against his cheek, then she went up on her toes and pressed a soft kiss against his mouth.

He found his hand was at the small of her back, bringing her even closer. But not only because he was hard for her—even though he was. He just couldn't bear the distance between them. He wanted her warmth and her scent, the sweetness of her physical presence.

She let him, and then laid her head on his chest—a gentle weight that somehow felt heavier than mountains. He wanted to wrap his arms around her. He wanted to hold her not for any other reason but the sheer joy and comfort of it.

He'd never wanted to hug anyone before, and he couldn't remember the last time anyone had hugged him. His mother had always been too interested in her tempestuous relationship with his father, and his father hadn't been a physically effusive man except with his wife. Asterion had clapped him on the shoulder in a brotherly way a couple of times, but that had been it.

So now, when Andromeda's arms slid around his waist, holding him, the weight in his chest, the heaviness of it, increased somehow. She was soft, and much smaller than he was, yet it felt as if she was the one anchoring him in place.

His resistance faded, his arms tightening around her, and then they were standing there, holding one another, her head on his chest, his lips brushing her hair.

He closed his eyes, felt something shifting inside him and settling into place, like the final piece of a jigsaw puzzle. By telling him how special she'd made him feel she'd given him a little piece of herself. It was a gift. *She* was a gift. And he needed to give her something in return.

No, that was wrong. He didn't *need* to. He *wanted* to.

'I wanted Michel's approval,' he heard himself say roughly. 'I was desperate for it. My father had always favoured Asterion more than me, and nothing I did seemed to make any difference to him. But I didn't have to do anything for Michel. He was proud of me no matter what. At least…that's what I thought initially. I didn't know he'd always wanted more.'

His arms tightened fractionally, holding her even closer against him.

'I didn't want him, and I told him so. But he pointed out all the things he'd done for me…said that one night was the least I could give him in return. I didn't know what else to do.' He paused, inhaling her familiar scent. 'After he cut off all contact, I thought I'd done something wrong.'

'You weren't stupid,' she murmured against his chest. 'What you said yesterday about yourself? Yes, you were young, but you weren't stupid and you didn't do anything wrong. He manipulated you.'

Poseidon didn't like how vulnerable that made him feel. How powerless. Intellectually, he knew it was true, that Michel *had* manipulated him. But even now, all these years later, it felt difficult to accept emotionally.

'Perhaps he did,' he said. 'Michel told me he only wanted a night…that it wouldn't matter, that everything would go back to the way it always was afterwards. And I believed him. I forced myself to believe him. Yet I came home the next day and spent an hour in the shower trying to get myself clean.'

The stain still lingers, doesn't it?

And that hadn't been the worst part. Despite what Michel had done to him—despite the trust he'd violated—Poseidon had still loved him like a father and had wanted their relationship to go back to the way it had been before.

Love. It was nothing but betrayal.

Andromeda didn't say anything, only held him tight, and somehow that was exactly what he wanted. Someone to hold him and to listen.

'I never told anyone,' he went on, and the words were getting easier, the urge to get it off his chest growing. 'I never told Asterion or Dimitra. I kept telling myself that it wasn't worth mentioning, that it was just a minor mistake. No big deal. But I think there was a part of me that never quite believed it. And I think there was deeper reason I never told anyone.' He took a breath. 'I didn't say anything because I was…ashamed. I felt dirty. It wasn't supposed to be a big deal yet it was.'

There was blackness behind his lids, but that was fine. The blackness was safe.

'And when he cut off all contact with me I felt…used. As if the rest of me wasn't worth anything. But even that wasn't the worst part. The worst part was that even after I gave him what he wanted, and he cut me off without a word, I still loved him.'

Andromeda turned her face into the hard wall of his chest and closed her eyes. She could hear the beat of his heart, faster than it had been before, betraying his agitation. He was warm, though, and he smelled so good, so familiar. Yet every one of those powerful muscles was drawn tight.

The crystals of her gown were pressing painfully into her, but she didn't want to move. His arms around her were tight, as if he couldn't bear to let her go, and she didn't want him to. She wanted to stand there all day, in the circle of his arms, and hold him right back. Because it felt as if her touch was something he needed.

She hadn't meant to tell him about her own jealousy, even though she'd told herself she wasn't jealous of her sister, only envious. How she'd always wanted to be the special one and never was. But she'd stood there in the gown Poseidon had bought for her—her wedding gown—and he'd looked at her with such blatant appreciation. A beautiful man, who'd treated her with so much gentleness and respect. A beautiful man who'd been hurt, and who was possibly afraid to admit it. She'd wanted to give him something.

She'd been going to tell him that she wanted to stop sleeping with him. She hadn't planned on giving him a reason, either, because she didn't want to tell him that if they kept on doing this she was in danger of falling for him and the thought filled her with dread. Mainly because he'd been so clear that a relationship was never going to be on the cards. Not that she was ready for a relationship anyway, but still…

But he'd kissed her neck, put his warm hands on her hips, and she'd known she couldn't tell him that she didn't want him, because that would have been a lie she couldn't bring herself to say. What she'd wanted was for him to feel as special as he'd made her feel, so she'd told him about his effect on her, even though it had felt as if she was baring a part of her soul and shouldn't be.

His eyes had flared then, as if what she'd said was a shock to him, and her heart had contracted in her chest— because did he not know how special he was? Did he genuinely not know?

Then his arms had come around her, almost hesitantly at first, then tighter, and he'd brought her close, and then he'd begun to speak, to tell her about Michel, and now she was crying. Pressing her face against his chest because she didn't want him to see her tears. He had enough to bear.

He was giving her something of himself too. Something he'd given to no one else—not even his brother.

You can't allow it to mean anything to you. You're already in deeper than you expected.

Oh, she knew that. But how could she allow what he'd said to mean nothing? This was something raw, painful, and deeply personal, and she'd heard the roughness in his voice. It had been hard for him to say, and yet he'd said it to her.

Of course it meant something, and to deny that would be wrong.

In that case, you have to be honest with yourself. You're in love with him.

Her heart was full and aching in her chest, a sweet agony. For him and what he'd gone through, and all alone.

It must have been a special kind of hurt too. Because even at twenty he would have been tall and powerful, no one's idea of a typical victim. But the force hadn't come from physical altercation. It had come, maybe even worse, from emotional manipulation. And he was a man of deep feelings, no matter how he insisted that he didn't care about anything.

It wasn't fair. It was wrong on just about every level.

And, yes, she loved him. She'd fallen for him a long time ago. Perhaps it had even been when he'd put his coat around her shoulders the day they'd met, in such a respectful and gentlemanly fashion, totally at odds with the man she'd thought he was.

But she knew now why he didn't want a relationship. Why he couldn't do love. Because love had been tainted for him by Michel. So perhaps it was best if she didn't tell him how she felt and kept that to herself.

It was going to make everything that much more painful, though.

More tears pricked her eyes, but she didn't let them fall. She wouldn't think about it, her stupid heart. He was the most important thing, not her feelings, and this moment was his, not hers.

'Nothing you did was wrong,' she said, her voice muffled by his shirt and his chest. 'And nothing you felt was wrong. He was the abuser. He manipulated your emotions and used them against you to get what he wanted. And love doesn't disappear instantly just because someone hurts you.'

She didn't look at him, because this was his private pain and she didn't want to force herself on him.

'Chrissy loved Simon right up until the end. Even though he hurt her and betrayed her.'

His arms still held her tightly and she felt his cheek press against the top of her head. Her heart ached. He was so much bigger than she was, so much stronger, and she felt almost enveloped by him. Yet he was holding her fast, as if he didn't want to let her go. As if he needed her.

For a long moment she stood there, listening to the beat of his heart, her eyes closed, breathing in his scent, loving his warmth. Then she felt his arms loosen around her and his body shifted. Only then did she look up at him, meeting his blue eyes, dark and depthless with an emotion she didn't recognise.

He didn't move away, only lifted his hands and cupped her face between them. 'And she hurt you, didn't she?' he asked gently.

The question was a shock. She wanted to deny it— tell him that it wasn't about her feelings. Because what did her feelings matter when Chrissy was gone? But the truth was that Chrissy hadn't listened, had ignored all her warnings, and if she hadn't things might have been different. And, yes, that hurt.

'She didn't listen to me,' Andie said. 'Mum didn't listen to me. Chrissy didn't want to believe that the path she was heading down was the wrong one, and Mum wouldn't hear a bad word said against her. I felt so helpless. So…useless.'

'You are neither,' he murmured, looking at her so intently she had no breath left. '*Asteri mou*, you're brave, and strong, and caring. You're special, Andromeda. You're the most special woman I have ever met.' He bent his head, brushing his mouth over hers. 'Let me show you how much.'

She didn't protest when his hands dropped to the zip on her gown, easing it down, then gently pulling away the fabric until eventually she was standing there only in her knickers.

Carefully, he draped the gown over the back of the couch, then came back to her, falling to his knees in front of her. He lifted his hands and ran them caressingly over her breasts, hips, and thighs, before leaning in and kissing her stomach. Then his hands moved to the waistband of her knickers and he pulled them down her legs, helping her step out of them before gripping her hips and kissing his way down between her thighs. He licked her, long and deep, his hands stroking and touching, mapping her curves with such reverence that the tears she was holding back stung once again.

He tasted her like wine, in slow sips that had her thighs quivering and cries of ecstasy gathering in her throat. He explored her tenderly, taking his time, holding her as if she was the most precious thing in the universe.

He knelt there and worshipped her, and when she was shaking between his hands he rose to his feet, picked her up and carried her to the couch. Then he laid her on the cushions, stripped his own clothes off and followed her down.

Andie lifted her arms to him, welcoming him as he stretched out over her. the slide of his hot, bare skin over hers was an intimate pleasure she knew she'd never get tired of. And when he positioned himself, she reached down and guided him home.

He slid into her and it felt perfect. So right. So good. She lifted her legs and wrapped them around his waist, holding him deep inside her. He stared down at her as he began to move, and she could see the desire, the depth of his hunger for her. She gloried in it, spreading her hands on his powerful shoulders and stroking down his muscled back, touching him with the same care and reverence he was using to touch her. His deep blue gaze was her entire world.

This magic they created between them would end soon, but she didn't want it to. She didn't want to lose this—she didn't want to lose him. Yet it was going to happen, and there was nothing she could do about it. He didn't want a relationship—he was so clear about that—and she couldn't insist. It wasn't her place and it didn't feel right, not given what had happened to him.

You'll have to be happy with this, because this is all you'll ever have.

Her heart felt raw and bruised, and there was pain beneath the pleasure. But she ignored all of it and let herself sink into the ecstasy, let herself feel, for the first time, as if she really was as special as he told her she was.

As the orgasm overtook her she clung tightly to him, and when she fell, he fell with her. As the pleasure drowned them both, she knew one thing: she was going to have her beautiful man, and she was going to have her beautiful gown, and her beautiful wedding, in a beautiful church. She wouldn't be able to keep any of it, but she'd be grateful for it nevertheless.

After all, it was more than her sister had ever had.

CHAPTER TEN

THE LITTLE CHURCH was full as Poseidon waited by the altar. It was mostly full of friends of Dimitra's and other assorted island aristocracy, since she'd insisted on inviting as many people as she could.

Asterion stood next him as his best man, a silent, steady presence, currently gazing with adoration at his wife, Brita. The exquisite ex-nun was sitting with Dimitra and gazing back at Asterion with the same sickening adoration.

Though Poseidon barely noticed. A curious tension sat inside him that felt almost like dread, but surely couldn't be. He was marrying Andromeda, and it was going to make Dimitra happy and the shares of the family trust secure, so what on earth was there to dread? And after the wedding they'd have a wedding night, then a wonderful honeymoon, before going their separate ways. There was nothing at all to fear.

To distract himself, he thought again of yesterday, and the feel of Andromeda's body against his, the way she'd fitted in his arms, her arms tight around him. Holding him as if he mattered.

He hadn't felt as if he'd mattered for a very long time—he could admit that to himself now. Michel had made him feel worthless, and yet Andromeda's simple acceptance of what had happened to him, her insistence that he'd done nothing wrong, that his emotions around Michel hadn't been wrong either, had eased a tightness in him in a way he couldn't articulate.

It was still hard to admit to himself that what Michel had done to him *was* a big deal, that it *had* been assault. Essentially, he'd been groomed—which was very difficult to accept, because he wasn't a victim in any way, shape, or form.

It was still hard to accept that his love for Michel wasn't wrong either, considering how it had been used against him. She'd told him that none of it was his fault but, again, while he knew that intellectually, emotionally it was a different story.

Yet there was a certain freedom in accepting what she'd told him, and he hadn't realised that until she'd said the words. It was as if a weight had been lifted. Subconsciously he knew that a part of himself had always thought he was to blame for what had happened, and now it was as if she'd given him permission to leave the blame behind.

He'd felt lighter the night before than he'd ever felt in his entire life, and yet now, as he stared down towards the entrance to the church, ignoring the buzz of conversation from the assembled wedding guests, that weight was back and he wasn't sure why.

He was conscious of Dimitra's far too shrewd gaze on him, as if she knew something he didn't—which didn't help.

She'd assisted Andromeda with her wedding preparations and had told him before the ceremony, with great certainty, that Andromeda was a fine choice because she'd never seen a woman so in love. Poseidon, she'd pronounced, had redeemed himself. The terrible Sea Monster was now tamed.

Yet right in this moment he didn't feel tamed. Something inside him was raging and he couldn't describe it. It was a strange not-dread, and a fierce anticipation, a raw possessiveness too, as if he would fight anyone who got in his way when it came to marrying Andromeda. Which was ridiculous—because who would stop him? She was going to walk down the aisle towards him soon, and then he'd take her off to his house for their wedding night and he'd keep her up till dawn. And after that their honeymoon in the Maldives, where he'd make love to her at every opportunity, wake up with her in the morning, talk to her about what interested her, what annoyed her, what made her passionate, her dreams, her hopes…

Then you will both walk away.

Yes. That was exactly it. That was the only reason all of that was even possible.

The church doors opened just then and in walked Andromeda. She was alone—she hadn't wanted anyone to give her away—and, in addition to the beautiful wedding gown she wore a silk veil that covered her face and extended down her back. She held in her hands some white peonies, with petals the same gossamer silk as her gown, and the first thing she did as she came into the church was look straight at him, her green eyes clear and steady.

A sudden rush of feeling gripped him hard by the throat. She knew his secret—the secret he hadn't even realised was a secret, the shame he hadn't been aware was shame. She knew and, despite knowing, she'd put her arms around his neck and kissed him, had let him into her body. She'd told him that he made her feel special, and in return she'd made him feel as if he wasn't that stupid boy he'd once been. The boy who'd believed the lies he'd been fed, who'd given away a part of his soul because he'd been so desperate for love.

She'd looked at him, seen all that shame and those feelings of worthlessness, and she'd accepted him despite all that. He hadn't been aware of how badly he'd needed that until now.

His chest ached as she came closer. He felt raw, undone, and violently possessive in a way he never had before.

You can't feel this. Not about her. Not about anyone.

It was true. He'd tried not to feel anything at all after Michel, because that was safer. He didn't want to be vulnerable to anyone—not again—and yet this beautiful, special woman had somehow found her way beneath defences he'd thought rock-solid. A mistake.

Perhaps going on a honeymoon with her was a bad idea. Perhaps wanting a wedding night was a bad idea. Perhaps right after the ceremony they should go their separate ways. Yet even as he thought this a part of him growled in silent rebellion, and he knew damn well he wasn't going to give up his wedding night or his honeymoon. It was selfish of him, and maybe a risk he couldn't afford, but he was going to have them. He was going to have as much of her as he could before it was time to say goodbye.

She walked slowly down the aisle to him and it was all he could do not to give in to the urge to meet her in the middle, toss her over his shoulder and carry her off, away from all these prying eyes. Take her somewhere private, where it was just the two of them, so he could sate his hunger for her over and over until this fierce, burning feeling was no more.

But he stayed where he was, because he wasn't an animal, standing rigidly beside the altar as she came to stand next to him and the ceremony began. When the priest joined their hands and said the prayers, the words echoed in his head, sounding like the truth instead of the lies they actually were. And when Asterion stood behind them and the exchange of wedding crowns was performed, he could hardly hear the priest through the thunder of his own heartbeat.

But then Andromeda glanced at him, her green eyes calm and direct through her veil, her wedding crown the perfect addition, and somehow the rush of blood through his veins steadied. And the platinum circle of his wedding ring felt abruptly like her arms around him the day before, anchoring him.

Then at last there was the trip around the altar three times, and finally it was time to kiss his new wife. Again he had to battle with himself not to ravage her mouth, lift her into his arms and carry her away. He would do that later. He could control himself. It was nothing. This feeling was nothing.

The way it was nothing with Michel?

No, this wasn't the same. This had nothing whatsoever to do with Michel.

His kiss was light, a mere brush of his lips on hers, as chaste as he could make it. Though when he lifted his head and found her looking up at him, with glittering sparks of heat and amusement in her eyes, he almost kissed her again, because she was so beautiful and he wanted her so badly.

There would be photos and register signings after the ceremony, and a reception to get through, but Poseidon decided then and there that the reception could be damned. He wanted to take his new wife back to his house, where they could be alone. Dimitra wouldn't mind. All she'd see was a couple in love who were desperate to be together.

Once the formalities were over, he grabbed Andromeda's hand and pulled her down the church steps to the wedding car. 'I don't want to wait until after the reception,' he murmured as he pulled open the door. 'I want my wedding night now.'

She went pink. 'Now? But everyone will know exactly what we're doing.'

'Good,' he said. 'I hope they do. It'll only add to the illusion.'

It's not an illusion, though, is it?

He ignored that thought too, pulling her into his arms as soon as the car door was shut behind them. She was warm and sweet, relaxing against him, her veil draped over his arm, her head against his shoulder, and he kissed her long and deep and hungry.

'You're my wife now, Andromeda,' he murmured against her mouth. 'And I need to claim you.'

'You've already claimed me.'

Her voice sounded husky, and when he raised his head and looked down at her there was something fierce and glittering in her eyes, an emotion he couldn't name. It made his own heart clench like a fist in his chest.

'You claimed me the day you came out of your building and put your coat around my shoulders.'

His throat tightened. The dread that had gripped him at the beginning of the ceremony was creeping up on him again and coiling in his heart. Because although he might tell himself all he liked that he didn't know what emotion burned in her eyes, he knew all the same. She felt something for him, didn't she?

'Little siren,' he said, his own voice as husky as hers, 'this will end, remember? We will have a magnificent wedding night, and a glorious honeymoon, but after that this affair of ours will be over.'

Her gaze flickered a moment, then steadied. 'Yes. I know. You told me.'

'I can't give you more.'

He didn't want to have to repeat himself, but that look in her eyes… She couldn't feel anything for him. That was only going to end in pain for her.

Her hand came up, her fingertips touching his cheekbone lightly. 'I know you can't.' Her voice was clear and steady, and yet there was a note in it that made him ache. A note heavy with yearning and regret.

She wants more.

But he couldn't give her more. He *wouldn't* give her more. And if she already felt something for him, then it made their eventual parting even more inevitable.

Which means you should say goodbye to her now. She deserves someone to make her feel special for the rest of her life, not just tonight. Not just for the next two weeks.

Ice crawled through his veins. He was a selfish man— he'd always been a selfish man—and taking a wedding night, having a honeymoon, was all about feeding his own lust, his own hunger.

You're just like Michel in the end.

The ice solidified, hardening inside him. He *was* like Michel, like her sister's boyfriend Simon. Men who used the emotions of others against them in order to satisfy themselves. He'd done it from the very beginning—from the moment he'd come out of his office to see her chained to that statue, shouting into her megaphone. He'd used her love for her sister and her grief to make her do something she didn't want to do. Then he'd used their chemistry to satisfy his own desire for her.

It didn't matter that she'd agreed to it all. It didn't matter that she'd told him he'd treated her with respect, that he'd made her feel special. He'd still made her do something she never would have even considered and he knew what that felt like. How in the end it made you feel dirty and used and worthless.

He couldn't do the same thing to Andromeda. He'd rather die.

Carefully, even though every part of him was stiff with denial, he eased her from his lap.

Her eyes widened. 'What's wrong?'

An ache was settling inside him, making his chest tight, even though he tried to ignore it. He had to do this now and he had to do this quickly—it would be better for them both.

Poseidon met her gaze. 'I'm sorry, Andromeda. But I've changed my mind. I think it's best if we end this now. I'll take you home and you can gather your things. My jet will be available to take you back to London tonight.'

* * *

Andie had no idea what had happened. She'd been in his arms, relaxing against him, relishing his heat and strength. The next moment he'd put her out of his lap and told her he was sending her home.

What had she done wrong?

When she'd walked through the church doors and seen him waiting for her at the altar, it had felt like a dream come true. No, it *was* a dream come true. She'd been wearing a beautiful dress, in a beautiful church, and was marrying a beautiful man, and then they were going off on a wonderful honeymoon.

The spectre of leaving him waited in the distance, but she hadn't been thinking about it. Their separate ways could wait. She wanted to enjoy what she had now.

Except then, in the car, in his arms, she'd watched as the heat in his eyes had dimmed, become dark, and he'd pushed her out of his lap. Told her there would be no wedding night, no honeymoon. That she would be leaving now.

He did understand that she'd accepted that their affair would end, didn't he? She knew he couldn't give her more. She wasn't asking for more, anyway, and she was fine with it.

You're not fine with it.

Well, no, but she wasn't going to push. She never would—not with him.

Her heart was beating fast and she wanted to reach for him, pull his arms back around her, but she kept them in her lap instead.

'Why?' she asked, trying not to sound demanding. 'I thought we were going to have a wedding night at least.'

'I thought so too.' The vivid blue of his eyes was darkening into black now, the lines of his face becoming rigid. 'But, like I said, I changed my mind.'

Her throat tightened, a stab of pain shooting through her. 'Is it me? Was it something...?'

'No,' he interrupted quickly. 'It's nothing you did—nothing at all. A wedding night was something I wanted, Andromeda. In fact, I demanded it. Just as I demanded this wedding. You didn't want to marry me—you didn't want to have anything to do with me. But I made you. And I used your grief for Chrissy to do it.'

She knew immediately what he meant, and everything inside her turned cold. 'Poseidon, you're not him,' she said very clearly. 'You're not.'

He gave her a cool look. 'Am I not? Michel used my feelings for him, my love for him, against me. He used it to manipulate me into giving him what he wanted. Aren't I just doing the same thing to you?'

'No.' She couldn't keep the fierce note from her voice. 'No, you're not. You gave me a choice. You never forced me into it. Yes, part of it was my feelings for Chrissy, but *I* decided whether to do it or not. And you didn't threaten me with anything if I said no.'

'I wouldn't have given you the money if you'd refused.'

'That's not manipulation, Poseidon. You were very clear the whole way through about what you were prepared to give me and what you wanted in return. Even in Monaco you were clear. You didn't spring anything on me that I wasn't expecting.'

He shook his head. 'Perhaps. But what I'm doing now is definitely manipulation. I want that wedding night, Andromeda. And I want that honeymoon too. But it's not fair of me to take it when you want more.' He paused a moment, his gaze searching. 'And you *do* want more, don't you, little siren?'

Her heart lurched at the gentleness in his voice and there were tears in her eyes. She didn't want to cry, though, so she blinked them fiercely back. 'Look, I know what you said about us going our separate ways afterwards, and I can handle—'

'Andie,' he said very softly, 'that's not what you really want.'

She wanted to get angry, deny it. Tell him that he couldn't speak for her, and ask him what did he know about what she wanted anyway? But she couldn't find her anger now—and besides, what would be the point? She couldn't hide what was in her heart. Not when she felt this strongly, this powerfully. She'd always striven for honesty.

'No,' she said in a husky voice. 'You're right. That's not what I really want.'

A muscle jumped in his jaw. 'I can't give—'

'I know you can't.' This time it was her turn to interrupt. 'And I'd never force you or manipulate you into it.' More tears prickled, and this time she didn't blink them away. 'But I… I can't lie. I do want more. Because the truth is that I've fallen in love with you, Poseidon Teras.'

His gaze had darkened almost into black, but he didn't say anything. So she went on, because she might as well.

'I always told myself that it was Chrissy who had the white wedding dreams, not me, but that was a lie too. A lie I told myself because I didn't want to admit that I'm more like my sister than I should be. I wanted a handsome man to sweep me off my feet. I wanted the white dress and a beautiful church. And I wanted to be some-one's wife. To be loved.'

His black lashes fell, his features tightening as if she'd delivered a mortal blow, but she hadn't said everything that was in her heart yet, so she continued.

'I love you, Poseidon. But not because you need sav-ing, or because I can heal you, or because you're a cause I'm giving my all to. I love you because you listen, and you're thoughtful. Because you're intelligent, and you disagree with me, and that makes me think. You surprise me, and you respect me, and you make me feel special. And no one has ever given me any of those things.'

'Andromeda—'

'No, I haven't finished.' She took a shaky breath, gaz-ing at the pure lines of his profile. 'I'm selfish. I want to keep all of it. But… I don't want it if you don't.' The tears escaped, sliding down over her cheeks, but she made no move to brush them away, just as she didn't try to keep the hoarse note of pain from her voice. 'The last thing I would ever do is force you to give me something you don't want to give.'

His lashes lifted then, and he looked at her. The ex-pression on his face tore at her. Intensity burned there, along with something longing, something yearning, and a regret that broke her heart.

'I'm sorry, my beautiful little siren,' he said, his voice as husky as hers. 'I wish I could give you what you want. But I made a promise to myself years ago that the only things I will ever let myself care about are my brother, my grandmother, and my company. I can't give anyone anything more.'

He lifted a hand to her cheek and gently brushed away her tears.

'You deserve to be with someone who'll make you feel as special as you really are. Who'll give you all the love you deserve for the rest of your life. You deserve to have someone who hasn't been broken like I have.'

Her heart was tearing itself in two, pain radiating through her entire body. She'd had no idea it would hurt this much.

'You're not broken, Poseidon. Don't allow Michel that power. You're an amazing man, and don't let anyone tell you any different.' She leaned into his hand, allowing herself this one last touch. 'But I understand. And I want you to know that if there's one person in this world who loves all of you, every part of you—even the part that you think is broken beyond repair—that person is me.'

A raw and anguished expression flickered in his eyes, and for a second she thought he might change his mind.

Everything in her went still.

But then his hand dropped from her cheek and his gaze shuttered. 'Find someone who feels that way about you, Andromeda. That's the very least of what you deserve.'

She couldn't find even the slightest spark of anger with which to argue. Not that she wanted to get angry with him. He'd made his choice and, since that choice had been taken from him once before, this time she had to let him make it. She couldn't—wouldn't—force him or guilt trip him into choosing differently.

It wasn't his fault that she wasn't enough to make him change his mind. She hadn't been enough for Chrissy, either.

But one thing was clear. For her own sanity she needed to put as much distance between them as possible, as quickly as possible.

He was right. It was time for her to go home.

She looked down at her hands, twisted in her lap. The silk of her wedding dress was spotted darkly with tears.

'I don't want to go back to your house,' she said. 'Just take me to the airport. Please.'

CHAPTER ELEVEN

POSEIDON SAT IN the darkness of his living room, clutching the tumbler containing his third straight whisky while he stared at the wedding ring circling the third finger of his left hand.

It was his wedding night, but he'd been as good as his word. Andromeda had wanted to go straight to the airport so that was where he'd taken her. And now she'd left for London, flying away from him into the night, and that was as it should be. That was what he'd wanted.

Yet recalling her face, and the tears streaming down it, ripped something apart deep in his soul. There had been a peculiar agony in watching her go up the stairs into the jet, the skirts of her wedding gown clutched in her hand, and he hadn't expected that. He'd thought he'd be relieved, if anything, because he had what he'd wanted at last. Her name on a marriage certificate, someone legally his wife, Dimitra's challenge met.

But the feeling in his heart wasn't relief, but pain. As if she'd taken a piece of his soul with her when she left. He didn't understand why. She loved him, she'd said in the car, and that had made a part of him leap in wild hope, while another part had felt frozen from the inside out.

What was hopeful about love? Love made you feel

dirty. Love made you feel used. Love was agony. Love was a vulnerability that could be used against you when you were least expecting it. Love was power—a weapon that could deliver a mortal blow—and he would never willingly put that kind of weapon in anyone's hands ever again.

Losing his parents had left him vulnerable, because he'd loved them. Michel had taken advantage of that love. Michel had used it for his own ends. And Poseidon couldn't make the same mistake a second time.

So he'd had to let her go. He couldn't give her the love she needed, the love she deserved, and keeping her for only a wedding night and a honeymoon, knowing that she loved him, would only be to visit the same kind of emotional torture on her that Michel had visited on him.

He couldn't do it. He wouldn't. She needed to be free to find someone better than he was. Someone who could love her for the amazing woman she was and who had more than just sex to offer her. God knew, that was all the value he had. Michel had taught him that.

He had nothing else to give anyone.

Poseidon sat there for a long time, waiting for the pain in his heart to go away, but it didn't. It felt like grief, which was odd, because no one had died.

Finally, he heard voices in the hallway—his housekeeper's and another, much deeper. Then, at last, a tall figure strolled into the room.

'Emulating me, brother?' Asterion said, coming over to where Poseidon sat before settling into the chair opposite. 'I have to say, brooding doesn't suit you.'

Poseidon's fingers tightened around his tumbler.

One day he'd have to tell Asterion about Michel, but he couldn't face it now.

'What are you doing here?' he demanded gracelessly.

'Someone said they saw Andromeda boarding the jet. By herself. So I thought I'd come and see what the issue was.'

'The issue is that she's gone,' he said flatly. 'So I suppose that's that.'

'I suppose so,' Asterion observed. 'If by "that" you mean drinking yourself into a coma.'

'It's a party.' Poseidon lifted his tumbler and tried pasting on his usual smile, but it took so much effort that he stopped. 'Please join me.'

'Thank you, but no.' Asterion leaned back in the chair and stretched his long legs out. 'I don't do pity parties.'

Poseidon tried his usual laugh too, but it came out sounding hollow. 'It's not a pity party. What are you talking about?'

Asterion's blue gaze, so like his own, merely stared back. 'Of course it is. You're sitting here, brooding like Heathcliff, drinking yourself into a stupor because your wife has left you.'

Poseidon decided to give up pretending. 'She didn't leave me. I told her to go.'

Asterion looked at him with mild curiosity. 'Why on earth did you do that? Any fool can see you're madly in love with her.'

A shock went through him like lightning, sharp and hard. 'I'm not in love with her,' he said, ignoring the way his heart was pressing painfully against his ribs and how the words felt like lies in his mouth.

'Of course you are,' Asterion said patiently, using his

elder-brother voice, as he'd used to do when Poseidon was very young. 'I saw the way you looked at her the moment she entered the church. And I saw the way she looked at you too. Even Dimitra did. So, again, why on earth did you tell her to leave?'

His brother was wrong—just flat-out wrong. He didn't love her. He *couldn't* love her. Love was a choice and he'd decided it wasn't for him.

'One day I'll tell you.' He lifted his tumbler and took another sip of his whisky, the alcohol burning like fire inside him. 'But now, suffice to say, I decided it was better for her if she left.'

Asterion frowned. 'Better for her how?'

He took another swallow of whisky. 'Let's just say I wouldn't wish love on my worst enemy.'

'Thank you for intimating that I am even worse than your worst enemy.'

Poseidon stared at him, trying to ignore the pain in his heart. 'How do you bear it?' he asked abruptly. 'How *can* you bear it?'

'Love?' Asterion smiled, as if he was remembering something very pleasant indeed. 'I don't "bear" love. I take it. I embrace it. I cover myself with it. I have it and it is more precious to me than anything else in my entire life.' He leaned forward, elbows on his knees. 'Love is a good thing, my brother. Believe me, I know. Don't be afraid of it. We lost our parents so young, but don't let those scars stop you from taking a chance at happiness.' His gaze, always serious, became even more so. 'And you deserve happiness, Poseidon. So does she.'

His heart clenched tightly in his chest, the ache in it getting even worse. Love was a good thing? Love meant happiness? Perhaps for Asterion it meant those things, but that hadn't been his experience. And what was happiness anyway?

She loves you. She made you happy.

He stilled. She *did* love him—she'd told him so. And her love had never made him feel guilty or dirty or ashamed. It had never caused him pain. Those things were also true. Her love was grounding. It made him feel good. Made him feel as if he had value. And in her arms he'd tasted something more than mere physical pleasure...something deeper...something that had felt a lot like...happiness.

She would never do to you what Michel did.

The knowledge settled in him like a stone thrown into a lake, sinking straight to the bottom and lying there, heavy with truth.

She was nothing but honest, nothing but straight up. She could have used his desire for her against him and she hadn't. Not once. And at the end, in the car, with tears streaming down her face, she'd let him make a choice. He hadn't chosen her, and even though that had caused her pain she hadn't protested, hadn't argued. She'd only told him once again that she loved him and then had let him push her away.

It was never about her, though, was it? It was always about you.

Poseidon's throat tightened, his heart weighted and achingly heavy. Perhaps that was right. Perhaps it really *was* about him. About his fear...about how, after Michel had cut off contact with him, he'd felt worthless. If there was nothing about him that anyone would want, why did he think he had anything of any value to offer Andromeda?

'Don't allow him that power. You're an amazing man. Don't let anyone tell you any different.'

That was what she'd told him in the car and he hadn't believed her. Because if he was so amazing, why had that man forced himself on him and why had he lied to him?

You're still giving him power. You're still letting him take your choice from you. Because if he hadn't been in your past you wouldn't have let anything come between you and Andromeda.

Understanding burst through him, so powerful that he could hardly breathe let alone speak. Because it was true. If nothing had happened with Michel, he would have brought down heaven if it had meant he could be with his siren.

All these years later and he was still letting Michel make his choices for him. Still letting him have power. And that wasn't love—he could see that now. Love *wasn't* manipulation. It *wasn't* a weapon.

Love was Andromeda's arms holding him.

Love was the look in her green eyes as she'd walked down the aisle to meet him.

Love was the tears that streamed down her face as she'd told him she would never force him to do something he didn't want to.

Love was the reason she fought her battles, for her sister, and he knew that she'd fight them for him too.

And love was the raw, passionate feeling in his heart, the pain in his soul. The grief he'd felt watching her walk up the stairs to the jet and fly away from him.

He loved her.

He loved her so much it was sweet agony and glory all rolled into one. It was standing on the edge of a cliff and jumping off into the terrifying void, only to fly...

Asterion nodded, as if Poseidon had spoken every word of his thoughts aloud. 'I think you understand now, don't you?' he said comfortably.

Poseidon lifted his tumbler, drained it, then put it back on the table next to him with a firm click. 'Tell Dimitra I have to go to London to retrieve my wife,' he said. 'It appears we missed our honeymoon flight.'

Asterion smiled. 'And your plans for a quick divorce...?'

'Are on hold,' Poseidon said as he strode for the door. 'Indefinitely.'

There was some muck-up with the flight plan and the jet ended up being diverted to Paris, where they sat on the Tarmac for what seemed like hours. Not that Andie was taking any notice of time.

She'd held it together until after the jet had left the island kingdom, then she'd burst into tears, watching the little island get smaller and smaller through the window of the plane.

She felt raw, and hollow, and she knew she was going to have to pull herself together when she landed in London, but for now all she wanted was to cry. She missed Poseidon so badly it hurt.

They hadn't spoken a word the rest of the interminable journey to the airport and he hadn't touched her again. And then, once they got to the airport, she'd got out of the car and hadn't looked back. She hadn't been able to bear to.

Now it felt as if a part of herself had been ripped from her chest, and she wished so badly that she could get angry about it. But, again, all her anger seemed to have gone. The only thing she felt was grief for what might have been.

You'll recover. You'll move on. That's what you did after Chrissy died.

She had—it was true. But if there was one thing she knew it was that grief changed you. You were never the same person after it had got its claws in you, and she wasn't the same woman who'd landed on the island a few days earlier.

She'd fallen in love with a man she'd never thought she'd even like, let alone love, then had her heart broken by that same man. It hurt. It hurt so much. Yet she wouldn't change it. Poseidon Teras was a man worth loving and she had no regrets. She wasn't going to stop loving him either. She'd probably continue to love him until the day she died.

Soon the flight plan mix-up was solved and the jet climbed into the air again, on towards London.

Andromeda wiped her tears away as they came in to land and hoped she didn't look too wrecked. She'd have to call herself a taxi or get a ride via the app on her phone. Hopefully she wouldn't get a chatty driver.

Then the stewardess—who'd politely left her alone for the flight, just surreptitiously passing her tissues when she needed them—opened the door of the jet and Andie, still in her wedding gown, gathered the skirts up as she got to her feet.

She went to the jet's door and stepped out onto the metal stairs. In the dimming light of a dull London evening she could see a long black car pulled up on the Tarmac, and a man leaning back against it with his arms folded.

A tall man. A *very* tall, powerful-looking man. And he was still wearing a morning suit.

Her heart gave one heavy, painful beat.

Poseidon.

Shock pulsed through her and for a long moment she just stood there, the wind tugging at her wedding gown, staring at her husband. Who stared back.

Then he pushed himself away from the car and straightened.

She was too far away to see the expression on his face clearly, so she began to walk down the stairs, and as she did so her absent anger suddenly burst into life inside her.

What on earth was he doing here? And how dared he? How dared he break her heart into pieces by telling her to leave, only then to turn up here at the airport to meet her? What did he want? Had he forgotten something, perhaps? To stomp on the pieces of that heart of hers that he'd broken?

She'd sworn she wasn't going to be angry, but this was a step too far.

She reached the Tarmac and strode across it towards him. His face was set in fierce lines, his blue eyes were burning like gas flames—every part of him the intense, passionate man she knew he was deep down.

'What the hell are you doing here?' she demanded.

But he didn't give her a chance to go on, because by then he'd taken a couple of steps towards her and, before she could say another word, he'd swept her up and into his arms, holding her there so tightly she couldn't escape.

'What the hell am I doing here?' he echoed, his gaze burning down into hers. 'I'm here to tell you that I love you, Andromeda Lane. And that I made a mistake. I should never have let you leave and, now that I have you, I'm never letting you go.'

And just like that all the fight went out of her, taking her anger along with it. She looked up at him, her heart aching, the warmth of his body seeping into her and stealing all her resistance.

'I thought that love wasn't something you could give,' she said huskily.

'I thought that too,' he said. 'But then Asterion came to give me a piece of brotherly advice. He didn't understand why I'd let you go when it was clear I was in love with you and you with me.'

Her throat closed. 'Did you tell him…?'

'No. I will one day, but not yet.' His arms tightened around her. 'He made me realise that the problem wasn't love, *asteri mou*. The problem was me. The problem—as you so astutely put it in the car after the wedding—was me still letting Michel make my choices for me, and all because I was afraid.'

She couldn't resist it. She lifted her hand to his beautiful face. 'Oh, Poseidon…'

'And I knew that. Because if Michel hadn't been in my past, there wouldn't have been anything in heaven or earth that would have stopped me from being with you.'

He turned her to the car that was parked there, the driver having already opened the door.

'So I decided that I had to stop letting him steal choice from me. I decided that there is only one man in the entire world who gets to love you, to make you feel special, to give you all the things you've always wanted. And that man is me, little siren.'

He smiled, and his smile was warm and brighter than the summer sun.

'I am devastated to report that from now on I must insist on being your husband for the rest of your life.'

Her heart felt full, a flower unfurling and blooming inside the cage of her ribs, and there were tears in her eyes yet again.

'I don't get a choice?'

Poseidon lowered her into the car and then followed her inside, shutting them both in the warm interior. Then he pulled her straight back into his arms.

'Naturally. You always get a choice, my beautiful wife.'

'Good,' she murmured as he bent his head to kiss her. 'Because in this instance my choice will always be you.'

EPILOGUE

POSEIDON SAT WITH his brother in the shade of the olive grove, enjoying another of the magnificent summers that the island put on, and listening to the sound of various children creating havoc around them. There appeared to be lots of screaming going on—something about a toy that his daughter Leni wanted, which one of her cousins had stolen from her or some such.

Leni was always screaming. She was definitely her mother's daughter.

He smiled indulgently as her older brother, Nico, at ten much more contained and grown-up than his six-year-old sister, came to the rescue.

Definitely his son, that one.

His sister-in-law Brita was sitting cross-legged on the grass, showing the other children the basics of a bow and arrow—most of them were Asterion's, except for the twins, Poseidon's youngest, Christa and Carlo, who were watching with big green eyes.

Archery practice was apparently now mandatory for a Teras child.

Asterion was watching his wife with adoration, but Poseidon didn't find it sickening any more. Mainly because his own little siren was curled up at his side, chatting with a by now very elderly Dimitra about how they were opening up a few new Chrissy's Hope services in the States and planning some for Australasia as well.

Andromeda's charity was doing brilliantly, as he'd known it would.

Just then Leni came over and flung herself, still weeping, into Poseidon's lap.

He closed his arms around her. 'Poor little one,' he murmured, stroking his daughter's red-gold hair. 'Papa has you.'

Asterion glanced at him then, and the brothers shared a smile. Because now they both had what they hadn't even realised they wanted. Contentment. Happiness. Joy.

And in the end Dimitra had been right. Her choice of wife for both of them had been the right choice—the *only* choice.

Though it wasn't marriage that had tamed the Monsters of the Mediterranean.

It was love.

* * * * *

COMING SOON!

We really hope you enjoyed reading this book.
If you're looking for more romance
be sure to head to the shops when
new books are available on

Thursday 23rd May

To see which titles are coming soon, please visit
millsandboon.co.uk/nextmonth

MILLS & BOON

MILLS & BOON®

Coming next month

TWINS TO TAME HIM
Tara Pammi

Sebastian rubbed a hand over his face. Any momentary hesitation he'd felt about having two little boys to care for, to nurture and protect, dissipated, leaving behind a crystal-clear clarity he had never known in his life.

Whatever instinct had propelled him to demand Laila marry him…it carried the weight of his deepest, most secret desire within it.

For his sons to be happy and well-adjusted and thriving, they needed their mother and he needed them. Ergo, his primary goal now was to do anything to keep Laila in his life.

And while he'd never have admitted it openly to his brute of a father, Sebastian had always known he could be just as ruthless as his twin.

He was keeping his sons and he was keeping their mother in his life, even if it meant he had to seduce every inch of logic and rationale out of Dr. Jaafri. And he would make sure she not only enjoyed the seduction but that she had everything she'd ever wanted. He would make all her wishes and dreams come true. It was only a matter of getting her to admit them.

Continue reading
TWINS TO TAME HIM
Tara Pammi

Available next month
millsandboon.co.uk

From showing up to glowing up, Afterglow Books features authentic and relatable stories, characters you can't help but fall in love with and plenty of spice!

OUT NOW

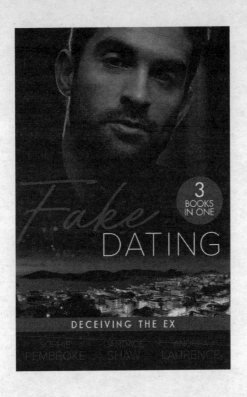

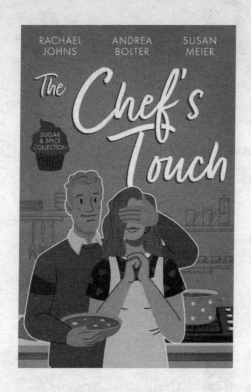

LET'S TALK
Romance

For exclusive extracts, competitions and special offers, find us online:

- **f** MillsandBoon
- **X** @MillsandBoon
- **◉** @MillsandBoonUK
- **♪** @MillsandBoonUK

Get in touch on 01413 063 232